P9-BZG-570

SHE WAS WISE
IN THE WAYS
OF MAGIC,
BUT POWERLESS IN
THE ARMS OF
THE KNIGHT
COME TO STEAL
HER SOUL....

"I SHALL MAKE YOU VERY SORRY YOU EVER CAME TO WALES," WYNNE BEGAN.

Fighting the urge to rub the spots where his hands had touched her, she went on. "I am not called the Seeress of Radnor for nothing. *I* am the Welsh Witch you spoke of, and I have powers at my command you cannot begin to fathom. I sensed your presence in these forests long before you arrived. And I can predict already the tragedy that shall befall you and your men if you linger here."

Cleve studied her for a moment, then grinned. "You are a superstitious people. No doubt the folk around here believe such things of you—maybe you even believe some of it yourself. But you'll not frighten me off with such wild tales."

"Then you are more fool than I thought," Wynne replied with a smug smile of her own. She lifted her chin proudly and put her hands on her hips. "You've been given your only warning. I'll not feel the least remorse for the hardships that shall plague you and your men now."

To her dismay, however, he only smirked and let his eyes run boldly over her. "If you would put the same effort into seducing me with your considerable charms as you put into scaring me away with your questionable powers, you would no doubt succeed far better." Then he reached out and caught one long tendril of her loosened hair and wound it around his finger. "Have you a husband?"

THIEF OF MY HEART

"WONDERFUL. . . . I truly enjoyed this one and you will too!"
—Affaire de Coeur

"CHARMING. . . . This steamy battle-of-wills romance will tug at your heart and keep you turning the pages as fast as you can."
—Romantic Times

"SUPERBLY CRAFTED. . . . This one fulfills every woman's fantasy while sustaining the sensuality of the well-developed characters."
—Rendezvous

MY GALLANT ENEMY

"A LOVE STORY OF OLD to thrill and delight. Much intrigue and an awesome, arrogant but lovable hero and the lady who turned his heart upside down."
—Affaire de Coeur

"SENSITIVE, REALISTIC AND PASSIONATE, *My Gallant Enemy* is a delicious medieval love story. Rexanne Becnel is sure to take her place in the ranks of well-loved medieval romance writers."
—Romantic Times

REXANNE BECNEL

Where Magic Dwells

A Dell Book

Published by
Dell Publishing
a division of
Bantam Doubleday Dell Publishing Group, Inc.
1540 Broadway
New York, New York 10036

ISBN: 0-440-21565-X

Printed in the United States of America

Published simultaneously in Canada

June 1994

10 9 8 7 6 5 4 3 2

RAD

1

Radnor Forest, Wales, A.D. 1172

There was a stranger in her forest. Wynne ab Gruffydd looked up from where she knelt in a tall bed of Olympia fern and a shiver snaked down her spine. Her hands stilled at their task of delicately uprooting the bulbous growths on the fern roots.

There was a stranger in her forest; she knew it with a certainty that had never failed her. She knew it without seeing him or hearing him. She knew it even though the fat red squirrels still chattered at their daily work and the doves called down in their familiar mournful tones.

Perhaps it was that the falcon circling so high above had suddenly dropped lower and now only skimmed the high tops of the oak and ash and thorn trees. Or maybe it was the pair of rabbits that had paused in their browsing for new fern fronds and wild strawberry leaves. Wynne did not bother to wonder about her knowledge. A man had entered the forest—perhaps more than one man. And he came by horseback.

Normally that was not cause for alarm. It could be Druce or even the Fychen family, coming as they always did during the waxing of the moon to collect the rare forest herbs she gathered and prepared for them. But she knew it was not them. This man was a stranger to her. And though she sensed now that it was indeed a group of men, one of them came through to her more clearly than the rest.

Wynne stood up abruptly, absently brushing the dried and clinging fern fronds from her deep green woolen skirt. Without realizing it she began to rub the familiar amethyst amulet that hung, heavy and reassuring from a chain around her neck. She had a sudden and uneasy premonition, stronger than anything she'd ever sensed before. This man spelled trouble for her. Though she'd long ago grown used to the inexplicable feelings that often assailed her, she'd also learned to trust them. Still, she'd never before felt so vivid an impression as this.

The devil's-apple she'd hoped to gather would have to wait, she decided at once. She could collect them another time. Right now she must get back to Radnor Manor.

Wynne did not take the deer path that led through the low fern beds and past the Old Circle, the huge granite boulders that were her secret place. She avoided the stream path and the ancient rocky road—the Giant's Trail. She had assumed the strangers would be traveling down the Old Roman Road. But now she was unsure just where these men were, and more than anything she knew she must remain hidden. So she picked her way down the hill, through the gorse and thorn grove, but avoiding the expanse of heather that grew in a sudden clearing. She clung to the thickets and deep woods, as familiar with them as any of the wild creatures might be. This was her home, her Radnor Forest. The man who traversed it now was a stranger to this wild part of *Cymru*—of Wales. He was a stranger and unwelcome, and Wynne's wariness swiftly expanded to include anger. What right had he to be here?

As Wynne approached the sprawling manor house, she spied Gwynedd standing at the edge of the clearing waiting for her. Her great-aunt knew, she thought with relief. She'd sensed the man as well. Somehow that was a comfort.

"Wynne?" the old woman called, although Wynne approached on completely silent feet. "Come here, girl. Give me your hand."

Wynne took her aunt Gwynedd's gnarled hand in hers and held it tight to still its constant tremor.

"I feared for you, girl. What is it?"

"There is a stranger—or strangers—in the forest. I felt their presence and I'm certain they bode ill for us. Did you sense them also?"

Gwynedd shook her graying head. Though her eyes followed the sound of Wynne's voice, Wynne knew they saw little more than shadows and light. "I sensed only your fear, *nith*. Tell me what you saw."

"I saw nothing," Wynne answered as she led her great-aunt slowly to a smooth log. They sat down together. "But I felt . . ." She paused and tried to organize the vague and troubling feelings that had risen inside her. "I felt something stronger—something clearer—than anything I've ever felt before. Yet it was still indistinct. There are a number of men, and yet only one of them came to me." She stared down at her hands, stained green at the fingertips, and rubbed a spot of dirt away. Then she turned to her elderly aunt.

" 'Tis the oddest vision I've ever had. I wish I could explain it. I wish you could still . . ."

Gwynedd smiled and patted her niece's knee. She stared at Wynne with her strange unfocused gaze. "My time is past. It has been these several years. But even if my powers were strong, there's naught to say that I would sense the same from this man that you do."

"But it's so strong. You would have been able to make something of it."

The old woman shook her head. " 'Tis different for each of us who have been blessed—or cursed, some would say—with the Radnor visions. You know that. We each have had our strengths and our weaknesses. All we can do is use our gifts as best we can. Mine is fading, just as my sight has faded. But you are young. You are strong."

They sat in silence a few minutes as Wynne pondered her aunt's words. Then she sighed. "He frightens me," she confessed in a low voice, disturbed that this unseen man held such power over her.

"He may have his strengths, my child, but you also have yours," Gwynedd reminded her. "Let us wait and see what he is about. And now, what is that I hear?" She cocked her head, and Wynne looked around.

" 'Tis Druce, back from the hunt. Perhaps he'll have news."

Druce ab Owain and three other men from Radnor Village filed into the manor yard. Two of them carried a long pole between them, from which hung a gutted stag. Druce and his younger brother each had a brace of rabbits slung over their shoulders. They were dirty, and their leather hunting tunics bore the stains of their successful hunt. But they were not concerned with their appearance. The hunt had been good and their spirits were high.

"Wynne. Wynne!" Druce called when he spied her. A huge smile lit his dark face, and he changed his direction toward her, holding his catch high for her to see. "This shall see all who reside at Radnor Manor well fed for the next few weeks!"

"Indeed!" she exclaimed. "Just feel what Druce has brought us, Aunt Gwynedd." Wynne brought the older woman's hand up to the several rabbits. "And he also has a fine stag."

"Ah, Druce. What a good lad you are to see to the needs of your neighbors." Gwynedd smiled and nodded blindly in his direction. " 'Tis best that I gather up the young ones. They must help Cook and the others in the preparation of the meat. The skinning. The carving." Then she turned to Wynne. "What say you? Are the twins to be banned from this, or is their punishment done?"

Wynne's pleased expression changed. Rhys and Madoc. Of the five orphans she raised at the manor, those two were by far the most mischievous. Riding the poor cow, Clover, as if she were a destrier. Scattering the already wild chickens. This time had been the worst, however, for had little Bronwen not alerted her in time, they might be dead by now. Or at least maimed. In exasperation Wynne thrust one hand through her heavy hair, further loosening the midnight tresses from her knitted coif.

"I'm not certain they've learned their lesson at all," she muttered. "But then, I doubt even a week of scrubbing hearths and cleaning the animal pens will wean them of their recklessness."

"They're but high-spirited lads," Druce said in defense of the twin boys. "Why, every lad worth his salt has swung down from the Mother Oak on wild vines, trying to make it to the other side of the Devil's Cleft. I did it, and so shall—"

"You were nearer ten," Wynne broke in. "Rhys and Madoc are but six years old. And barely that," she added, becoming frightened once more for her impish charges.

Druce shrugged. "They would have been fine. Though

I doubt they would have reached the other side, they would not have been hurt."

"They might have fallen!"

"They would have slid down the vine, only a little frightened for their adventure."

He gave her a lopsided smile, and as always Wynne found herself struggling to hold firm against it. Though Druce was one year older than her, he still seemed a boy, young and reckless. Fun-loving. He'd been the wildest lad in Radnor Village, and she'd been close behind him in daring. Had he not ordered her away those long years ago at the Mother Oak, she would have clambered up after him and tried to swing across the Devil's Cleft herself. It was the first time he'd acted as the other boys usually did, reminding her that she was only a girl. When she'd become incensed, he had threatened to tickle her. When that hadn't worked, however, he had used the ultimate threat. He'd vowed to kiss her and then stepped forward to prove he meant it.

She'd fled in horror, just as he'd expected. He had made the daring swing from the tree and had come home to the village a hero, swaggering and proud. His father had bragged endlessly, and his mother had been dismayed. Wynne, however, had been devastated, for everything had changed after that. Druce had joined the older boys' games and assumed more and more responsibilities among the men, while Wynne had slowly become more a part of the village women's world and the accompanying chores. Not until after the English attack and her move from the village to Radnor Manor itself had she and he recovered their old friendship. And even then it had been different.

Of course everything had been different since the English had come to Radnor Forest that day nearly seven years ago. Her parents had both been killed, and then later her sister, Maradedd, had died too. Yet Maradedd had been murdered by the English just as surely as if they had left her bleeding and lifeless on the day of the battle. The mere fact that she'd survived another nine months meant nothing.

With Maradedd's death Wynne's transition from wide-eyed child to embittered woman had been complete. She, instead of her sister, had moved into Radnor Manor with the Seeress, her aunt Gwynedd. At the age of thirteen she had begun to assume the responsibilities for the manor and the string of little English bastards that had found their way to her door. Now, six years later, she was Seeress of Radnor, with both the problems and the privileges that position conferred.

With a sigh Wynne gazed up at Druce's waiting face. "All right, the children shall help. Even Rhys and Madoc. But I shall fetch them myself," she added, frowning. "And, Aunt Gwynedd, I hope you give them the hardest and dirtiest task of all. Those two need to learn some caution."

"Spreading dirt over the bloodied yard is not likely to teach them caution," Druce taunted her, but Wynne purposefully ignored him. He was very likely right, but what else was she to do? She so often felt inadequate to the task of raising them. Though she tried to fill the role of mother to them all, most of the time she felt more like a beleaguered older sister.

"Come along." She sighed, taking her aunt's arm. "We've kegs and pots to assemble, and brine to prepare. Cook can't do it all alone." They started toward the squat kitchen building just beyond the two-story cruckwork manor house, but then Wynne remembered the strangers in the forest and turned back, letting her aunt proceed alone.

"Druce," she called, hurrying across the dusty yard to catch him. "Druce, did you see anyone in the forest? Any travelers? A group of men?" she added in a quieter tone.

He pushed a handful of coal-black hair back from his brow. No trace of teasing was left on his face, for he was a firm believer in the Radnor vision, which had been passed down through the women in Wynne's family. "A pair of barefoot monks riding jennets were on the Old Roman Road headed north. But that was in the morning, right after we left Radnor Village. They can be nowhere near here by now." He frowned. "What did you sense?"

Wynne shook her head, and a shiver snaked up her spine. "I cannot quite say. A man—actually, several men —are somewhere in our forest. What they want and who they are is a mystery to me. But they—" She broke off. To say they frightened her was not quite accurate, she realized. They unnerved her. *He* unnerved her, whoever he was.

"We saw no one out of the ordinary," Druce said. "Trystan ab Cadawg of Penybont Village was fishing on the far bank of the Waddel. And old Taffy was checking his traps." He paused, searching his mind. "No," he finally said. "No one else. Where were you when they came to you?"

"In the low meadow. Almost to Crow's Moor. I was picking the earliest curls of fern and had planned to search for devil's-apple. Mandrake," she clarified.

He grimaced at her mention of that feared root. "Do you still feel these men?"

Wynne forced herself to become still. She grasped her amulet as she exhaled a long breath and closed her eyes, willing away the everyday sound of the manor grounds.

She listened to her own breathing and tried to hear the steady rhythm of her heart. After a moment she raised her face to stare at Druce.

" 'Tis different from anytime before," she murmured, more to herself than to him. "I do not sense him, and yet I know he's there."

Druce considered that. "Maybe he is harmless. Is it only the one man?"

"No, 'tis a group. I'm almost certain. But only one of them comes to me."

"Maybe they mean us no harm. Maybe they are just passing through, bound to one or the other of the villages in the forest."

Wynne left it at that. As she hurried off to her own tasks, she hoped Druce was right, and yet a part of her knew he was not. This man had come to Radnor Forest for a reason. He was not simply passing through. Yet with nothing to go on, she could only sit and wait. Druce promised to check the area around the manor before he and his brother and friends returned home to Radnor Village, but Wynne suspected he would find no one.

She sighed as she sought out Rhys and Madoc. What would be, would be. She believed that, and life had proven it to be true over and over again. She would face whatever threat this man brought when it came to pass—if indeed it was a threat at all. But at the same time she would prepare herself and all the children. They had their hiding places. They had their own peculiar weapons.

And perhaps her fears were unfounded. Perhaps it was only another Norman holy man come to purge the Welsh of their lingering pagan practices. Wynne smiled at that thought. How she would love to terrorize some pompous priest or bishop with a mysterious fire that burned green instead of yellow and red, or purge him with a sweet wine laced with fairy cap.

Feeling better, she broke into a run, working off her nervous energy. It was a beautiful day, unmarred by clouds or rain. The five orphans she raised were healthy and strong. They had fresh meat, thanks to the villagers, and Radnor Forest provided them with everything else they needed. What more could she want from life?

" 'Tis the land of dragons, they say."

"And of witches."

Cleve FitzWarin heard the mutterings of his men, but he refused to acknowledge them. They'd camped last night on the eastern side of Offa's Dyke, the steep-sided ditch that marked the border between England and Wales. All day they'd ridden deeper into the wild hills of Wales, and all day his men had become increasingly uneasy. Even Cleve could not totally dismiss their apprehension. The hills rose higher, turning now into craggy outcroppings and ancient mountains. This was the home of the irrepressible Welsh folk—the people who'd sent King Henry home a beaten man with a crushed army. And here Cleve was, venturing into the very heart of Wales with but seven men behind him. God, but he must be a complete fool.

No, not a complete fool. Just one determined finally to win lands of his own.

Behind him he sensed his men growing more and more anxious. He pulled his tall charcoal-gray destrier to a halt and leaned forward in the stirrups. The men clattered to a halt around him.

"What now?"

"By Saint Osyth's soul—"

A sharp wind whistled around a craggy granite boulder,

sounding for all the world like a woman's high-pitched keening, and all the muttering ceased. Wales was surely a cursed land, Cleve decided, not for the first time that day. All the tales of ghosts and dragons, of heathen folk as wild as any animals, which he'd dismissed as the talk of fools, seemed suddenly believable. And yet, ghosts or no, dragons and heathens notwithstanding, he'd come here for a purpose, and he'd not leave until he'd succeeded. He pushed his woolen hood back and shook his head in irritation.

"We'll camp there," he called to his huddled men above the sound of the wind. "There looks to be a stream past those elms where it's low and wet. John, Marcus, see to a fire and food. Henry and Roland, see to the horses. Richard, you, Derrick, and Ned scout the area."

The men scattered to their tasks, but Cleve remained on his mount, leaning forward, squinting toward the mist-shrouded mountain ahead of them. His horse stamped once, then twice, on the rutted cart track, but still Cleve stared, looking and listening for something he could not name. He'd been troubled these last two hours and more. He was troubled still.

Sir William had been vague. He'd spoken of a place southwest of Stokesley Castle, a forest called Radnor. But he'd not remembered the specific village name, and Cleve had found that there were several within the forest. Nor had Sir William even known the woman's Welsh name. Yet now, maudlin fool that he was, he had sent Cleve to find the child of their union. Angel was the name he'd called her. But so far Cleve had found no one who remembered a woman going by that name. And so he yet searched.

Cleve grimaced to himself, disgusted once more by the history of the English in Wales. He'd been more than glad seven years ago not to have been a part of King Henry's luckless campaign against the Welsh. His own mother had been Welsh, and though he and she had always lived on English soil, she had kept both the language and the culture of Wales alive in her only child. At her death the English father he'd seen but twice had grudgingly arranged a minor position for his bastard son, Cleve, in a decent household. Through the grace of God—and the intervention of Lady Rosalynde and both her husband and father—Cleve had risen above his lowly beginnings. Yet he'd avoided the war against Wales, even though it had offered a chance for him to win recognition and reward. Something in him simply had not wanted to make war on his mother's people.

Now it appeared that his Welsh heritage, which had always been considered shameful, would be his good fortune, for it was Cleve's knowledge of the Welsh tongue—rusty though it was—that had given him this opportunity.

Were it not for the promise of reward, Cleve would have dismissed Sir William Somerville's odd mission as foolish beyond belief. To find a child, sired in wartime to some Welshwoman, and if it was a boy bring it back, was a fool's quest by anyone's standards. And yet, for the promise of lands—a castle and demesne of his own—Cleve would have searched out the devil himself and wrested him back to England.

As if to underscore his black thoughts, the wind whipped more viciously than ever, lifting the ends of his heavy wool mantle and causing his destrier to start in alarm.

"Be still, Ceta. 'Tis naught but the wind." But it was a formidable wind, Cleve thought, cold and relentless, just like the land.

With a sharp curse he hauled Ceta around and followed

the trail his men had left. They would sleep and regroup. Tomorrow they would find this place called Radnor, and one by one he would investigate each and every household there. They would trade their good English coin for information if necessary. And they would purchase the rare herbs and potions several of Sir William's daughters had demanded he search out for them. But above all else they would find the child that Sir William so desperately sought.

Though Cleve did not truly wish to steal the child from its mother, he was nevertheless prepared to do just that if it proved necessary. He would not forgo his prize for one woman's stubbornness. And after all, Sir William's bastard would become heir to all the Somerville name had to offer. Sir William was adamant about that. No doubt his sons-in-law were disappointments to him, Cleve speculated. But whatever Sir William's reasons for wanting his bastard son, one thing was certain: the child would never suffer the lack of family, name, or property as other bastards did.

As Cleve did.

No, any pain the child and mother might feel on parting would swiftly heal in the light of all the boy would gain.

And in the process he, too, would gain, Cleve reminded himself. He would win the hand of Sir William's youngest daughter—Edeline was her name, he remembered. More important, however, he would win the dowry lands that came with the girl. He would be lord of his own lands and people, and his children would be born to those same lands. There would be no bastards from him, he vowed, only sons and daughters, raised in the security of their rightful home.

He dismounted and turned back to stare up at the mists

that hid the mountain peaks from view. Somewhere in these vast, forbidding hills lay the key to all he wanted in life. Nothing and no one was going to prevent him from gaining it.

2

Wynne awoke with a start. Her heart pounded in her chest, and she gasped for breath as she lay there on her straw truckle bed. Had she been dreaming? Yet she could not recall any dreams, certainly not anything that could have caused this sudden, fearful thudding in her chest, nor the dampness of her palms and brow.

She sat up, trying to focus in the dark room. Was it one of the children? She rose at once and padded on bare feet from her small chamber to the fireplace, where she quickly lit a candle. Then up the steep stairs she went on sure feet, to the nursery she'd fashioned beneath the broad eaves in a loft above the hall.

Once she was in the low-ceilinged room, she moved slowly from bed to bed, letting the light fall briefly on each of the children's faces. Bronwen and Isolde slept side by side in a shared bed, the one sprawled sideways, wrapped in the wool coverlet, the other curled in a ball, shivering from the cold. With a small smile Wynne tugged the cover from Isolde and tucked Bronwen into its warmth.

How different the two girls were, she thought fondly.

Her niece, Isolde, with her dark hair and flashing eyes, was a little tyrant at times. She was Welsh through and through, just like her mother, Wynne's sister, had been. Bronwen meanwhile had the coloring of her father. So far that had not been a problem, but Wynne feared the girl's strikingly fair hair would forever mark her an English bastard.

With a sigh she turned to the boys on the other side of the room. As she expected, Madoc and Rhys faced each other on the truckle pallet they shared. It was as if they plotted mischief even in their sleep, yet Wynne could not deny that they looked more like angels right now than the little devils she knew they could be. With their dark, curling hair and equally dark eyes, they would no doubt cause many a heartache in the years to come.

Then there was Arthur. What was she to do with Arthur? He was already so wise that it was frightening, and yet there was a sensitive side to his nature that worried her. Though the other four children made allowances for his dreamy inclinations, she knew he would always be one easily taken advantage of, especially by other boys.

But what could she do? She had willingly undertaken to raise the five of them, five wonderful, exasperating six-year-olds who would not be placated by her explanations about their absent parents forever.

Though the invading English had ultimately been routed and driven from Wales, they yet survived here in the blood of their bastard offspring. One day she must explain it to the children, and yet it was still hard for her to understand herself. How did you explain to a child about war? About rape? How did you make a little child understand that your father had not created you with love and respect, but with hatred and violence? How did you explain that your father and his people were the worst enemies you would ever have?

She suppressed a shiver, then reached out to cup Arthur's cheek. He was warm and so sweet. They all were, and she loved them as fiercely as if they truly were her children. Just the feel of his soft breath was reassuring, and she swallowed the uneasiness that had plagued her the whole day through and on into the night. Everything would be all right. She was sure of it. Whoever it was who trespassed upon her forest would not be there forever. He would wreak whatever mischief he might be planning, but he would not disrupt their lives for long.

Hers was a race that had survived many a foreign onslaught. Besides, it was not an army encamped in her woods. She knew that instinctively. A few men were no real threat.

Perhaps they would be gone by sunset today.

Cleve squatted beside a narrow brook, watching a deep, still pool just downstream from him. Someone was coming, and his naturally suspicious nature prompted him to observe the traveler a little while before revealing himself.

With a remarkable absence of sound a man picked his way down a barely visible trail. On his shoulders he bore a small, oddly made boat. The Welsh called it a coracle, Cleve remembered. It was an awkward-looking craft woven of willow and covered with leather.

The man was alone, which was good, and he appeared to carry only a small dagger in a leather sheath strapped to his thigh. When he put down his light craft, Cleve was surprised to see, however, that he was an old man, a graying grandfather come to do some fishing. This was a good sign, for an old fellow like this would surely know all the goings-on in these parts. Cleve eased his hand from the carved bone hilt of his own dagger.

"Good morrow, father," he called, rising to his full height. The old man started and then warily drew back. But Cleve smiled and walked forward with no threat in his demeanor. "What manner of fish do you seek this fine day?"

The old man stared at him as if he were an oddity never before seen, and Cleve frowned. Was his Welsh so bad as to be unintelligible?

"I mean you no harm," he tried again, enunciating carefully.

"The English always say that," the man replied warily.

Cleve's expression lifted in relief. He was not surprised the man identified him as English, for he knew his pronunciation gave him away. But at least he was able to make himself understood. "Our leaders are not at war," he replied. "Neither should we be."

The man snorted in answer. Whether his disdain was aimed at Cleve or at the English and Welsh leaders was hard to say.

Cleve tried again. "Is this the Radnor Forest?" He squatted down a little distance from the man and began idly to toss bits of twigs into the dark water.

After a long minute's consideration the man nodded.

"Ah, that is good. Mayhap my journey is near to its end."

The man began to ready his boat for launching, but he nonetheless kept a wary eye on Cleve. Finally, as if he couldn't bear not knowing, he spoke up. "And where is it ye journey to?"

Cleve tossed another twig into the water. "I'm not certain. Somewhere around here." He peered at the man, noticing his worn-down boots and the ragged hem of his ill-fitting tunic. Perhaps he should take a chance.

"I'm looking for a child about six years old. Born to a woman who was sometimes called Angel. I'm willing to pay for information." For emphasis he stood up and patted the purse that hung beneath his own mantle.

The man stared at him. "There's a lot of children to be found around here."

"This one would have been fathered by an English soldier."

Cleve sensed that the man knew something, for he stiffened slightly and his eyes darted away. Sure he was on the right path, Cleve went on. "The father seeks this child so that he can provide for him. He's a very powerful and wealthy man." He loosened his purse and crossed nearer to the man. "Would you know of such a child?"

The old man licked his lips, and his eyes darted back and forth between Cleve's face and the clinking purse in his hand. "There's many an English bastard in these parts, left over from the wars. How can you know which one it is? Or don't you care?" the old man added with a shrewd gleam in his eyes.

Cleve kept his face carefully blank. He'd had the same thought himself, and more than once. How *would* Sir William know whether any young boy he brought back was truly his son or not? And yet Cleve knew he could not foist just any child off as Sir William's.

However, it was not for Sir William's sake that he wanted to find the right child. It was for the child's. Every child deserved to know his father.

His own father had been a poor enough parent, and yet at least Cleve knew who he was. How much worse not to know him at all.

"I want the correct child, so I warn you, do not send me to just anyone. I'll pay only for the truth."

When the old man looked carefully about, as if he expected to find someone listening, Cleve knew he'd won.

"There is this woman, not far from here. She keeps several of the English bastards."

"She has several bastards? Are any of them about six years old? Are any of them boys?"

"They're all six or so, come from your King Henry's last foolish attempt to subdue our lands." He snorted in disdain at the English king's idiocy. "And aye, she has boys."

When Cleve returned to his men, he was brimming with renewed optimism. For a dozen English pennies the man had given him directions to Radnor Manor, a large house just beyond Radnor Village. They'd passed near the place only yesterday, and it was there that a number of English bastards resided under the care of some woman. The Seeress of Radnor, the old man had called her. A witch come from a long line of Welsh witches.

Cleve laughed out loud as he spied his small band of followers. Wales was indeed as wild and pagan as the priests so often preached. In Norman England a woman so widely regarded as a witch would have been roundly castigated—probably excommunicated and either driven out or else put to death by the ordeal. Yet that old man, Taffyd, had seemed both respectful and ambivalent about her. What was to be made of such a people?

"We ride back to where a thicket of impenetrable thorns encircles a solitary oak," Cleve called out. "A rough trail leads north, and with a bit of good fortune we shall reach our destination by midday."

At that moment a watery sun broke through the low-lying mists, and for a few minutes Cleve was able to see the beauty of these strange lands. The damp woodlands sparkled as if the finest of jewels had suddenly been strewn about by a mighty and benevolent hand. The grimness of the land was softened, and Cleve felt a surge of excitement in his chest.

Wild this Wales might be, but it held the key to all he longed for. Though he was not one to believe in signs and omens, he was certain this boded well for him. The old man. This unexpected sunshine. Everything he had struggled for was almost within his grasp.

She knew long before Rhys and Madoc came running and tumbling down the hill that the man was coming. She'd sensed it just as she had yesterday, only this time it was even stronger. Despite her fear of these unknown intruders on her lands, however, Wynne could not ignore the equally overpowering sense of curiosity she felt. Who was this man she sensed so vividly—more vividly than anyone or anything she'd ever sensed in her nineteen years?

Rhys gasped for breath. "Druce says to find all the women—"

"—and children. And get inside," Madoc finished excitedly.

"Somebody's coming—"

"But don't worry, Wynne, we won't let them get anybody—"

"The bloody English bastards."

"Rhys!" Wynne exclaimed. "Where did you learn to use such language?"

Both boys stared up at her in quick chagrin. If it were not for the tiny scar on Rhys's left eyebrow, Wynne would have been hard-pressed to tell them apart. It was Madoc who responded in a defensive tone.

"Druce says they're bloody English bastards."

"Well, I don't care what Druce says. If I hear such talk from either of you again, I'll wash your mouths out with soaproot. Do you understand?" When they reluctantly nodded, she sighed. "All right, now. Did Druce give any other instructions? Did he say anything else?"

"No. Can we go with Druce?"

"Absolutely not. Are you sure he didn't give you any further message?"

"He said . . ." Madoc screwed up his face as if he were trying to remember. "He said you didn't have to worry. He wouldn't let anything bad happen to you."

"And then Barris told Druce maybe you would give Druce a big wet kiss if he saved the day," Rhys added.

Both boys stared up at Wynne as if they weren't precisely sure what a big wet kiss was, but Wynne was not about to enlighten them. "Barris has no business saying such things," she fumed as her face grew hot with embarrassment. Druce was her childhood friend. A few years ago he'd been willing to explore other possibilities between them, but she hadn't felt the same. She thought of him more as a brother than anything else, and once he'd understood, he'd treated her as a sister. But the teasing of his brother and friends could easily make things uncomfortable for them all.

Besides, a husband was the last thing she needed. Even if someone was willing to marry the Seeress, he would hardly want the five children that came with her. And anyway, she didn't have time for a husband, nor the desire. She wasn't sure she ever would.

Hiding her discomfort as best she could, she took both of the twin boys by the hand. "Go find your sisters and then get inside the manor house. Where's Arthur?"

"I want to see the bloody English bas—" Madoc broke

off in the nick of time, but Wynne was too worried to scold him again.

"The English are a horrible people," she warned. "You don't want to see them." Then she relented, for she knew her words would only fire the imagination of this irrepressible pair. "If Druce brings them to the manor, you may see them. All right? But only if you do what I tell you, as soon as I tell you." Then she pulled each of them near for an urgent hug and a heartfelt kiss upon their sweaty brows. "Now, off with you both. Go find Isolde and Bronwen while I look for Arthur."

Arthur was not in the stable loft. He was not in the cedar grove beside the spring, nor did she find him on his favorite boulder next to the hay field. Wynne saw Rhys and Madoc, followed by Isolde and Bronwen, go into the protective walls of the sturdy manor house. She saw Gwynedd's sightless eyes searching for her, listening and sensing her. But Wynne couldn't turn back. Where on God's green earth was Arthur?

A cloud passed over the sun, and a rabbit shot across her path. She stopped where she was and fought down the fear that rose so swiftly in her chest. This was not a time for panic or for believing in omens, she told herself. This was a time for calm and for concentration.

She closed her eyes and subdued her rapid breathing, willing her mind to clear of all but the need to feel where Arthur was. When she lifted her head, she was calmer, though no more certain where he was. All she knew was that he was not in danger. But though she took comfort in that knowledge, she nevertheless could not abandon her search. She would not relax until he was back in her care.

With a clearer sense of direction, Wynne headed back to Arthur's boulder. It was here he lay in the rare sunshine and dreamed his fanciful dreams. It was here he created his wild tales and observed the world with his amazingly observant eye.

She lay a hand on the flat place where he always sat, pressing her palm down hard, searching for some direction. When nothing came, she looked around in frustration. Perhaps he'd heard the commotion about the English and had gone nearer the Giant's Trail to investigate.

Though she devoutly hoped she was mistaken, Wynne headed down the gently sloping hill, into the deep woods that surrounded Radnor Manor. She was careful as she walked, pausing to listen and notice which way the grouse and harriers and ravens flew. She maintained her calm as she went, but if Arthur *had* gone this way, she vowed to punish him severely. But only after she had given him the tightest and most grateful of embraces.

Wynne was nearly to the Giant's Trail, growing more and more agitated, when she suddenly halted. A squirrel high above her scolded in its high-pitched tone, then just as quickly became silent. From above the tree line came the screaming call of a chough, but where were the woodcocks and goosanders?

Then the gay laughter of a child—of Arthur!—came to her, and she had her answer. He giggled again, and an enormous tide of relief rushed over her. She started forward, but then she froze in mid-stride, for a low voice murmured a reply to Arthur, something she couldn't quite make out.

As quickly as relief had come, so now did it flee. A cold hand seemed to clench around her heart. The voice was not one she recognized, and she belatedly remembered that Arthur was not a child given to carefree laughter.

She shrank away, touching her amulet—the deep purple jewel her mother had worn, and her mother before her. Instinctively she pulled back into the protective embrace of a prickly holly, but all her senses strained forward, needing to know who was with Arthur. She heard the movement through the woods, the sound of a large animal traveling without fear in a straight path. He was mounted, she realized. But above all else that she sensed about this unknown person with Arthur, the most overwhelming was that this was the man. This was the one she'd felt since yesterday.

"Are you often allowed to wander so far from home?"

His voice was deep and mellow, though Welsh was clearly not his usual tongue. Yet Wynne nonetheless detected a small edge of tension in his tone. Or perhaps anticipation was a better description.

"No," Arthur admitted. "But now that I'm past my sixth birthday, I think it's all right. Don't you?"

Had the circumstances been different, Wynne would have smiled at the odd mixture of childish lisp and mature phrasing that was so typical of Arthur. As it was, she only stood there as still as stone, waiting for them to come into view and promising to put the fear of the Lord into Arthur once she had him safely back.

"I think six is too young to be alone in the woods," the man replied to the boy. "How do you think your mother and father will feel about your absence when I bring you home?"

He intended to bring Arthur home! That was all Wynne heard. It was all she needed to hear. She pushed away from the holly and moved toward their voices.

"My real mother is dead. And I don't have a father," Arthur replied matter-of-factly. "Well, really, I had two, but neither of them wanted to keep me. I figured that out from what people said in the village."

"Arthur!" Wynne moved into the path of the big horse. She was as stunned by Arthur's casual revelation as the man and boy were by her sudden appearance. But she was determined to brazen her way through this situation. She would deal with Arthur and what he actually knew of his parentage at another time.

"Arthur, where have you been? I've been searching everywhere for you," she said, her hands planted on her hips. Then she looked directly at the man, giving him what she hoped passed for a grateful smile. "Thank you for finding him. I'm sorry if he caused you any trouble, but I'll take him off your hands now."

Her eyes met his, and then could not pull away. They were dark eyes, she saw, yet not that deep black-brown so common to her people. These were warm brown eyes, and yet they were opaque and impenetrable right now, as if he purposefully shuttered his thoughts—and motives— from anyone's prying eyes.

But though she could not guess at his reasons for being in her forest, there were many other aspects of him that she recognized at once. He was English, just as she'd predicted. His studded bliaut, tall boots, and leather gloves proclaimed it. But he was no monk, nor was he some fat and wealthy lord. This was a man who lived by his sword, she realized with an uneasy shiver. From the hard planes of his jaw and steely quality of his gaze to the obvious strength of his body and ominous presence of his dagger and sword, he was a man of war.

Had he come to make war on them?

"Don't be angry with me, Wynne," Arthur pleaded, breaking into her disturbing thoughts. "I was following a red kite. I wanted to find her nest. And then I got stuck—"

"I found him up a tree," the man interjected. "He couldn't go up and he couldn't get down."

Wynne took a settling breath. His voice was calm and

comforting, but she would not be deceived by his reassuring tones and his handsome face.

And it was a handsome face, she had to admit. Strong and lean, with a square jaw and a straight nose. Even his dark hair, which was long and tied back, was clean and shining in the sunlight that streamed down through the oak branches.

She frowned, forcing herself to concentrate on what was really important here. How he looked certainly did not matter.

"Thank you, milord. I'll take him off your hands now. You need not trouble yourself with him any further."

" 'Twas no trouble," he answered, making no move to hand Arthur down. "Arthur and I have become fast friends, haven't we?"

"He said I have the hands of a horseman," Arthur said brightly. "He said gentleness and a light touch are very important to the horse."

"So they are," Wynne agreed. "But you must come down. Right now, Arthur."

"I am Sir Cleve FitzWarin," the man said, still not making any attempt to relinquish his hold on the boy. "I know this is Arthur. Are you his mother?"

Wynne peered at him. There was something about his question that bothered her, and yet she could not determine what. On the surface it was the most natural inquiry in the world, and yet she sensed again that strange air of anticipation about him.

"No, I'm not his mother. As Arthur has already informed you, his mother is no longer living. He's in my care now."

When he quirked one brow questioningly, she reluctantly continued. "I'm Wynne ab Gruffydd. Arthur and I live at Radnor Manor."

"Then you know this area."

"Of course."

"Good. Perhaps you will be kind enough to allow me and my men a place to rest our horses the night and fill our water pouches."

Wynne's eyes narrowed, and she stared hard at him. He was manipulating her, pure and simple. She knew it, and she could tell by the sudden glint in his eyes that he knew she knew. But that didn't perturb him in the least. Though a bubble of anger rose to her lips, she forced herself to suppress it. He wanted to see Radnor Manor, did he? Well, then, she would let him. That would give her time to determine what he was up to, for she was certain he had some hidden motive for being here. That's why she had sensed him so vividly. She would invite him to stay on the manor grounds. Maybe she would even provide him and his men with a fine feast of fresh venison and birch wine.

She fought down a slight smile and nodded her head. "You and your men are most welcome at Radnor Manor," she said in a far friendlier tone than she felt.

And if time proved them to be unwelcome, perhaps those fairy caps she'd planned for the next pompous churchmen who came through would do better for this English knight and his followers, wherever *they* were. Fairy caps or witch seed or even blue violets.

She turned to lead the way and let her smile break through. Oh, yes, she would just love to play with this mighty knight from England. When he finally left her portion of Wales, it would be with the sincere intention never again to return.

3

Surely not even Wales's greatest leaders had ever presided over so uncomfortable a gathering, Wynne thought sourly. She cast an eye at Druce and his scowling fellows, all gathered to one side of the main hall's wide fireplace. He looked ready to toss down the gauntlet at any moment and take the English on in battle, no matter that he was outnumbered.

The English knight, however, seemed completely unfazed by the hostility of the Welshmen. Wynne stared at him and his men clustered on the other side of the fire pit, their faces lit by the flickering fire and the torchiers that circled the hall. To her distinct unease she could not escape the feeling that this Cleve FitzWarin was very well pleased to be feasting tonight at Radnor Manor.

She heard a murmur behind her, then detected the stealthy movement of a six-year-old body. "Sit still, else you shall all go to bed," she whispered as softly as was possible to do and yet still maintain control of her charges. Unfortunately instead of quieting the restive children, her words seemed only to draw the Englishman's gaze.

"I beg you, do not admonish them on our account," he protested. "I would rather you introduce them than suppress their natural curiosity about the strangers in their midst."

Wynne started to respond, then promptly clamped her mouth shut. She and Gwynedd had agreed that her aunt should take the lead role in any discussions with the English knights. Druce was there to counter any physical threat, while Gwynedd and her calm manner would ease any tension. And perhaps the older woman would be able to draw this Cleve FitzWarin into revealing more of his plans and motives than he intended.

Gwynedd smiled in the direction of her guest, then gestured to the children. "Come forward, my lambs. Come to my side."

Like eager kittens the five children tumbled from their shadowed positions behind Wynne, their eyes bright with curiosity. For once Arthur did not hang back, for he already considered the English leader his special friend. Not to be outdone, Rhys and Madoc jockeyed for position, pushing their way to the fore. They were not afraid of the "bloody English bastards." At least not here in the security of their own comfortable home.

Bronwen and Isolde were not as aggressive as the boys, yet even their curiosity could not be misread. Isolde stood as one of the boys might, hands on her hips, staring straight at the English. Only Bronwen, sweet, shy child that she was, stood demurely to the side. She held a puppy in her arms and kept her gaze more on the fat, sleepy animal, only glancing up now and again at the strangers across the fire.

Once the children had introduced themselves, Gwynedd clapped her gnarled hands, drawing the squirming youngsters' attention. " 'Tis late now. Far past the time for all good children to be in their beds. Off with you now. All of you," she added before Rhys and Madoc could make their customary protestations.

Wynne was relieved to have the children away from the Englishman. His easy way with Arthur and his deliberate interest in the others somehow bothered her. She would rather he abandon this farce and reveal the true purpose of his presence in Wales. And in Radnor Forest.

Torn between needing to supervise the children and not wanting to miss even one word of what went on around the fire, Wynne gnawed at her lower lip.

"Arthur. Isolde. I'm putting you two in charge. Make sure everyone washes themselves and goes to the privy pot. Then everyone had better go directly to bed. Directly," she added, raising her brows and staring pointedly at the twins.

"But we're not sleepy—"

"—or dirty," Rhys finished for Madoc.

"And make sure you take off your shoes before you get into the bed," Wynne continued, ignoring their protestations. "I'll be up to the loft in just a little while, and whoever isn't ready for bed shall suffer the consequences tomorrow. Is that clear?"

" 'Tis not fair," one of the quintet muttered.

"We never have *any* fun."

Even Arthur was surprisingly vocal. "Why can't we stay up, Wynne? Just this once?"

Wynne was hard-pressed to stifle her exasperation. Only by reminding herself that it was the Englishman she was irritated with, not the children, was she able to suppress a sharp retort.

She squatted down among them, commanding their attention with her eyes. "You have to go to bed now, otherwise you'll be too tired to get up tomorrow and go down in the Cleft with me."

"Down in the Cleft?"

"The Devil's Cleft?"

"Shhh, shhh," Wynne cautioned, but she couldn't help smiling at her enthusiastic young charges. "You've been clamoring to go, and since I'm climbing down there tomorrow to dig for skirret root, I'll take all of you along with me. But *only* if you go to bed right now."

Once more Wynne was reminded of gamboling kittens as the five of them competed to see who could get out to the wash bucket the fastest. Even demure Bronwen leaped gaily, caught up in the excitement, while her puppy ambled along after them all.

But Wynne's moment of pleasure fled when she turned back to the circle of adults. The meal was long over, and Gwynedd was now relating an oft-told tale of Radnor Forest and how the manor came to be built more than two centuries previously. Although her tale of the Radnor dragon and how the Giant's Trail had come to be had the other Englishmen enthralled, and even Druce and his comrades who knew the story well were drawn in by her eerie singsong retelling of it, the one man—that Cleve fellow—was clearly not listening. He was watching Wynne instead, and once more she felt that odd shiver of anticipation.

"—of these forests," Gwynedd was saying. " 'Tis a place well known for the magical power invested in its secret places. Our herbs are more potent. Our oaks are more holy. Even the mistletoe grows thicker and more freely in these woodlands."

The Englishman's gaze finally turned away from Wynne, and he smiled at the older woman. "I've heard also that a woman of Radnor is known for her strange abilities. Some have gone so far as to term her a witch."

He paused, and in the silence there was a restless shifting among the Welshmen. FitzWarin's eyes flicked briefly over them and then back to Gwynedd. "Are you the one named the Seeress of Radnor? The Welsh Witch?"

If only Druce had not jerked to look over at her, Wynne was later to fret. If only he had not stared at her in alarm, the Englishman might have been satisfied with Gwynedd's reply.

As it was, the old woman's rambling response, that she was indeed blessed with the sight and possessed of a darker knowledge than that given to most mortals, did not seem to convince him. Though he questioned Gwynedd with polite deference and even remarked in a friendly tone of caution that Norman priests would not countenance her claims, and indeed might even brand her a witch and subject her to the "trial," Wynne knew he did not believe Gwynedd.

He maintained their conversation out of curiosity and to ferret out whatever he could. But he knew Gwynedd was no longer the Seeress, and judging from the way his gaze wandered constantly back to Wynne, he guessed that *she* was.

Well, what matter if he did? she thought vengefully. Gwynedd *had* relinquished that role to her long ago. Everyone within hailing distance of Radnor Forest knew that; there seemed no reason to hide the fact from these English. Both Gwynedd and Druce were too cautious by far. No matter the reason this Englishman had come to Radnor asking questions about the Welsh Witch, she was well able to handle him.

A show of her power was what was needed here, she realized. Something to set him back on his heels. Something that would make him think twice about tangling with the Welsh, and remind him that the English had been sent fleeing from Wales seven years ago for a reason.

She shifted on the rough three-legged stool and smiled faintly, anticipating once more how she might curtail this man's threat. It never ceased to amuse her what a violent flux of the bowels could do to a person, and she knew just the portion of snakeroot required to get the job done.

She lifted her gaze to the Englishman, and this time she didn't even try to hide the smug expression on her face. The fact that he was staring at her with an equally triumphant expression hardly bothered her at all. Men were always smug in their dealings with women, especially Englishmen. Well, she would just see how long his arrogance lasted in the face of her "witch craft." She'd not had a cause to make any mischief since she'd frightened old Taffydd from trapping hares in her special part of the forest. An oil of fireweed soaked into his trap lines had burned his hands with two days of itching. She had not kept her actions secret from the old man. He knew now that her warnings were not to be taken lightly. Now also would this Englishman be forced to admit as much.

The Englishman was talking, something about tin mines and the special properties of the black wool of Builth Wells, but Wynne knew it was just part of the farce he played. She stood up abruptly, drawing everyone's gaze.

"As much as I enjoy this company, I fear I must check on the children. Also, since tonight is the quarter moon, and it didn't rain today, nor was there even a dew, I want to check the shutters again."

Neither Gwynedd nor Druce reacted to her words other than to watch her and wait. As she expected, however, the Englishman looked around as if for some explanation. Then he asked her directly.

"The quarter moon?"

She inclined her head slightly toward him, then casually shook out her full kersey skirt. "When the rain does not wash the air clean on the day of the quarter moon, there are often strange occurrences in our forests. Not always," she hastened to add, as if for reassurance. "But sometimes . . ."

FitzWarin frowned at the sudden restless shifting of his men, but when he looked back at her, she saw the glint of comprehension in his eyes. He knew what she was trying to do.

For an instant her resolve wavered. Her confidence weakened. In the wildly flickering firelight his dark features had taken on a decidedly wicked cast, as if it were *he* who was possessed of some secret powers over her and not the other way around. He knew she was preparing to fight him, but he was not in the least concerned.

But Wynne was no weak-willed female, nor one to fold at the least sign of difficulty. Maybe that was what he was accustomed to in England, but he was in Wales now, and women here were afforded far more rights than in other lands. She especially, as Seeress of Radnor Forest, had been raised to expect a position of importance and respect in her society. This fool of an Englishman had no idea with whom he had chosen to tangle.

She nodded deliberately at him, holding her smile steady.

Had she simply turned then and left, she would have come out the clear victor in their silent battle. But she hesitated too long, and through the long hours of the night she was to regret it most dearly.

For Cleve FitzWarin had not nodded back at her as she had anticipated. Instead he'd let his dark, unfathomable eyes slip down the length of her, slowly and thoroughly measuring her with his impertinent gaze, not as a foe to be reckoned with but as a woman to be desired, pursued, and then mastered. It had taken her completely off guard, and when he'd finally finished his rude appraisal and returned his gaze to her face, she knew her shocked expression had given her away.

She'd snapped her gaping mouth closed, and her expression had turned furious, but it was too late. He'd seen her moment of uncertainty and discomfort, and no doubt he'd marked it well as her vulnerability.

She had whirled and stalked away, silently cursing him with every step she took and trying to convince herself that she'd not really lost anything in this first round. If anything, he would only grow more confident, making it easier for her ultimately to make a fool of him.

But in the end the only comfort she found was in reassuring herself that he could not possibly know how profoundly that one look had affected her. He could not know that her entire being had responded to him. Her breath had come shorter. Her stomach had tightened somewhere deep down and low. Even her breasts had tingled and her nipples had grown small and hard, as if from the cold. Only she hadn't been cold. Anything but.

Yet the fact that he could not know of her physical response to him was in truth small comfort. For no matter how she tried to rationalize her reaction, she could not. She'd sensed the danger of this man since yesterday. Now he was here, and her fear of him only increased. Only it was not precisely fear—at least not the sort of fear she'd experienced in the past when Englishmen had come to

Wales. Then she'd feared for her safety, for her physical safety and even for her life.

Now, though it was completely illogical . . . now she feared for her soul.

4

The Englishmen had camped in the cedar grove just beyond the kitchen. They'd kept their own guard posted all night, two men to watch over their horses. Wynne smirked at the sight of the hunched-over figures, barely visible in the cold, misty dawn. For all their professions of friendship and peaceful intentions, they clearly trusted the Welsh no better than Wynne and her people trusted them.

But this wary sort of truce, as unpleasant as it was, was still better than the inhuman cruelties of war.

Inhuman cruelties of war. Wynne sighed and turned away from the window. The problem was, the cruelties of war were entirely human. She, who was so familiar with the mountains and forests, with all the wild places and wild creatures of Wales, knew better than most that no animal was so cruel as was the common foot soldier.

In her more charitable moments she could understand it. Fear was the most powerful of human emotions. It drove a person beyond ordinary strengths, beyond the ordinary boundaries of civilization. Yet even blind, terrifying fear could not justify all the horrors inflicted in the name of war, for it was invariably those most unable to strike back who received the worst treatment. She'd seen helpless prisoners tortured in the most vile and unbelievable fashions. She'd seen infants and children garroted by drunken soldiers.

And she'd seen terrified women—some not even old enough rightfully to be called women—raped repeatedly by men gorged on both their fear and their power. Her own sister . . . No amount of charity or understanding could ever justify such sickening behavior.

She shuddered and wrapped her wool knitted shawl tighter around her shoulders. She didn't want to think about it. She didn't want to remember that monstrous time when Radnor Forest had been overrun by the English. Those had been days of violence and horror and never-ending fear. Though she'd been but a girl of twelve, she remembered it in chilling detail. How could she ever forget? The day of the attack, then the long weeks—the endless months—of the English occupation.

And what had come of it in the end? she wondered now as she'd wondered so many times since then. What had resulted from all the misery they'd lived through during that most dreadful of years?

In the end the English had left, withdrawn by a sullen king who'd been soundly defeated at some distant battle in the north. Slowly life had been restored to a modicum of its previous normalcy. The ordinary cycles of life had returned. The sheep were shorn in the spring. The fields were prepared, and eventually the barley and pease and corn were reaped. But life had never truly been the same since then. How could it be? So many dead. So many maimed. She'd lost her own parents.

And then there were those whose lives had been destroyed in far less visible ways.

She sighed, then looked up as a slight noise came from the loft. Her melancholy lifted when a rosy face peeped down and, upon spying Wynne, broke into a sleepy, gap-toothed grin. On silent feet Isolde made her way backward down the steeply slanted ladder, and as Wynne watched the child's slow descent, she smiled to herself. The only good thing to come of those times was the children, no matter the violent way in which they were conceived. For her they were the only proof that a God did indeed watch over the world from His heavenly throne. Without them she would gladly have reverted to the pagan ways of the beasts, worshiping only the wind and the rain and fire, respecting only what affected her life in a real and lasting way.

But her five little children restored her faith in God, for God had truly blessed her when He'd sent them to Radnor Manor. Though He'd taken her parents and sister from her, He'd given her these five orphans to take their place.

She smiled as Isolde padded on bare feet over to the fire, then perched on a stool next to the hearth and basked in the warmth of the strengthening flames. How like her mother, Wynne's sister, she looked.

"Do you want a mug of warmed milk and honey, love?" she asked, reaching over to rub her niece's back.

Isolde shook her head, and her thick black hair stirred softly around her face. "I'm still too sleepy," she murmured.

"What woke you so early?"

The child yawned, then sighed. Her gaze was clearer when she looked at Wynne. "You said we could go down in the Devil's Cleft with you today."

Wynne's fond smile widened as she stared at the little girl. She was such a lovely child with her wealth of hair and vivid green eyes. Though it would probably have been better for all of the children if they'd had the coloring of only their mothers—the dark hair and eyes of the Welsh people—it was hard to begrudge Isolde the rare beauty of her unusual eyes. Even the others—Arthur with his English coloring of brown hair and hazel eyes, and Bronwen with her flaxen tresses and dark brown eyes—were lovely in their very uniqueness.

At least Rhys and Madoc appeared thoroughly Welsh with their more typical coloring and sturdy builds. They would not suffer the same insecurities of being different that would plague the other three all their lives. She, of all people, knew how hard that could be.

And yet hadn't she turned that very difference to her own advantage? Her visions were real enough. Her knowledge of plants and herbs and all the wild creatures was vast. But had her eyes been an ordinary brown or black, her position as Seeress of Radnor would not be nearly so strong. It was her eyes—the strange clear blue of the sky, she was told—that lent credence to her predictions and spells.

She had her father to thank for that. He was from the far north, but had been beguiled into staying in Radnor Forest by Wynne's mother. Though her mother's powers had never been strong, her oldest daughter, Maradedd, had been blessed with the Radnor vision. Wynne's own talents had not been as strong nor as important. But when Maradedd had died, everything had fallen to Wynne.

She sighed and bent toward Isolde and turned the child's face up to hers. Yes, those green eyes had the same possibilities, she decided. Whether or not the Radnor visions would affect Isolde was not yet known. But she *was* Maradedd's daughter, notwithstanding the tainted English blood that also ran in her.

"What's the matter?"

Wynne started from her deep thoughts. "Oh, nothing. 'Tis nothing at all. Only this hair caught on your cheek." She smoothed the child's hair back, then rose with a determined smile.

"Will you help me with the breakfast porridge? Then we can rouse all those lay-a-beds up there and get on our way."

"Can I stir the pot? I promise I'll be very careful of the fire. I'll be really careful this time. And even if I get splashed like last time, I won't cry," Isolde added. "I'll just get the goatweed oil like you did and spread it on the burn."

Wynne smiled once more at her sweet, innocent niece and stroked her head again. "Very good. You remembered that very well, Isolde."

The child beamed. "I'm going to remember everything you show us today. Everything. I'm going to learn all about the plants and the forest, just like you. And when I grow up, I'm going to be just like you."

As they began the morning routine, Wynne couldn't help but wonder if Isolde's words would prove an accurate prediction. And if they did, should she be pleased for the child or worried for her? Being Seeress brought such responsibilities. Sometimes Wynne wished she could simply be an ordinary maiden looking forward to a perfectly ordinary life. She wouldn't have to preside over the court held four times a year in the three villages within the forest. She wouldn't have to meet everyone's expectations of what being Seeress meant. But an ordinary life was not what fate had in store for her. As for Isolde, well, what was meant to be, would be.

Mist still lay on the land when they started out. The ground was wet and the sun but a blurry yellow-orange ball on the horizon. With the five children trailing her like bright-eyed little ducklings, Wynne led them around the manor, carefully avoiding the English encampment.

In the dark comfort of her bed last night she had decided to leave the English knights to Gwynedd and Druce after all. It would be best for her simply to follow her normal routine, to care for the children, give them their lessons, and see to her herb gathering. Today's journey to the Cleft would accomplish all three of those tasks, and if it also thwarted the Englishman, so much the better. That man's interest last night in the children still troubled her. Keeping them well out of his way seemed the best choice open to her. His disturbing interest in her as well gave her reason to avoid him at all costs.

She heard a giggle and glanced back at the straggling line of children. "Everyone must keep up," she admonished. "Remember, we're practicing how to walk silently in the forest. How to avoid stepping on twigs and dried leaves. How not to alarm the creatures or leave a trail. I want all of you to concentrate on every single step, all right?"

"But what about the dew?" Rhys called to her in a half whisper.

"It sticks to our shoes and leaves a mark in the grass," Madoc finished.

"Once the sun comes up, it won't matter," Arthur explained. "All the dew will be gone then."

"Very good, Arthur. And it was very observant of you two to notice it," she added to the twins.

"Stay in line, Rhys," Isolde scolded.

"Don't be so bossy," his brother scolded right back. "We have a lot more to carry than you do."

"Well, my stuff is more important," she retorted.

Wynne turned to face them, her hands planted on her

hips in frustration. "Every squirrel, every rabbit, badger, fox, and deer will flee long before we approach anywhere near if you keep up this chatter." When they all stared at her with the proper expressions of chagrin, she nodded. "That's better. Now, let's begin again. And this time I promise a reward to each of you who remains silent and walks carefully."

"What kind of surprise?" Madoc ventured in a hushed whisper.

Wynne shook her head in exasperation, though a smile struggled its way to her lips. "Extra stew of cooker pears tonight," she finally relented. Then, before any of them could question her further, she turned and resumed their trek.

Though the morning was cool, by the time they reached the dense thorn wood that protected the Cleft, Wynne was well warmed. The children were too preoccupied by their exertions to do more than follow her instructions and try to keep up with the demanding pace she'd set.

"Shall we take a little rest before we climb down?" she asked, hiding a grin as best she could.

"Yes," Arthur answered at once.

"I'm tired, and my feet hurt," Bronwen added.

"I'm not tired," Rhys boasted.

"Me neither," echoed his twin.

Isolde glared at them. "Don't tell such fibs! You *are* tired; you just don't want to admit it."

"We are not!"

"We could climb down there right now," Madoc retorted.

"Or even swing down on a long vine—"

"Rhys and Madoc!" Wynne's sharp tone drew everyone's attention. "If I hear even one more word about swinging on vines over the Devil's Cleft, your confinement to the sleeping loft the other day will seem like nothing at all compared with the punishment you shall have this time. Is that perfectly clear?"

Amid much shifting of both feet and eyes, the two adventurers mumbled their understanding. Wynne was just congratulating herself on her success when another voice joined in.

"Had I a mother like you, I'm certain I would not be possessed of nearly so many scars as unfortunately I am."

Wynne pivoted around at the words, her heart pounding a sudden, fearful rhythm. When she spied a man in the shadows beside a thick oak trunk, she reached instinctively for the dagger that hung in a sheath from her girdle. But then she recognized the man, and her emotions made a quick and inexplicable change from fear to an unnerving panic. The Englishman. How had he followed her so easily? Why hadn't she heard him or at least sensed him?

Her gaze narrowed as he moved nearer, and she willed her heart to slow its thunderous pace. She did not have to fear physical harm from him. He had startled her, that was all. He had taken her by surprise. But she couldn't help remembering the slow, assessing gaze he'd slid over her last night. Only the quick flare of her anger prevented her from succumbing to the same stunned silence as on that previous uncomfortable occasion.

"You followed us," she began in an accusing tone.

"Hello. Remember me?" Arthur interrupted her excitedly. "Where's your horse?"

The Englishman squatted on his heels as Arthur came up to him. "I decided to walk. I've been trying to catch up with you, but you've all been walking so fast." He glanced up at Wynne, not trying in the least to disguise the gloating expression on his face.

"Yes, we're very fast walkers," Bronwen agreed, moving up alongside Arthur. Wynne stared at the girl in surprise. Shy Bronwen speaking up so eagerly, and to a complete stranger? In a moment the other three crowded forward as well, all chattering and bragging, asking questions and cautiously fingering his odd English clothing.

"Can I ride on your horse when we get home?" Isolde asked as she elbowed Madoc aside to get nearer the man.

"Why did you come to Radnor Manor?" Arthur interrupted before the Englishman could answer her.

"Can we—"

"—hold your dagger?" Rhys finished for Madoc as the two of them eyed the man's finely carved bone-handled weapon.

"Are you married?"

It was Bronwen's inquiry, so innocently stated, that brought the questioning to an abrupt end. Rhys and Madoc started laughing. Even Arthur, who was not one to take sides in boy-girl arguments, joined in.

"Knights don't have time to get married, Bronwen," he explained importantly. "They have to go riding around, fighting fights and doing other . . . well, other knight stuff."

"As it happens, I'm not married," the man said, chuckling. For an instant his eyes met Wynne's, but although the moment was fleeting, a sharp jolt of awareness passed between them. She felt it all the way to her toes.

"But I do plan to marry one of these days," he continued, addressing Bronwen. "Don't you?"

"Oh, yes," replied the child, breaking into one of her rare and beautiful smiles. "I want to have lots and lots of babies."

"Me too," Isolde broke in. "I want lots and lots of babies too."

The man chuckled again. "With such a large family as you already have, I would think you'd get tired of being around so many brothers and sisters all the time." He studied them all with a more watchful expression. Then he looked back at Wynne. "How did you come to have all these children under your care?"

Wynne hesitated. He already knew the answer to that; she was sure of it. So what was he up to? Her eyes narrowed, and she squared her shoulders. Two could play at these cat-and-mouse games of his. With a careless shrug she turned away from him and sat down on an exposed shelf of limestone.

"The children are all orphans."

"They all appear to be the same age," he prodded her.

"We're all six," Arthur announced.

"But we're—"

"—the oldest," the twins announced.

"They were born on the very same day," Bronwen explained. "They're twins."

"But just because they're the oldest, that doesn't mean they can order us around," Isolde stated quite firmly.

Wynne could not restrain herself any longer. Enough of this friendly chatter. "I'm the only one who does any ordering about," she interjected. She sent the children a cautionary look, then addressed the Englishman directly. "Is there a reason that you followed us?"

The smile on his face changed ever so slightly. He'd been amused and charmed by the milling children; now he seemed equally amused by her question, but in a somehow more challenging way. Wynne, however, had decided to take control of this game of his, and she waited patiently, vowing to play the role of cat today, not of mouse.

He cleared his throat. "I don't often have the chance to

take a ramble in the forests just for the pleasure of it. It's a welcome change from the company of men and horses."

Wynne did not even try to disguise her skepticism. "You've come all the way from England to take a walk down a woodland path with a Welshwoman and five children?"

"Maybe he came to find the dragon," Arthur suggested helpfully. "To slay the fire-breathing dragon Druce told us about. The one that lives in the caves of Black Mountain."

Arthur's expression was so serious that Wynne was no longer certain she wanted the man to answer her question. At least not while the children were around. For whatever perverse reason, the children all seemed to like him. Especially Arthur.

She should take heart at that, she knew. She'd always noticed an innate ability in both children and animals to distinguish between good and evil, so the children's unrestrained acceptance of this man should ease her worries. He did not mean to harm them. But there was still something he was hiding.

"If the Englishman seeks the dragon of Black Mountain, we can point out the cart track that leads that way." She stared pointedly at the man. " 'Tis just beyond the moor you crossed. On your way back you'll see it off to your right."

He nodded slightly, not saying a word, but only studying her until she grew decidedly uncomfortable. "For today I'll forgo the dragon. And I'm Norman, not English."

Wynne lifted her brows. "Really? Tell me, why is it English nobility still identify themselves with Normandy? 'Tis at least a hundred years that you've been in England, yet you refuse to call yourselves English."

"We're *Cymry*. Welsh," Isolde boasted. She moved

nearer her aunt, and Wynne drew comfort from the child's loyalty.

"Perhaps then I should term myself Norman English," he conceded. "And I have a name," he went on. "I'm Cleve FitzWarin. I'd like you to call me Cleve."

Wynne gave him a contemptuous look. "Well, *Sir Cleve*, the children and I have a purpose for being here today. As interesting as this conversation has been, we must be about our work."

"May I be of any help? Wynne," he added with subtle but still obvious emphasis.

She bristled at once. "I have enough help."

"Then perhaps I can help you shepherd the children," he replied smoothly, not at all affected by her simmering anger. "I'm certain they won't mind."

"We don't—"

"—mind at all!"

The other three children looked less sure than the twins, for they'd obviously sensed the animosity between the two adults. Arthur in particular appeared distressed by the tension between Wynne and the Englishman, and Wynne was immediately sorry that she had let this man bother her so. What had happened to her plan to be the cat and not the mouse?

She gave him a tight, even smile. "If you wish to join us, you may." Then she turned abruptly away, unable to pretend to a calm she hardly felt. "Let's be on our way. The trail down into the Cleft is very near."

As they made their slow and careful descent along the rocky face of the Devil's Cleft, Wynne reluctantly admitted to herself that FitzWarin's presence was useful. She'd known the climb down would be awkward with five children. She could safely shepherd only two or three at a time. But with the Englishman's presence they could all go down together.

She led the way, followed by the children, with him bringing up the rear. Though the trail was not difficult for a careful adult, she knew that the children might be too excited to be as cautious as they should be. It was almost a relief, then, to have another far more stern voice to instruct the rambunctious quintet.

"Rhys, don't crowd your brother. Arthur, keep your eyes on where you're going," he ordered from somewhere behind her.

"Oh, look! Look at the big butterfly!" Bronwen exclaimed. "It's as yellow and orange as a fire."

"Catch it. Catch it!" Rhys and Madoc cried.

"No! Leave it alone," Isolde said, hurrying toward the two boys. "You'll hurt it, and if you do, then I'll hurt you!"

Wynne turned to stare up at the trio. "Isolde, I'll handle this. Rhys and Madoc, we're only collecting what we need. Nothing more. If we can't use it for food or medicine or something else, then we leave it where it is. You know my rules."

At once they became contrite, and she nodded approvingly, then smiled at them. "I know you're excited. There's so much to see down here. But we want to leave it here so we can come back to see it again and again."

It was in that unguarded moment, when she was thinking only of the children and the land that sustained them all, that her eyes met the Englishman's. To her surprise his expression was actually approving. Then he smiled at her—a mixture of admiration and camaraderie—and she felt the oddest reaction in her stomach. This was not the bold, assessing gaze of last night, and she was hard put to be angered by it. But dismayed . . .

She was unnerved and put off balance by his steady stare, and with an uncomfortable swallow she turned away.

Once they had reached the lush green floor of the narrow ravine, Wynne purposefully set the children to their separate tasks.

"Rhys and Madoc, I want you to scrape away as much of this soft dark-gray stone as you can. See how it flakes off if you drag a piece of sharpened granite on it? That's right," she said as the boys mimicked her action. "Put what you scrape into this leather sack.

"And Arthur, you need to pick the youngest, smallest fern fronds. Here's one. See how the end is still curled? Only take the ones that are about as long as your hand. Here's a cloth you can lay them on. Afterward I'll wrap them up for you."

"What about us?" Bronwen and Isolde chorused.

"Let's see. Oh, I know. I need spiderwebs. Can you collect them for me? Or, no. Maybe I'd better do that. Why don't you girls dig for skirret. Here's a spade. You can take turns. One of you can hold the leaves aside like this while the other one digs for the roots." She pulled free several of the white, fleshy tubers. "Just pull some of it off, then pat the rest of the roots and the plant back into place."

"So they can grow more of those fat things for us for next time," Isolde reasoned.

"Precisely. I've been taking skirret roots from this bed of plants for years."

She brushed the moist earth from her hands as she stepped back and surveyed her industrious brood. Although she could probably collect everything she needed in less time than her five helpers could, she was glad she'd decided to bring them along. Six years old was not too young to be contributing to the welfare of the family. Every child needed to learn responsibility, as well as to know that they were important to the family, even when it was not the most typical of families. That lesson could not begin too soon, especially for these orphans who must eventually know the difficult truth of how they came to be and how unwanted they once were. But they were wanted now. Very much so. She couldn't love them more if they were truly her own.

"Have you no task for me?"

The Englishman's low voice just behind her caused Wynne to jump in alarm. She nearly trod in a bed of young Olympia fern, so startled was she.

"You . . . I . . . no." She fought to compose herself. "No, I have no task for you. You may leave anytime you like."

He raised one dark brow at her brusque remark, and Wynne was immediately embarrassed by her rudeness. He had, after all, aided her and the children in their precarious descent into the Cleft.

Still, he'd followed them here uninvited. She owed him no more than the minimal courtesy.

"Thank you for your help, but I'm sure you'll find our activities extremely boring. We'll be gathering plants and minerals the entire morning. You need not linger to help us."

"Ah, but 'twould be my pleasure to do so," he answered, mocking her forced politeness with an excessive display of courtliness. "If you would but direct me, I'm certain I can be of some assistance to you."

Wynne's eyes narrowed in frustration, to be rewarded only by the faintest shadow of amusement in his warm brown gaze. He was laughing at her, and it galled her to no end.

"Perhaps there *is* one task," she said as a truly wicked idea came into her head. Though she knew she should not be so unkind, even to this Englishman, some devil seemed to drive her. She consoled herself with the reminder that he had no business being here in the first place. Nor even in Wales. He'd brought this trouble down upon himself.

"I need to replenish my stores of parsley fern. Only the leaves, mind you. I'll find a plant, and perhaps you can fill this pouch with the newest leaves. Just the tiny pale-green ones."

"What do you use them for?" he asked as he followed her.

For causing a severe rash on those who think to cross me, she thought spitefully. But her answer was more evasive. "Oh, for medicinal purposes."

"For coughs? Or bleeding?" he prodded.

"No." She searched her mind for an answer that was not precisely a lie. " 'Tis invaluable for expelling worms. Here." In relief she pointed toward a plant. "Here's what I'm looking for. And there are more over there." Then she turned and hurried back toward the children.

Perhaps his reaction to the irritating juices of the fresh leaves would not be too severe, she rationalized as she searched for the sturdy webs of the tree queen spider. Perhaps the itching would only last a day or two. But even as she began to carefully remove one web from the limbs of a young elm tree, Wynne could not escape the feeling that she would somehow come to regret the devious trick she was playing on him. He had the look of a man who could be as ruthless and vengeful to his enemies as he had proven to be kind and patient with the children. It would not take him long to determine what she'd done, and then he would surely group her among his enemies.

She glanced back at him, biting her lip doubtfully. At

the same instant he looked up and met her eyes. For a long moment their gazes remained locked, and she was assailed with that strange and vital awareness of him that had affected her long before she'd ever laid eyes on him. There was some link between them, she realized with a sinking sense of dismay. What that link was remained a mystery to her, but it did not change things. They were connected by fate. She was certain of it.

Yet she feared that by this casting down of the glove, as it were, she had irrevocably directed that fate down the path of outright warfare.

Still, she knew there was no other way. Her hand went to the ever-present Radnor amulet that hung between her breasts. He was English; she was *Cymry*. They were destined to clash.

5

The morning seemed to stretch out forever. Though the children were surprisingly diligent in their efforts, and the linen bags and leather pouches she had brought were swiftly filled, Wynne could take no pleasure in it. She kept stealing glances at the Englishman and veering between regret and righteous anger. She should have warned him to wear gloves with the parsley fern; he would be furious with her and was bound to find a way to retaliate. And yet he would at least recognize that she was a more than worthy opponent. He would think very carefully before tangling with her again.

"I'm hungry," Isolde announced as the midday sun began to find its way into the deeply shadowed ravine. "Can we eat now?"

"What did you—"

"—bring to eat?" the twins asked.

Wynne looked up, relieved for a break from her warring emotions. "We've Gwynedd's barley bread, cheese, herring, and dried raisins. There's a small spring beyond that hanging vine—right up in the wall. Why don't all of you wash up there? Wash especially well and get any grit or plant stains off your hands," she added with a guilty glance at the Englishman.

Cleve FitzWarin was sitting back on a thick carpet of moss, and the sun shining through the tree branches above dappled him with light. Wynne was uncomfortably aware once more of the vital strength of him. What was worse, however, was that he watched her now with the most discerning of gazes. The leather pouch she'd given him was filled, but she couldn't help wincing at the sight of his green-stained fingertips.

"You'd better wash too," she muttered reluctantly. "Here, use this soaproot."

He caught the stringy bit of root mass she tossed him, then handed it to Arthur. "Go along, lad. Do as Wynne says. I'll wash in a bit."

When Arthur scampered off, FitzWarin turned his disturbing gaze back on her. He scratched the back of one hand idly, and Wynne swallowed uneasily. It was just a matter of time before his skin reacted to the irritating sap. She wanted to be back at Radnor Manor before that happened.

"I'd like to know more about the children," he began, surprising her with his directness.

All her mixed feelings fled, and she gave him a wary look. "Why? What concern are they to you?"

"They're the offspring of English soldiers, are they not?"

Wynne's jaw clenched. "The bastards of a vile and cruel army," she hissed, though not loud enough for the children to hear. "The forgotten by-blows of a heartless invading people."

For once, he was not able to completely hide his reaction. She saw a faint flush cross his jaw, and his throat worked as he swallowed hard. So she had made him uncomfortable. Good.

"I am told your people do not hold a child's parentage against him," he responded, his tone low and mild in comparison with hers.

"And I'm told your people do," she snapped back.

His gaze did not waver under her furious glare. "There are those of us born on the wrong side of the sheets who yet manage to rise above it."

"You?" she exclaimed. "Are you saying that *you* were bastard-born?"

He nodded once, and for a moment Wynne stared at him in ill-disguised shock. She could see his admission had not come easy, and that fact touched her with unexpected sympathy. How foolish were the English, she thought. To blame a child for his parents' actions was so unfair. The pain of it clearly lingered long after the child grew to adulthood.

Yet she knew that she could not afford to let this man's own troubled childhood affect her judgment. She forced herself to sound firm. "Be that as it may, your similarity of situation in no way gives you the right to pry into the lives of these children."

"Perhaps not. But the expressed wishes of one of their fathers does."

"Their fathers?" Wynne stared at him, not quite understanding what he meant. "What do you mean, 'their fathers'?" Then she gasped, and her hands tightened into fists. "They *have* no fathers," she snapped, hardly able to believe that anyone, even an Englishman, could believe that those men's wishes mattered in the least to her.

"One of them has a father who wants him," the English knight countered with maddening persistence. "I'd like your help in determining just which one it is."

"A father who wants him?" she sputtered, still in shock. "A father who wants him? If that were not so poor a joke, I'd laugh in your face!"

" 'Tis not a joke. I have good reason to believe one of these children you raised was sired by my liege lord. He but wants the child of his loins."

"The child of rape, you mean. He gave up all rights to any child when he joined the godless horde that stormed across this land, killing, raping, and pillaging!"

He had the good grace to pause at her angry words, but then he pushed on. "What's done is done. Would you punish the child now by denying him the rights of his parentage?"

At that very moment Rhys and Madoc came tumbling back toward them, racing to see who was the faster. Only by the most stringent effort was Wynne able to bury her burning emotions. But her hands balled into fists and her jaw tightened painfully as her eyes glared her bitter feelings at him. Though she held her tongue, however, her mind seethed with vengeance.

Deny the child his parentage. What a fool this man was. Did he truly believe that anyone of *Cymru* would ever consider an English heritage valuable? Only the arrogant English would see it that way. And now this most arrogant of all Englishmen had come to her, wishing to take one of her children back to England with him!

Had she all the abilities attributed to her by the gossips, she would have turned him into a viper then and there, or at least struck him down with an affliction of the gut. Maybe blinded him or caused his tongue to swell and thicken, then rot and fall out. But she did not possess such dark powers, and she'd never thought it such a pity as she did now.

"Wynne, Wynne. Madoc didn't wash with soaproot,"

Isolde shouted as she, too, ran up. "He only wet his hands a very little, then wiped them on my skirt!"

With a last cutting glare at FitzWarin Wynne turned to the children. "Madoc, go back and wash up properly. And if any others of you have done a poor job of it, back you go as well."

As Madoc turned reluctantly back toward the spring, Wynne remembered the parsley fern and felt a quick glimmer of satisfaction. This Cleve FitzWarin thought he could simply ride his tall destrier into Wales, pick out some child, and return to England with it, did he? Well, he was in for a bitter lesson, and she was only too happy to be the one to give it to him. By the time she finished with him, he would consider the uncomfortable itching of his hands nothing at all. She would see him and his men retching from the food they ate, purged by the drink they took, and made dizzy by the smoke they breathed. Their skin would itch and their bowels would burn. Even sleep would not give them peace, for she knew where to find the black mold that caused dreadful dreams to both the waking and the sleeping.

She turned to look at him, and a thin, gloating smile lifted her lips. He would rue the day he ever crossed her path, thinking to steal one of her children from her.

But if he wondered at her odd and unexpected smile, or suspected the wicked thoughts and plans that fostered it, his expression did not reveal it. He only nodded at her once, then rose to head toward the spring.

Let him wash, she thought, following his tall form with her vengeful glare. It would only soften the effects of the parsley fern, not banish it. Besides, that was only a taste of what she had in store for him.

* * *

They left the Cleft shortly after their meal. Wynne led the way up the rocky wall, followed again by the children and the Englishman. Once she clambered over the rim, she turned to help Isolde out, and then Bronwen. Rhys and Madoc insisted on climbing the last steep section unassisted. When Arthur peeped over the edge, he, too, declined her help.

"I can do it," he insisted, panting from his efforts. He reached for the same exposed root the other boys had grasped, but when he pulled on it, it gave with a sudden snap.

"Arthur!" Wynne cried, grabbing wildly as he teetered backward. But she couldn't get there fast enough, and as she watched in horror, he began to fall.

"Where do you think you're going?" With a quick movement FitzWarin caught Arthur's tunic. For a moment the boy dangled, arms and legs flailing in fear. Then the man pulled him against his chest, holding him safely next to the rough wall of the ravine.

"You're all right now, my boy. Just catch your breath a bit."

Wynne heard the labored rush of Arthur's breath and was equally aware of her own relieved gasp for air. It had all happened so quickly, yet she felt now as drained as if she'd run a league and more. "Give him to me," she demanded in a voice that shook.

The Englishman met her frightened eyes, and for an instant their gazes held. Gone was her anger, replaced now by an immense gratitude. How could she have been so careless? She knew Arthur did not have the physical skills of the twins. If this man had not been there . . .

She forced her gaze away from his and instead peered down at Arthur. "Are you all right? Here, take my hand."

Once he was safely out of the Cleft, she pulled him into

a smothering embrace. "Oh, Arthur, you frightened me so," she murmured into his soft, wavy hair as she fought back a rush of tears. She breathed in the scent of him, of dirt and little-boy sweat and barley bread.

"Wynne!" He exclaimed, squirming away after a moment. "I'm not a baby, you know." He slipped away from her, then glanced over at FitzWarin, and his pale face lit up with a smile of admiration. "It's my good fortune that you were there," he said, in his more usual adult phrasing.

"Yes, it was," the Englishman answered gravely. Then he extended one hand to Arthur. "Do you think you could give me a hand up?"

Arthur leaped to the task, an eager grin on his face. Forgotten was that moment of terror, Wynne realized. Forgotten was everything in the face of this man's easy way with the boy. In that same instant she reluctantly recognized how much Arthur needed a father. How much they all did.

Coming as it did on the tail of the Englishman's revelation of his purpose in Wales, that admission was nearly her undoing. They needed a father, even the girls. No matter how hard she tried to mother them, she couldn't change that fact. Yet giving up even one of them to their English father was not the solution.

Unable to deal with these new and troubling thoughts, Wynne rose abruptly to her feet. "Let's be on our way then. Rhys, Madoc, come away from that vine. If you two think you're going to try that foolhardy feat again— Here, I want you two separated. Rhys, you shall go with Bronwen. There, up ahead of me. And Madoc, you and Isolde stay behind me—"

"I'll walk with Sir Cleve," Arthur piped up.

"No, you shall walk with me," Wynne retorted. She crossed to Arthur and took his hand in hers, pulling him clear of the Englishman. Sir Cleve, indeed! It seemed the English gave titles to baby-stealers now. What a godless race they were.

"You're hurting my hand," Arthur complained. He pulled hard against her. "Wynne!"

In sudden confusion Wynne stared down at the child. His eyes were wide and frightened. The other children, too, were watching her with expressions ranging from uncertainty to fear. She released Arthur at once, then clasped her own hands together. Anything to stop the awful shaking that had suddenly overcome them.

"Are you all right?" the Englishman asked in a quiet voice. When she didn't answer, he turned to the children. "The five of you start up the path. You know the way. Go slowly and stay together. Wynne has had a little scare, that's all. We'll follow shortly."

The children obeyed at once. Though Wynne would like to have called them back—to gather them all in her arms and draw strength from their very nearness—at that moment all she could do was stand there, trembling.

"Are you all right?" he asked once more.

Again Wynne didn't answer. She couldn't. The truth was, she was not all right. Her life, which had seemed so even and calm, so predictable, now was shattering all around her. And all because of this man.

He put a hand on her arm and turned her to face him, but at his touch she jerked away. Though she'd had a strong sense of his presence before she'd even laid eyes on him, that was as nothing compared with the effect of his touch. It was so strong, it shook her to her very core. Even as she backed away from him, she could still feel the individual impressions of each one of his fingers.

"Stay away from me," she whispered, not sure whether it was her fear or the threat she intended that came through in her voice. "Stay away from me and my children."

"Listen to me, Wynne." He stepped forward, arms open in appeal. "Let me tell you everything, and then you'll understand."

"I understand all I need to understand," she retorted. "You've come here to steal one of my children. That makes you my foe, and . . . and . . ." Her voice wavered, and she knew she sounded more like an emotional woman than an enemy to be feared. But still she plunged on. "And I'll fight you with every fiber of my being."

She started to step back and turn away. He was too close. He was too big and too intimidating. But before she could move, he had her by both arms. Once more that unexpected charge of energy shot through her, catching her off guard. Then he lowered his face to the same level as hers and glared back at her.

"I don't want to fight you," he snapped, giving her a slight shake for emphasis. "One of your children was very likely sired by Sir William Somerville. He's a very powerful and rich man, and he wants to give his son all the benefits due him."

"You can't be sure it's one of my children."

"He left a woman here in Radnor Forest, a woman who was heavy with his child. He called her by the name Angel, and even though I've searched the whole forest, she's nowhere to be found. But you've got five English orphans of those times." He shrugged as if that were proof enough, and indeed it did give Wynne pause. But she would never give her children up to an Englishman.

"That proves nothing at all. Besides, the English hate their bastards," she spat back at him. "Everybody knows that. Didn't your father hate you?"

She knew at once she'd scored a blow, for his hands

tightened around her arms. "You little witch," he muttered through gritted teeth. " 'Tis my very bastardy that guides me in this. Those boys—all of them—need their fathers. They need a man to look up to. To receive approval from."

"They have men—real men who do not rape and murder and torture! Druce is there for them, and they look up to him."

"He's *not* their father." He gave her another shake. "And *you're* not their mother."

Had her hands been free, she would have struck him for that. As it was, all she could do was glare bitterly at him. Perhaps she wasn't their mother, but she was the nearest thing to it they had. Still, in the angry silence Wynne couldn't help but recall her own thoughts of just minutes before. They did need a father, and not just the boys. But this Englishman was not the one to decide who that father would be.

She took a deep, steadying breath and willed herself to be calm. Then she fixed him with a narrow, glowering stare. "I shall make you very sorry you ever came to *Cymru*—to Wales," she began. "You think you may come here, dangle the thought of a title and lands before me, and thereby justify stealing one of these children from the only home they know. Do you honestly believe I will idly sit by?" She let out a harsh laugh, then shrugged out of his loosened grasp.

Fighting the urge to rub the spots where his hands had touched her, she went on. "I am not called the Seeress of Radnor for nothing. *I* am the Welsh Witch you spoke of, and I have powers at my command that you cannot begin to fathom. I sensed your presence in these forests long before you arrived. And I can predict already the tragedy that shall befall you and your men if you linger here. Sickness. Madness. Even death if you are not swift in your retreat," she added for good measure, though at that moment she considered it no exaggeration. She would murder him with her own hands if that's what it took to drive him away.

He studied her for a moment, then grinned. "You are a superstitious people. No doubt the folk around here believe such things of you—maybe you even believe some of it yourself. But you'll not frighten me off with such wild tales."

"Then you are more fool than I thought," Wynne replied with a smug smile of her own. She was feeling stronger and more in control now, and he was playing right into her hands. She lifted her chin proudly and put her hands on her hips. "You've been given your only warning. I'll not feel the least remorse for the hardships that shall plague you and your men now."

To her dismay, however, he only smirked and let his eyes run boldly over her, lingering on her outthrust breasts and then her lips before returning to her shocked eyes. "If you would put the same effort into seducing me with your considerable charms as you put into scaring me away with your questionable powers, you would no doubt succeed far better." Then he reached out and caught one long tendril of her loosened hair and wound it around his finger. "Have you a husband?"

Wynne hardly felt the sharp pain on her scalp as she turned and fled. She did not notice the path as she plunged headlong through the forest after the children. All she knew was that this Englishman possessed some awful power over her, one she'd never allowed any other man to have. She'd firmly rebuffed any man who approached her in that way, and none of them had ever thought to anger the Welsh Witch.

But this man . . . With only his slow, heated gaze he caused her mouth to go dry and her mind to go blank. He turned her anger into a terrible burning in the depths of her stomach, leaving her unable to focus. Did he have powers of his own? Some ability that was stronger than hers? She'd heard of wizards and warlocks, but she personally knew of no men possessed of such powers. Only women.

His chuckle followed her, but she determinedly shut it out. Let him laugh. At least she knew that it was only his touch and his potent gaze that weakened her. If she stayed away from him and never met his eyes, she would be all right. She would plot in private. She would devise all sorts of miseries for him, and eventually she would drive him away.

Yet even as she caught up with the children, she was not totally reassured. He was very determined. But then, so was she. And she was on her homelands, surrounded by people who would help her.

Then she breathed a sigh of relief. Gwynedd. Her aunt Gwynedd would help her. She would know what to do. Wynne chanced a glance back and saw him not far behind. He was watching her with a confident, assessing expression on his face. It was enough to destroy her recovering calm.

"Hurry, children," she said, a false note of gaiety in her voice. "The first one back to the manor shall get a double serving of pears tonight."

But she would cook up a special recipe for the Englishman, she vowed. And she would make him very sorry he ever heard of the Welsh Witch.

6

Gwynedd awaited them in a woven chair of rye straw draped with sheepskin, which had been placed outside in a pleasant, sunny spot. Her head tilted back against a down-filled cushion, and her eyes were closed.

How could she be asleep? Wynne fumed as she herded the children forward. How could she nap so peacefully, so unaware of the terrible situation they were in? Surely she should sense it.

"Children, leave your bags and pouches on the big table in the kitchen. Then go look for Druce." She shot an angry glance at the Englishman, who stood so straight and tall, surrounded by the children. "And stay away from the English encampment."

As one, the five children looked from Wynne to Sir Cleve, then back at her. To her enormous relief they did not question her words. She supposed even a group of six-year-olds could not mistake the pure animosity that emanated from her toward that man.

She glared at him in silence as the children trotted off to the house. Then, still not speaking, she turned and walked away. When she reached her great-aunt, she knelt down before her, sneaking a quick glance back at the Englishman. He was still watching her, but then the shivery sensation up her spine had already told her that. What was this disturbing effect he had on her?

"Aunt Gwynedd," she whispered urgently, even though he was too far away to hear. "Aunt Gwynedd, wake up!"

"What? Ah, *nith*, did I doze off?" The old woman patted Wynne's hand, which rested on her arm. "Ah, well, 'tis one of the pleasures of old age, I suppose. You gather the herbs while I rest in the sunshine."

"Aunt Gwynedd, I know now why that Englishman has come. He wants to take one of the children away. One of the boys."

Gwynedd pushed herself a little upright. "What do you say? He's taken one of the children?"

"No, no. Not yet at least. But he will. He says one of them is the son of some English lord. And that this lord wants his son back."

Gwynedd stared at her, all vestiges of sleep gone from her sightless eyes. "One of our lads is heir to an English lord? How can he be sure?"

Wynne shook her head in frustration. "I don't know. I don't think he knows which one it is. He's probably not even sure it *is* one of our boys, he's only hoping. You know how the English are." She snorted in contempt. " 'Tis only sons they value. Women are but chattel to them, little better than brood mares to give them more of their precious sons."

Gwynedd's gnarled hand tightened around Wynne's. "There is a reason for all things, child. The English pass their lands to the eldest son. 'Tis but a device to avoid conflict among several sons. Here in Wales a man's holdings go to his most powerful son. 'Tis a tradition that cannot help but promote warfare within a family. You've seen it yourself. Kant ab Fychen rules only because he broke his brother's fighting arm. Were Anwyl able still to fight, one or the other of them would by now be dead."

Wynne stared at her aunt in frustration. What had Fychen's boys to do with anything? It was these boys she was concerned with. "Didn't you hear what I said? That man—the English bastard—would take one of my children back to England with him! A son of *Cymru* forced to live in that godless land!"

Gwynedd sat in silence for a moment. Her very lack of emotion, however, only incited Wynne more. How could she be so calm? But before Wynne could speak again, Gwynedd turned her blind eyes toward her niece. "The English are not a godless people. Their ways are different than ours, to be sure. But they love their sons, their children. If one of our boys *is* heir to a title and lands, who are we to deprive him of it?"

"What?" Wynne sat back on her heels, stupefied by her aunt's words. She could hardly believe her ears. She would have pulled her hand free of Gwynedd's except that the old woman gripped it so warmly.

"They are not yours, Wynne, these children you were given to raise. You have tried to be both mother and father to them up till now, but they are not truly yours. You know that. You've always known. Children are a gift from the Mother—from God, if you will. But they're ours only for a while. Some die young; the rest grow up and leave us." She gave a sad, understanding smile. "Perhaps it is the time for one of our five to leave."

"No!" Wynne leaped up, hurt and angry and confused. Of all people, she would have expected Gwynedd to understand. She was certain her great-aunt would sense the same danger, the same threat that she sensed from this Englishman. Yet her aunt felt nothing. And now she was willing to give up one of the children to some English monster. What matter that he was a lord and possessed of lands and holdings? What matter if he were the English king himself! He was English and therefore a plague upon the face of the earth—or at least on the face of Wales.

"I will not surrender any of my children to this English *lleidr*," she vowed in a voice that shook with emotion.

Gwynedd sighed. "Not even to the child's rightful father? Every child deserves to know his own father."

Too consumed with fury and a deep-rooted fear, Wynne ignored her aunt's words, though they mirrored her own earlier thoughts. "They are all children of *Cymru*. Their mothers were *Cymry*, and so are they, no matter if *all* of their fathers come for them. Those despicable *cnaf* have no claim on them now. 'Tis too late." She turned to leave but stopped when Gwynedd spoke.

"*Nith*, I ask only that you hear him out. Do not make this decision in pain and anger. You decide a child's life here. Do not make a choice which that child shall someday blame you for."

Wynne stood a moment, not willing, even in anger, to show disrespect to the great-aunt who had been so good to her these past seven years since her own parents had died. Only when Gwynedd sank back into her chair did Wynne give a curt nod, then stride away. Yet she could not hide from the new fear that the old woman had roused with her parting words.

These children would not always be children. The day would come when they would be men and women, capable of their own choices and decisions. She'd always dreaded the day that they must know the truth of their births. But she'd never imagined that they might wish to meet their fathers. In her eyes their mothers were saints, martyred one way or another at the hands of that devil's horde—the English. Their fathers they would hate, just as she hated them.

But *would* they hate them? The idea that they might not, that they might actually be curious about them, was too painful for her to accept. Already it seemed Arthur had heard something of his parentage, if his conversation yesterday with the Englishman was any indication.

Upset as she hadn't been in years, Wynne was not conscious of her direction as she fled the manor grounds. She only knew she had to get away, to be alone and collect her thoughts and lick her wounds. What her aunt was suggesting went against everything she felt. The past seven years had been hard ones. Orphaned and surrounded by the devastation the English had wrought, she'd managed as best she could. Parents gone; sister swollen with the seed of the very enemy who had caused their misery. And then Maradedd had been found at the foot of that cliff, her body broken and lifeless, while her baby had lain, strong and alive and demanding, in Wynne's arms.

How Wynne had hated that child. If she'd never been born, at least Maradedd would still have been alive. Thank God, Gwynedd had stepped in, naming the child Isolde, forcing the thirteen-year-old Wynne to care for her. Forcing her, Wynne knew, to love her. And she did love Isolde. She loved them all. How could Gwynedd now expect her to be able to give any of them up?

She came to a breathless halt at a small stream. Clear and cold, it gurgled past a tangle of gnarled oak roots, then dropped past a shelf of stones to run through a quiet moss-lined glade of ash and wych elm. Wynne stared about her as if she'd never truly seen the place before. She knew where every rabbit hole, goosander nest, and fox den was, and yet the place seemed somehow wholly new to her.

Were there places like this in England? Wild places where it was quiet and safe? She'd never thought it possible, yet her rational self knew there must be. The land was still the land. It was different everywhere you went, yet even in that it was the same. It was people who shaped it, who made it a wonderful place. Or else a terrible one.

The English people were who made their land so awful, she told herself. And they would make life awful for an orphan of *Cymru*, thrust so young and defenseless among them.

She took a deep breath of the familiar damp air. Even to conceive of one of her children in England was madness. They would be frightened and alone, away from the only family they'd ever known. Besides, their fathers had forfeited all rights to them when they had fled Wales in the wake of their defeat. If the children should ever wonder about their fathers, then she would simply face that problem when it arose. She would tell them the truth, and then, well, then they would just see.

Feeling suddenly exhausted, Wynne pulled her coif from her head and shook her hair free. Then she made her weary way to the low-hanging branch of an ancient oak. For as long as she could remember, this had been her special spot. She would sit on this branch, pushing with her heels, making it dip and sway in a slow, ponderous rhythm. It was soothing and it was always there, unchanged, with moss beneath her feet and trails of mistletoe above her head. She'd cried a thousand tears in this place. She'd cursed the English to hell and back, venting her anger and her pain and her overwhelming sorrow.

Perhaps that was why the mistletoe thrived so well, she thought. All her darkest emotions flying around in the air, making the mistletoe's power even stronger.

She reached up to run one finger lightly around a waxy

green leaf, outlining its shape against the dark gray-brown of the oak bark. "How shall I best dispose of these devils?" she mused out loud.

Then the hair on the back of her neck prickled, and with a sinking feeling she jerked around. There on the edge of the clearing—her clearing!—stood the very demon who sought to ruin her life.

"Leave this place," she hissed, her voice filled with deadly menace.

"We have to talk."

She gave him a murderous glare. "I have nothing to say to you," she began, "save that you are truly a witless fool to think I'd give up any one of these children to a pair of heartless *lleidr* such as you and this . . . this . . ."

"Lord Somerville," he supplied.

"Yes, this Lord Somerville. What fools you both are. Do Englishwomen give up their children so easily? Are they so cruel and unloving? Would your mother have given you up had your father wanted you?" She pressed on, hoping to hurt him again as he was hurting her. "But no, I forgot. Your father never did want you, did he?"

She smiled smugly, sure she'd wounded him. But his expression was shuttered. He only gave her a steady look, then moved forward.

"You're quite correct, my father did not want me anywhere near, and as a boy that knowledge tortured me. 'Tis not easy growing up knowing your father cares more for the beasts in his stable than he does for you."

She stiffened and steeled herself against the opening she'd given him. Just because he'd wished to know his father better meant nothing. He was only one person, and everyone was different. And anyway she loved her children enough to make up for the absence of their natural parents.

But he seemed to read her thoughts. "My mother loved me dearly. And when she did marry, her husband was more than good to me. But after my mother's death, when my father, in a weak moment, had me sent to be a page in a good household, I was only too eager to oblige him. So you see"—he spread his hands in appeal—"you cannot prevent these children wanting to know their parents. You can put it off, but you can't prevent it happening eventually."

A hard hammering began in Wynne's heart. Fear and desperation combined to rob her of the power to deny what he said. She gripped a rough branch and clung to it for strength. "There must be a hundred other bastard children from that war. You can't be sure any of mine is the one you seek."

"It was Radnor Forest. And I've searched all the villages within the forest—Radnor, Penybont, Llandrindod Wells. None of the other women I found fits his description of the woman." He stared at her. "But you have five orphans. It's one of your children. They're the only ones left."

The certainty in his voice turned her blood to ice. "Leave here," she muttered between clenched teeth. "Leave here!"

"No. Not until you listen to me."

"No!" she spat back, conscious that her voice held a wild, almost hysterical note. "I refuse to listen to anything you have to say!"

"By damn, but you will listen," he swore. In an instant he was before her, trapping her legs between his as he pressed his thighs against the thick tree branch. She leaned away, nearly falling backward, but he caught her arms and held her steady.

"Lord William's son deserves to receive his inheritance.

Do not deprive him of it. He may hate you forever if you do."

"My sons—mine!—love Wales."

"They are not your sons," he bit out. "Once they know they're half English, they're bound to be curious about their fathers and their fathers' heritage."

"They will never want anything that is English!"

"God's teeth, woman. Just think. What has Wales to offer Lord William's child? No lands of his own. No castles or even manors. Shall he be happy with a cottage built of mud and straw when in England he could be lord of all he can survey? Can you think to compete with that?"

"That won't matter to them. They have this manor house to live in. They have this forest to make their homes in, and it provides all they'll ever need," Wynne insisted, though she trembled now with the fear that his words might prove true. "We Welsh despise everything English."

"By damn," he swore once more. Then his grip tightened, and his brown eyes bored into hers with a new determination. "You no doubt believe what you say. But even you, Welsh Witch that you purport to be, are not immune to all things English."

With a quick movement he pulled her upright, sliding her to stand between him and the slowly swaying branch. As the heavy limb swung forward, it thrust her intimately against him, and he pressed back when the branch moved the other way. "There are some attractions bound by neither political boundaries nor even our own wishes. This for instance."

Before she could think to escape, his face lowered to hers, and he caught her lips in a bold, searching kiss.

If he meant to silence her, he succeeded. If he meant to prove his point about the perverse attractiveness of at least some things English, he did that as well, for from the very first touch of his lips to hers, she was undone. Like some dark magic, his power overwhelmed her, robbing her of her ability to think, flooding her senses with feelings she could not begin to control. Heat, cold; a soaring lightness and a sinking, drowning sensation—all these and more did he invoke with that warm, intimate connection.

She felt his tongue searching the seam of her mouth, sliding seductively, demanding entrance. Though she had no experience in such things—indeed, some rational part of her warned her to turn her head, to pull away, to run as fast and as far as she could from him—she could not do it. Her lips parted, longing to discover how deep and dark his magic went, and with a sweet surge he took complete possession of her mouth.

The damp bonding they made as his tongue met hers shook her to the very deepest part of her. Body and soul, she was rocked. A fire caught in her belly, and a trembling began in every part of her.

He was not fighting fair, the last remnant of her rational self deplored. Yet the part of her that believed in what could not always be seen or explained knew it did not matter. Magic was magic, a power to be used just as a keen eye or a fleet foot was used. And for once she'd met someone whose magic was as strong as hers.

When his hands moved from her arms to circle her, then slid down her back to cup her derriere, she amended that thought. His magic was stronger than hers, she admitted as she dissolved beneath his touch. It was an ancient and primeval magic, and she was helpless against it.

She was not conscious that she had lifted her arms to circle his neck. She was too overwhelmed by the torrid feel of his tongue sliding in and out of her mouth. He nibbled and sucked at her lower lip, then lured her tongue out to meet his. When he drew it into his mouth, Wynne pressed forward eagerly, unable to help herself. Had he not broken the kiss, allowing them both to gasp for breath, she was not sure where it would have ended. As it was, when their eyes met, she became abruptly and acutely aware of their intimate embrace and the firm press of his arousal against her belly.

"You are indeed a witch," he murmured in a tone that sounded both taunting and wondering. "For you have surely cast a spell on me."

She had cast a spell on him? Wynne could not credit that at all, not when she was feeling so overwhelmed and without the ability to speak or move—or even think, it seemed. She stared up into his deep brown eyes, captivated by the tiny gold flecks that lent them their warmth, and still inflamed by the way he made her feel. In her wildest, darkest imaginings she'd never—ever—imagined that a man could affect her in this way. And an Englishman, no less!

She'd made enough love potions for enough lovesick maidens to be well acquainted with the effects of physical attraction. The girls sighed and giggled and spoke in hushed voices about the way their various love interests made them feel. Warm, tingly, like they would die if he didn't pay attention to them. She'd even made love amulets for girls to entice Druce—dear, reliable Druce. If he only knew how many girls sighed over him—or perhaps he already did.

But never had she herself experienced those feelings. Not for any man. Even now she was not certain it was truly that simple. He must possess some power. He must! It was the only explanation. Otherwise when he lowered his face a second time, she would have torn herself from their embrace. She would have been able to stop the kiss before it began.

Only she couldn't. When his lips met hers once again, she was as drawn in by their warm seduction as she had been the first time. But this time she knew what was to come, and the anticipation had her skin on fire and her insides all hot and jumpy.

To her dismay, however, he ended this kiss almost before it could properly begin. His lips parted hers, and his tongue probed almost violently before he pulled away.

"A witch," he muttered, shaking his head as if to clear it. "If it's your plan to sway me from my purpose, I warn you, Wynne, it will not work."

"What? Sway you?" For a moment her thoughts were too scattered for her to grasp his meaning. Then she shoved him away from her. Once removed from the power his touch held, she found her wits, and she searched her mind frantically. He feared *she* was swaying *him* with that kiss? Did that mean he was as affected as she? She peered at him warily, noting his quickened breathing and the bright gleam in his eyes. She could not mistake the telltale bulge in his braies either, but though she rejoiced in the proof it gave her, she could not ignore the very odd, very disturbing quiver that snaked through her at the sight. Yes, she had affected him, but he had easily done as much to her. Was the power of two witches together more than the sum of the two individuals alone?

She didn't know. Indeed she didn't want to know. Above all, she reminded herself, he was her very worst enemy, and she must always deal with him as such.

She forced herself to raise her chin and hoped she appeared more confident than she felt. "You will gain nothing by lingering here. Indeed, you have much to lose, for I will never—*never*—give up any of my children. And I will fight you even unto death, if that's what it takes."

Instead of responding to her mounting anger with anger of his own, the Englishman sighed and raked his dark hair back with both of his hands.

"I only want what is best for this child. Once you recover from your initial shock, you will see that. A veritable kingdom awaits this child—if he is a boy. He will not forgive you when he learns what you have cost him."

Wynne ignored his last words, for they were too uncomfortably close to Gwynedd's warning. Instead she latched on to another point. "*If* he is a boy. *If!* If this man has sired only a girl, then he doesn't even want her. What kind of a parent is that?"

FitzWarin had the good grace to look at least a little discomfited. "He already has four daughters. But I'm certain he would take this child if it proved to be a girl. He would care for her—"

"He doesn't even *want* her," Wynne broke in. "If she's a girl, he doesn't even want her. You know that's true."

There was a brief, charged silence as they stared at each other. "Which child is his?" he finally asked. "Don't lie to me, either, for I'll find out. Which child is his?"

Wynne glared at him. Then she let out a harsh and bitter laugh. "The truth is, I don't know. I doubt if even their mothers knew. The English were rather indiscriminate in where they spread their wretched seed. Any woman would do. An old crone. A budding girl. Even pregnant women!" she spat.

He absorbed that with a closed, stony face. "There must be a way to determine their parentage. Were any of their mothers called Angel? Where are their mothers?"

Their mothers. The very thought of her children's mothers caused Wynne's blood to run cold, stifling the lingering vestiges of their brief, fiery interaction. "They're dead. At least three of them are. And none of them was called Angel."

"Angel wasn't her real name. It was what he called her, though."

"Are you saying he didn't even know her real name?" Her eyes narrowed in contempt. "All right. I'll tell you about these women you English raped and abandoned. Let's see. I'll begin with Arthur. His mother had other children, and she bore her pregnancy fairly well, or so we thought. But then she tried to end it—using a sharp stick. She nearly died, but God saw fit to keep her alive, at least until the child was born. She bled to death at the birthing. Naturally her husband did not want the English bastard that had cost him his wife and made orphans of his children. And so Arthur was given to me.

"Then there's Bronwen," she continued, though every word felt like a fresh wound. "Her mother had only just reached that first moment of womanhood. She was so small, she nearly died bringing her child to life. Had the baby not been so tiny—" She broke off, swallowing the hard lump of bitter feelings that gathered in her throat. "Her parents told her the babe was stillborn. They gave Bronwen to me.

"Rhys and Madoc came later. Their mother bore them and kept them. Her betrothed husband married her despite the stain upon her honor. The stain upon *her* honor!" she repeated furiously.

She took a steadying breath and forced an ironic smile. "She died a year later, trying to give her husband a child of his own. He did not want the twins after that. So they, too, came to me."

She stared at him, daring him to speak a word about the rights of an English lord to his abandoned bastard child.

"Why did they all come to you?" he finally asked. "And what of Isolde?"

Wynne suppressed a shudder, and for a moment her eyes closed as she remembered the terrible moment of Isolde's conception. Her sister's hysterical screams. The men's coarse laughter. After what seemed like the longest time, Maradedd's cries had subsided to helpless whimpers. The men's laughter had been reduced to crude grunts.

Wynne had heard it all from beneath the pig trough. She'd stifled her own cries by biting down on her hand. But she'd never been able to forget the sounds of the awful day.

Taking a shaky breath, she forced herself to face him. "Isolde is my niece, daughter to my only sister. But she could just as easily have been mine. You see, my sister hid me. She sacrificed herself to the . . . to the English swine who meant to have *me*—" Her voice broke, and she turned awkwardly away from his scrutiny. She hadn't meant to cry before him. It was the last thing she wanted to do. But even her boundless fury could not overshadow the piercing pain of these memories.

"Wynne," he began in the gentlest of tones. It stiffened her resolve at once.

She stared at him over her shoulder and continued in a voice gone as cold as ice. "My sister bore the child. Then she leaped from a cliff. She ended her own life—"

Her voice failed her, and in frustration she clenched her jaw, willing her emotions away. "I took Isolde as mine, and the other children were brought to me when their families heard of it. I raise them all as mine—they *are* mine. And no one—not you nor your powerful lord, nor even your damnable king himself—shall take them from me."

He seemed to be without words, and for that Wynne

was enormously grateful. One more minute of this conversation would have seen her dissolved completely in tears.

Even as she willed him to leave, she heard his footsteps crossing the quiet glade. His step grew softer as he crossed a mossy bank, then made his way from her private bower. She would like to have rejoiced at his disappearance and to have believed he would now depart for good. But she knew this was not over. He had been moved by her impassioned recital, it seemed, but she feared he had not been chased off.

And why should he? she berated herself. He'd seen her at her weakest, both emotionally and physically. He'd touched the raw wound that seven years had yet to heal. That was bad enough. But she'd also let him see into that closed part of her, that deep, private place no one else had seen before. He'd felt her tremble in his embrace.

In that moment, in that quiet glade where only the wind and the movement of wild things interrupted the silence, Wynne knew that this battle would be far worse than she'd anticipated. His reason for being here was enough to make him her foe. But his new presence in her life—his prying with his watchful eyes, disturbing touch, and overpowering kiss—made him her mortal enemy. She was fighting for her very existence.

But even if she won—and she would—she nonetheless knew that her life would never be the same again.

7

"Gwynedd says you are to come to her."

Wynne looked up from dark thoughts of fairy cap and the black mold to see Isolde and Bronwen watching her with wide eyes and grave expressions. She would have been alarmed by their serious demeanors, except that they didn't appear in the least frightened.

"Well, and what is this all about?"

"I think you're in trouble," Isolde answered.

"Gwynedd says that was a very wicked thing you did," Bronwen added.

That, at least, brought Wynne out of the wretched mood she'd been in since the Englishman had left her glade yesterday afternoon. So he'd awakened to find his hands aflame from the parsley fern, had he? Good. That would prove to him that her threats were not to be ignored.

Isolde clucked her tongue, sounding very like Wynne when she was about to scold one of the children for a naughty prank. "You should know better than to be mean to our guests."

"Sir Cleve is a very nice man," Bronwen interjected. "Why did you make his skin itch?"

Because he's not really nice at all, Wynne wanted to correct the little girl. *Because he has no honor or morals and would willingly steal one of you from me.*

But she couldn't say that to them, so she only stood up slowly, shook out the skirts of both her plain kirtle and her plunket cloth bliaut. Then she pushed her narrow sleeves up to her elbows. "Well, shall we go see what his problem is?"

It was easy for Wynne to be smug and self-righteous with only the children around. But at the manor, under Gwynedd's disapproving stare, sightless though it might be, she was considerably more uncomfortable. He was getting only what he deserved. But Gwynedd obviously did not agree.

"You have a gift," the old woman began in her soft, lilting voice. " 'Tis not for you to misuse in such a fashion."

Wynne frowned. "Run along, girls," she told the two watching children. Once they were gone, she replied to her aunt.

"He wishes to take one of our children back to England. I told you what he planned, and now, even though I told him in no uncertain terms that I will not allow it, he is nonetheless determined to do it. He wants to know which child was sired by this English lord of his. As if I will help him determine such a thing!"

Gwynedd took in Wynne's impassioned words without a change in her expression. "What you did was wrong. What plant did you have him handle?"

Wynne stared at her aunt disbelievingly. "Haven't you heard anything I've said? Don't you care at all that he wants one of my children?"

Gwynedd sighed and raised her gnarled hands to press against her clouded eyes. "Of course I care, *nith*. But these children will not always be children. They will grow; we will die. They will have to make their own way in this world and make their own decisions. His quest is not without merit." She stared straight at Wynne. "Now, what plant is it that irritates his hands so?"

Wynne had never felt so powerless. Of all people, she would have expected Gwynedd to understand and support her against this English enemy. " 'Tis parsley fern that brings him such misery," she revealed most reluctantly. "But he shall consider his present discomfort as nothing compared with what I have planned for him if he doesn't flee Radnor Forest soon," she finished belligerently.

"We shall see about that," Gwynedd answered with un-accustomed sharpness. "Now, help me up."

Wynne could not deny her great-aunt's request. When the old woman's hand closed around her arm, however, she felt an odd mixture of reassurance and dread. Gwynedd's hold was firm, and the old sensation of power seemed to flow from her into Wynne. Her aunt was deter-mined to let this man have his way, Wynne realized. And she was still a force to be reckoned with.

"I want you to prepare a cleansing wash and then a poultice to ease his pain," Gwynedd ordered as they made their way toward the capacious stillroom. "You know what is needed, and I depend on you to do a good job of it. As good as if it were Druce or Barris or even one of the children who was so afflicted."

"I'll *not* aid him. If you wish to heal him, then you may do so. But I shall not."

"You will, girl. You caused his pain and you shall undo it."

"But Gwynedd—"

"Is this the way you would abuse your gifts? Is this the example you would set for Isolde? She may one day be Seeress here. Do you wish her to learn that her skills may be used as readily for spite as for good?"

" 'Tis hardly spite to protect your family," Wynne retorted.

But Gwynedd was unaffected. "*You* will be the one to ease his pains. You."

Had it not been for the five observant faces that greeted her just outside the stillroom door, Wynne would have argued further. But their confused and watchful expressions bothered Wynne even more than Gwynedd's accusing tone. The children did not understand how she could have pulled so cruel a prank on someone they all liked. Arthur especially stared at her with a hurt expression on his innocent face.

Oh, how could she ever make them understand?

With an unhappy sigh she squared her shoulders and lifted her chin. "I'll see to him," she muttered. Then she and her conscience escaped into the comforting privacy of the stillroom.

What was it about that damnable Englishman? she fumed as she snatched up pottery containers with unaccustomed vehemence. He was the villain, and yet Gwynedd seemed prepared to forgive him anything! She slammed a leather pouch down on the table, then repressed an oath when its seam split, releasing a quick puff of a pale orange powder. Just look what he'd made her do now! Even after she had a clear wash of moth herb in rosewater, and an ointment of bittersweet and yellow dock prepared, she was no less irate. But as she made her way toward the English encampment, she vowed to suppress it. Anger would not help her, but cool, calm reasoning could. He needed to determine which child was sired by this Lord Somerville. Well, there was no way he could ever know without her help. And even if she did cooperate —which she wouldn't—she wasn't certain they could ever know for sure. It was hardly likely that any of the children's mothers had known their rapists' names. Certainly her sister had not. There'd been too many of them. Besides, three of the four mothers were dead.

Even with that thought uppermost in her mind, she could barely repress the shiver of fear that snaked up her back when she entered the English encampment. So many men, and every one of them her enemy. Cleve FitzWarin especially was glaring at her with undisguised animosity. But it was that very anger of his that helped to banish her fear.

"I hear that you have need of my healing skills," she said in English, not trying in the least to hide her amusement. She swept the other men sitting before the low-pitched tent with a slow, appraising stare. "As anyone in Radnor Forest will tell you, I have uncanny skills as a healer."

When they all shifted uncomfortably, she turned her smug expression back on the man who was the true focus of her ire. Ignoring the dangerous glitter in his eyes, she went on. " 'Tis fortunate for you that I have this gift, for such an affliction as you have would surely test the skills of a lesser healer. As Gwynedd has told you, the magic of this place imbues both the plants and the people with powers quite beyond the ordinary."

His eyes narrowed. "Leave us," he snapped to his men, though his eyes bored into hers. Only after the men scrambled hastily to obey did he address her directly.

"While your performance may impress my soldiers, it holds no weight with me. Play the role of seeress or witch or whatever you wish. But understand this, Wynne ab Gruffydd. I know you for what you are."

His eyes moved over her, from her now angry face, down the full length of her body, thoroughly examining every aspect of her appearance. When he at last raised his insolent gaze back to her face, she was burning with outrage, as well as a distinctly more uncomfortable emotion. How dare he look at her as if he meant to . . . meant to consume her.

As if he sensed her discomfort and was pleased by it, he relaxed back against the massive cedar tree behind him. "Here are my hands, O witch of the Welsh forests. You've done your worst on them. Now come heal them."

Hiding her fury as best she could, she drew nearer. He obviously knew Gwynedd had forced her to help him. But he couldn't be completely sure that she would comply. If nothing else, she could make him wonder, and at least wipe that smug and arrogant look off his face.

" 'Tis my pleasure to heal you, my lord," she said with exaggerated sweetness. She glanced at his red, chapped hands, and though she was successful in restraining her grin, her eyes gleamed with malicious delight. "Oh, dear, how dreadfully that parsley fern affected your fingers." She knelt down beside him and spread out her medicinal concoctions. "Is your skin always so sensitive?"

Without warning he grasped her chin and jerked her face up toward his. "Not always. It depends on the particular stimulus. For instance, my hands react to your parsley fern. Other of my parts react directly to you."

He released her chin, and before she could respond, he let his raw knuckles stroke ever so lightly down the column of her throat, a slow, possessive exploration.

She would have scrambled back from him at once, but

he grabbed her wrist. "Oh, no, you don't, my little Welsh witch. Your work is not yet finished here."

Wynne had never felt so trapped. She'd known not to look into his eyes. She'd known she mustn't let him touch her. Yet here she was, doubly caught by him once more.

For a long, trembling moment their gazes remained locked. She felt the heat of his hand on her skin and the heat of the angry emotions in his eyes. Yet the fire that leaped between them burned hotter than it should have. It was his damnable magic, she knew. This terrible, powerful magic he possessed.

Though her heart pounded and her mouth was unaccountably dry, she forced herself to reply. "If you will release me, I'll do as my aunt has requested. But if it were left only to me . . ." She didn't finish the sentence. But then, there was no need.

With a snort of disgust he let her go, but it was clear he was far from pacified. He started to scratch his left palm, then thought better of it. "Heal this bloody itch," he growled. "And no tricks, or you shall pay a severe cost."

Removed from both his touch and the mesmerizing power of his bottomless brown eyes, Wynne felt the slow return of her equanimity. She still seethed with fury, yet she knew she must remain calm with this man. She must control her emotions and thereby control the situation. As she soaked a small square of linen in the cooling wash, she counted silently to ten. First in Welsh, then in English.

"Hold your hands over this bowl," she ordered, pleased by the steady sound of her voice. She smiled as she lifted the dripping cloth. Though the wash was healing, she knew that at first it would sting his irritated skin. She squeezed the cloth over his outstretched hands, but when he only flinched ever so slightly, she glanced up at him in surprise.

The gaze that met hers was cool and appraising. A little threatening too. "The sting is no doubt necessary to the healing." He made it a statement, not a question.

"It must burn away the evil spirits," she automatically mouthed the answer she always gave her patients. "The more it stings, the better it is working . . ."

Her words trailed off as she realized he didn't believe a word of it. She jerked her eyes away from his too-aggressive stare and concentrated on her odious task. "Turn your hands palm up." She squeezed more of the wash over his hands. Though she would have been perfectly happy if her preparations did not work in his case, a part of her was nonetheless unable to do less than her best.

It was not that she wished to help him. Far from it. But he clearly thought she was a charlatan, that her claims for powers beyond her herbal remedies were false. Though logically it did not matter what he thought, some irrational and emotional part of her wanted to prove him wrong. She wanted to shock him with the strength of her gift and then rub his face in it.

She glared at his red, chapped hands, willing them to heal as she continued to drizzle the moth herb and rosewater wash over them. He would see. She could ease pain just as well as she could cause it. Better in fact.

With a determined expression on her face, she glanced up—but only briefly. She must avoid meeting his eyes and touching him. "Now let your hands dry in the air. Don't touch anything."

"That's it?" he exclaimed in disbelief. "They burn worse now than they did before."

"When your skin is completely dry, I'll apply this ointment," she snapped, shooting him an angry glare.

But that proved to be a mistake, for once their eyes met, she seemed unable to look away. Though her eyes re-

flected her icy rage, he seemed easily to absorb that emotion in the fathomless depths of his velvet-brown stare.
Anger, fear, loathing—all those emotions of hers he accepted and swallowed up in his steady gaze until she had
nothing left to throw at him. She blinked, conscious that
he was looking deeper, all the way inside her, it seemed.
Muttering an imprecation, she jerked her eyes away.

He laughed. "*Cnaf.* That means 'knave,' does it not?"

Wynne bristled at the amusement evident in his words.
He would not bait her again. She worked in silence, giving the thick yellow ointment another stir, then placing it
on the ground between them.

He mocked her, did he? Well, she would just see about
that. She pressed her fingertips briefly to her eyes, then let
her hands circle three times above the small pottery dish.
"Come into me, O Mother of us all. Come into me and
through me. Work your healing powers on this man who
seeks your aid." Then she leaned forward, placing her
hands palm down on the mossy ground on either side of
the bowl, and let her unbound hair fall forward, forming a
curtain as her amethyst amulet swayed in a slow circle
above the bowl.

How long should she hold the pose? she wondered. If
he were a superstitious old woman seeking a poultice for
her aches, or a nervous young man desiring a love potion
to captivate the girl he longed after, she would remain
thus until their nervousness was palpable. But he was a
cynical Englishman. Best not to overdo it. She would have
further opportunities to drive home her point.

When she raised her head, she was careful to maintain a
serene expression, completely devoid of any emotions.
Nor did she meet his gaze, though she was acutely conscious of his eyes searching her face.

"Rub a light coating of this into your skin. Once now,

and again before you retire for the night. Your hands should be recovered by morning." She pushed the ointment nearer to him and began to gather her other things to leave. But then, as if some devil goaded her, she added, "You should have no difficulty handling your horse when you and your men leave here tomorrow."

She saw his reddened hand reach for the bowl, but he did not speak. After several silent moments she realized that her breathing had ceased as she awaited his response. She forced herself to exhale, then slowly drew a breath. What was keeping him? she wanted to shout. Why didn't he tell her one way or the other whether he was giving up on this ridiculous plot of his?

She was close to exploding when he abruptly reached out and grasped her wrist. With only one sharp tug he had her off balance. Her free hand braced frantically against his thigh so that she wouldn't fall onto him, and her face ended up but inches from his.

"We have unfinished business, Wynne. I'll not leave until it is settled." He paused as their gazes clashed, but he didn't loosen his hold. "And it's more than the children now. It's you and me."

" 'Tis you who have started this war, not I," she hissed. "But if you imagine that I shall back down, then you're even more addle-brained than I had supposed."

He laughed at that, and she felt the warmth of his breath on her cheek. "What a fierce little warrior you are, *cariad*. But it is not war I want to make with you. 'Tis love. Hot, hard, sweaty love." His voice dropped to a low, husky whisper as he leaned even closer. "Just you and me. And perhaps some special potion you can prepare to prolong the pleasure of it." Then he took her earlobe lightly between his teeth and gave it the most erotic tug.

When he pulled back from her, Wynne was too unnerved to do more than gape stupidly at him. As if her body were no longer hers to control, she knelt there gasping for breath, conscious only that her heart was thundering, her mouth had gone dry, and somewhere, deep down inside, an inferno was just beginning to burn. She was completely undone by his intimate threat, shaking with feelings she didn't understand and bewildered by what was happening to her.

Only when his smile broadened and he leaned toward her as if to take another nibble, did she come out of her stupor.

"No!" she cried, jerking away. But his grip on her wrist held. Beneath her other hand she suddenly became aware of his thigh, so hard and firm beneath the thin layer of his fine woolen braies. So warm and unfamiliar.

"Let go of me," she muttered, refusing to meet his eyes.

His hand shifted slightly upon her skin, but did not loosen. "Only after you complete your ministrations," he answered, amusement clear in his tone.

She resisted the urge to glare at him, for in her present unsettled state, she feared the devastating impact of his eyes. "Let me go now!"

"Only after you put the salve on my hands," he replied with maddening persistence. "You deliberately sent me to that bed of noxious weeds. Now you shall see me healed."

In the end Wynne deemed it prudent to comply. Though she was infuriated by his bullying tactics and dismayed by his bold overtures, she could think of nothing else to do. If she went along with him, he would let go of her wrist. If she just slapped the potion onto his hands, she could escape his overpowering presence.

And at the moment escape was the most important thing. She *had* to get away from him.

Yet even submitting to his demand did little for her peace of mind. As she scooted back from him, glancing swiftly—almost desperately—around for any sort of help, he chuckled.

" 'Tis only you and I, my fair Welsh witch. No one else is near, so do not try to delay. Apply your wondrous ointment with its mystical healing powers. Heal me where I burn."

She scowled at him. "I despise you," she hissed as she snatched up the small pottery bowl. She scooped out a glob of the yellow goo and practically flung it onto his hand.

"Careful. My skin is *very* tender. And be sure you work it between my fingers. Here also, in the creases of my palms."

In anger she grabbed his outstretched hand, hoping she hurt him with her rough handling. But when his hand curled around hers, his fingers twining with her own, she knew she suffered far more discomfort than he, for her entire being seemed to jump with awareness of him.

"This spot in the very center of my palm is especially sensitive," he murmured, holding her eyes captive with his. "Rub it in very gently."

Wynne hardly remembered applying the salve. She had never worked so quickly—nor fumbled so badly. Once the task was done, however, she jumped up and backed away.

"I despise you," she vowed once more, though that vehement statement was sorely weakened by the shaky quality of her voice.

His mocking eyes raked over her. "I desire you," he replied. "Very much."

Wynne did not stay to hear any more. He was the most horrible man she'd ever had the misfortune to run across, she swore as she fled to the manor house. A godless heathen. A heartless bastard. A man who would steal babies and seduce women—

Cleve's thoughts followed a similar path to Wynne's as he watched her flee. She was truly a witch, worshiping ancient gods not known to the one true faith. But she was heartbreakingly beautiful. Though he'd come here to procure Sir William's child from her, at the moment all he could think of was how much he wanted to touch her. How badly he needed her in his bed.

She was as exquisite as any rose, though she bristled now with thorns. But if he could just get near enough and get past those sharp edges of hers, he knew his reward would be sweet indeed.

8

Beyond the open door of the stone kitchen building, Cook bustled back and forth, busier than was normal with her tasks. The manor household numbered only six adults and five children, so the seven English visitors had a profound impact on her work, Wynne realized. Added to that, Druce—loyal friend that he was—had come up from Radnor Village with his brother and two others. Although Wynne was pleased by his show of support in the face of the English threat, it did, however, complicate things for her.

She clutched the small pouch in her fist as she peered into the kitchen. How was she going to manage it? She dared not involve Cook or her helper in this plot. Gwynedd would be furious enough, and Wynne did not wish for her aunt's anger to fall on anyone else. She herself would shoulder the blame—the credit, she amended bitterly. But how she would manage to sicken only the Englishmen was proving a most difficult problem.

She ruled out the gravy for the venison. Everyone would partake freely of it, and besides, if one of the men proved to be a glutton, he could easily take too much. She glanced down anxiously at the ground root of yew in the pouch. She didn't want to do any permanent harm to the Englishmen. She just wanted to frighten them away.

Maybe in the wine. If she slipped it into one of the ewers and then was careful to fill the Englishmen's goblets from only that particular ewer . . .

She knew she couldn't put it in the pears or the soft cheese. The children too often sneaked a taste before the meal or begged Cook for an extra serving afterward. No, it had to be the wine. None of the children would be tasting the wine.

She lifted her chin and squared her shoulders. This was the only way, she reassured herself. She had to rid them of their enemy, no matter how Gwynedd might react.

She still could not understand her aunt's easy acceptance of the loss of one of the children. Though Gwynedd had never married or had children, the old woman had raised the orphaned Wynne as her own. Would Gwynedd have given her niece up to the first Englishman who'd come along, claiming her as his own? Wynne knew she would not. And Wynne was just as unlikely to give up one of *her* charges. Why couldn't Gwynedd understand that?

She saw Druce across the yard—speaking to that despicable Cleve FitzWarin. Shoving the pouch into the working purse that hung from her girdle, she strode toward them, the hem of her bliaut flaring. She was determined that the Englishman not try to smooth-talk Druce as he'd obviously done with Gwynedd. To a poor Welsh lad like Druce, the Englishman's offer to make one of the children so wealthy might sound awfully enticing. Castles. Vast demesnes. She could not take the chance that FitzWarin might try to sway her one ally away from her.

"—tin mines. But that's farther south," Druce was saying in a guarded tone as Wynne drew near.

"I've also orders for potions and special herbs," Cleve said.

Druce looked up at Wynne's approach. "You should speak to Wynne about that. She's the one who knows the herbs. She gathers them and prepares them to suit her customers. She's received orders from as far away as Anglesey—"

"Could you seek out the boys?" she interrupted Druce. "If you'll recall, you promised to help them make bows and a target."

Druce gave her a steady look. "Are you sure you wouldn't rather I stay with you?" He gestured with his head toward Cleve as though the man were not there.

Wynne shrugged, emulating Druce's nonchalance. "I've no intention of lingering to speak with him."

"Actually I want to speak to you about purchasing some specific herbal remedies," Cleve stated, ignoring her words completely.

"I'm not selling anything to you. *Anything*," she repeated dismissingly.

"I've come with coins to pay," he insisted. His lean face showed the faintest hint of a grin, trebling her irritation. He hefted the purse hanging beneath his tunic.

At the clinking sound elicited, Druce's brows arched in interest. "You know, Wynne, you do have a need of coin. Remember? You were saying just last week—"

"I'll thank you to let me decide what I do and do not need." She made an exasperated face at him.

Druce sighed and gave a frustrated shake of his head. He glanced from her to Cleve. "Talk or don't talk. You're both on your own." Then, avoiding meeting her furious glare, he ambled away.

Wynne would have left as well, for in spite of her irritation toward Druce, at least she'd succeeded in separating him from the Englishman. Druce was her only ally. She didn't want the Englishman to win him over with his glib promises. But as she turned on her heel, she was halted by FitzWarin's hand on her arm.

"You're always fleeing me, Wynne," he said, drawing out her name in a manner that was far too familiar. "We've business together."

"I'll not do business with you," she vowed, shrugging out of his grasp. "Not this pretense of purchasing herbs, nor the true purpose of your presence here. I've nothing whatsoever to sell to you!"

"By damn, but you are a fiery little dragon, aren't you? But for once you'll hear me out. Now, the women of Kirkston Castle had me commit their orders to memory." He dragged her over to a wooden garden bench and pushed her down upon it. "Don't interrupt my litany, or I'll be forced to begin again."

Though she glared at him, not attempting in the least to disguise her outrage to be manhandled thus, he released her and straightened up with a half smile. "Lady Anne wished shepherd's-heart and thousand-leaf. The Lady Bertilde desires althea root and lad's love for her babe, and something for her husband's ailment: ground thistle, sea parsley, and Juno's tears."

Wynne snorted contemptuously at that. Lady Bertilde's husband obviously needed to improve his performance in the marriage bed if his wife sought Juno's tears. But Cleve's quick scowl warned her to silence before she could speak.

"Catherine asks only for woodruff. And Edeline—" He broke off, and for a moment Wynne actually thought he looked uncomfortable. But why?

"Edeline wants a decoction of rose hips. Plus linden flowers to keep her complexion clear; chamomile for a hair rinse; and belladonna to deepen her eyes." He shrugged as if to say he had no idea what deepening the eyes meant, but Wynne knew. Almost any portion of that plant, properly prepared and taken in small drops, caused the center of the eyes to grow larger, giving a mysterious dark-eyed cast to an otherwise ordinary woman. But it was a dangerous remedy, even for medicinal purposes. Using it for cosmetic reasons was completely foolhardy.

"This Edeline, she is vain and frivolous, I take it."

To her surprise her scornful words only increased his discomfort. But he quickly hid it behind his reply. "Her only failing is that she is very young. She will settle down once she is wed."

But Wynne was in no mood to be charitable to anyone, least of all a vain and frivolous English girl who'd probably never suffered a moment's want in her entire life. No, nor any heartbreak, pain, nor suffering either.

"Why, Sir Cleve," she sneered. "You speak as if *you* are the one who must wed her but do fear to admit what a pitiful pairing you do make."

She'd thought only to make a general attack on the horrible nature of all English people by her criticism of the absent Edeline. But the oddest sensation suddenly overwhelmed her. Not a vision precisely. Still she knew at once that he did plan to marry this silly English noblewoman.

Wynne should have rejoiced at her discovery and laughed out loud to know what a misery awaited him in England. But instead of mirth she felt only another spurt of unreasoning anger toward him.

"So I am right. Well, perhaps when I make up the belladonna for your Lady Edeline, I should also prepare something for you. Something that will fire your ardor a little higher. Or no, maybe what you need more is a good portion of thorn apple, so that you may attract some more congenial woman to your side."

She tapped one finger against her chin and paused as if in consideration, not in the least dismayed by the warning look in his eyes. If anything, his growing temper urged her on. "You know, it could be only that your manners are so crude. I've noticed that myself. If your wooing were less rough and more persuasive instead . . ." She leaned back and gave him a disdainful glance. "Oh, well. I doubt even *I* can help you in your plight. Englishmen haven't the vaguest notion of how to please a woman—"

"I pleased you." He bit out the words, giving her an insultingly thorough once-over. "Very well, as I recall. And Wynne, *you* pleased me."

"That's not—I didn't—you—" Wynne broke off her sputtering under his gloating stare. Though she knew her cheeks were stained with heated color, she shook her head in denial. "I loathed that kiss," she swore, though she knew it was a complete lie. "No doubt your tepid bride will loathe them as well!"

They glared at each other from across a span of only inches, her eyes bright with anger and his darkening now to fury. He was taller, stronger, and clearly able to punish her for her hateful words, but at that moment fear was the last emotion she felt. She was filled instead with a strange exhilaration, as if she were girded for battle, ready to ride out and face her enemy, even though it might be a fight to the death. Blood surged in her veins; every muscle in her body tensed for the conflict.

When he jerked her to her feet therefore, pressing her fully against him and lowering his head to hers, she was completely unprepared for the response that ripped through her. Oh, this was indeed a battle, she dimly realized when his mouth caught hers. The struggle for dominance, lips against lips and tongue against tongue, was never so fiercely fought. His arms sought to still her; his violent kiss struggled to make her submit. But Wynne was a warrior, too, and as her mouth opened to the wondrous onslaught of his tongue, she thrust back, seeking to make *him* submit this time.

In this oldest of struggles they were the newest combatants. He found fresh territory, cupping her derriere and pressing his fingers, despite the bulk of her skirts, into the unchartered place between her thighs. She fought back by circling his neck with her hands, claiming his thick hair with her fingers, holding his head where she would have it, preventing him from ending the kiss.

They strained together, chest to breast, rigid loins to concave belly, until their need for breath broke them slightly apart.

"You are drug enough," he muttered against her temple, seeking her ear with his lips even as he gasped for breath. "Do you know, my fiery little dragon, my thorny rosebud, just how you fire my blood? Do you know all the things I would like to do to you? With you?" He punctuated that with an almost painful tug on her earlobe with his teeth, then a slow, stirring kiss in the same place.

Wynne arched instinctively against him. It was as if every portion of her body were connected to and controlled by the touch of his mouth. No matter where he used it—upon her lips, her neck, her ear—she had no defense against it. Nor did she want one either. For that one perfect moment when he pressed her belly hard against the rigid arousal beneath his braies, she understood the thrill of battle that men spoke of. The blood lust they described with glowing eyes and raised voices. She wanted to wage this battle ceaselessly, to fight him in this sultry, drowning manner until they were both burned to cinders in the fire.

She turned her face toward his seeking lips, blindly groping for more as her hands tightened around his neck. But he pulled slightly away and held her, with one hand tangled in her hair, so that she was forced to stare deep into his eyes.

"Where can we go?" he murmured as his eyes roamed her flushed face. He bent forward to capture her lower lip very briefly, sucking on it but refusing to satisfy her with the deep kiss she wanted. "Where can we be alone to finish this—"

"Wynne!"

The sharp cry of an alarmed child sent Wynne and Cleve stumbling apart. For a moment she was too disoriented to respond. She only stared at the worried faces of Rhys and Madoc, looked back at Cleve, then turned once more to the confused twins.

"Rhys. Madoc. What . . . ah . . . that is, did you— did someone need me?"

Madoc continued to stare at her with mouth agape. But Rhys turned to scowl at Cleve. "What did you do to Wynne? If you hurt her, then . . . then I'll hurt you back." He started toward Cleve, followed after only an instant by his brother.

"No. No, Rhys. Wait, boys," Wynne interjected. "It's all right. He wasn't . . . he wasn't hurting me."

They stopped, still confused by the situation, but obviously relieved that the man they'd grown to like had not betrayed them. Little did they know, Wynne thought as a wave of humiliation washed over her. Not only would this man willingly rip them from their home and family, but she—she who loved each of the children so desperately— was apparently ready to capitulate in his favor at the mere touch of him.

She took a shaky step back, pressing one hand to her

throat and the other to her kiss-swollen lips. What had possessed her to behave so with him? And why, even now, did her very blood seem to run hotter and faster in her veins?

"Was that . . ." Madoc's gaze turned curious. "Was that a wet kiss? You know, like Barris said?"

"Madoc!" Wynne risked a glance at Cleve only to see him beginning to grin at the boys.

"That was indeed a wet kiss, Madoc. But where have you two heard of wet kisses before?" Cleve asked.

Rhys answered. "Barris said that if Druce chased the—well—the English away, that maybe Wynne would give him a reward. You know, a big wet kiss—"

Wynne wanted nothing more than to creep into the thick grove of beechwood behind them and disappear. Why must her children choose now to practice their honesty? Why couldn't they be as evasive with this man as they so often could be with her?

"Go on back to the manor," she interrupted before they could say anything further. But Cleve was apparently enjoying himself too much to let them leave just yet.

"Wait, lads. Just tell me whether Wynne rewarded Druce as Barris had suggested." He turned the full force of his grin upon her, watching her with a gloating expression and yet still somehow conveying the very disturbing impression that he could devour her with only his eyes.

"Well, of course not," Madoc replied with the simple reasoning of a six-year-old. "He didn't chase you away. You came here, so he can't get his reward."

"Is that why you got the reward from Wynne?" Rhys piped up. " 'Cause Druce didn't chase you away?"

Cleve chuckled softly. "It's often difficult to say why a woman rewards a man with a kiss. Perhaps Wynne can explain it to you."

The fulminating glare she sent him did not shame him in the least, and Wynne was hard put to suppress her frustration. But Rhys and Madoc were watching her, their innocent faces curious.

"I . . . I really think six is too young to be discussing such . . . such things," she stammered. "Perhaps when you're older."

"But Wynne—"

"—we're big boys now."

Cleve moved over to the boys and stood behind them with a hand on each of their shoulders. "It's always best to answer a child honestly," he said, though his high-minded admonition was completely offset by the cheeky expression on his lean face.

"What would *you* know of raising children?" Wynne countered. "Have you any?"

"No. But I have not forgotten the lessons of my own youth. One way or another, a child can always deal with the truth. 'Tis lies that linger and continue to cause pain."

There seemed at that moment to be a whole host of new emotions in the air between them. His gloating and amusement at her expense had fled, to be replaced by a dark and disturbing candor. Her frustration and anger at the awkward position he'd put her in—and the inappropriate feelings he'd roused in her—were overtaken by a reminder of the deeper conflict between them. Cleve wanted at least one of her children to know his father—no doubt that was the "truth" he spoke of. But she wanted what was truly best for all her children, and an English father could not possibly fall into that category. This was one case where the truth would only hurt a child. And she was determined that no one should hurt her children.

She drew herself up and gave him a chilling look. "Rhys, Madoc. 'Tis time we returned to the manor. We shall finish this discussion later," she added, forestalling the protestations she sensed coming from them. Then, not giving them a chance to object, she grabbed each of them by the hand and marched stiffly away.

"Wynne, what's the matter with you?" Rhys complained once they were inside.

"Why are you mad—"

"—at us?"

A sudden wave of complete weariness settled over Wynne, and she stared down at the mutinous pair. "I'm not mad at either of you," she answered. She leaned forward impulsively, hugging them both close. "I'm not mad at you. I love you both too much ever to be mad at you."

Rhys pulled a little back so that he could look at her. "You were mad at us when we tried to swing on that vine," he reminded her.

"Oh, that. That was different, sweetheart. I was afraid for you, so I reacted angrily. But it was only because I love you so much."

Madoc's face creased in confusion. "Are you mad at Cleve because you love him too?"

At that ridiculous statement Wynne's mouth dropped open in surprise. "Love him! Love him? That's . . . that's too silly to imagine. Madoc, I didn't mean to imply that I love everyone I act angry toward. You and the other children, well, I get worried for you, so sometimes I appear to be mad. But I always—always!—love you. Even when I punish you. But as for Cleve FitzWarin—"

She broke off, not sure how to explain her anger toward the Englishman without revealing too much of his purpose for being in Wales. "Cleve FitzWarin is from England, and England is an enemy to Wales. You know that already."

When they both nodded, she felt marginally reassured.

At least she was on the right track. "It's very difficult for me to trust any Englishman. Even though they act like our friends now, I worry that they might turn back into our enemies once more."

There was a short silence as they digested that.

"Druce doesn't act mad at them—"

"—at least not anymore."

"Yes, but I'm sure Druce is still being very careful, just in case."

"But . . . but why did you give Cleve the reward?"

"Yes, Wynne, why did you give him the wet kiss that Druce was supposed to get?"

That deflated her all over again. She reached for her amulet and began to rub it nervously. "It wasn't a reward. And anyway, Druce didn't want—"

"Is Druce gonna be mad 'cause you gave his reward to Cleve?" Madoc interrupted.

"No!" Wynne exclaimed. Then she bit her lower lip in indecision. "But I don't want either of you telling him about it either."

"But why?"

"Well, you see, Druce is very protective about some things, and he might get angry with the English."

"But why?"

"Because . . . because he doesn't want the English spending too much time in Wales."

"But why?" the two dark-haired boys chorused.

"Because . . ." She heaved a sigh of futility. "Just be-cause." She crouched before the twins and tried her best to appear animated. "It can be our little secret. Our spe-cial secret. How about that?"

The boys shared a look. Then they nodded in unison. "Druce will never guess that Cleve got *his* reward."

"We'll never tell him."

"You can't tell *anyone*," Wynne insisted. Though she wished more than anything that she could correct their childish impression that the kiss had been a reward, she knew it would be impossible. Once the twins had an idea in their heads, nothing could shake it loose. Swearing them to secrecy seemed her only hope. "You can't tell anyone at all," she repeated. "Promise?"

"We promise," they replied.

She sighed again and stood up. "All right, then. Run along now. I think Druce is going to help you make bows and arrows. But remember your promise," she called after them as they scrambled out the door.

Wynne stood staring after them as they chased each other across the dusty yard. They stopped once to stalk a wary hen caught away from the shelter of the trees and undergrowth, but when she began to squawk in earnest, they quit and turned back to their original direction. Rhys stopped to pick something up from the ground, and it was at that exact moment that Madoc took off running as fast as his six-year-old legs could carry him. Rhys took up the challenge at once, shouting all the way that Madoc was a cheater.

Not until they disappeared beyond the kitchen did Wynne's fond smile fade and her thoughts return to the problem of Cleve FitzWarin. She reached instinctively for the small leather pouch in the purse at her waist and gave it a reassuring squeeze. More than ever it was essential that she send the English packing.

Cleve was becoming ever bolder.

And she was clearly weakening in her ability to resist him.

It was almost as if he sensed her weakness and grew even stronger because of it.

She jerked the pouch out of her purse and stared at it,

feeling as if it were her last resort. Tonight she would somehow dissolve it into the ale. She had no choice. She had no chance fighting him on his own terms. He was clearly too strong. But if she could move the struggle to another battlefield, she might win.

She clutched the precious pouch of powdered yew root tightly in her hand and pressed it to her chest. She had to succeed. She had to! She was battling for her family as surely as any man who'd ever wielded dirk or sword in battle.

And like any warrior, she was prepared to fight her enemy to the bitter end.

9

The taut bit of twine made a satisfactory twang, and Druce grinned as he handed the completed bow to Arthur. "There you go, lad. Now the three of you can practice to your hearts' content. Only be careful always to stand your bow in a corner when it's not in use. Never lay it on the ground, for some clod's foot is bound to find it."

"Yes, Druce," the boy answered dutifully. He stared at the half-sized instrument through serious hazel eyes, and it was obvious some question brewed in his quick mind.

"Does it hurt when the arrow hits the rabbit or deer? Or any other animal?"

Druce stared at him for a moment. "Animals don't have the same feelings people do."

"Well, they know when they're hungry," Arthur reasoned. "And when they're scared, 'cause they always run away from hunters. So they must know if it hurts them when the arrow hits into their body."

"Well"—Druce cleared his throat—"I suppose it might hurt a little. But we need them for food and fur and lots of other things. That's why God gave us animals, so we could use them to survive. Arthur, why don't you run along with Rhys and Madoc?" Druce finished.

Arthur looked at him with a wise-old-man expression, then obediently turned to comply. But as he made his way toward his brothers, his brow was creased in thought.

"I hit it! I did. I hit it!" Madoc shouted, cavorting around and around the three sheaves of hay that had been propped up as a target for the boys.

"Watch me. I can do it too," Rhys yelled back at him.

"Wait, Rhys!" Isolde ordered. "Arthur, get out of the way."

Bronwen looked up from the puppy and kitten she playfully baited with a long stalk of tall grass. "I hate boys," she muttered, more to herself than to Isolde. "They're so loud, and they always do such stupid things." Then she giggled as the kitten pounced on the puppy's waggling tail.

"They get to do all the fun things," Isolde countered grumpily. "And they think they should *always* be the boss."

"You *want* to shoot a bow and arrow?"

Isolde glared at the rowdy twins. "I bet I could do it even better than they can."

Bronwen shook her head at such a silly idea. "Well, go get Arthur's bow. He'll let you use it."

Sure enough, Arthur was more intrigued by how the placement of the feathers on the end of the arrow shaft affected its flight than by the actual use of the weapon. He shrugged at Isolde's request and didn't even look up when she walked off with the bow and another arrow. Only when a shouting match ensued near the target did he abandon his study of the arrow.

"I can, too, shoot!" Isolde yelled at the twins. They stood shoulder to shoulder in front of the target, and if their scowling faces were any indication, they were just as mad at Isolde as she was at them.

"Girls don't shoot longbows—"

"—only boys!"

"You're just afraid I'll be a better aim."

"Am not!"

"Are too!"

"Am not!"

"You better shut up, Rhys," Isolde warned.

"Stupid girl."

"Ha! Girls are a lot smarter than boys. All boys know how to do is make noise and get dirty and hunt. But girls can do lots of things."

"Girls are stupid."

"We are not!" Even Bronwen joined the fray. Arthur drew nearer, but he didn't say anything. Isolde and the twins were always arguing like this, and no one ever won.

"Girls don't know anything," Madoc taunted them. He shot Rhys a conspiratorial look, and in that strange way they had, he seemed to convey to his twin his very thoughts.

Rhys continued. "That's right. We know something you don't know. So who's smartest now?"

"Oh, you don't know anything," Isolde accused. "You're just making it up."

"Oh, yes we do," they chorused.

"Okay, then prove it."

For a moment they didn't reply, and Isolde pounced on their hesitation. "You see? I told you." She turned toward Bronwen and Arthur, a superior expression on her face. "I knew they didn't know anything."

"We do too!" Rhys shouted at the back of her head. "We saw Wynne give Cleve—"

"—the reward she was supposed to give Druce."

The two girls looked at them, not comprehending. It was Arthur who spoke. "What reward? For doing what?"

"It was a wet kiss."

"A real long one too."

Arthur looked skeptical. "What's a wet kiss?"

"I think it's when they open their mouths," Bronwen answered. "You know, they touch their tongues together." She smiled at the wonder of it all. "You only do that with someone you love."

"Or that you like a whole, whole lot," Isolde added, nodding her head wisely.

Arthur grimaced. "What a lie. Why would anybody want to touch tongues? It sounds stupid."

"You don't just stick your tongue out and touch them together," Rhys scoffed. "At least, that's not how *they* did it."

"Oh? What did they do?" Isolde asked.

"Yes," Bronwen added breathlessly. "Tell us all about it. Tell us everything."

Madoc gave them a taunting smile. "We saw the whole thing, didn't we, Rhys?"

"Uh-huh. And they were hugging and squeezing each other. And Wynne's hair was all messed up."

"But what about the wet kiss?" Bronwen interrupted.

"Well, they pressed their mouths together—like a regular kiss, only a lot, lot longer."

"And you could tell they opened their mouths—"

"—and that's when their tongues were touching."

Isolde and Bronwen looked at each other, then abruptly broke into giggles.

Arthur just shook his head. "That doesn't make any sense. What was she rewarding him for? And what about Druce? Why would she want to give *him* a wet kiss?"

Even after Rhys explained what Barris had said to

Druce about Wynne and a wet kiss, Arthur still looked skeptical. But Isolde and Bronwen chattered excitedly.

"Maybe Druce and Cleve both love her."

"Yes, but she didn't kiss Druce. She kissed Cleve. So she must love him back."

"Wynne would never love an Englishman," Madoc said in an exasperated tone. "She hates the English."

"Boys are *so* stupid," Bronwen retorted with equal exasperation. "Don't you know? You can't help who you fall in love with."

"But the English are our enemies," Madoc exclaimed.

"So? Cleve likes us and we like him," Isolde replied.

"And Wynne *really* likes him." Bronwen giggled.

"He could marry her," Arthur mused, more to himself than to the other children. "And if he did, well, then he'd be our father." He was quiet a moment, still mulling over that idea. Then his thin face broke into a huge smile, and his serious eyes glowed with excitement. "He'd be our father!"

Rhys and Madoc looked a little disconcerted by that possibility. Even Bronwen and Isolde appeared taken aback, despite their previous rapture over the idea of Wynne and Cleve being in love. But Arthur was thrilled with the idea.

"He'd be our father, and . . . and we'd be like a real family."

"We *are* a real family," Madoc stated. "Wynne says so all the time."

"But real families have fathers."

Rhys and Madoc shared a look, then they both shrugged. "He *is* nice to us—"

"—almost as nice as Druce."

"But Wynne doesn't love Druce," Bronwen interrupted. "She loves Sir Cleve."

Rhys looked at Madoc. "She *did* give Cleve the reward she was supposed to give Druce."

It was that indisputable fact that finally convinced the others. Wynne loved Sir Cleve, and he loved her. They would get married and then they would all be a real family. Arthur kept that happy thought uppermost in his mind as he clambered up onto his thinking boulder. In the field beyond him Rhys, Madoc, and Isolde continued their target practice amid much good-humored rowdiness. Bronwen made a little cottage on one side of his boulder and tried to get her kitten and puppy children to sleep in the straw beds she fashioned for them all. But like all children, her two didn't wish to go to bed precisely when their mother ordered.

Arthur heard her gentle scolding only vaguely, however, and was equally unaffected by the noisy play of the other three. His quick mind turned over and over this new turn of events.

Wynne certainly hadn't acted as if she liked Cleve FitzWarin up to now. Isolde and Bronwen had told him earlier that Wynne had caused Sir Cleve's hands to get all itchy. Surely she wouldn't do that to someone she liked. But then, there was that kiss. She wouldn't give a big wet kiss to someone she didn't like an awful lot.

He sighed, and stared up at the sky, watching the high, circling movements of a falcon of some variety or other. Some things were just so confusing. There were times when he thought he'd never figure the world out. But he was determined to try. He wanted to know everything about everything—even though some things were very puzzling. But that only made figuring them out even more fun. He didn't understand how Wynne could want to hurt Cleve and then want to kiss him—but then, he didn't understand anything about why men and women fell in love. Maybe that was how they were supposed to act.

He frowned in concentration. That must be it. Wynne had never acted so strangely before. But she'd never kissed anybody before either. At least not that the children knew about. Yes, it must be the kiss that did it. She was in love with Cleve, only she just wasn't used to it yet.

He sighed and smiled in contentment. A father. Not until he'd met Sir Cleve in the forest and he'd helped him down from that tree, then given him a ride on his big horse, Ceta, had Arthur even thought about having a father. But now it seemed the most important thing in the whole world. He wanted a father, and he wanted it to be Cleve.

Wynne peered at Arthur suspiciously from across the well-lit hall. He'd been watching her like a hawk the entire evening. So had all the children. Could it be they suspected what she planned to do? But surely they couldn't.

She bit her lip in uncertainty and fiddled with the stem of her plain pewter goblet. Arthur was possessed of an almost uncanny intelligence, it was true. But he'd never evidenced any particular interest in her herbal remedies. He was too busy trying to determine how birds could fly, where the sun went every night, and why the ocean didn't drain off the edges of the world.

In the warm, golden light cast from the several torches that rimmed the hall, she saw Isolde whisper to Bronwen, and then both girls giggled. Perhaps Isolde suspected. Yes, it must be her, for she already showed an intense curiosity about the healing arts. Wynne was certain she would eventually show signs of possessing the Radnor vision.

She caught her breath. Maybe this *was* that first sign. Maybe Isolde simply *knew* what Wynne planned.

Just then all the men filed through the pair of heavy oak doors of the manor for the evening meal, drawing Wynne's attention. Cleve and Druce walked together, conversing in a congenial manner, much to her disgust. Both of them sent her a smile. While Druce's was sincere and without guile, though, Sir Cleve's was clearly mocking and smug.

How dare he court her only ally? she fumed, jerking her eyes away. But when her gaze fell on the children, her anger fled, to be replaced by dismay. For all five children were staring at Cleve with the oddest expressions on their faces. They were at once both happy and wondering, excited and nervous. But why?

She looked back at Cleve, then over at Druce. Something was afoot, but she had no idea what it could be. For some reason the children appeared to be more enamored of Cleve than ever.

Her gaze narrowed upon Rhys and Madoc. Had those two revealed to the others about the kiss they'd witnessed?

A frustrated sigh escaped her. If that was the case, there was no telling what their childish imaginations had put together from that. But they simply couldn't know about the powdered yew in her pocket.

Once everyone was well settled at the long trestle tables, Gwynedd turned her head toward Wynne and nodded, signaling that the evening meal could begin. Though Wynne was Seeress now, Gwynedd still presided over all the meals, as befitted the matriarch of the family. Sightless she might be, but her ears were sharp, and she knew when everyone was assembled and seated at the long plank tables that formed a great U in the spacious hall.

Wynne rose and made her way to the surveying board,

where the various platters and ewers waited for serving. Cook and her two helpers were ready with their hair freshly bound and clean cloths wrapped around their waists.

"Enid, you serve the wine. Cook, take the meat tray while Gladys takes the cheese and breads. I'll serve the children their milk and cheese. Just put some meat and bread on this smaller tray for them."

Wynne had decided to do the deed after the men had eaten their fill. It would make the effects of the poison more dramatic. Messier, she thought, wrinkling her nose. But this was a desperate situation and therefore called for desperate measures. She would slip the powdered root into a ewer of ale or wine, whichever they called for, and serve them herself. Then she would just see.

Wynne did not delude herself that she would escape blame. Cleve would know at once. So would Gwynedd. But that was not the point. She wanted to show the Englishmen that she was serious. The parsley fern had been but a mild warning. This would be more serious. Plus, it had no easy antidote. They would mend only when they had purged the poison completely from their systems.

How far she was willing to go in this war with them was a question Wynne wasn't quite ready to answer. In her head she was convinced she would fight Cleve FitzWarin to the bitter end. To the death, if it came to that. But just the thought of his warm mouth against hers made her doubt that. He was so alive and vital. So warm all over. And despite her quite reasonable hatred of him, she could not deny that he roused the most incredible answering heat within her.

She frowned as she poured goat's milk into the children's wooden cups.

"Do you have a headache, Wynne?"

Wynne stared down into Isolde's innocent face. "Why, ah. No. No. I was just, um . . . just thinking. That's all."

"Can we have extra meat tonight?" Madoc asked.

Wynne nodded absently, then was even more bewildered by Rhys's response. "You're a very good mother, Wynne."

"Yes. I'm so glad you're my mother," Bronwen echoed.

Wynne finished serving them amid their beaming approval. It was Arthur's shining gaze, however, that confirmed her fears. He kept glancing from her to Cleve, then back again. From the first he and Cleve had seemed to connect in some indefinable manner. It was clear now that he imagined some attachment between her and Cleve, some attachment that would make Cleve a part of young Arthur's life.

Wynne almost groaned out loud. How had things gotten so out of hand?

She forced a stern look to her face. "I want all of you to leave the hall as soon as you are finished with your meal. Once you've finished your chores, you can wash up and then go to bed."

"Oh, Wynne, do we—"

"—have to do chores?"

"It's little enough. Bronwen, you put the puppy on a rope so he won't pester the chickens. Boys, each of you bring a bucket of water to the goat shed. A full bucket, mind you. And Isolde, you carry the kitchen scraps to the chickens. You see," she finished, "it won't take you but a minute or two each."

For a moment she was disconcerted by the steady stares of the five of them. Then they all began to nod and agree. Bronwen giggled once, but stopped when Isolde nudged her.

Oh, but they weren't the least bit subtle. No, not at all.

Still, that was the least of Wynne's concerns. When the Englishmen all became ill, the children would know it was she who'd caused it. What would they think of her then? They thought Cleve FitzWarin was just wonderful. She knew they would never understand.

She shoved her hand into the folds of her skirt and patted her purse reassuringly. Maybe it was time for her to tell them the truth. Maybe they were old enough to understand about their parentage and why she must chase this English knight away.

Rhys bumped Madoc's arm, and his milk sloshed onto his hand and the table. Isolde shook her head at their rowdiness, and Bronwen picked up her bowl so that the milk wouldn't run under it. As Wynne quickly wiped up the spill from the ancient wooden table and tried to restore order, however, she studied Arthur's rapt expression. He was staring at Cleve with an almost painful longing.

In that moment she knew she must tell them. There was no avoiding it any longer. She cleared her throat as she poured more milk into Madoc's cup. "I've something to talk with you about. Tonight when you're ready for bed, I'll come up, and we'll talk then. All right?"

"Yes, Wynne," they all chorused. Between their beaming faces and clear agreement of thought, she was doubly dismayed. This would not be easy.

"Good. Well, here's your stew. And the bread and cheese. Eat your whole bowlful before you have any of Cook's pears, understand?" She nodded as they began to eat, then turned back to the adults' tables. There was no backing out now. Things had gone much too far.

The meal passed in good humor—at least for everyone but Wynne. Though they were soldiers of lands with a long history of off-and-on disharmony, both Druce's and Cleve's followers took a cue from their leaders, and there was no indication of any strain between the two groups. Even the language barrier was not a problem, for the Welsh warriors all knew a smattering of both English and French, and they were happy to teach their difficult Welsh words to the Englishmen. The stumblings over the foreign sounds made for much laughter and jesting, and the high-arching ceiling echoed the good cheer.

When Druce told a bawdy joke, which Cleve translated for his men, the entire gathering dissolved into laughter. That is, the entire gathering excepting Wynne and the five children. The children simply did not understand the double meaning of the words. As for Wynne, she understood, but she was not in the mood to appreciate such humor. The pouch in her purse seemed to be burning a hole into her thigh, prodding her to get on with it—to just pour it into the wine and serve the Englishmen a generous portion.

Her hands were sweating when she finally pushed away from the table. Her own trencher of food was hardly touched, for her nerves would not allow her to eat. Steeling herself, she made her way to the surveying board, waving Cook to remain at her own meal. This was one serving she must do herself.

As she passed alongside him, she could not prevent herself from glancing at Cleve. He was watching her, but she'd known that already. Every time his gaze rested upon her, she was acutely aware of it. It might have been an actual touch—a long, slow caress—so distinct was the feeling it gave her.

This time, when their eyes met and held, the feeling was trebled. For a moment she profoundly regretted the fates that had cast their destinies at such variance. For a moment she wondered about the possibilities this powerful connection between them might offer.

But it could go nowhere. She knew that.

With a wrenching effort she forced herself to look away from him. But the burning intensity of his dark gaze would always remain with her, she thought sorrowfully. She doubted any other man would ever look at her in such a way. Nor that she could ever respond in so basic and visceral a manner.

At the surveying board she paused, keeping her back to the diners. She filled a tall pewter ewer half full with red wine, then swiftly emptied the ground root of yew tree into it. Before she could reconsider, she swished the ewer several times, then filled it to the top with more wine so that the powder was well dissolved. With a resolute sigh she finally squared her shoulders and, with the ewer firmly in hand, turned toward the Englishmen.

Just as she approached them, however, a small, slender form shot past her. She looked over in dismay to see Cleve beckoning to Arthur, a warm smile on his face. Almost without invitation Arthur perched on Cleve's knee, causing Wynne to stumble to a halt. Now what was she to do?

"Ah, fresh wine. Just what I was hoping for," Cleve said. He stared boldly at her, but she swiftly looked away. "Here, fill my cup, Wynne. And perhaps just a taste for my young friend, Arthur."

Wynne looked up in horror. "No—" she blurted out.

"No? You mean no wine for me, or for Arthur?"

"For . . . for Arthur. He's . . . he's much too young."

"I've tasted wine before, Wynne," Arthur broke in importantly. "Druce has let me, and so have you."

"Yes . . . well. But not tonight. Now, be off with you, Arthur. You and the other children have chores, remember?"

"But dinner isn't done. What about the pears?" he protested. "Besides, Cleve says I may have some wine."

"Come, Wynne. Don't be so difficult," Cleve prodded, drawing her tortured gaze. He held his cup forward, a taunting smile hovering on his lips. "Serve the wine."

"Yes, serve the wine," Arthur echoed, holding his own small cup out as well.

Wynne's grip on the ewer was so tight that her knuckles showed white. And yet still it shook in her hand. He knew! Somehow he knew what she planned, and now, heartless bastard that he was, he used Arthur's innocent trust as a shield. Her jaw clenched as she glared her rage at him, but he answered her with an even more mocking expression. He'd caught her and he knew it. What was worse, he was going to make her squirm like a worm on a hook before he let her go.

If he let her go.

"It appears Wynne is not listening," Cleve commented to Arthur.

"What's the delay?" Druce called from several seats down. "I'll have some of that wine, Wynne, even if you won't serve Arthur. He can steal a sip from my cup when you're not looking."

At that moment Wynne regretted not taking Druce into her confidence. He was ruining her plan. "It appears you've already had too much wine," she snapped at him. "You all have," she added in frustration.

She jerked around and marched stiffly back to the surveying board, for she knew no other way to get out of this predicament. She couldn't let Arthur get even one slight sip of the tainted wine, although at the moment she wouldn't have minded if Druce had some. How could he be so obtuse?

Cook came up beside Wynne at the board. "Is aught amiss?" she whispered.

Wynne shook her head. But when Cook sought to take the ewer from her, Wynne tightened her grasp on it. "No. Not this wine—" She sent a furious look toward Cleve FitzWarin. "I fear it may be tainted," she muttered so that only Cook could hear.

Cook's eyes widened at that, and it was clear when the woman made the connection in her mind. But when Isolde came up to Wynne with a hurt look on her face, Wynne knew that even the children had guessed what she had attempted to do. Although Wynne didn't care at all what the other adults might think of her actions, the children's confusion cut her deeply. The other three at their small table stared at her in dismay. But it was Arthur's pale face and his expression of hurt and betrayal that struck her the deepest.

She saw him pull away from Cleve and run from the hall. Cleve stood up and, after sending her an exasperated frown, followed the boy.

Druce stared about him in confusion. The wine he'd already consumed made him slow to comprehend. When he did, however, he shook his head in resignation.

"Ah, Wynne. I fear you may have to accept that for once you might be wrong."

"What has happened?" Gwynedd asked in the oppressive silence.

But Wynne could not remain to answer. She wasn't sure she knew anymore. Only a few days before, her life had been wonderful. Peaceful and routine. Uneventful. But now everything was wrong. Everyone doubted her—first Gwynedd, now Druce, and even the children.

Panic suddenly overwhelmed her, and unaccustomed tears stung her eyes. Whirling about, she fled the hall, just as Arthur had, running away from a truth that was too painful to accept. Though she was an adult and Arthur only a child, at that moment she felt as bereft as she had those seven years ago when she'd been the abandoned one.

Once more, it seemed, the English had destroyed her family. Only this time she could not deny that she was as guilty as they.

10

Once again Wynne found herself searching for Arthur. But it was dark now with only a gibbous moon to light the way. She stared up at the half-hidden orb, which danced in and out behind the high, wispy clouds. A storm brewed somewhere out over the sea, and soon it would strike here. How fitting that was.

She sighed, unaware how dejected she appeared with her shoulders slumped and her face so pale. The only thing that mattered to her was to find Arthur and try to explain. She closed her eyes, grasped the amulet all the women in her family had worn, and tried to sense his whereabouts. But it didn't work. She was too unsettled for the visions to work. All that came to her was a vague awareness of . . . of . . . of the Englishman!

"*Cnaf,*" she muttered, not bothering to hide her feelings. Why should she? He was indeed a knave. Had he not ridden in here on his heartless mission, none of this would have come to pass. But come he had and, *cnaf* that he was, he seemed somehow to invade her very thoughts.

She scowled, trying to ignore the disturbing shiver that began somewhere deep inside, then slowly snaked out to encompass her entire being. The scoundrel was not far away. Perhaps on the edges of the meadow—

At Arthur's thinking rock! No doubt he'd followed Arthur there.

At least Arthur was safe, she realized. The Englishman would not let any harm come to him. But that acknowledgment only depressed her further. The man truly seemed concerned for the children. He was completely misguided about wanting to take one of them back to England of course. But his intentions were at least not malicious.

Still, as she approached the rock, moving silently through the tall, damp meadow grasses, she dreaded the coming confrontation—both with Arthur and with Cleve. But she'd behaved badly, and now she must pay the price.

As the rock loomed ahead and two quiet voices murmured from the darkness, she steeled herself. It was Arthur who was important here—nothing else. If she must reveal the terrible truth of his conception to him, so be it. Perhaps now he and the other children would understand her suspicion and hatred of the English. Perhaps this really was for the best.

When she halted before the big, flat rock, however, Wynne was not at all convinced of that. As she'd expected, Arthur was there with Cleve. But she'd not anticipated that he would be sitting in the big man's lap, cradled gently, if awkwardly, while the two spoke, their heads bent near. A pang of intense longing struck her to see one of her children comforted by someone other than herself. He was *hers* to raise. She was the one who loved him most.

She had to forcibly stop herself from rushing over and snatching Arthur away.

Cleve looked up first, then Arthur. The boy shifted slightly, leaning nearer to Cleve, it appeared to her. That simple movement drew her up more abruptly than any words might have. Once more she felt the unwelcome sting of tears. She, who so rarely cried, now seemed ever on the verge of a veritable flood. Like a statue she stood there, staring at them, knowing her emotions were plain on her face, but unable—and unwilling anyway—to hide them.

"Arthur," she spoke his name tentatively. A long-eared owl hooted three times from the lurking blackness of the forest beyond them. The meager light of the moon gleamed for a moment as the clouds cleared before it, and Wynne could vaguely make out the closed expression on Arthur's face. She also recognized the irritation on Cleve's.

"Arthur," she tried again, moving a pace nearer.

She saw Cleve's hand tighten slightly on Arthur's arm. "Don't be rude, lad," he murmured gently.

Arthur lifted his chin a fraction, and Wynne tried to take heart. At least Cleve was not trying to interfere between them. "Arthur, I . . . I know you're angry with me—"

"You tried to kill Cleve!"

His accusation made her swallow hard. No doubt that's how it must appear to everyone. "No, I didn't try to kill him. I just—"

"Yes, you did!"

"Hush, lad. Let's listen to what Wynne has to say."

Wynne crouched down at the edge of the low rock so that her face was just a little below Arthur's. "I did put something in the wine," she admitted in a low and miserable tone. "But only to make him ill—"

"He *might* have died!"

"He would only have retched for a while. And had the runs," Wynne added weakly. "But he wouldn't have died.

I just wanted to frighten him and his friends away from here." She searched Arthur's shadowed face, desperate to make him understand. "I only wanted them to go back where they came from and leave us alone."

There was a brief silence, and it wasn't until Arthur spoke that Wynne realized she'd been holding her breath.

"But why?" the child asked in a suddenly trembling voice. "Why would you want him to go away?"

Wynne's eyes flitted to Cleve's, and though she couldn't read his expression, she knew he waited for her to tell the truth—to reveal everything to Arthur. Before she could answer, however, Arthur continued.

"Is it because of the kiss? Because he took Druce's reward?"

Wynne closed her eyes. Oh, how could she possibly explain *that* to the children? She reached out a hand to touch Arthur's knee. "It goes far beyond what has happened during the past few days, Arthur. There are things I need to tell you and the other children." She bit her lower lip nervously. "If you'll come with me now, we'll all of us have a long talk, and I'll answer every one of your questions."

To her chagrin Arthur did not respond at once. He looked up at Cleve as if for permission. Only when Cleve patted the boy's shoulder reassuringly did Arthur look back at her.

He sighed. "All right. I'll go."

Wynne stood up, her hands clenched together at her waist, while Cleve lifted Arthur down, then stood up himself. "Go along, lad. Wynne and I will catch up with you in a moment." Then he caught Wynne's wrist to make sure she didn't leave. "Go along," he repeated, rumpling Arthur's hair fondly. "Find the other children so they can all listen to what Wynne has to say. I'll see you in the morning."

Wynne watched Arthur disappear across the dark meadow with a sinking feeling in her chest. It wasn't bad enough that she must face the five children tonight and explain the terrible circumstances of their births. Now she must also deal with Cleve.

As if to underscore her dismal thoughts, he jerked her to face him, none too gentle in the movement. "Now, mistress witch, are you going to end this ridiculous campaign of yours to chase me away? It should be clear by now that the only ones you hurt by your actions are the ones you are supposed to care for—your children. Only they're not really your children, are they?"

"They *are* mine," Wynne bit out angrily. "And no *lleidr* Englishman is going to steal them away on the pretext of bringing them to their father—if indeed this lord of yours is truly father to any of them."

"If I wasn't convinced he sired one of these five children before, I'm convinced of it now. We've found no other bastard offspring of the English of this age anywhere in Radnor Forest. I've spoken to Druce and Gwynedd and even old Tafydd."

Wynne felt as if his words were a noose tightening around her. "The child might have died long ago. Or this woman your lord claimed bore his seed—she might not have brought the child to life. She might have lost it—perhaps even forced it from her womb as soon as he was gone."

Even in the dark she could see the distaste on his face. "No God-fearing woman would do such a thing."

"If she felt she bore the devil's seed, she would. And no one would blame her for it! These were children of rape, remember? Brutal rape," she went on, growing more and more hysterical. "Sometimes over and over again, by an endless stream—"

"Stop it!" he snapped. Then, in an unexpected movement, he pulled her hard against him, holding her there with one strong hand on her back and the other cupping her face to his chest. "Don't dwell on a past that was so terrible. No good can come of it. You must think of the future now. Of these children's future."

Though his words came out in a harsh growl and his tone was demanding, Wynne found a most perverse comfort in them. More than anything she would like to put that dreadful time behind her, never to think of her sister's tortured cries or her long months of suffering and horrible death. But how could she forget? The children were a constant reminder. And now *he* was here, confusing her, stirring up all these awful emotions. Old hatreds. New longings. And most of all fear. She was terrified of the new future that threatened to take from her everything she cared about.

For a moment longer she let herself rest against his strong body, not ready to resist him just yet. She was simply not strong enough. Then she took a shaky breath and forced her hands against his chest.

He didn't budge. Nor did he loosen his grip in the least.

"Unhand me," she muttered, embarrassed that she'd let herself go weak against him for even a moment. She should never have given him a glimpse of her vulnerability. Men like him—Englishmen—always took any advantage they could. She shoved at him harder. "I said, let me go!"

But for all her efforts she succeeded only in leaning far enough away to meet his inquisitive gaze. That was hardly her goal, but when she tried to look away, he tangled one of his hands in her loosened hair and forced her head back so that their faces were but inches apart.

"I'll release you when you've heard me out and not before, Wynne. Do we understand each other?"

She glared rebelliously into his darkened face, yet she knew as well as he did that the choice was not hers. When he was satisfied by her silence that he had her attention, he cleared his throat.

"You must give them the truth, Wynne. Not colored by your own feelings or prejudices."

Her jaw clenched. "And do you think the truth will not damn your people?"

She felt his sigh, for her breasts were pressed firmly against the gray kersey bliaut that covered his broad chest. "The children will not understand the horrors of war," he replied. "Nor the horrors of rape. They're too young to understand that such things happen, nor why."

"Understand *why?*" She scoffed at the idea. "No woman can ever understand *why* rape happens. Nor war either. How can we? Only men understand those things—or at least they pretend they do." Her gaze bored into his. "Maybe you can explain it to me, Sir Cleve. Why *do* men make war on each other? Why *do* they rape?" Then, unable to stop herself, she blurted out. "Have *you* ever raped a woman?"

He stiffened, and his hands tightened painfully on her arms. Then he thrust her an arm's length away, as if she were a burning brand against his body.

"No! No, never." He shook his head as if he sought to shrug off his anger. "Not all men are the same. Surely you know that. What of your friend, Druce—"

"Don't you dare to compare the foul deeds of those English soldiers to Druce, nor to any of my people! We *Cymry* are a people apart from the likes of you!"

Once more he shook his head, but this time, even in the face of her contempt, he seemed to feel sorry for her. "You call yourself Seeress. The people of Radnor look to you for advice and guidance. Wisdom, even. And yet was ever a woman so unwise? So naive and innocent? We English are not so unlike you Welsh. There are both good and bad among us. Honest and dishonest. Loyal and disloyal." He gave her a little shake, and his eyes burned into hers. "We are not so different, Wynne. There are men of Wales who rape and pillage amidst the insane glories of their wars. Do you think there are no Welsh bastards in the outlying villages of England?" He shook her again. "It is not right, not for either side. But we cannot change the fact that it has happened. These children you raise have English fathers. The fact that one of their fathers wishes to right the wrong he's done should not condemn him in your eyes."

"Nor should it exonerate him," she answered, though the heat of anger had somehow fled her voice.

"He can't change the past, Wynne. But he can change the future."

But I don't want him to, Wynne wanted to cry. Only she couldn't.

A cold fear of that very future seemed to grip her, filling her with a terrible dread. She shivered, and when she did, he folded her into a warm embrace.

"I know this is hard for you," he murmured against her hair.

Wynne squeezed her eyes tight against the tears that fought for release. "No, you can never know . . ."

She felt the movement of his throat as he swallowed, and against her chest his heart thudded strong and steady. Why had he come here? He'd disrupted her life thoroughly, and yet at that moment she was comforted by his presence. For a moment she could almost believe he was right and that his quest was a good one.

But to give up one of her children . . .

Her emotions were so raw, so tangled and painful, that she could hardly think straight. When he tilted her face up to his, she stared at him through eyes damp with tears. "I love them so," she whispered, unable to control the tremble in her voice and the fear in her soul.

"I know," he murmured back as his gaze swept her shadowed features. "And I . . ." He took a sharp breath, then groaned. "And I've been waiting to do this too long."

The kiss he abruptly forced on her was not entirely unexpected, nor did Wynne pretend to herself that it was unwanted. A part of her had longed for this ever since their kiss earlier in the day, and yet she'd suppressed the very idea. It was too traitorous of her. Too absolutely foolhardy.

But now as his lips came down on hers without the least semblance of gentleness, she shed the need for pretense. It was too, too glorious, this press of warm, damp flesh to warm, damp flesh.

His lips parted hers so easily, as if it were always meant to be thus, and at once their tongues met in a wet and fiery battle. He pulled her tongue wholly into his mouth. Then when she surged excitedly to him, he thrust back, taking full possession of her mouth, filling her in the most erotic manner imaginable. He surged in and out, rubbing the sensitive inner surface of her lips, and something deep in her belly leaped to fire.

Unaware of what she did, Wynne pressed her belly hard against his muscular thighs and hips. He responded with equal fervor, and she felt the rigid contours of his quick arousal. He bit at her lip, then lifted her up off the ground, holding her fully within his grasp.

He kissed her as if this were a battle they fought, and some distant part of Wynne's mind knew he fought to win. Yet in succumbing to him she felt not vanquished, but rather victorious.

He lifted her higher, with one arm tightly wrapped under her buttocks. Only when her face was above his, when she was lifted into the dark mist of the night, looking down into his face, so faintly lit by the silver moonlight, did she consider what she did. Her arms were wrapped about his neck. Her hands were filled with his hair. One of her legs was lifted, curved wantonly about his lean flank, and had anyone been about, the conclusions would have been obvious. They would be lovers. It was ordained by whatever powers governed both the earth and the stars —God the Father in heaven, or the Mother Goddess of the earth.

His eyes shone up at her with the most possessive of lights. Then he lowered his face and nuzzled the fine wool fabric that covered her chest. Nudging her amulet aside, he rubbed his cheeks against the soft peaks of her breasts, nipping at the loose, braided neckline with his teeth.

"Ah, woman. You are indeed a witch. Can you not make these unwieldy garments of ours disappear so that we may properly finish what we have begun?" Once more he rubbed against her breasts, seeking the taut nipples with his teeth.

"Oh," she groaned as he found one, causing her to arch in mindless pleasure. "Cleve . . . oh, please . . ."

"Yes, yes. You do please me well. And I want nothing more than to do the same to you," he murmured against the bared skin of her collarbone. His tongue found the gentle indentation above the bone, then trailed small, heated kisses along it to the soft hollow of her throat. She swallowed, and he marked the undulation with more fiery kisses up to her chin and then on until he found her lips once more.

"I want you, Wynne ab Gruffydd." He kissed the words against her mouth. "My sweet seeress. My wicked Welsh witch . . ."

"Wynne? Are you out there?"

Like an icy stream of water, Druce's voice brought Wynne to reality with an abruptness that had her sputtering. "Oh! Let me down! I must . . . I can't . . ."

But Cleve would not let her go. He only let her slide down along the hard length of him, all the while holding her fast in his arms.

"Wynne is just discussing something with me," he called through the darkness to Druce. "We'll be in very shortly."

There was a pause during which Wynne was acutely aware of every inch of Cleve's body melded so intimately to hers. A part of her still yearned for more of the seductive thrill he filled her with. But the practical side of her struggled to break free.

"Shhh," he admonished her with a forceful kiss that left her breathless all over again.

But Druce was not done with them. "Wynne?" he called once more, a trace of concern clear in his tone.

"I . . . I am here," she managed to choke out. "Wait for me. I was . . . I was just coming in."

She met Cleve's still-ardent gaze and felt a sinking desperation when she spied the frustration on his face. One of his hands forced her face nearer his until their breath mingled. She truly thought she would faint from the terrible pull of too many divergent emotions.

"Ah, witch. You have but prolonged the moment when

we shall find our pleasure in one another. If it is your intention to torture me, then you have well achieved your aim. But know this, *cariad.* My turn will come. And I promise you a sweet torture of your own."

Then he kissed her hard and possessively, as if he meant never to release her. When he finally did set her free, Wynne stumbled back, disoriented, confused, and unable whatsoever to marshal her thoughts.

"Wynne!" Druce was nearer now, and his tone had become demanding.

"Yes . . . I . . . I'm coming," she managed to answer him, though her eyes were riveted upon Cleve. The man was a sorcerer in his own right, her disjointed thoughts decided. And he was far too strong for her to stave off.

She jerked about and walked stiffly toward the distant lights from the manor, toward the vague outline that was Druce. At that moment Druce appeared a gift from a protective God, a savior sent to rescue her from the clutches of the devil himself.

"Are you all right?" he whispered when she reached him.

Wynne could only nod. She did not stop nor even pause. She only fixed her stare on the distant manor and continued across the meadow, unmindful of the tall grasses that parted before her and of the two sets of male eyes that followed her. She wished only to find a safe and private place where she could hide from prying eyes and try to mend her shattered nerves.

"What did you do to her?" Druce challenged when Cleve drew abreast of him.

Cleve gauged the other man's reaction before answering. "I did what any hot-blooded man would do to her, given half a chance. I kissed her." When Druce's gaze narrowed, he went on. "Are you telling me you've never once tried to do the same?"

To Cleve's surprise Druce looked away in quick chagrin, and his words came out awkwardly. "I've wanted to, I'll admit as much. Most of the lads in the village have wanted to. But no one's ever boasted of succeeding."

A sudden rush of possessive feelings caught Cleve unaware. She'd not kissed another as she'd kissed him!

He and Druce fell in step together, both aware of the slight form that hurried on ahead of them. Cleve cleared his throat. "Has she not been promised to any other man, then?"

Their muffled footsteps and the cry of a nighthawk somewhere beyond the tree line was the only sound for a few moments. Then Druce sighed as if in resignation. "This is not England. While a father may deny his daughter permission to marry a man of whom he does not approve, no Welshwoman may be forced into a marriage she does not want. As Seeress, and with no father to guide her, Wynne's choice is even more her own." He shrugged. "Though at one time or another we've all thought to win her, she's never allowed any man to court her. We thought perhaps she never would. But now . . ."

His words trailed off into the night air, but not before they had imprinted themselves on Cleve's brain. Court her. Was that what he was doing? He suppressed an uncomfortable spurt of guilt. He was betrothed to Lord William's youngest daughter—or at least he would be, once he succeeded in returning Lord William's bastard son—or sons—to him. So why was he dallying with this woman whom he must necessarily abandon?

Wynne's earlier words suddenly rang in his memory. "Have you ever raped a woman?" she'd asked. Though he had not, he knew nonetheless that he had deliberately seduced more than his fair share. And he'd very nearly succeeded in seducing Wynne tonight. If Druce had not interrupted them . . .

"I'll bid you good night," Cleve spoke curtly to Druce as he veered toward the English encampment.

"Wait. I would know—" Druce broke off, then after a moment's consideration continued. "What are your intentions toward her?"

Cleve took a slow breath. *What indeed?* "She is a beautiful and intriguing woman."

"I doubt you've any maidens in England quite like her," Druce boasted, abandoning his cautious tone. "If you've a mind to win her over, well, I wish you good luck. You shall need it," he added with a lighthearted chuckle. "Mind you, however, do not press her beyond where she would go, else you shall answer to me." Then he turned and walked away, still laughing despite his last warning.

But though he had heard Druce's words, and even wondered at the man's amusement, Cleve was too consumed by his lingering desire for Wynne to think clearly. How he wanted that woman, prickly rose though she was. Yet he could not escape the guilty feelings that assailed him. He would have her if he could, and then what? Leave for England with one of her children in tow? What if there was a child of *their* joining?

She could avoid that, he told himself. She was a healer, after all—a witch, as she so often proclaimed. She must know all the methods to avoid bearing an unwanted child.

Yet if she was as untried as Druce said . . . If she was truly a virgin . . .

Cleve flung himself down on his blanket, curled one arm beneath his head, and stared up at the faint form of the moon behind the high, leading clouds. Of course she was a virgin. Why should he ever have thought otherwise?

That was one more reason why he should abandon this mad pursuit of her.

Yet the uncomfortable tension in his loins was too insistent to ignore. He shifted, trying to find a more hospitable position. But as the moon wended across the sky and the clouds followed, growing heavy and threatening, he couldn't help cursing the perverse God who'd offered him the wife and lands he'd always hungered for, then turned around now to tempt him with a woman the likes of which he feared he might never find again.

When he finally slept, it was to toss fitfully beneath the gathering storm clouds, dreaming of a field of the sweetest roses. But when he sought a resting-place amid them, he was ever held back by their thorns.

11

Wynne had no easy answer for Isolde's question. "I don't know why the English king wanted to make Wales a part of his country," she finally replied.

"Because he's a bloody English bast—" Madoc broke off when Rhys elbowed him in the ribs.

But Wynne was too troubled by what she must tell the children to be concerned by Madoc's language. She sighed and reached out to rub Isolde's foot. "I suppose King Henry felt Wales was a threat to his people. If he could make the people of *Cymru* his own, well, I suppose he thought he wouldn't have to worry about us anymore. We would be English then.

"But that's not what I want to talk about," she added. She glanced at Arthur, and her nerve almost abandoned her. Though he'd done as asked, and all five of the children had been gathered in their sleeping loft waiting for her to come up, Arthur kept himself aloof. Like the others he was dressed only in his oldest shift, the one reserved just for sleeping. But unlike his brothers and sisters he sat apart, his knees drawn up to his chest. The others sat in various poses around her, all curious and bright-eyed

about Wynne's odd behavior. She usually made them go
to sleep long before now.

A single rush-light illuminated the low-ceilinged space
with a warm glow, yet from Arthur's corner there came
only an ice-cold chill. Wynne cleared her throat.

"War is more than two armies battling with swords and
battle-axes. It's more than just men fighting against other
men. Other people get hurt too."

"Even little children?" Bronwen ventured.

Wynne nodded. "Sometimes even little children."

Madoc and Rhys shared a slightly alarmed look. "Are
we going to have—"

"—another war with England?"

"Oh, no, sweetheart. That's not going to happen. At
least not anytime soon. And not here," Wynne hastened
to add. "No, you're all very safe in Radnor Forest."

"Then why are you talking about war?" Isolde asked.

"Well, I'm trying to explain about your fathers."

"They were soldiers, weren't they?"

Wynne looked up at Arthur's belligerent question.
"Yes, they were soldiers."

"I knew it!" Madoc crowed. He jabbed at Rhys with an
imaginary sword.

"And we'll be soldiers too."

"Listen to me," Wynne pleaded, reaching forward to
still the irrepressible pair. "Listen to me," she repeated
urgently.

Perhaps it was the sadness in her eyes that finally registered on them, for Rhys and Madoc grew silent, and
Isolde and Bronwen leaned nearer one another. Even Arthur finally met her gaze, and she saw both the fear and
longing in his eyes. He wanted to know, but in his wise-
old-man fashion, he knew the truth would be unpleasant.

Otherwise she would have told them all of this long before.

Wynne took a fortifying breath. "You are all Welshborn. Never forget that. And though I am not your true mother, I am your mother in every other way. Your birth mothers were Welsh also. But your fathers . . . your fathers were all English soldiers."

Complete silence seemed to envelop every corner of the low-ceilinged loft. Only the dancing flame of the solitary rush-light gave any indication of movement. Not sure how this news affected them, Wynne plunged on. "Seven years ago the English overran our portion of Wales. They were here off and on for several months. Many of us hid from them. Others resigned themselves to the invaders' presence and simply tried to make the best of it."

Isolde frowned and bit her lip, trying to understand. "Well, if the English soldiers married our mothers, how come—"

"They *didn't* marry them, stupid!" Arthur jumped up with a furious expression on his face. "They *didn't* marry our mothers! That's why that bully Renfrew called us little *bastards* when we went to the village with Druce. That's why Druce got so mad at him. He didn't want us to hear and figure it out. But I figured it out . . . I figured it out, didn't I, Wynne?" He trailed off in a frightened voice.

She stared at him through eyes filled with tears. There was such pain in his voice, such hurt on his young face. Then she nodded and held her arms out to him.

In an instant Arthur had barreled into her lap, sobbing against her chest. Isolde and Bronwen began to wail and squeeze against her, and even the twins began to sniffle and edge nearer. When she extended a hand to Rhys and

Madoc, they, too, burrowed into the heap of weeping children.

They didn't understand, not really. But they understood enough to realize that things were not as they should be. Wynne knew she had to tell them everything—at least as much of it as they could make sense of.

As usual Arthur understood far too much for a six-year-old. She'd often thought that was why he was so sensitive. His quick mind was so logical that he easily reasoned things out. But his little-boy emotions did not so easily accept. After all, he was but a little child—they all were. It was not right that they should have to deal with such difficult facts at so tender an age.

"Oh, my sweet babies," she crooned, rocking back and forth with them. "I love you all so much. Everyone at Radnor Manor does. You must ignore bullies like Renfrew. What does he know?" she added, smoothing Arthur's fair hair with one free hand.

Isolde lifted her head and looked up at Wynne. A tear trickled down her cheek to hang trembling on her tiny chin. "But . . . but what's a 'little bastard'? I don't understand." She began to cry again.

Wynne forced down the lump in her throat. Arthur met her gaze, and she saw in his teary face no trace of his earlier anger. Time to explain, she reluctantly admitted to herself.

"Here, let's all dry our eyes first and catch our breath. All right? Then I'll explain everything to you and answer all your questions."

It was a subdued group who faced her, once they were all settled down. "When a man and woman marry, they commit to living their lives together and raising a family. Usually the woman begins to have babies and . . . and they raise their children, and, well, that's it. But you don't *have* to get married to have a baby."

"That's not what Cook says," Isolde murmured.

Wynne gave her a wan smile. "What Cook means, sweetheart, is that you *should* marry before you have babies. Both God and the Church prefer it, and it's best for everyone concerned. But sometimes women have babies before they get married."

"Babies like us," Arthur said solemnly.

"Yes, babies like all of you. But don't blame your mothers," Wynne hastened to add.

Bronwen shook her head. "But I don't understand."

Wynne exhaled a noisy breath. How was she to go about this? "All right. We all know that birds and rabbits and deer have babies, don't we?"

They all nodded, their eyes steady on her, and she was reminded of a nest of magpies. "The mother and father bird—or whatever—don't get married. They just decide to have babies. Well, it can happen that way with people too."

"But how?" Rhys and Madoc chorused.

Arthur shot them an exasperated look. "Haven't you ever seen the goats? You know, when the ram climbs on the ewe and . . . and wriggles all around?"

The other four children all nodded, but their blank expressions told Wynne that they still did not understand. In frustration she tossed her hair behind her shoulders and leaned forward earnestly.

"People are like the animals. The man must plant his seed within the woman so that it may grow into a babe. The Church tells us that he must marry her before he puts his seed into her. But some men don't wait. They put their seeds in women—"

Wynne broke off, for the memory of her sister's cries of

terror and pain came back to her too clearly. The cries had eventually subsided to mere whimpers as man after man had taken her. "Planting his seed" was far too gentle an image for the bitter truth of that day.

Wynne closed her eyes against the revulsion that filled her. Then Isolde lay a hand on her arm, and Wynne forced herself away from the past. She had been given Isolde, she reminded herself. No matter the terrible circumstances of her conception, Isolde was still precious to her. They all were.

"Is that what our fathers did?" Isolde whispered the question.

Wynne nodded. "Yes. That's what they did."

"And then when the war was over, they left." Arthur frowned a little. "Didn't they even want to see us?"

Oh, God, she thought. How could she hurt them this way? "They had to go back to England. They left before any of you were born."

The twins looked at each other. "Where are our real mothers?" Rhys asked.

"Isolde's mother fell on some rocks and died," Wynne answered at once. They'd heard that abbreviated story before, she knew. But now to explain the others.

"Arthur, your mother died a few days after you were born. Sometimes that happens. And Rhys and Madoc, your mother died too, when you were both only a year old. But all of your mothers are in heaven right now, watching over you all the time. They love you so much."

She felt a tug on her skirt and turned toward Bronwen. "What about *my* mother?" the sweet-faced child asked. "What about me?"

Wynne sighed, and stroked a silky strand of blond hair back from the girl's brow. "Your mother was very young.

Too young to raise a baby of her own. That's why you were given to Gwynedd and me to raise."

"You mean an English soldier planted his seed in a little girl?" Isolde asked askance.

Wynne had to force herself to appear calm. But inside she seethed once more with impotent rage. Put that way, in the innocent words of a child, the crime seemed tenfold worse than it already was.

"Yes," she spoke the word tightly. "Yes, that's what happened."

"But . . . but she wouldn't want . . . I mean, did she want . . ." Isolde's voice trailed off.

"No, sweetheart. She didn't want him to. None of your mothers wanted the English soldiers to plant their seeds in them. But the soldiers didn't care. When that happens, it's called rape, and it's a very cruel thing to do to a girl or a woman."

"But how can he give her his seed if she doesn't want it?"

To Wynne's relief it was Arthur who answered Isolde. "You've seen the sheep and goats. The ram is bigger and stronger. Even if the ewe doesn't want him to, he can still do it."

"But most men aren't like that," Wynne hastily added. "Most men marry a woman first, and she agrees to have a baby with him. They love each other, and the man is gentle and kind to his wife."

"Are Cleve and the English soldiers going to do that to Isolde and Bronwen—"

"—and you?" Madoc finished for Rhys. Both of their faces reflected their horror.

"No! Oh, no, don't worry. Cleve would never hurt any of us. Nor will his men." For all her conflicting feelings about him, Wynne knew without a doubt that in this she was absolutely correct. Cleve FitzWarin might be an English soldier, but he was no rapist.

Once again it was matter-of-fact Arthur who tied their discussion of the past back to the reality of the present. "Well, then, why *did* Sir Cleve come here?"

Wynne averted her eyes and stared unseeingly at her tightly clenched hands. Why indeed? She forced herself to show no emotion. "Sir Cleve FitzWarin is a knight. He was sent here by his English overlord to find a child whom this lord thinks may be *his* child."

The children stared at each other curiously. "One of us?" Arthur asked.

Wynne nodded. "He thinks maybe one of you is this man's child, and . . . and he wants to take whichever one of you it is back to England with him. To live there with this man."

Bronwen shrank back in fear. "But . . . but I don't want to go."

Isolde, too, clung tighter to Wynne's side. "You won't let him take us, will you, Wynne?"

Wynne forced a reassuring smile for the children's sake. "I'll never let you go. Don't worry. No one can take any of you away from me." But inside she was not nearly so certain as she sounded.

Arthur shifted and rubbed his foot, which must have gone to sleep. "I wouldn't mind if Cleve was my father."

Wynne saw again the painful longing on the child's face. "Cleve is not searching for his own son, Arthur, but for someone else's," she gently explained.

Arthur shrugged. "I know. But still . . ."

Much later, when the rush-light had been doused and all five of them were asleep in the curved truckle beds, Wynne sat at the edge of the loft contemplating Arthur's last words. He wouldn't mind if Cleve were his father.

That was not really surprising. Cleve had touched something in Arthur that no one else had. Even before Cleve had saved him from that dreadful fall, Arthur had already begun to look up to him. Now it was a powerful case of hero worship.

And why not? she wondered disconsolately. The man was certainly everything a boy would look up to. Tall and handsome; strong and in command. He rode a powerful destrier like one born astride, and carried his weapons with a confident air. He was not overtly threatening, and yet anyone could see he was not a person to dismiss lightly. To top it off, he was patient and generous with each of the children, free with both his time and his good humor.

Only with her did he display the darker side of his temperament.

A shiver snaked through her, and Wynne sighed. The dark side of his temperament. He certainly brought out *her* dark side as well. So much so that if she were not more careful, she might soon be the one carrying his seed to fruition in her belly. Only it would not have been planted there against her will. That she could not deny.

"Dear God," she groaned as she pulled her knees up to her chest and wrapped her arms about them. What had she done to deserve such a curse be sent down upon her? Why did he have to come here?

But she knew why, and the answer chilled her anew. He wanted one of her children—not her. He had a maiden awaiting him in England. Edeline was her name. Oh, but the man was a completely selfish bastard. He wanted his English bride. He wanted one of Wynne's own children. And now he wanted her to grace his bed. The man wanted what he wanted, and when he wanted it, no matter who was hurt in the taking.

Yet that was not precisely true, she had to admit. He was indeed bastard born—he'd admitted as much to her. As a result he seemed truly to care that this English lord's bastard child receive the full portion of his due. She grimaced in frustration. If only he could see that lands and castles were not everything to desire from life.

But how could he? He himself clearly longed for those very same sorts of possessions, so he assumed everyone else must as well. To be fair, most people did. But not her children, Wynne vowed. Not hers. They were Welsh, and they would reject everything English, as did she.

Only they didn't. And if she were honest, she would admit that she didn't either.

"Lleidr," she muttered under her breath, picturing in her mind Cleve's smiling visage. The man was indeed a thief in every sense of the word. He'd stolen her confidence and thereby weakened her reassuring hatred of the English. He'd stolen kisses and more from her. Now he'd stolen her children's loyalty—especially Arthur's.

He'd even stolen her heart—

No. That was not true, not even close to true, Wynne decided angrily. He'd fired her ardor perhaps. But only a little. Her heart, however, remained untouched.

Troubled by her thoughts, Wynne forced herself to rise. It was long past time for her to seek her own bed. As she made her way down the sturdy ladder from the loft, with one last look at the sleeping children, she realized it was raining. Good, she thought as the wind thrust belligerently against the shuttered windows. If it rained and blew hard enough, the Englishmen might be washed away. A tent was not too hospitable a lodging in such a storm as appeared to be brewing outdoors. Nor would the tiny lean-to stable afford any better shelter.

She made her weary way across the shadowed hall. The

embers of the evening's fire glowed hot. Cook had banked it well before retiring to the stone cottage she shared with her husband, Ivor. Gladys and Enid were bedded down in Gwynedd's small antechamber.

Wynne looked over at the heavy wooden doors that led outside. How were Druce and his fellows faring in the storm? she wondered. She should invite them to bed down in the hall.

As if attuned to her niece's thoughts, Gwynedd's form materialized from the entry to her chambers. "Bid the men to sleep within," she said in a voice muffled by sleep. She pushed a long gray braid over her shoulder and moved as if to return to her bed. Then she paused. "Invite them all, *nith. Cymry* and English alike. 'Tis not a night fit to sleep without."

Wynne did not respond. She knew her duty as hostess well enough. Besides, Druce's friendly attitude toward Cleve would probably make it impossible for her to leave the English outside anyway. With a frown on her face and a strange and fearful anticipation knotting her stomach, she found her mantle and working clogs, then made her way to the door.

The wind was in fine form tonight, she thought as she forced the door closed behind her. It tore at her skirts and pulled violently at the full mantle. Like a living thing it was, strong and vital, and angry too. And yet somehow aimless in its direction.

How fitting. It mirrored her mood precisely.

She lifted her face to the stinging rain and let her eyes accustom themselves to the pitch-blackness of the storm. Even through the heavy clogs she could sense the gravel path that led toward the animal sheds. A hedge of roses, bent almost to the ground in the wind, loomed to her right, and she knew that the cedar grove was off beyond it.

A sudden flash of lightning lit the low-hanging clouds from above, then another. For a moment the manor grounds were lit with a pale and ghostly light. There was no color. All was shades of gray, light and shadow, with everything wet and washed out. Yet still she saw plainly the English encampment, shared now by the Welshmen as well.

Their fire was long gone, marked only by a blackened heap and a circle of lumpy forms. Each man was huddled under his own blanket, taking what miserable rest he could under the circumstances. The white tent Cleve had brought was flapping wildly, revealing several more huddled men crowded into it.

Wynne felt a flash of sincere compassion for them all. In the two minutes she'd been outside, her feet and lower legs had already become soaked. It wouldn't take long for even her heavy mantle to be wet through and through. She hurried toward the camp, holding her hood in place with one hand and the front of her mantle snug with the other.

"Druce. Druce!" she called though the rain pounded in her face.

"I'm here, Wynne," he answered from the edges of Cleve's tent.

She gave him a disapproving look. Better that he be huddled in the storm than to be housed in an English shelter. But then, he seemed to be more in agreement with Cleve FitzWarin these days than with her.

"Come inside the manor," she shouted, though without the least amount of graciousness in her tone. "You needn't sleep in this storm."

Another man moved to Druce's side, and when lightning flashed again, she knew it was Cleve. Though she had only that instant of recognition, she read a wealth of emotions in his piercing stare.

"Thank you," his voice came to her from the returning darkness.

She would have loved to have excluded him then and there, to tell him that only Welshmen were welcome in Radnor Manor. But she knew she could not. Besides, it was such a childish and emotional reaction. She'd displayed too much childish emotion to him already. It behooved her to play the role of Seeress with more dignity than she had so far.

How that would aid her cause, however, was very difficult to comprehend.

In an instant the men—English and Welsh alike—were scurrying en masse toward the manor. Wynne stood a moment more in the abandoned camp, clutching her mantle to her and wondering what the morrow would bring. Then a firm hand grasped her arm, and she found herself face-to-face with Cleve.

"Come with me to the stable," he said. "I want to check the horses, and we can speak privately there."

"No." Wynne hung back, but it did not affect him at all. Through the muddy yard he propelled her, and at once any thoughts of dignified behavior flew right out of her head.

"Let me go, you vile wretch! I do not wish to speak privately with you!"

"That I can believe. But don't worry, at least I do not plan to poison you."

That caused her to dig her heels in even harder. In her struggle her mantle gaped open, flapping around her like the wings of a startled bird. But he was too strong and too determined. As if oblivious to her opposition, he dragged her relentlessly on through the downpour, her mantle trailing behind her.

At the stable door she caught the edge of the opening with one hand. "I shall scream," she threatened in a furious voice. "I'll scream, and Druce will be here in an instant. Do you really want to provoke the fight that shall surely ensue?"

She'd thought to best him with that. She'd thought it the one threat that would stall him. But Cleve only let loose a harsh, merciless bark of laughter, chilling her with his complete lack of concern.

"No one shall hear you over this storm, Wynne, so scream as loudly as you wish. Besides, I told Druce I required a word with you. Alone. He'll not trouble us for a while." Then he gave one last tug, and to her horror she found herself trapped in the stable with him.

"Now, shall we make ourselves comfortable?" So saying he began boldly to unfasten the ties that held her mantle on.

"Stop that! Don't you dare—" She batted at his hands to no avail. The mantle was already drenched and heavy from the rain. Once loosened, it fell from her shoulders to land in a sodden heap behind her.

"You wretched man! You horrid *cnaf!*" she cried. " 'Tis not your place to order me about. No, nor to handle me in so vile a manner." Her hands curled into fists, though he held her wrists firmly in his grasp. "Were I a man, I would challenge you to battle, and I would cut out your villainous heart—if indeed you do possess one!"

"Ah, but you are not a man, are you, my Wynne?" For emphasis he surveyed her slowly and thoroughly, from the top of her rain-soaked brow to the muddy tips of her now-bare feet.

With just those few words and that piercing look, she

was undone. She realized just how she must appear to him, with her hair loose and wild, her clogs lost in their muddy struggle, and her plain linen kirtle thoroughly soaked. She was an absolute mess, and yet she was most convincingly displayed through the wet linen as a woman fully formed. That was the one thing he seemed to notice most. Her breath caught in her throat, and she swallowed convulsively.

"This is not proper," she managed to whisper, straining away from him. But his hold was unyielding.

"No, 'tis far from proper," he conceded. "But I fear it is nonetheless inevitable." He pulled her nearer, then reached out one hand to touch her face. His palm slid down the length of her wet and tangled hair, down past her neck and shoulder, along the length of her arm to rest finally at her waist. "The things I wish to do with you are far from proper."

He frowned then and exhaled a long breath. Wynne had gone from cold with the rain and her icy rage to an uncommon warmth. Though she understood the actual workings of a man and woman's joining, she had never understood the desire that was spoken of by other women in such hushed and giggling tones. What she remembered were her sister's cries of fear and pain. Beyond that she'd never comprehended.

But this man made her understand.

No, not "understand." She would never understand why he made her feel this way. She knew only that he did. Without thinking she stepped nearer, into the circle of his arms. He was so warm, even more so than she. She turned her face up to his, wanting the kiss that she knew was coming. Wanting it though every logic told her it was all wrong.

But Cleve did not kiss her. He only pulled her near,

tucking her head under his chin. For a moment they clung together, while the storm beat tirelessly against the small thatch-roofed barn. The animals shifted now and again in the few crowded pens, but within the barn there was a certain peace and comfort. Nothing could touch them here, not the most violent storm flung at them. The sturdy walls held the world at bay, and Cleve's strong arms protected her from reality.

She burrowed nearer, not wanting to think at all, but only to be close to him.

"Ah, woman. How easy it would be to lose myself in you," he murmured low and very near her ear.

In response she turned her face up to his once more. But when she met his gaze, she knew he would not kiss her. Not this time. With a groan he banked the heated ardor that burned in his eyes. Then he stepped carefully back, only holding her at arm's length.

"As much as I would like to lay you down here and now and bury myself in your sweetness, I gave my word to Druce."

At her shocked, and then humiliated, expression he grimaced ruefully. "First we talk, Wynne. We talk and settle this business once and for all. After that . . . well, after that we shall just see."

12

"Sit over there."

Wynne obeyed Cleve's command only because she did not know what else to do. She had careened from one difficulty to another the whole day long. From one uncontrollable emotion to the next. Now it was the dead of night, she was trapped in the stable during a nasty storm, facing a man whom she desired in the most frightening manner, but who perversely seemed to wish only to talk.

She heard the sharp click of flint to steel as he worked to light the horn lantern that hung from a peg near the door. When the light finally caught, the low-ceilinged interior of the barn filled with a thin, yellow light.

Wynne slumped dejectedly and stared down at the wet linen that so clearly outlined the curves of her thighs. No village whore had ever looked so shamelessly wanton as she did at that moment. Any proper woman would be relieved beyond the measuring that a man would not take immediate advantage of her vulnerable situation—especially given how obviously willing she had been. Yet she . . . she could not deny that she was crushed with disappointment.

Ah, sweet Mother, what in the world was wrong with her? While her head rejoiced that Cleve had thrust her away, her body fairly hummed with desire for him. Like a desperate hunger it was, and she was no longer able to ignore it.

She looked up at Cleve and noted the strained expression on his face. He, too, was wet, and his chainse clung to his wide shoulders and finely muscled torso. He'd pushed his long hair back from his brow and wiped the rain from his face. But his eyes burned into hers, and she knew that his distraction was not caused by the rain. It was her, and she took what meager satisfaction she could from the knowledge.

He paced the narrow width of the stable's central aisle, then turned back the other way. With a frustrated oath he finally stopped and faced her.

"The thing is, Wynne, no matter your objections, Sir William has the right to know his son—his child," he amended. "The law supports this—"

"Whose law?" she demanded, shedding her tumultuous emotions for the far safer feelings of anger. "England's or Wales'?"

"Both, dammit. And beyond the laws of men, there is the law of God. Or do you presume to deny that law as well?"

"Where does God proclaim that a rapist has the rights to his child? Where?"

"Bedamned, Wynne. You but make this harder than it already is," he muttered, raking both hands through his wet hair. Then he fixed her with a penetrating stare. "What is the Fourth Commandment? Honor thy father and mother. But you would deny this child the chance to honor his father."

"And you deliberately choose to interpret the Commandments in their most narrow sense," she countered. "I raised these children to respect and honor those who care for them. That is all that God asks."

He straightened with a scowl. "That is not the point. These children deserve to know whatever parents they have, especially if that parent is willing. And Lord Somerville is willing."

Wynne sighed, and for a moment she closed her eyes against the pain that gripped her so intensely. "He may be willing, but I am not," she finally answered in the merest of whispers.

There was a silence between them, when only the howl of the wind could be heard and the distant roll of thunder. She watched him uneasily, waiting for an angry response from him. To her surprise, however, he took a three-legged milking stool from its perch astride a half-wall and set it on the hard-packed dirt floor directly in front of her. She leaned back in alarm when he seated himself on it, then took her two hands between his own.

"Listen to me, Wynne. Just listen. This has gone beyond your ability to control. This child *will* go back with me. Gwynedd knows it must be this way, and so does Druce. And now, by your own recklessness, you have made the children wonder at your reasoning. Tell me, how did your talk with them go?"

Wynne swallowed hard and looked somewhere past his left shoulder. She could not avoid this awful conversation, but she didn't have to look into his far-too-perceptive eyes.

"I talked to them."

"Did you explain their parentage to them?"

She nodded.

One of his hands rubbed hers. "So they know why I am come to Radnor Forest?"

She shifted her gaze back to his, not trying at all to hide the pain he was causing her, nor the anger either. "They know you've come to steal one of them from the only home they've ever known."

He exhaled noisily, but when she tried to withdraw her hands from his warm grasp, he only held her tighter. "So which one is Sir William's child?"

This time she did jerk her hands free. "I don't know!"

"Wynne, this is pointless. Tell me the truth."

"That *is* the truth, *cnaf! Lleidr!*" she added for good measure.

"Knave, perhaps. But thief?" He eyed her grimly. "No, I am no thief, Wynne, and even you, in your heart, must eventually concede that point."

Unable to bear the thought that he could be right, she leaped to her feet. But he caught both of her arms and with a rough jerk forced her to sit again. His brow lowered, and he gave her a thunderous look.

"You cannot run away from this, Wynne. If I have to drag every fact from you, so be it. But you will avoid me no longer!"

Though she struggled to remain calm in the face of his fury, Wynne feared he could see through her. She had pushed him into a corner, and now he was pushing back.

"Now." He released her, but continued to lean toward her, one hand propped on each of his knees. "Isolde is your niece; you've told me that. And her father—" He broke off, suddenly disconcerted.

"Her father is unknown," Wynne finished for him in a strained tone. "He could be any one of many English soldiers who . . . who raped my sister."

He cleared his throat. "Lord Somerville speaks of a woman who he kept as his . . . his companion during the three months he was in this area. She was dark-haired—"

"So are most *Cymry* in these southern mountains."

"Yes, but he said she was called Angel."

"That's hardly a Welsh name."

"I think he may have called her that as an endearment."

She gave him a scathing look. "How uniquely English —to give endearing names to your victims."

"Bedamned, Wynne. You're only making this harder for us both." He glowered at her. "Now, you said Bronwen's mother was very young."

"Twelve," she spat. "Twelve when she had her babe. But only eleven when she was raped!"

He gritted his teeth. "That rules out Bronwen, then, for Sir William said Angel was a young woman, but she was not a child."

Wynne lifted her chin contemptuously, though inside her dread only increased. "How convenient for you. You came in search of a boy, and now both girls are ruled out. I fear, however, that you can narrow your choice no farther. The boys' mothers are both dead. They were not from villages but from individual households deep within the forests and hills. And I'm certain none of them was ever called Angel."

He studied her a minute, and she felt a renewed shiver of fear. "What were their names?"

"I don't know."

"You lie."

"I do not! I was but a child myself at the time. Ask Gwynedd. Oh, but you've already done that to no avail, I'd wager." She smiled bitterly. "So you see. No one knows their names. The trail runs cold, Sir Cleve. Your fine English lord can never know which of these boys is his true heir—if indeed any of them is."

For a brief moment she savored her victory, for his frown conveyed most clearly his frustration. But then his eyes narrowed, and his expression grew determined.

"Perhaps Sir William could determine his heir were he to meet the boys. Some feature, perhaps, that can identify whom he sired."

"He will not be welcome here. Don't you even think to bring him to Radnor, for I'll—"

"Your threats are futile, Wynne, so do not waste your breath. Besides, I did not think to bring him here."

"Then how—" She broke off as the awful truth of his intentions struck her. "You cannot mean to— No, not even *you* would be so cruel as to attempt to take them *all.*"

But that was what he intended. She knew it from the way he sat back and averted his eyes from hers. He knew it was wrong and even felt a certain amount of shame for it. But what was a small portion of shame when weighed against the reward that awaited him in England? Wynne had to catch her breath at the pain that welled up in her chest. How could he think to take all three of her boys from her? How could he? And yet the ache was caused almost as much by her profound disappointment in him as it was by her fear for her children. Despite the depths of their conflict, Wynne had still—foolishly, she now knew —attributed some sense of honor to him. Some shreds of nobility and decency. But now . . .

She shook her head in disbelief, staring at his shadowed face. He was lit on the one side by the lantern, while the other half of his face was cast in darkness. Like good and evil. Like beauty and the ugliness it often hid. He was as fair and handsome a man as she'd ever laid eyes upon. But his soul . . . his soul was black as sin.

"I will never allow it," she warned in a voice that shook

with the strength of her feelings. "Never," she repeated, willing him to raise his coward's gaze to hers.

"Once the truth is revealed, the other children will be returned to Wales," he said when he met her menacing glare. But his words were not all that Wynne heard. His face was carefully blank, displaying neither triumph nor guilt. His every emotion appeared under tight control and hidden behind his shuttered eyes. Yet as clearly as if he stated them, Wynne suddenly sensed his thoughts.

She should have rejoiced, for her Radnor vision had been none too active these past days since he'd arrived. Only once since she'd foretold his presence in her forest had she felt even a glimmer of the unnamed sense that usually helped her, and that was when she'd realized he planned to wed one of his Sir William's daughters. Now, however, she sensed that he not only planned to take her three boys with him to England, he also planned to take her.

She drew back in alarm, filled suddenly with an overwhelming fear. England—source of all her pain. The place she'd hated forever. The very thought of venturing there caused her to cringe inside.

"I will not go," she swore earnestly, though the words came out faint and breathless. "No, I will not, and nothing you can do or say could ever force me to."

One of his brows cocked higher, and he stared at her in surprise. "How did you know—" Then his jaw tightened. "It doesn't matter. Nor does it matter that you object. The boys will go with me. Would you have them travel alone? Would you choose not to be there to meet their father, to see the home that awaits them?" He leaned nearer. "To be certain that the right child becomes heir to all those lands?"

Torn by both her concerns for the children and her own

crushing fears, Wynne scrambled back, tangling her legs in her wet gown and falling into a pile of straw in her haste to put a safe distance between them. But what was a safe distance? Though his eyes were lost in the deep shadows of his face, his thoughts seemed still to reach out to torture her.

Come with me, Wynne, the silent message came to her. *I will have you one way or the other. We both know it's inevitable.*

"No, no," she muttered, still stumbling back into the darkened reaches of the barn.

But like the devil himself, he was fast upon her, reaching out to catch her close to him, holding her effortlessly though she fought him with both arms and legs, flailing, using every bit of her strength. Only when she was exhausted by her efforts and her hands were firmly trapped between his chest and hers, did he catch the long length of her wet hair in one of his fists and force her face up to his.

"Damn you, woman. If you would but listen to me!"

"Why!" She practically sobbed the word. "So you may twist the truth to suit what you want to believe? So you may assuage your guilty conscience?"

She felt his labored breathing and was acutely aware of the rapid rise and fall of her own breath and how their chests pressed ever closer together, the ancient crystal resting between them.

For a moment she did not need the Radnor vision to know what thoughts ran through his mind. Her body sensed them on its own, and with a perverseness she could not fathom, it strained toward him in answer.

At once he let loose a vicious oath. Then he thrust her an arm's length away. "You *will* go, Wynne. If only to see that it is best for Sir William's child. You will do it to make sure that either Arthur or Madoc and Rhys adjust easily to their new home. You will do it because it is best for your children."

With that last he thrust her even farther away and clenched his hands into fists at his side. "Now, begone from here, else I will not be accountable for my actions. Not to Druce nor to you."

Wynne did not wait to be told a second time. Unmindful of the storm and not caring that her mantle lay forgotten somewhere on the stable floor, she whirled and dashed for the door. Into the downpour she fled, though the rain blinded her with its fury and the winds tore at her drenched gown. She ran for the only shelter she knew, the only comfort she'd had in the past seven years.

Aunt Gwynedd was her only hope. She bolstered herself as her bare feet fought for purchase on the muddy ground and slippery rocks. Aunt Gwynedd must help her in this. She must.

Wynne stood as rigid as stone, staring toward Black Mountain, seeing its uneven twin peaks in her mind's eye though low clouds yet obscured them. The muddy yard before the manor house seethed with activity. Horses were packed with provisions. Soldiers checked the saddles and straps on their mounts. The children shouted and ran, interfering with everyone in their excited attempts to be of help.

Cook was weeping, dabbing her face with her apron even as she pressed another wheel of hard goat's cheese into Druce's hands. But she was the only one, Wynne bitterly acknowledged.

Though Wynne kept her back to the frenetic activity in the yard, she did not have to see what was going on to know. Gwynedd no doubt was seated in her favorite chair, enjoying the meager traces of watery sunlight that occasionally broke through the early-morning clouds. She had called each of the children to her one by one and spoken quietly to them. Druce also and his brother, Barris, had received their instructions from Gwynedd.

Now she awaited Wynne, but Wynne did not think she could force herself to an amiable farewell. How could Gwynedd expect it?

Yet Wynne could not even muster anger anymore, not at her aunt, nor at Druce, though they well enough deserved it. She was too drained, both emotionally and physically, to do more than stand apart from them, wrapped in her loneliness and misery.

She'd been abandoned by those she'd always thought she could rely upon. Both Gwynedd and Druce had sided with that black-hearted Englishman. Through the dark hours of the storm she'd argued with first her aunt and then her onetime friend. She'd sworn and shouted. She'd bullied and threatened, and then when that had not worked, she'd pleaded and cried.

Yet throughout her emotional scene the two of them had remained firm—although Druce had more than once appeared hesitant. It had been Gwynedd who'd kept them fast to their position. This Somerville was willing to pass his considerable holdings to his son, though the child was but a half-Welsh bastard. What an opportunity for the child, Druce had argued time and time again. What a benefit to Wales, Gwynedd had pointed out repeatedly.

Though Wynne had refused to agree, she'd nonetheless been overruled. What was one woman to do when faced with the combined might of both her enemies as well as her own people?

She swallowed hard, stringently willing any hint of tears away as she grasped the Radnor amulet. She'd cried the very last of her tears, she told herself. From his place in the main hall Cleve FitzWarin had no doubt heard every angry word she'd said in her aunt's chamber, as well as every tearful plea she'd made. But he'd not heard her tears this last night past. Those she'd shed in silence, muffled in her bed linens, until she was completely drained.

Yesterday she'd seen little enough of FitzWarin, for she'd kept to the forests, hiding her pain and seeking solace in all her familiar haunts. But it had been for naught. Now the day of departure had arrived and she was no better prepared to go than she had been before.

"Wynne?"

At the tentative sound of Isolde's voice, Wynne looked down to her left. She tried without success to smile and settled instead for taking her niece's hand and squeezing it.

"I . . . I think Aunt Gwynedd is waiting for you."

Wynne took a shaky breath, then nodded. "Yes. I know." Then, determined to appear as undeterred as ever, Wynne proudly lifted her chin and turned toward her elderly aunt.

The dozen or so horses were ready, she saw. The children were gathered together. English soldiers and Welsh alike stood waiting to mount. Waiting for Cleve to give the order, she thought. And he was waiting for her to take her leave of Gwynedd.

For a moment she wondered how long he would wait. What if she refused to go to her aunt? What if she refused to mount her horse? But that was only a foolish hope. There was no putting off this moment any longer. With all the arrogance and pride she could summon, she gathered her plain caddis traveling skirts in one hand and stepped carefully across the muddy yard.

"Good-bye, Aunt. I wish you good health in my absence."

When there was no response, Wynne's resolve faltered a bit. From its determined focus somewhere beyond her aunt's shoulder, Wynne's gaze slid to meet Gwynedd's sightless gaze. Only then did the old woman speak.

"We shall be well enough. But it is your return we shall await every long day of your journey."

"Even though I return less one or perhaps two of my sons?"

Gwynedd did not react to the condemnation in her niece's low tone.

"It could be that you will return with even more than you departed with," the old woman said enigmatically.

Wynne started to make a sarcastic reply, but then halted with her mouth still open. She bent nearer her graying aunt. "Have you had a vision?" she asked, all trace of hostility vanished.

Gwynedd's face settled into the familiar serenity Wynne had known and trusted every day of her childhood. "I am an old woman, *nith*. Both my eyesight and my visions have all but abandoned me in recent years. But some things are seen more clearly with the heart than with the head. This journey you begin in such pain shall end in joy. I feel it here," she finished, pressing one gnarled fist to her bony chest.

Wynne's eyes widened, and a tiny spark of hope came to life inside her own heart. She knelt beside her aunt, unmindful of the mud upon her skirts, and grabbed one of Gwynedd's hands. "Does this mean that perhaps . . . perhaps *none* of our boys was sired of this English lord? Perhaps once he sees them, he'll know—"

She broke off when the old woman began sadly to shake her head. "Oh, child. 'Tis you who are more blind than I, for you see only the solution you wish for. Haven't I taught you that the Mother—and the Father as well—see far better than do we? Can you not trust them to guide you?"

Wynne sat back on her heels. As quickly as she'd found hope, so now did it abandon her. "Trust them?" she scoffed. "They have sent the English here twice. Once they deprived me of my parents—and also my only sister. Now they seek to deprive me of my children. Trust them?" She shook her head. "No, I'll not trust them again."

The old woman sighed. "The gods did send you these children to replace the family you lost," she reminded Wynne in a voice that revealed some of her frustration. "If you would be Seeress here, you must feel beyond your emotions. You must learn to see with more than your eyes."

But Wynne was in no mood to listen. She rose abruptly and stepped back from her aunt. "Farewell, then. It appears everyone is eager to depart. Save, of course, me."

For a moment their eyes met and held, the one pair clouded with age, yet seemingly clear of purpose, the other young and bright, yet filled with uncertainty and fear. And pain.

"Come kiss me, then," the old woman said, holding one arm out.

Wynne bent forward stiffly and brushed her aunt's lined cheek with her lips. Despite her anger with her aunt's obstinacy, however, she felt a sudden surge of love for her.

Gwynedd, too, must have felt it, for she smiled as Wynne straightened. "Trust in the future, my child. Trust in the Mother, and the Father also. The fates, if you like."

But though Wynne tried to take comfort from her aunt's words, it was impossible. She crossed the yard to mount the gentle mare that Druce held for her, avoiding both his gaze and that of FitzWarin. She looked instead at the children, who for once were quiet, and smiled as reassuringly as was possible at them.

Then everyone mounted. Isolde and Bronwen rode before Druce and Barris. Rhys and Madoc sat before two of the Englishmen. She'd meant for Arthur to ride with her, but he'd insisted on riding with Cleve. Before she could object, Druce had interceded, reminding her that she'd not spent much time on horses and that maybe it was better this way, at least until she became a more confident rider.

A lump formed in her throat; never had she felt so alone. As they filed from the manor yard, she heard the fond calls from those left behind—and the loud wailing of Cook. But Wynne stared straight ahead, blinking hard and fighting back tears.

Trust in the fates. The sad fact was that there was only one person she could trust, and that was herself. If she was to save her children from the clutches of this heartless English lord, she must trust only herself.

And what of saving herself from the clutches of Cleve FitzWarin?

The oddest sensation shivered up her spine, but she staunchly beat it down. One of her hands slid to the heavy purse that hung from her waist. She carried a few of her precious store of coins in it. But more important, she had a veritable stillroom packed within its leather folds. Just let him try to confuse her with his devastating touch and mind-stealing kisses. She would be ready for him this time, for she'd selected carefully. The strongest powders. The most potent roots and oils. She could carry only the smallest portions, and she had to be alert for any opportunity. So she'd selected the most powerful and effective preparations from her vast stores. And there was also the forest to add to her choices.

She lifted her chin and narrowed her gaze on the back of Cleve's head. In the strengthening sunlight his dark hair glinted, and she was unexpectedly reminded of the way those long strands had felt between her fingers.

Oh, but she was perverse!

She jerked her eyes away from the accursed Englishman and instead focused on Black Mountain off to her left. They had four or five days' journey ahead, Druce had told her. Four or five days to plot against this Sir William.

But it was not just the English she fought any longer, she reminded herself. Druce and Gwynedd would not let this matter drop. Her task now must be to convince the English lord that none of her boys was his.

And if that did not work?

If that did not work, then the dangerous medicines she carried in her purse would not help her in the least—save for revenge.

If that was all she could have from them, however, then that's what she would take.

13

Cleve felt Arthur's head slump back against his chest. For the past hour the boy had been fighting sleep. Each time it had overtaken him, he'd struggled back, asking an endless stream of questions about the towering trees they passed beneath, the birds and creatures they flushed from their activities, and most of all about the place they journeyed to.

But this time Arthur remained quiet, and Cleve smiled when he glanced down at the child. Fast asleep he was, with his little face peaceful and his limbs gone slack.

He was a most astounding lad, Cleve thought once again. Far too intelligent for his few years. It was clear Wynne was responsible for encouraging the boy's curiosity and strange imaginings. Then, as he too often did, Cleve found himself wondering about the thorny woman he was bringing to England with him.

The situation could not have turned out any better—or any worse, he admitted with a frustrated sigh. She was coming to England with him, something that pleased him in the most inexplicable and perverse way.

He resisted the urge to turn around to see her. No, it

was not inexplicable. It was very clear and very basic. He desired her. He wanted her with an intensity that was overpowering—and exceedingly stupid. What of Lord Somerville's youngest daughter, the one he would wed once his task was completed? How did Wynne fit into that situation?

Gripped with a sudden frustration, he pulled his mount to a quick halt. When Wynne's mare drew alongside him, he sent her an angry look.

"Take Arthur," he muttered. For a moment he met her wary gaze, and he became conscious of her lack of color and the shadows beneath her eyes. He was hurting her by what he was putting her through. That was obvious enough. And yet what else could he do?

Muffling an oath, he placed Arthur before her, then abruptly jerked Ceta about. But though he sent the eager destrier bounding forward and was soon beyond view of the slower-traveling group, he was unable to outrun the guilt feelings that assailed him.

He wanted her and he would do whatever was necessary to have her. Earlier this morning Druce had made him vow not to force Wynne in any way, but Cleve knew how easy it would be to seduce her. She could be made willing; that had been clear on at least two occasions already.

"Bedamned!" he swore as he brought Ceta to a stiff-legged halt. If he did not curb his randy thoughts soon, this ride to Kirkston Castle would be the worse sort of torture for him.

But every time he thought of her—so eager and soft in his arms, so warm and responsive to his kisses—his loins fairly ached. Then his mind would begin to imagine them finishing what they'd begun, and he could hardly bear it.

With another vicious oath he slid off Ceta, then just leaned heavily against the beast, willing his raging passions away. By Saint Osyth's soul, they were but two leagues gone on this journey. How was he to survive?

Wynne's fury knew no bounds when Cleve deposited the sleeping Arthur on her lap, then rode so abruptly away. What right had he to treat her in so rude a manner? But then, why should she expect any better of him? He needed no reason to be cruel. It was a part of his nature.

Yet even as she settled Arthur more comfortably between her arms, she was unable to cling to her righteous anger. Some other aberrant emotion seemed to worm its way into her heart, and she only ended up feeling even more alone than before. She hugged Arthur tighter than ever, praying she would not lose him to this English lord, then glanced back at the twins and prayed just as fervently that she would not lose them either.

Men and their sons. Why could they not be as pleased with their daughters? Why couldn't they be as content to pass their properties through their girl children?

But they weren't, not Englishmen, nor Welsh. Nor any other country she'd heard of either. Men invariably chose to pass their hard-won lands to their sons. It was as simple as that. Would her boys be as rigid when they reached manhood?

She glanced over at the two girls who rode with Druce and Barris. They were both every bit as smart as the boys, though they were as different as night and day. What would become of them in the years ahead?

Indeed, what would become of all five of them? What would they do; where would they live? For an uncomfortable moment she wondered if perhaps she was being selfish. What endless possibilities might this Lord Somerville's wealth provide for one of her young charges? But just as quickly as it surfaced, so did she bury that weak thought. Her children did not need English wealth to be happy. Radnor Forest and the vast lands at their disposal would provide for them, as it had for so many others.

Besides, the children clearly were not concerned with the future just now, for all of them were nodding and very near falling asleep.

Arthur shifted, and Wynne felt a twinge in her left arm. She could not carry him this way for long. Her arms were not strong enough. A quick glance at the sky told her that it was near midday. Time enough to stop for a rest and something to eat. Without a word to anyone, she turned her mare off the ancient road and toward an inviting stand of young beeches.

"Wynne," Druce called in a loud whisper. "What are you doing?"

She glared over her shoulder at him. She did not plan to forgive him anytime soon. "I'm tired and hungry. So are the children. We're stopping here."

He hesitated for a moment and glanced at Barris for support. But his brother only shrugged and turned to follow Wynne. In short order the Englishmen also followed her lead.

She had them spread rugs for the children in a shady spot and urged her charges to continue their naps while she prepared them a meal. But once disturbed, the twins could not doze off again. Before very long all five of them were wide awake and curious about their new environs.

"Look at these rocks," Rhys said as he kicked at the edge of the road.

"They look like coins, so flat and round," Madoc said.

"Let's play market day," Bronwen suggested as she squatted down and began to place the newfound coins one by one onto her lap.

"I'll sell medicines and herbs," Isolde said. "And love potions and magic spells," she added with a grin.

While the others busied themselves with their new-found sport, however, Arthur only frowned and looked around their little campsite.

"Where's Cleve?" he asked, directing the question to no one in particular. When he received no reply, he tugged on Wynne's skirt.

"Where's Cleve?" he demanded suspiciously.

"He rode on ahead," Wynne answered in an even tone, though she, too, wondered where the man had gotten to.

"He hasn't left us, has he?"

Wynne turned at the panicked sound in Arthur's voice and at once put aside the knife and loaf of bread she held. She took the child's hands in hers and looked earnestly into his eyes. "He'll be back, sweetheart. Don't worry. He's probably just scouting ahead to make certain we don't go the wrong way."

Arthur sighed in relief. "Yes, that must be it. He'll be back soon."

He scampered off after that and joined the other children at their play. But his new contentment only increased Wynne's concern. It was plain that Arthur adored Cleve. What had begun as simple hero worship seemed to have grown now into a much stronger emotion. But instead of putting an end to it, her failed attempts to discourage Cleve in his cruel mission had somehow served only to strengthen the bond between him and Arthur.

She concentrated on preparing the simple meal, dividing bread and cheese into five child-sized portions, but all the time she worried. In the end Cleve and Arthur must part. Whether she kept all her boys with her or—God prevent it—any of them remained in England, Cleve would not stay a part of Arthur's life. Yet with every passing day the connection between them seemed to grow stronger.

By the time she had them settled at their meal, she knew that she must speak to Cleve about Arthur. Though she considered the arrogant Englishman the most hateful and selfish man alive, he *did* seem to care for the boy. Perhaps if she appealed to that side of his nature, he would recognize the harm he did by befriending Arthur.

Her chance did not come until evening. Though she caught a glimpse of Cleve several times during the long afternoon ride, he stayed a good distance ahead of them. Once Druce rode up to confer with him, but Druce was soon back with the rest of their party, a thoughtful expression on his face.

"Well, and what has that Englishman to say for himself?" Wynne had asked, unable to disguise either her irritation or her curiosity.

Druce had shrugged. "He's thinking, was all he said."

"Thinking? Hah. More than likely he's plotting some new and nefarious scheme to convince this Somerville that one of my boys is his son." She glared at the empty road ahead, trying to spy the object of her ire, but when she failed, she turned her anger toward Druce. "But I forget myself. You no longer care which of my boys goes to this English rapist, do you? So long as the lad becomes heir to the man's wretched lands. No doubt you'd call him father yourself if it would gain you a castle or two!"

Druce had not replied to that. He'd only slowed his horse and let her go ahead so that she rode alone. And so she'd ridden the whole day, her anger and fear festering inside her like a bitter and untended wound.

Now, as she turned her mare over to the English soldier called Derrick, she plotted her next move. Poisoning would not work, at least not at the moment, for though she might not balk at killing the Englishmen, she knew she could not endanger Druce or Barris that way. And as long as Druce and Gwynedd supported Cleve's quest, her children would not be made safe by such actions. No, the only way left to her was to make all of the Englishmen fear her and her powers and, in their fear, hesitate to take one of her children into their midst. It was a weak plan, she glumly realized, but it was all she had.

Meanwhile, however, she and Cleve must discuss Arthur's inappropriate affection for him.

Cleve was standing with his back to her, deftly removing the saddle and sidepacks from his tall gray destrier. She knew, however, that he sensed her, for his broad shoulders tensed when she drew to a halt but three paces from him.

"I would have a word with you."

He did not respond to her demand at once, but only slid the sidepacks to the ground, then squatted on one knee to unfasten the girth strap.

"I would have a word with you." *Uffernol cnaf,* she silently added.

He pulled the saddle free, then turned slowly to face her. For a moment he didn't answer, but simply stared at her with the most intent expression on his face. His eyes slid down the entire length of her, from her sunburned cheeks and nose, down along her dusty traveling gown to where her muddy boots peeked from beneath her skirts.

For the merest fraction of a second she felt the oddest and most inappropriate emotion begin to unfurl within her. From belly to breasts to the very tips of her fingers and toes, the feeling raced, and she found herself wishing she did not always look so bedraggled in his presence.

But as quickly as those unreasonable emotions flared, so did she beat them down. He, too, seemed to reconsider the boldness of his gaze—no doubt because she looked so wretched—for he scowled and heaved his saddle to the ground between them.

"What now?" he barked as he once again turned his back to her and began to tend his horse.

Uffernol cnaf, she thought with even more vehemence than before. Hellish knave. She adopted her iciest tone. "There is a problem with Arthur."

He twisted his head to meet her glare. "What do you mean, a problem? Is he hurt? Or ill?"

Wynne felt an edge of her tension ease. At least in this she was correct. He did care for the boy. Now, if she could only convince him that the attachment between them could come to no good.

"No, he is not ailing. But I fear . . ." She clasped her hands nervously. How she hated making this appeal to him. "I fear he becomes too attached to you. And no matter the final outcome of this . . . this quest of yours, one thing is certain. You will not remain a part of Arthur's life. Whether he resides with me or with this . . . this Englishman who seeks a son of his own, *you* will not long be around."

He studied her for a moment, but his face revealed no hint of his thoughts.

"If Arthur is the one that stays in England, I will see him. I'll make it a point to check on him."

"You will be too busy with your own wife—and children," she threw back at him. "If you marry this Edeline, you'll probably reside in another place and will soon forget about Arthur. But what of him? He would be left all alone in a strange place, surrounded by strangers."

"He may not be Sir William's son. It might be the twins."

"Perhaps," Wynne conceded. "And perhaps *none* of them is his son. But even so, Arthur will be hurt the most.

For when we return to Wales, you will be out of his life. Forever. The fact is, this affection you show him now will only hurt him later. You think to comfort him, but when you are gone from his life, he will be left with a new and painful emptiness."

Cleve frowned. "What would you have me do, then? Cast him aside? He's but a lad and in urgent need of a father."

"But *you* can never be that father, so don't pretend to be," Wynne snapped in a rising tone. She glared at him, her hands clenched into fists. She was prepared to fight for Arthur—for all the children—in any way she had to. But Cleve's next words took all the wind from her sails.

"What if you stayed in England—with all of them?"

She blinked, not understanding in the least what he meant by such an outrageous suggestion. "Stay in England! Me?" Then she frowned. "You are truly addled, Englishman. Have you perchance eaten of the black mold? For your mind does twist in fanciful directions. Stay in England, hah! I'd rather reside in hell."

He stepped over the forgotten saddle. "England is not so unlike Wales, but you will see that soon enough."

Her gaze narrowed at the odd, almost coaxing tone in his voice. "I'll not stay. No, not even one minute beyond what I must. Once this matter is done with, we shall take our leave from there, even though the skies fall upon us and the winds threaten to blow us away. Nothing could keep me there."

She stared challengingly up at him. But in the short silence she grew uncomfortably aware of his nearness. She swallowed once and started to step back, but he caught her by the arm.

"You could stay with—" He broke off and cleared his throat. "I could find you a place to live. Someplace where you can see Sir William's son—or sons—as often as you like."

Wynne felt a sudden rush of blood through her. Whether it was caused by his touch, as had so often been the case, or by the very thought of leaving one of her children behind—or by the idea of staying in England and being near to Cleve—she could not be sure. All she knew was that all of her logical arguments seemed to fly right out of her head.

With a movement that was rooted more in self-defense than in any lingering anger, she jerked out of his grasp and stepped safely away. But there was no safety to be had merely in keeping her distance from him, for Cleve's gaze followed her, and she was unable to break the hold of his mesmerizing gaze.

"Give it some thought," he said in a voice low and far too soothing. Seductive. "Give it some time, Wynne. We'll cross the Dyke tomorrow and be in England. You'll see then that the forests are as thick and green as your own. The birds and beasts are familiar. The land but becomes a little gentler, and you'll see more roads and villages. Give it time—"

"No!" She shook her head adamantly. "A hundred years would not be enough time to sway me to your way of thinking."

"Listen to me, Wynne." He stepped forward as if he meant to take her in his arms and convince her in the same way he'd managed to convince her in the past. His kiss made his words seem not so misguided. His intimate caress dissolved all her protests every time. Yet knowing that, Wynne was nonetheless unable to prevent the erratic leap of her heart, nor a hot surge of the most unwarranted feelings from deep within her belly. But he stopped before he reached for her, and though the sudden arrival of Arthur made it clear why he'd halted, Wynne was consumed by the most acute sense of disappointment.

"Cleve! Where were you all day?" the child asked. He smiled up at the man in a way that clearly revealed the depths of his affection, and Wynne at once berated herself for becoming sidetracked from her original goal. She sent Cleve a speaking look, willing him to somehow rebuff Arthur. Gently, of course. Just firmly enough so that Arthur did not invest even more of his emotions in the wrong man.

But Cleve ignored her. He knew precisely what she wished him to do, but he very deliberately refused to comply. Wynne watched as he squatted down to face Arthur on the child's own level.

"Hello, my boy. How did you enjoy this long day in the saddle? Still convinced you wish to be a knight and spend your life astride?"

"I didn't get tired at all," Arthur boasted. "And my bottom doesn't hurt either."

Cleve grinned, glancing up at Wynne as he did so. "Just wait until tomorrow. Then we'll see if you sing the same song." He looked back at the boy. "Tell me, did you see any new types of birds?"

Wynne wanted to stalk away in anger—to hide her pain from Cleve's probing gaze. How could he be so cruel to Arthur? She understood that he might wish to punish *her*, but not Arthur. So why was he courting the child's affection in this way? It would only make their separation far worse for the child.

Then, however, she recalled his odd suggestion that she stay in England. Even though she'd turned him down, she'd been very close to succumbing to his sensual appeal. Oh, how very, very stupid she was, she realized as complete understanding came to her. He wanted her to stay in

England for his own personal reasons. For his own very intimate and physical reasons. That was what this was all about. He was going to make it as hard for her to leave him as possible, and he was not above using the children to help him do it.

Her mouth gaped open at the realization, then snapped shut when she recognized how easily—how willingly— she'd been playing into his hands. What an absolute fool she was. What a complete and utter goose.

It wasn't as if she'd not been approached by well-favored men in the past. She'd been pursued by two or three handsome and eligible lads from the village. But she'd been smart those times and she'd kept both her heart and her wits well in hand. Why couldn't she be as smart with this man?

". . . but if Offa's Dyke is so easy for us to cross, I don't understand. How does it keep the English on their side and the Welsh on theirs?" Arthur was asking when Wynne focused once more on their conversation.

"Well, it's not so hard for a few men on horseback to cross it. But an army, well, that would be more difficult. The carts, the wagons of supplies, and also the siege engines can't be brought across a steep-sided ditch nearly so easily."

"Oh." Arthur pondered that a moment. "A bridge would have to be built."

"That's right. Or else the Dyke dug down and used to fill in the ditch."

"But then *both* armies could go back and forth."

"Bright lad." Cleve grinned at Arthur and then again at Wynne. "You've got the makings of a true soldier here, Wynne. One who will think with his head before he strikes with his sword."

Wynne only frowned more fiercely at his words. If

Cleve meant to irritate her endlessly, he was succeeding very well, for Arthur was beaming under the attention and praise from his idol.

Yet anger was but one of the emotions roiling within her. More and more she was feeling trapped. Outfoxed. Defeated by this bold Englishman with his handsome face, seductive words, and breath-stealing kisses. Her defenses were becoming weaker, and her own plans to defeat him appeared nigh on to impossible. Only one hope remained for her, and that was to prevent him from proving that any of her boys were sired by this English lord of his.

No, that was not her only hope. She must also hope and pray—and struggle against any temptations to the contrary—that she could continue to resist his ever-bolder advances.

He did not mean to cooperate where Arthur was concerned. Indeed he clearly meant to use Arthur in this struggle between the two of them. Well, so be it, she sighed. She could accept any adversity so long as she still had hope. And she did still have hope. She did.

"Arthur may have all the makings of a soldier," she said, dismissing Cleve with a haughty lift of her head. "But for the moment he appears more suited to fetching water. Gather the other children, Arthur. I have chores for all of you."

Cleve ruffled the boy's brown hair and rose to his feet. "Aye, lad. Do as Wynne says. I, for one, am hungry enough to eat a bear. We must all help her prepare the meal."

Wynne waited until Arthur raced away before she fixed Cleve with a carefully aloof and appraising eye. "So you expect me to prepare your meal. I commend you for your bravery, Sir Cleve. Or do you intend to let Arthur test-taste your food before you partake of it?"

His dark eyes gleamed with devilment. "You will not try the same trick again, witch. Too many of us are watching you now."

"How smug you are." She laughed. "I need but a pinch of witch seed to lay you low. No more than I could easily hide beneath my thumbnail. Are you so certain you wish to take that chance?"

She noted with pleasure that his smile wavered just a bit, and a shadow of uncertainty showed in his eyes. "You are more talk than anything else, woman. We shall all of us eat from the same pot. You cannot take the same chances here that you did at Radnor Manor."

He might as well have thrown one of his steel-and-leather gauntlets at her feet, so blatant was the challenge he put before her. Her eyes narrowed and glinted with a fiery blue light of their own. "I shall enjoy bringing you low more than anything I have ever done in my years as Seeress."

He grinned as if her threat did not faze him in the least. "Lay me low? I would like nothing better, my sweet Welsh witch. Perhaps tonight?" he finished with a hopeful tone in his voice and a hot gleam in his eyes.

Wynne, however, was not amused. Ignoring the disturbing warmth in her belly, she glowered at him.

"Gloat now, Sir Fool. But we shall see who gloats in the end."

"Yes," he replied to her stiff, retreating back. "We shall soon see."

14

They camped the second evening just beyond Offa's Dyke, on English soil. Cleve and his men were relaxed and boisterous that night, lighting a huge fire to celebrate their homecoming, though they were still three days' journey from Kirkston Castle. Even Druce and Barris joined in the high spirits, and the children were hard-pressed to stay in their beds, given the gay songs and rowdy laughter coming from the fire.

"England is a very merry place," Arthur said from his end of the tent they all occupied.

"Everyone does seem very happy," Isolde agreed.

From her position, seated on a rug just inside the tent opening with her arms wrapped around her knees, Wynne could see the dark silhouettes around the dancing flames. "I suppose anyone—even an Englishman—is happiest on his own homelands. Though were they to live any length of time in Wales, they would fast change their opinion," she added.

"Are we supposed to be sadder because we've left Wales?" Bronwen asked.

Wynne smiled ruefully and reached through the darkness to where she knew the little girl lay. She rubbed Bronwen's knee. "No, I don't think we have to be sadder, sweetheart. We can miss our own home and yet still enjoy our journey. 'Tis quite an adventure for us, and we should endeavor to learn as much as we can from our time in England. Such as improving your skills in the language."

"We learned a—"

"—new word today," the twins said.

"I heard you speaking with Derrick," Wynne said.

"Ned taught me the word *whore*," Madoc boasted.

"What! He taught you a word like that?"

"Well . . . I mean, sort of. He . . . he said it to Marcus, and I asked him what it meant."

"And what did he say?" Wynne demanded.

"Well, he . . . he said it was a woman who kisses lots of different men. Lots and lots of them."

Wynne felt a small relief at that, but her anger did not abate at all. A group of hardened soldiers was poor company for such young and impressionable children as these. Not for the first time she wondered why she'd relented to the girls' pleas that they be allowed to come along. Bad enough that the boys *had* to come. She should have left Isolde and Bronwen with Gwynedd.

But it was too late now for second thoughts. She must make the best of things, and her first order of business tomorrow would be to speak to Cleve about his men's foul language before her children. Hopefully he would respond better to that than he had to their aborted discussion about Arthur's affection for him.

The very thought of that conversation—especially the note on which it had ended—caused her stomach to knot. He was so insufferably confident! It would be best if she had Druce there to back her up. Cleve would not dare be so bold with Druce there.

Yet Druce's involvement in this whole business was not entirely without suspicion. She recalled something Cleve had said to her that night in the stable when the storm had struck. He'd promised Druce that he would not take advantage of her. Druce! As if he were her father or brother. But it was not Druce's protection that bothered her, for to be honest, she appreciated that. But there was something else implied, something that disturbed her enormously.

Was Druce aware of Cleve's personal interest in her? And if so, did he actually approve?

Wynne straightened up and squinted toward the fire. She heard Madoc whisper something to his brother, but he received no reply. The children were finally dozing off, it seemed, but Wynne was wide awake, and her mind turned round and round this absurd new possibility.

It was one thing for Druce to act the part of her brother when it came to protecting her and her children. Both their lifelong friendship and the fact of their common Welsh heritage demanded no less of him. But to seem to give approval to some Englishman who courted her—if what Cleve pursued could very loosely be termed courting —was going much too far. The very idea made her blood boil.

First thing tomorrow she would set Druce straight. Then once he was sufficiently reprimanded, the two of them would approach Cleve FitzWarin.

A bark of laughter drifted to the tent, and she glared at the men who made merry. Someone stood up across the fire, and she recognized Cleve. His wide shoulders and long dark hair set him apart from the rest. He lifted a mug and said something she could not make out. The others laughed and lifted their mugs in reply. Then they all drank.

Cnaf, she brooded. Knaves, the entire lot of them. She

turned away, pulling the flap of canvas down to close them off. But even as she lay on her mossy pallet and pulled her cloak over her shoulders, she was keenly attuned to every sound the men made. Every muffled word, every laugh or toast, only blackened them further in her eyes. Were it not for their necessary part in maintaining the human race, she decided, the world would be better off without any men in it whatsoever. There would be no wars. There would be no need for weapons or armor or even destriers. Nor castles, moats, or dykes. The world would be a peaceful and pastoral place, with no voices raised in anger, nor fists either.

But even as she counted the sins attributable to the male of the species—of *all* the species, rams and stallions and bulls included—she could not shake one immutable fact: Life would certainly be dull without them.

"Wynne . . . Wynne." It was Druce's impatient voice that roused her from discordant dreams of towering castle walls overrun with wild mistletoe vines. Only the mistletoe sprouted roses every now and again, and it grew so fast that she became caught up in the vines, trapped within the dark walls of the massive castle. When Druce's voice broke through to her, she clung to it as if it were a lifeline.

"What . . . what is it, Druce?" she mumbled as she sat up and pushed her hair from her eyes. Then, when she recognized the urgency in his tone, she blinked the sleep away. "Is aught amiss with you?"

"Not me. No. But one of the Englishmen is ill, and two others of them. . . ."

She poked her head out of the tent. "Ill? In what way?"

He shrugged. "He has puked his guts out the whole night long. And two of the others are beginning to feel the same way."

"They probably just drank too much." She thrust the wild tangle of her dark hair from where it fell once more over her eyes. "And it serves them right. I heard the lot of you, carousing long after more sensible persons would have sought out their beds."

But Druce shook his head. "No, 'tis not the pounding head of too much drink. I'm feeling that right enough myself. But Marcus, he has a fever. And now Richard and Henry do as well. He's sick, Wynne. All three of them are. Can you help them?"

Wynne stared past him toward the figures huddled around the remnants of the fire. In the pale gray light of early dawn the men appeared almost ghostly. Mist hugged the ground so that the man who lay curled on a crude pallet was barely discernible. The agitated cry of an oriole echoed from somewhere beyond, and a squirrel chattered, then skittered up the trunk of a towering beech, its tiny claws making a scratchy sound against the bark.

Morning was here, though the children yet slept. But what an interesting morning it would prove to be, the wry thought came to her. She'd not yet had the chance to use any of her potions on her enemies, yet here they were, falling ill but a stone's throw from the Welsh border. She almost laughed. How fitting.

She crawled from the tent, then shook off the last vestiges of sleep and rose to her feet. The ground was cold and damp, but she ignored that.

"So, three of them are struck low. But then, what could be expected when they seek to steal a child of *Cymru* from his home?"

Druce peered at her suspiciously. "Wynne, have you done something to cause this illness?"

"Of course not," she answered, though she smiled smugly. Let him wonder. Let them all wonder.

"Bedamned, Wynne. But this is foolish beyond anything you've ever done before."

"I tell you, I did not cause this illness they suffer. Have I had access to their mugs or trenchers? All my cooking has been in one pot. Everyone partook of the same meals. Although I may wish to strike them down, I would not risk you and Barris, or the children." She paused and sent him a deliberately disdainful look. "Well, I would not risk the children."

With a ragged sigh Druce ran a hand through his rumpled hair. "Do not jest in this. The Englishmen are angry enough already. They do suspect you," he added in a whisper.

Wynne lifted her head and stared at the English encampment. Her eyes glittered with undisguised glee. "I do not care *what* they suspect. I did nothing to cause this affliction they now suffer. At least nothing other than wish for it. I wonder," she mused, tapping one finger idly against her chin. "I wonder if my powers do grow stronger. Mayhap I can now wish ill on my enemies and see it come to pass."

Druce took a step back from her, and she noted that he looked appropriately impressed. "Do not say such things around them," he hissed. "You forget that we're in England now. They do hunt down those they suspect of witchcraft." He glanced over his shoulder and swallowed hard when he spied a tall form rise, then stare over at the two of them. "Especially do not say such things before Cleve. He sent me to fetch you. We'd better go now."

Wynne smiled. "Yes, we had better go. We wouldn't want to rile him, would we?"

But as she tied her hair back with a bit of odd ribbon and found her dirty boots, Wynne knew that riling Cleve was exactly what she wished to do. She found the purse she'd filled with herbs and slung her short cape over her unlaced gown. Then she turned to Druce, who awaited her.

"On another matter, Druce. We need to talk about our friendship. Yours and mine. I hope you do not imply to that English knight that you have any authority—either over me or over my children—which you do not truly possess. It would put me in the worst sort of temper if you did."

He shifted from one leg to the other. "Gwynedd specifically instructed me to have a care for you and the children."

Wynne lifted her brows slightly and pinned him with her icy stare. "Our physical safety, perhaps. But you are neither my brother nor my father. No, nor any of the children's either. This Cleve FitzWarin makes certain . . . well, certain overtures toward me."

"I warned him not to be too bold!"

" 'Tis not your place to warn him at all!"

His eyes narrowed to suspicious slits. "Why? Would you have him pursue you even more vigorously than he does?"

"No!" Wynne shouted. She gritted her teeth in exasperation. "I wish he would fall off the edge of the earth so that I might never be bothered by him again, so long as I live."

He stared at her a moment. "Then I will make my warning to him even stronger."

"No!" she protested once more. " 'Tis not your business to speak to him about me."

It was Druce's turn to grow angry. "You make no sense at all. You do not wish his attentions, and yet I'm to say nothing to him?"

" 'Tis not your place," she insisted, though even she

recognized how contrary she must sound. She frowned, then hugged her purse to her chest as she tried to explain. "When you speak to him about me—when you place limits on his behavior toward me—well, that implies a certain amount of approval. Which is not yours to give," she hastened to add. "For all practical purposes, you give him leave to court my affections."

He shook his head in confusion. "Would you have me abandon you in this? Not step in if he should be too bold?"

"No. I mean, yes." She sighed in exasperation. "Druce, I appreciate your concern. I am most relieved that you are here. But that man . . . that man has no right to pursue me, and therefore you have no right to make any rules for him about *how* he should pursue me. Does that make sense to you? Besides, he has a bride waiting in England for him. He's promised to wed one of this Lord Somerville's daughters in reward for stealing one of my children," she added scathingly.

"Now, Wynne, there's no use in arguing that point once again. And as for this other maiden, well, they're not yet wed, are they? I am certain he favors you."

"*Ffiaidd dihiryn!*" she swore. "You are truly the most loathsome of knaves. Don't you understand what I am telling you? I do not *wish* for him to favor me!"

His cockiness returned at that. "Now, now, Wynne. Do not lie to me. I have known you since you wore short skirts, remember? Every woman needs a husband, and you are no different. Cleve would make a good husband for you."

Wynne opened her mouth to challenge that ridiculous statement, then closed it with a sharp click of her teeth. It was useless to argue with Druce, especially when he had that stubborn look on his face. Oh, but she would get nowhere trying to reason with such an addle-headed fool as he clearly was.

With a cold, dismissive glare she turned and stalked away from him, fuming the whole way. Men were the most difficult of all God's creatures. Just look at Rhys and Madoc with their reckless adventures. They were so like Druce was as a boy, and no doubt they would favor him in manhood. Even Arthur was impossible to reason with once he had an idea fixed in his mind. Such as this attachment he'd formed for Cleve.

She glared at the object of her ire as she approached, unfazed by the sharp look he turned on her.

"So. Do you come to gloat or to lend us your healing skills?" He stood between her and the rest of the encampment, his legs slightly spread in an antagonistic stance, and his fists on his hips.

Wynne tilted her head up in a gesture of disdain. Let him posture belligerently. If he expected her to plead for the chance to help his ailing men, he was an even greater fool than she suspected.

"How astute you are, Englishman. If the truth be told, I *have* been gloating these last few minutes. However, if you require my assistance as a healer, then I will make my talents available to you. For a price," she threw in for good measure.

One of his brows arched in surprise, then he laughed. "For a price. You lay my men low with one of your heathen potions, then would exact a price from me to remedy your mischief." Then before she could react, he caught her by the wrist, and his brows lowered in absolute fury. "Heal my men, witch, or suffer the consequences—"

"Have a care, Cleve," Druce interrupted as he came up to them. "You've no cause to treat her so. She assures me that she did nothing—"

"I am able to speak for myself," Wynne snapped, sending Druce a furious look. Then she turned back to Cleve, a murderous glitter in her eyes. "Whatever ails your men is not of my doing," she stated, measuring her tone with acid precision. "No powder or oil of my hand made its way into their meals. If it had, more than three of them would now be groaning their misery."

His grasp remained tight on her arm. Painful even. But she matched him glare for glare, and slowly she sensed his anger begin to recede.

"You have tried it once before. I cannot believe you do not even yet wait for another opportunity."

She allowed a faint smile to curve her lips. "So I do. But it appears my powers do grow ever stronger. Perhaps it is the intensity of my emotions these past few days. I did but *wish* to lay you English low and . . ." She trailed off with a shrug and peered around him to view his three miserable men.

At once he jerked her arm, throwing her off balance before he righted her with a hand on each of her shoulders. "Enough of this talk of witchcraft. 'Tis but a ploy you use on gullible villagers—"

"And English soldiers," she added, not hiding her laughter in the least. She'd seen the alarm in the other Englishmen's faces. Even Barris had appeared suitably impressed by her claim to these new powers.

"Not all of us are fools, Wynne. You delude yourself if you believe we are."

They stared at each other, his dark brown eyes clashing with hers of vivid blue. But she refused to be cowed by him, even though she found his nearness almost suffocating. His hands held her body at his command, while his gaze seemed to fight for authority over her very soul.

He was no fool. She recognized that. But neither was she, and she refused to allow him to dismiss her as one.

It took Druce to break their impasse.

"Let her see to them, Cleve. If she says she can heal them, then she can."

"But will she?" he growled, still not removing his gaze from hers.

"If you do not wish my services, you have but to say so. Never fear, I shall not be crushed by the rejection."

"Oh, you shall heal them, all right," Cleve replied, his face very near hers. "Only I shall watch over your every move."

But although Cleve was willing, his men were not.

"No, not the witch," Richard groaned, managing, despite his weakness and pallor to stumble away from the camp. Marcus and Henry, however, were not even able to do that, though it was clear they, too, wished to escape her ministrations. Henry especially kept babbling as she spread her traveling stillroom out upon a small woolen rug.

"No, do not let her—"

"Be still, man. She but prepares a healing draft," Cleve muttered, sounding more impatient than reassuring.

"No, no. 'Tis a poison," the poor fellow mumbled, very near to tears. Even Wynne was moved by his terrible fear. Although she clung to her mysterious skills of seeress as her very last line of defense in this battle with the Englishmen, she nonetheless felt an uncomfortable pang of guilt. So much of healing was built upon trust and an abiding belief in the healer's skills. Her abilities owed as much to her people's faith in her as they did to her knowledge of herbs and her special sense for such matters.

But this man was too alarmed by her presence to be healed by her hands, and that knowledge bothered her.

With a small frown she sat back on her heels. "This will not work," she muttered as she stared hard at the fellow's sweaty face.

"You mean, you do not wish it to work," Cleve countered from much too close behind her. She jerked her head around to glare at him.

"If the patient will not cooperate, there is nothing I can do for him."

"He is afraid, damn you. Something you've deliberately encouraged."

"Be that as it may, I still cannot undo his fear."

"Just make the potion. I shall see that he takes it," Cleve added with a meaningful look at the frightened Henry.

"That will not be enough," Wynne muttered back at him. "If he does not will it—if he resists the medicine— then he will not heal."

Cleve gave her a long, steady look. He was squatting on his heels right next to her, and she could see the weariness on his face. He'd had too much to drink last night, then had been up before dawn's light. For a brief and startlingly intense moment she wished to erase the exhaustion and worry from his lean face. She wished to see his face crease in a smile, not a frown.

Then she blinked, and that instant of madness passed. If he was tired or worried, it was his own doing. He deserved all this and worse. She broke the hold of his disturbing gaze and concentrated on her little store of medicines.

"Perhaps there is a way," she murmured as a devious thought occurred to her. She lifted her head then and sent Cleve a taunting smile. "If you partake of the same remedy—if your men see you are willing to trust my healing skills—mayhap then they will not be such cowards. Unless, of course, *you* are too much the coward to do it." She laughed out loud and met his lowering gaze. "Yes, that shall be the price of my aid—you must partake first of the cure. Have you the courage?"

The silence that followed her challenge was all-pervasive. Even the shrill oriole seemed to hold its breath in anticipation of Cleve's answer to her outrageous suggestion. As Wynne stared at him, even she was not certain how he would reply. Nor did she understand where this strange idea of hers had come from. It could work of course. But she knew that it was not the welfare of Henry or his other sick mates that had prompted her. She'd already determined that they had contracted the same illness that had most recently affected a goodly number of people in the several villages in Radnor Forest. She'd dosed them all with a tea of liver lily for their vomiting, and yellow gentian and sallow bark for their fever. In two days they'd invariably been cured. No doubt they would have recovered even without her aid. It just would have taken a little longer.

But Cleve did not know that, and as she awaited his reply, she found herself praying that he rose to her challenge.

"What is this cure you propose?" he asked, a wary note in his voice.

"Liver lily. And a blend of two very effective herbs I just happen to have with me. A healthy person will still benefit from it, for it but soothes the stomach and clears the head. An ailing body, however, will benefit from it most markedly."

Their gazes remained locked for so long an interval that Wynne began to sweat from the very intimacy of it. But she refused to look away.

Then he smiled, and once more she felt the intensity.

Only this time it was relief, not yearning, and she could not keep from smiling in return.

"Do your worst, madam, while you have the chance. But I promise you, Wynne," he said, whispering this last for her ears only, "I shall expect from you the same sort of expression of faith in me. There will come that moment when you shall have to commit your trust to me." He lifted one hand and touched her cheek ever so slightly. "The time will come, and not too distant. Don't forget then that I trusted you today."

When he finally released her from his compelling stare, she turned at once to her task, for it was a supreme relief to concentrate on the measuring and mixing of the proper remedy for her patients. Anything to escape the overpowering sense of losing her will to this man.

He was her direst enemy, she reminded herself. A man paid by some marauding English lord to steal a child of hers. There could never be anything even approaching trust between the two of them.

Yet Wynne knew there was something building between them. Something that had begun as purely physical, but now was becoming emotional as well. Why else did her hands shake so?

She swallowed and glanced over at Druce. Where was he when she needed him anyway? Why wasn't he beside her, preventing Cleve FitzWarin from affecting her in so disturbing a fashion?

But Druce was easing his own ailments with a crust of bread and a slice of cheese. And anyway, she'd just told him in no uncertain terms not to involve himself in her dealings with Cleve. *Cnaf,* she muttered in frustration. Knaves, all of them.

When the tea was prepared, and the other two powders dissolved in a small amount of cold water, she finally raised her gaze back to Cleve. "Here it is; drink only one fourth of the content of each cup."

Henry watched with wary eyes as Cleve took the two cups she handed him. Richard and Marcus also stared at him, their pale faces cautious with hope. The other men, however—the ones who had not been so miserably afflicted—only appeared doubtful. From their tall, powerful leader to the small, mysterious Welsh woman their suspicious gazes flitted. Only Druce and Barris appeared confident about the outcome.

And Cleve, she amended. He looked completely confident as he took the medicines from her, letting his fingers slide over hers for an instant. Then he gave her a faint mocking smile and took a long pull from each of the vessels.

When he tasted the second preparation, however, his face puckered sourly. "My God, woman! Did you select only the vilest of your many remedies? It does taste like the overripened leavings of the garderobe!"

He wiped his mouth with the back of one fist and grimaced once again. But then he laughed and passed the two cups to Henry. "Show your mettle, man. Do not quake and quiver before this slight maid. She is more bark than bite. Drink up," he ordered with a grin directed at Wynne.

Though Cleve had risen manfully to her challenge, Wynne nonetheless frowned at his levity. As Henry cautiously sipped the remedies, she turned back to her medicines, collecting them and folding them back within her purse. In one fell swoop it seemed that Cleve had undone her. What had begun in wicked humor—a rare chance to best him—had somehow turned around on her. Like a fool she'd challenged him, but he'd risen to it.

What had she actually thought to win? she wondered as Marcus and Richard edged forward to take their portion of her remedies.

But more important, what had she lost?

15

They remained that whole day in camp. Four times did Wynne dose Richard, Henry, and Marcus with her foul-flavored concoctions, much to their complaint. But the very fact that they became more and more vociferous in their objections only proved to her that they did already mend.

The children enjoyed themselves very well, running and exploring; practicing with their bows; climbing trees. Arthur especially delighted in the break from their riding, for Cleve gave over several hours of his time to the child. They examined various forms of rocks until Arthur's collection bulged from the small haversack he carried. They located five different types of birds' nests, three of which were empty, but the other two were occupied with hungry little nestlings.

The other men, English and Welsh alike, also fell prey to the children's high spirits. Only Wynne stayed somewhat apart.

It was difficult for her to remain aloof, however, for there was little enough to do. Straighten the bedding in the tent. Prepare the meals. Measure and mix the medicines. In between times she sat upon the grassy edge of the uneven Dyke and stared across the narrow divide toward her homeland.

She pointedly ignored Cleve FitzWarin, and somewhat to her confusion—and even dismay—he ignored her. Just as well, she groused, setting her chin in her palm as she squinted to see any evidence of Black Mountain on the horizon. He was the last person on earth to whom she wished to speak.

Yet as the hours passed and the heat of the late afternoon came upon them, she knew that was not true. She tilted her head slightly so that she could spy upon him without appearing too obvious. He and Druce had returned from a short hunting expedition bearing three rabbits and four squirrels. They were in good spirits as they tossed the game to the other men for cleaning. Cleve especially looked exuberant, with his face brown as a berry and his dark hair tossed by the wind. He was so tall and straight, so strong and vital, with his tunic removed and his thin chainse clinging to his damp body.

Lucky the maiden who awaited him at Kirkston Castle, Wynne unhappily admitted to herself.

When he looked up, straight at her, she did not even try to look away. Only when he said something aside to the others, then started her way, did she turn her head to stare back at Wales.

She heard his footsteps and fancied she felt the very earth tremble as he lowered his long-legged frame to sit beside her. But she stared doggedly at the western horizon and the clouds that hid the downward arc of the sun but temporarily.

"Ah," he exhaled noisily, a contented, masculine sound. "I've had a hard time of it today, Wynne." He waited for her response.

"Oh?" She didn't look at him.

After another short silence he continued, undeterred by her obvious refusal to appear interested. "I could not decide the cause of my enormous good spirits this day. I thought it was my return to my homeland. But as I hunted, I found that my eyes were sharper and my aim truer. Then I realized that it was your doing."

"My doing?" She chanced a very brief sidelong glance at him, which she immediately regretted. Why must he plague her with his easy grin and relaxed posture? Why didn't he just leave her alone? She frowned and glared at a cloud shaped absurdly like a woman riding upon a dragon's tail.

"Yes, your doing. That vile stuff you mixed up is even better than you predicted. I have been invigorated the entire day, and the others do heal before my very eyes. Yes, 'tis of your doing. You are every bit as skilled as you did boast," he finished in a tone so excessively sincere that it rang false.

She shot him a suspicious look. "You are more bothersome than ever the most difficult child."

He laughed out loud, causing her frown to deepen. "Leave me be, Cleve FitzWarin. I do not wish your company."

She watched as, with an effort, he controlled his grin. "Ah, Wynne. I wonder if there is anything I could do to make you smile."

"I told you. Leave me be."

"I don't think that will make you smile," he replied. Then before she knew it, he took one of her hands into his. "Surely there is something else."

"There is nothing else," she vowed, once she had her wits back. "Let me go," she added, tugging hard to remove her hand from his warm and intimate grasp.

"Perhaps you would enjoy a stroll along the Dyke. We could watch the sunset," he continued as if she'd not said a word. "Or ride together. There is a meadow not far from here where the deer will come out to browse at dusk."

"No, I . . . I will not go anywhere with you," she stammered. She was conscious of the hard thudding of her heart and the heated rush of blood throughout her body.

He leaned nearer. "Smile for me, fair Wynne. Give us a smile. You do it so rarely, and it does light up your face in the most wondrous fashion."

They were like love words, soft and enticing, flirtatious and beguiling. Oh, why was he saying them to her?

"I cannot . . . I cannot smile at you," she managed.

"You mean you *will* not," he pressed on. "You are far and away the most stubborn wench I've ever met. But you've smiled on me before; you can do it again." He paused, and his dark eyes burned into hers with golden lights. "Must I kiss you again to bring that smile to your lips?"

"No!" She gasped the word as all the emotions she'd fought to hold at bay came tumbling past her weak barriers. Just the thought of him kissing her made her stomach tighten in the most unimaginable fashion. Like violent shivers, only come from the inside out and caused by heat, not cold, the waves of longing coursed through her. He lifted her hand to press against his chest, making it even worse, for the strong beat of his heart seemed to penetrate her fingertips and up her arms, then all the way to her own heart.

As if he knew the damage he was doing to her will-power—as if he could actually see her insides dissolving under his deliberately sensual attack—he kept his dark and glowing eyes steadfast upon her.

"Why no?" he prompted, searching her face, lingering at her lips. "Why don't you want to kiss me again? I was so convinced that you liked it those other times."

Wynne saw the slow, seductive grin that curved his mouth. She had liked those other kisses very much. Too much. And he knew it. Just this glimpse of his tempting grin brought all those feelings back to her, stronger than ever.

With a groan she closed her eyes. She simply could not be strong when he was so close and staring at her so boldly. But as if her lowered eyelids were a permission he awaited, a sign of her surrender, Cleve pulled her nearer until their faces were but inches apart and she could feel the very warmth of his breath.

"Open your eyes, my Wynne. See the one who would bring you every physical pleasure if you would but accept it." Then his mouth touched hers ever so lightly, and her eyes did indeed pop open.

"You see?" he murmured, moistening her lips sweetly with the words. "There is something between us—some fire—that no amount of denial can change. Here, open to me."

Like one mesmerized, she did as he said, parting her lips to his command, accepting the devastating thrust of his tongue within the sanctum of her mouth. Like the sleekest velvet it slid upon her sensitive inner lips. Like fire it licked into her, igniting the deep and smoldering embers of her darkest and most secret emotions. With unerring accuracy he stroked and roused her until she strained forward, accepting him wholly and wanting ever more.

In an instant she lay in his lap. One of his arms circled her back while the other cupped her face, tilting her backward to accept his thrilling caress. Her own hands gripped his chainse, and she felt the dampness of his skin. And the warmth. At that moment she would happily have crawled beneath the flimsy linen. Anything to be close to him, to touch his flesh with her own.

"Tonight, my fairest love. Tonight once the camp sleeps, I will wait for you," he murmured against her now-seeking lips.

Her answer was a long and hungry kiss. She didn't want words any longer, for there was no common ground for them with words. They were an ocean apart with words. Yet when they met like this . . . it was as if she were at last complete. A whole person. All her senses raised to new heights by his very nearness. Her skin fairly glowed from his touch. The taste of him, the unique scent. If she could but hear his voice every day of her life and see his smiling face . . .

But it went beyond even that. Far beyond. Like the most sharpened of her visions, the clearest sense of him came to her. Of him and her together, joined in the old way. Joined in the way men and women have joined all the ages of time. But better and stronger, and more right than was imaginable.

"Tonight." He kissed the word down her neck, heating the tender flesh there to new heights.

"Tonight," she answered somehow, though there was no breath within her to say the word. Yet even with the sound of her own voice, she knew it could not be that simple.

His hand slid down her side, skirting the edge of her breasts, then lower, past her waist to rest upon the swell of her hip. He pressed her harder against him so that she was aware of the rigid arousal beneath his braies.

It was both a wonder to her and fearsome as well. She did both long for and dread what he desired of her. How could a woman be so torn apart, so pulled in conflicting directions? Yet there was no denying the aching fullness in her belly and breasts. It was as if her very insides longed for the touch of him, and she knew at last why women could long for that very same act which in different circumstances could be so cruel and demeaning.

Groaning, she sought his mouth once more, and acting the aggressor, she held his head while she kissed him. He took her tongue into his mouth, then before she could taste her fill, thrust back, possessing her in a frighteningly aggressive manner. They slid a little way down from the edge of the Dyke, rolling slightly into the coarse grass so that he half lay upon her. One of his thighs parted hers, and she felt the hard pressure of his desire pushing against her belly. His tongue thrust too, filling her mouth, possessing it rhythmically until she was fair to bursting with unnameable desires.

"Sweet Mother," he panted, pressing his kiss against her eyes and cheeks and ear. "Ah, sweet witch, how I burn for you." He took her earlobe in an almost painful bite, then pressed his fiery kiss further, stroking into her ear so that she twisted convulsively beneath him. Squirming away from him. Squirming nearer.

His hard thigh slid against her legs, rubbing between them in the place where all her desires now seemed to be centered. Not conscious of her actions, she pressed up against him, for she desperately needed some relief to this cruel desire he'd fired in her.

"God, do not do that," he groaned against her ear. "Else I will no longer be able to control myself."

She turned her head slightly, silencing his words with a deep kiss, pouring all her longing and need into it. She wanted to consume him. She wanted him to consume her.

Someone cleared his throat, but she was only vaguely

aware of it. After a pause, however, the high, whistling notes of a familiar Welsh melody pierced her consciousness, and she went stiff with panic. Druce!

Cleve, however, was not nearly so alarmed as she. He only raised his head to peer over his shoulder, up toward the edge of the Dyke, above which the top of Druce's dark head was barely visible. "Begone from here, man."

The whistling stopped. "I need to speak to Wynne."

Cleve stilled Wynne's panicked attempts to rise with a stern look. "I need to speak to her as well. And she needs to speak to me," he added, giving her a lusty wink.

Druce cleared his throat. "I've no doubt at all that she does. However, I must act in her best interests, and at the moment I fear her . . . ah . . . her 'conversation' with you is not in her best interest."

Wynne felt her face go scarlet with shame. Druce knew exactly where she'd been heading. Though she'd told him not to interfere with her, at that moment she could have wept with relief that he had ignored her. Another kiss or two, another caress from Cleve, and she would have cast all caution to the winds.

She could not meet Cleve's eyes, but she felt his searching gaze upon her face. "Wynne?" he asked. Then, when he did not receive an answer from her, he moved his mouth nearer her ear. "Till later." He murmured the heated words in a sweet, sensual threat. Then he kissed her ear once again until she was arching in silent plea beneath him.

"Do not make this harder than it already is," Druce called impatiently.

Cleve chuckled before pulling back from Wynne. "That would be a physical impossibility," he whispered wryly.

But Wynne was too tormented by conflicting emotions

to reply. She was as limp as a well-worn length of old linen. Burned almost to ashes by the fire he'd lit within her, yet aflame still and not able to cope with the new and tumultuous feelings he'd roused in her. She stared up at him in helpless appeal, close to tears and yet still trembling uncontrollably with desire.

She saw the grim humor flee his face, to be overtaken by an expression closer to pain. "By damn, woman. Don't—" He broke off and scrambled to his feet. With a low but vicious curse he rounded on Druce. For a moment Wynne thought he meant to attack the younger man, and with a supreme effort she, too, managed to rise.

"No, Cleve. Don't you dare." She placed herself between the two and placed a hand on Cleve's chest. "Leave him be. Just . . . just go away," she pleaded as his dark gaze moved from Druce to her. At once she pulled her hand back. Touching him was far too dangerous. It weakened her so. It made her want to draw ever nearer.

She shook her head. "Just go away." She whispered the plea brokenly.

He took a long breath, slow and shaky. Then another. Finally he nodded and stepped back. His eyes flitted to Druce, who had moved closer, and Wynne felt the crackle of quick animosity begin slowly to ease.

"You told me, Druce, that an unmarried Welsh maiden is free to make her own choices."

Druce nodded. "So she is. But I did not say she was immune to advice from those who have had a care for her all the days of her life."

Cleve seemed to consider this, then he smiled ever so slightly, and his midnight gaze moved back to Wynne. "Your lifelong friend does wish to speak with you." He gave her an abbreviated bow. "Until tonight," he added in a tone reserved for her ears alone. Then he strode away.

Wynne watched him go. He headed along the edge of the Dyke, then made his way down and across it so that he walked now on Welsh soil. That simple choice of paths seemed a clear omen to her, and she felt a quiver of anticipation. But Druce was there, and she could not ignore him any longer. She turned to him, willing her heart to control its thundering and her nerves to ease their clamoring. Yet she could not quite erase the color from her cheeks.

"You've bits of grass and seeds in your hair," Druce said when they faced each other.

Wynne smoothed her wild hair back with hands that still shook. Why must he have such a knowing expression on his face? Why was he prolonging this lecture she was certain he planned?

"There. Is that better?" she snapped.

He gave her a thorough once-over, then grinned. "I suppose it depends on who's looking at you. I'd say your Cleve much prefers you with your hair loose and tangled in the grass."

"*Cnaf!*" she swore. "What do you want of me? First you do throw me at him and now you snatch me back. I do not understand you at all!"

To her vast irritation he only grinned and settled himself on the ground. "Do not turn your frustration against me, Wynne, for 'tis not of my doing. I do but act your friend in this matter."

"Hah!"

He looked up at her and shoved a hank of hair back from his brow. " 'Tis clear to me you want him. And he most desperately wants you. I do but ensure that his need for you overshadows any plans he has with this Lord Somerville's daughter."

Wynne stared at him in horror. How could he speak in

so reasonable a tone about such an outrageous plot! "You would not . . . Surely you do not . . ." She trailed off under his steady grin. "Druce. Listen to me in this. I do not under any circumstances wish to usurp this poor girl's place. He may marry her in all good faith—though that is not likely to happen. She is, after all, his reward for succeeding in his quest, and I shall make certain he does not succeed."

Druce snorted in exasperation. "How shall you make certain, Wynne? And why? So you may claim him for yourself?"

"No! I told you. She is welcome to him."

"Then what is it you plan to do with him? 'Tis clear even to a fool where you two were headed just now. What I cannot fathom—since you are apparently so willing to cede him to this English maiden—is *why* you were heading there with him."

"That should be plain, even to a fool such as you," Wynne hissed, her fists planted on her hips. "You *know* where we were heading. And how do you know? Because you've been there before yourself with some maiden— probably several. But you are not wed. No, nor even betrothed. Well, I seek no more than you've already found. I am well past marriageable age. But since I do not intend to marry, I see no reason not to exercise my freedom of choice. And if I choose to . . . to . . ."

"To what?" he asked quite pointedly.

"To . . . to . . . you know! Anyway, 'tis my choice to make. Not yours."

He stared at her, a steady, probing, and most disturbing gaze that seemed to strip away her weak defenses. She might have been but a child and he a wise and all-seeing parent, so patient and understanding was his expression. In frustration she spun away from him and stalked off in the opposite direction Cleve had gone.

Only when she reached a pair of oak trees that sprung awkwardly from the peak of the Dyke did she stop. It was her choice, she knew, and in the end if she chose to meet with Cleve in that most intimate joining of man and woman, Druce could do nothing to prevent it.

But why in heaven's name would she choose to do such a foolish thing?

She touched one finger to her kiss-swollen lips, then swallowed hard at the sweet thrill of remembered passion that at once rose from her belly.

The answer was unsettlingly clear. For this feeling, rising so unexpectedly in her, overtaking her body, her mind, and even her heart. That's why she was set on so precarious and destructive a course. She sought the culmination of these feelings he'd stirred to life within her. Yet what of the consequences?

She glanced over her shoulder to where Druce still stood, staring now back toward their homeland. He was right, of course. He was her friend, and though they did not agree on this matter of Lord Somerville—nor obviously on the matter of Cleve FitzWarin—she knew he wished only the best for her.

But who knew what was best any longer? Even if she eventually returned to Radnor Forest with all five of her children, nothing would be the same. She could never be the same anymore.

She sighed and touched her mouth once more. How could one man affect her so? How could he make her body sing and her heart beat faster just by his touch. Or simply from a solitary look?

Those were questions without any hope of answers. Yet the nearer they came to this Kirkston Castle, the more essential it became for her to decide what she was going to do about them. To lie with him as her body longed desperately to do would be an easy choice, one she knew she'd already made. It seemed only a matter now of when or where. But there was still the matter of her sons. Of Sir William's heir.

She looked back toward the camp, searching for the children. When she did not see them at once, her eyes darted about, seeking them with renewed concern. A shriek and a giggle, followed by a burst of laughter, put her racing heart at ease. There beyond the tent, beneath a canopy of beech boughs, Rhys and Madoc appeared, pushing and tumbling about, laughing and pointing back toward the shaded copse. Bronwen followed more slowly, looking back as well, but curiously.

Wynne turned toward them, wanting their company and reassuring presence around her. As she made her way through the thickly grown wild grasses, she saw Isolde and Arthur depart the shade of the beech trees. Isolde was scowling at the twins, a thunderous expression on her little face. Arthur, however, seemed lost in thought.

"You're both the stupidest boys in the entire land," Isolde shouted. "The stupidest in the whole wide world!" She turned back to Arthur, and her expression changed. "Don't pay any attention to them. They're acting like children."

Arthur rubbed his mouth with the back of one hand. "They *are* children," he replied matter-of-factly.

"Well, then. They're acting like babies."

"What are you children up to?" Wynne asked.

Isolde whirled around in surprise, and a guilty expression colored her face. Bronwen, too, looked suddenly discomfited by Wynne's unexpected presence.

But Arthur only shrugged. "We wanted to see what it was like."

Wynne's brow arched in inquiry. "What *what* was like?"

She saw Bronwen's eyes widen in alarm, and Isolde sent Arthur a quelling glare. But Arthur was squinting at a hawk circling high in the distance.

"Kissing," he answered unconcernedly. "We wanted to see what was so important about kissing."

That was the very last thing Wynne had expected, and her mouth gaped open in surprise. "You wanted to know about kissing?"

Isolde sighed in exasperation. "Arthur!" Then she peered up at her aunt. "He can't keep a secret for anything."

"Can too." He stared at her for a moment. "I just don't see why it has to be a secret—"

"What exactly *is* the secret?" Wynne interrupted. "Exactly what were you doing?"

When neither Isolde nor Arthur answered, Wynne turned toward Bronwen. "Well?"

Bronwen smiled timidly. "They kissed. Arthur and Isolde kissed. On the lips."

"Oh." Wynne pursed her mouth, trying hard to repress the smile that threatened to break free at such an innocent revelation. "And what did you think of it?"

Arthur shrugged. "It was all right. I suppose."

Isolde glared at him all over again. "It was very nice. Just like grown-ups do."

"But we aren't grown-ups," Arthur reasoned. He focused on Wynne. "It's all right, isn't it? I mean, we're not *really* brother and sister, because we have different mothers and fathers."

"It's just like Wynne and Sir Cleve," Bronwen said with a dreamy smile.

At once Wynne's amusement vanished. But before she

could form an appropriate reply, Arthur focused his watchful gaze upon her.

"If you kiss him, you must like him, Wynne. And if you like him, then why don't you marry him?"

"Oh . . . well, you see . . ." Wynne pressed her lips together, anything to stop such foolish babbling. Arthur's face was so earnest that she knew she must pick her words very carefully.

"Cleve is . . . well, he *is* an impressive man. Strong. Handsome. I like him well enough but . . . well, he's English and I am Welsh. We could never marry."

"So you only kiss each other?" Bronwen asked.

"But why can't you marry him?" Arthur interrupted. "I mean, if Rhys and Madoc have to stay in England, or even if I do, when we grow up, we'll probably marry English maidens. But we're Welsh."

"It's not precisely the same thing," Wynne began.

"You *can't* marry an English girl," Isolde broke in. "We've already kissed. You can't marry anybody but me."

Wynne looked from her niece to Arthur and then back to Isolde. "No one is going to stay in England," she vowed, though it was hard to feel the same conviction she'd felt in the beginning.

Arthur shook his head. "I think you might be wrong about that, Wynne. 'Tis very likely that one of us *is* Sir William's son. I don't think you'll be able to keep us if we are."

Of all the pronouncements, conjectures, and arguments advanced on behalf of Lord Somerville's quest, this one, coming from such an innocent yet wise young child, was the hardest for her to hear. "I shall keep you," she countered. "None of you belongs to this Englishman, no matter what he says."

"I don't want Arthur to live in England," Isolde began to cry.

"What about Madoc?" Bronwen joined in the wailing. "And Rhys?"

"Oh, don't cry, my darlings. Come here." Wynne gathered the two weeping girls into her arms. "Everything is going to be all right. You'll see."

As she hugged them tight, she met Arthur's serious gaze. "I . . . I don't really want to live in England," he admitted. She could see he was struggling to control his emotions. "But it wouldn't be so terrible if *you* were here too."

She reached an arm to him, and he quickly scurried to her side. But she had no answer to his words. She could never stay in this godforsaken land. Never.

But a part of her would stay, she realized. Her heart would be torn into bleeding pieces if any of her children remained behind.

She swallowed the lump that formed in her throat and hugged the children all the tighter. Beyond the copse of trees in the distance someone came into view. It was Cleve, she recognized at once, the one man who appealed to every part of her—to every one of her senses.

But not to her head. She knew in that last bastion of reason that he was all wrong for her. Every moment she spent with him, looking at him, or even thinking of him was all wrong.

Worst of all, however, was her knowledge that even if she did return to Wales with her little family intact, she would still leave a huge portion of her heart behind. Cleve would have it always, though he would never be aware of it.

If nothing else, she must never let him know how thoroughly he possessed her heart.

16

Dark came early to their encampment. Heavy clouds pressed low, although Wynne knew there would not be rain. The birds did not hurry at their feeding. The air was soft with the humidity, not oppressive with the surging energy of a storm. At worst they might receive a light drizzle, a soft, cooling bath for the heated summer earth.

Wynne sat in the entrance of the tent, staring out at nothing in particular, hearing only in the most superficial sense the rising buzz of the grass crickets and the comforting rush of the night winds in the arcing branches of the beech trees above them.

The men had all departed to their bedrolls, and no voices carried to her any longer. At least no spoken voices. But in her head—no, in her heart—she felt herself being called, as clearly as if a voice rang out in the dark silence, calling her by name.

What was she to do?

Already her body fairly hummed in answer to that call. Would she truly lose anything by giving in to it?

She turned her head slightly, smiling fondly at the sprawl of six-year-old bodies that took up the entire floor of the tent. They were all blessedly asleep, lulled by the healthy exhaustion so typical of children. How she wished she could tumble into that same oblivion they'd found and experience the same deep peace. At the moment, however, peace seemed far beyond her.

Refusing to think about where her actions might lead, she rose on silent feet and eased out of the tent. The air was cooler, and the breeze caught at her unbound hair, lifting it as if in a caress. She moved on sure feet, heading toward the Dyke and the same familiar hummuck she'd perched on most of the day, staring toward Wales.

Cleve was waiting there.

He'd spread a rug upon the grass, and he lay on his back, his arms crossed beneath his head. When she stopped but one pace from him, he looked up at her. It was dark, and the moon was partly hidden by the clouds, yet she saw him almost clearly. He saw her too, for she felt the vivid imprint of his gaze moving down her body. From the top of her dark hair past her eyes and mouth to her breasts and belly and all the way down to her bare feet. Then up again, stroking her entire length until he stopped at her face.

"I've prepared a nest for us, love. Come lie beside me." He sat up and reached a hand to her.

But Wynne would not take it. She wet her lips nervously, and only when he lowered his hand back to his side did she speak.

"The thing is, we must talk. We must understand each other."

"I understand far more than you think, Wynne," he answered in a voice so low and husky that her knees began to tremble. "You also understand. Come here beside me and you will soon see."

Wynne shook her head. "Not yet. Not until we have agreed."

He rolled to his side and propped his head on one hand. "Agreed? 'Tis clear we are in complete agreement. I am here. You are here."

" 'Tis not so simple as that."

He sighed and ran a hand through his hair. "You do but make this more complicated than it is."

"And you would rather believe it is as simple as . . . as an easy tumble with some . . . some whore!" A sudden fit of trembling caught her in its grip. "Oh, I am a fool even to be here."

She turned, prepared to flee, to run and hide her awful shame. To lick her wounds. But Cleve was faster than she. Before she'd even reached the crest of the Dyke, he bounded up, caught her arm, and forced her to a halt. Her chest heaved with both emotion and her efforts to get away as she stood before him. Though she faced him, however—forced to do so by his unrelenting grip on both her shoulders—she did not look at him.

"I know it is not simple, Wynne. Anything but. There is a vast chasm between us. But there is also this . . . this passion. It's been there since I first laid eyes on you in the forest, looking like some wild, magical creature who might disappear at any moment. Like one of your Welsh fairies, a figment of my imagination, not wholly of this world."

Her eyes raised to his, drawn by the compelling force of his words. He'd wanted her from the first?

Their eyes met and locked, trading secrets in the darkness of midnight. "I should not . . . should not feel this . . . this passion for you," she whispered. "You are my enemy."

He shook his head. "No, I'm not your enemy. I could

never be your enemy." His voice became more husky. "I could never be your enemy."

She had become less and less rigid in his grasp. Now, as he pulled her closer, Wynne felt herself fairly dissolving into his arms. When he lowered his face to hers, she leaned against him, more than ready for his kiss. Then his lips met hers, and she sighed with relief, though the turmoil inside her increased a hundredfold. But it was a different sort of turmoil from before, demanding, not doubting. Joyful, not fearful.

He pulled her fully against him so that they met, belly to belly, chest to breast. How could they fit so perfectly together? a part of her wondered. He was so tall and hard; she was so much smaller and softer. He was the wrong man, from the wrong country, and with all the wrong ideas. Yet he made her body sing and her heart soar.

His tongue pressed urgently against the seam of her lips, probing for entrance, demanding more from her, and Wynne opened at once. She wanted him there inside her, awakening all her senses, bringing her alive with the erotic play of his lips and tongue. The stroke of his tongue filling her mouth fully, then pulling away, rubbing her sensitive inner lips like warm, rough velvet cloth, aroused the most sinful of feelings in her.

He held her in a fierce embrace, with one hand covering her derriere and pressing her hard against his loins. Fire leaped between them there, and without being conscious of her actions, Wynne slid one of her hands down his back to the curve of his muscular buttocks. He jerked in reaction, a convulsive response to her artless caress.

"Sweet Mother, but you have tortured me too long," he breathed in her ear. His lips found the delicate edge of that orifice, then his tongue. Wynne gasped and arched in helpless pleasure—or was it pain? The two seemed so very much alike. The desire that built within her seemed ludicrously about to explode beyond the meager confines of her body. Yet she was certain that explosion would nonetheless be exquisite, and she wanted it more than she'd ever wanted anything before.

"You torture me now," she panted, sliding her hands up along his back. Through the soft linen of his chainse she could feel every muscle, every ridge and curve and hollow of his torso. The warmth of him was there too, like a fever, a contagion that would soon consume them both, for the fever was now in her as well.

"I shall torture you more and more. The whole night long will I torture you," he vowed, interspersing his hoarse words with an erotic trail of kisses. Down her throat the trail moved, down along her collarbone, pressing against the hollow at the base of her neck, then lower, nuzzling the neckline of her kirtle down until he pressed his hot lips to the upper swells of her breasts. Only then did he pause.

"You are indeed a witch, my wild Welsh rose. A witch who has me in her thrall. A seeress who has enchanted me." Without warning he lifted her into his arms. His strides were swift and sure through the dark and the high grasses. He only stopped when he reached the rug he had prepared for them.

"You've bewitched me," he murmured. "Whether with some dark potion or just the dark glow in your eyes, I don't know. But I must have you, Wynne. There can be no other way."

He set her upon her feet, then pulled her once more against him. His hands stroked slowly down her back, melting her, she thought through the fog of passion that had her in its grasp. But his touch, though lingering, was no less urgent. "Lie with me, love. Here and now. Forever," he added in a soft, heated breath against her ear.

"Forever?" She sought his lips with hers, probing within his mouth, seeking to undo him in the same wanton manner with which he always managed to overwhelm her. Then she pulled a little away from him. "There can be no forever," she whispered, as much to remind herself as to let him know. "There is only now. That's all there can be for us."

But Cleve ignored her words. As if he fought their dampening effect on both himself and her, he captured her lips once more. "We shall see," he murmured. He pulled her down upon the rug so that they were kneeling face-to-face, their thighs touching, her breasts pressed against his chest. "We shall see."

Wynne, however, fought the overpowering effect of his touch. "No." She shook her head. "There can be only now. You must know that."

There was a pause. "There can be more, Wynne. If you'll just let there be."

Like a cold rush of wind between them his words drove her a little farther back from him. "You are a fool to still believe that," she whispered, her heart breaking from the intrusion of reality into this sweetest moment of unreality.

"Bedamned!" he swore, though he did not release her from his grasp. "If you believe that, why do you come to me this way? If you would keep me your enemy by day, how can you come to me as a lover by night?"

Wynne did not have an answer, at least not one she could express to him. She could hardly say that he was the one man in her life whom she would cherish above all others. She could never reveal that her feelings moved far beyond mere passion. An avowal of love would gain her nothing, and perhaps cost her everything.

But her silence only increased his agitation. "Why do you come to me?" he demanded, shaking her for emphasis.

"I would . . . I would see this passion to its fruition!" she cried in frustration. " 'Tis nothing more than that. No, nothing," she insisted.

"You are untried, are you not?"

Wynne gritted her teeth. "I am a virgin," she confirmed. "But what has that to do with it?"

"In England a maiden such as you is kept well away from men. Her purity is a prize reserved for her husband."

"We are not in England!" she cried, exasperated by this pointless discussion.

He laughed. "Ah, but we are in England, my love. Just beyond the Dyke is Wales, but where we sit, this is English soil."

He had her there. But even so, Wynne did not see the purpose of this conversation.

"Do not expound your English values to me. If the English valued virgin maidens, they would not rape so freely. And what of you? You do not value my purity, else you would not be trying so adamantly to take it!"

He studied her a moment in the darkness. "I do not have to try very hard."

"Oh! Why you . . . you utterly wretched man!" She tried to jerk free of his hold, but he had a merciless grip on her. A part of her knew he spoke very near the truth. Yet she refused to shoulder all the blame.

"If you believe I am so . . . so free with my . . . my . . . myself, then begone from here! Leave me be."

For a long moment they glared at each other. Then he gave a self-deprecating chuckle. "I cannot," he admitted. "Whether you tempt me in order that I will lower my guard against your bloodthirsty ways, whether you think to sway me to your way of thinking regarding your children—it hardly matters. I want you, and that is all. I want you and I must have you."

Like a blast of hot summer air his profession of desire melted her icy rage. It kept coming back to that. They desired each other beyond all logic. She trembled despite her best efforts to appear composed. "You do not trust me, and I most assuredly do not trust you. All we have is this shared passion. Must there be a reason beyond that?" she finished in a soft, almost pleading voice.

He regarded her steadily. "Ideally, no. A shared passion should be enough reason." Then his thoughtful tone grew more businesslike. "But it seldom works that way. Especially with untried maidens."

"We Welsh do not view it in the same way you English do. We believe a girl's purity is hers for the giving, not something her father or brother may barter away."

"So why are you giving your purity to me?"

Wynne swallowed hard. They had come full circle, it seemed, back to the one subject she could not discuss with him. "I . . . I am curious," she answered, but rather weakly.

His hands ran up and down her arms, making her aware of the great contrast between the cool night air and his warm touch. "There is no other reason?" he asked. "No ulterior motive?"

She stiffened. " 'Tis not my intent to poison you, if that is what you fear."

Once more he laughed. "No. If anything, I fear you will do me in with your truly lethal kisses and devastating touch. I may expire from the pure pleasure of your body pressed against mine." He pulled her closer and bent to kiss the tender flesh at the side of her neck. "Would you do that for me, Wynne? Kill me with the exquisite pleasure of your sweet body?"

Wynne's breath caught in her chest, and she arched her neck to better accommodate his searching lips. How could a man be at once so exciting and so exasperating? She licked her lips as a wave of fiery warmth flooded through her. "If you wish me to do you in that way, then . . . then I shall try." She gasped the words out.

In a trifling moment he had her on her back, the rug prickly beneath her and his hard body warm above.

"Do your worst, then, sweet witch."

With those words he seemed to release all the repressed passions within her. Like one being they communed. His hands found those areas of her body that most desired his touch. His lips brought a sort of heavenly salvation to her starving flesh.

Likewise did he respond to the bold ventures of her hands upon him. When one of her palms slid beneath his chainse, up the straining muscles of his back, gliding over the damp flesh there, he groaned and shifted. One of his hands found the hem of her kirtle and raised it to bare her legs. She felt the rough wool of his braies on the tender skin of her inner thighs. Like a threat and a caress it was. Something both to fear and to desire. Then when his hand followed, she gasped out loud.

"Cleve . . . what . . . wait."

"Wait for what, sweet witch? Until we are both melting from this heat between us? If we wait any longer, I fear there may be nothing left of us but a puddle in the grass. No." His hand slid higher, into the unchartered place between her thighs. "There is no time left for waiting."

He was right. She knew it when his fingers found the damp center of her, and she cried out in wild abandon, arching convulsively. There was no time left for waiting.

His magic was too strong for her. He was seducing her with it, making her bend to his touch, and there was nothing more she wanted in the entire world.

She heard his gasping breath. He sucked in air in time with the terrible, wonderful stroking he was doing to her, sliding over the entrance to her most private self. Then he slipped farther, thrusting his finger right up into her, and she nearly came up off the rug.

"Relax, my sweet. Don't fight it. Just let it come to you. Let it come," he murmured. He pressed her down on the rug, capturing her mouth in a deep and penetrating kiss that mirrored the thrusting rhythm of his touch down there.

She was sinking, drowning in the pure ecstasy of the sensations that bombarded her. It was too much to bear. It was not enough.

"Touch me." She heard his ragged whisper in her ear. He moved his head down and found the rigid peak of her left breast through the linen of her kirtle. He teased it at first, then took the nipple wholly into his mouth. Then he bit lightly at the aroused nub.

"Touch me," he ordered in an almost painful tone. "Touch me, Wynne."

She did as he said, finding his hard arousal instinctively. Wynne understood about how things worked between men and women. She knew from raising three boys how men were formed. But what she discovered now, so hot and stiff beneath Cleve's strained braies, was something beyond her meager knowledge. It was at once something quite apart from him and yet most integral too, something essential to this mysterious and powerful attraction between them.

Was this the answer? she wondered as her fingertips traced the long length of him. It felt too large, too threatening to fit where she knew it must fit. Yet with just the touch of it she felt herself growing even more wet with desire.

Cleve groaned against her neck when she flattened her palm upon the pulsing length of him, then began to rub up and down, adopting the same rhythm of his intimate stroking of her. At once his fingers stilled within her, and he bucked hard against her hand.

"Sweet Mother!" he rasped out. "Damn, but you . . . you bewitch me."

Wynne smiled and became even more bold. This was a power she had over him. It was not solely the other way around. Yet the giving of pleasure to him only seemed to increase her own desire. She moved against his hand, and he began once more the slow, exquisite stroking deep inside her.

When she whimpered her pleasure, he caught the sound in another stirring kiss. Only when she was breathless and limp beneath him did he pull back. She was so befuddled by the voluptuous sensations that gripped her, she hardly noticed when he pulled her hand away from him.

" 'Tis too fast, woman. I shall surely explode if you touch me again."

"Cleve . . ." She breathed his name like a prayer and reached up to his face. He caught her hand against his cheek, then turned his head slightly to press a hot kiss to the very center of her sensitive palm.

"You are verily a witch," he muttered, his voice half wondering and half—half what?

Half angry, Wynne realized.

"Please . . . oh, don't be angry with me."

He laughed, but mirthlessly. " 'Tis not you, sweetheart. No." He stood and quickly shed both his chainse and his braies. Before her eyes could trace the full beauty of his virile body, he lay on the rug again, partially covering her half-clad body with his warm, naked flesh.

He kissed her, hard and possessively. " 'Tis not you who are to blame, but I."

Without waiting for her response, he pulled her kirtle high, dragging it over her head and casting it aside. One of his hands began to stroke and tease, down the center of her chest, circling her full and aching breasts until her nipples were taut and erect. He wet his finger and touched one nipple, then the other, bringing Wynne in arching desire up off the rug.

"Cleve . . . oh, please . . ." she panted.

"Shhh, my love. Just be patient," he answered in a low, breathless gasp of his own.

Then his hand slid, palm down, fingers splayed, past her breasts to her waist, then over her belly. With excruciating precision he cupped the soft mound of dark curls, curving his fingers toward the aching entrance to her woman's place. One finger slid into the sweet dampness, and she lifted up to meet it. But he withdrew it and instead began to stroke the small hidden nub that seemed suddenly to become the focus of every sensation she'd ever experienced.

"Do you like that?" he whispered, punctuating his words with an erotic kiss to her ear.

She swallowed and nodded, hardly able to respond, so incredible were the feelings building in her.

"Haven't you ever touched yourself here, Wynne?" When she only rose up more frantically against his hand, grasping the rug in her fists and digging her heels in, he kissed her ear again. " 'Tis your sweet spot. The source of your deepest magic. The one place too many men neglect

in their haste to satisfy themselves. Am I too hasty?" he
murmured.

There was no answering him. Wynne was too caught
up in the power he wrought with just that one finger, with
just his simple touch, his flesh to hers. She was swept
along into a storm of emotional and physical sensation. It
enveloped her entire body, from her fingertips to the ends
of her toes, from deep inside her belly to every square
inch of skin that covered her. Yet it was also centered
where his finger stroked in an ever-increasing rhythm.

She heard his harsh, gasping breaths—or were they her
own? Then in a shattering vortex it came, like lightning
striking down at the earth, unexpected even though the
storm had raged all night. It struck, and she cried out in
the most exquisite agony.

"Cleve . . . Cleve . . ." She sobbed his name out
loud, over and over, while her body convulsed in violent
reaction.

"I'm here," he whispered, cupping her once more with
his entire hand, seeming to hold all her feelings, all her
emotions in his comforting grasp. "I'm here," he repeated, sealing his words with a kiss that was sweet and yet
more intimate than any other so far. He touched her heart
with that kiss, and without hesitation she threw her arms
around him, pulling him down upon her.

"I lo—" Her artless avowal was swallowed in his hungry kiss. Wynne was so filled with love and gratitude, with
the warm need to fill him with the same wondrous happiness with which he'd filled her, that she opened completely to him. Mouth, arms, heart, she took him to her.
When one of his thighs edged her legs apart, she did not
hesitate. When the heated center of him probed for entrance, she pressed up in response.

"Put me in," he instructed in a voice thick with need.

She found him with her hand, and for a moment she just held him, wrapping her fingers around that overheated flesh, wondering at the smoothness there when so many other places were rough with hair. He jerked against her touch and, if anything, grew even hotter than before.

"Put me in, Wynne. Now."

She guided him to the damp entrance to her, feeling as she did her own need returning.

This was truly amazing, she thought in a passion-induced fog. The most amazing thing that had ever happened to her. This was truly magical.

Then his erect manhood began to slide into her, and her eyes came open in shock and then dismay.

"Wait," she gasped as he pressed into her, filling her with his burning flesh, threatening with his very size to rip her asunder. "Wait!"

"I cannot wait any longer," he muttered.

Yet he paused even as he spoke. For a moment they seemed suspended awkwardly, somewhere between coming together and pulling apart. He was half within her. The frantic pressure of her hands against his chest were but an insignificant barrier to the completion of the act they had begun. But he held back, and though Wynne was overwrought with too many confusing emotions to be sensible, she did appreciate that fact. His arms trembled with his restraint. Every one of his muscles strained and beaded with sweat, but he held back.

"Just relax, Wynne. Relax and you shall see how good it will be."

She shook her head, unmindful of the salty tears that trickled now past her temples to be lost in her hair. Just inches from her own, his eyes burned down into hers, willing her to pliancy.

"Just try to relax," he murmured again.

" 'Tis too . . . too big," she confessed, feeling an abject shame at her admission. A woman was meant to accept her man this way. Was something wrong with her that she could not? "I liked your finger better," she revealed, and she began to cry in earnest.

"Don't cry. No, Wynne. Sweetheart. Don't cry. Here." He sought out her mouth with his and slowly began to kiss her. Wynne responded at once to the stroke of his lips and tongue. This was a pleasure she'd come to understand. This was something she knew brought only pleasure.

Bit by bit, as their kiss grew deeper and more passionate, Wynne shed her tension. Her panic faded, and as it did, she was once more, steadily and inevitably, filled with that heated rush of desire. Her hands slid from his chest to circle his neck and pull him nearer. Her legs eased from their taut resistance, and with that he began to slip naturally within her.

He was careful and gentle, and though Wynne was conscious of the hard delving of his manhood all the way into her, she no longer feared it. He filled her to overflowing. She was so tight and he was so hot, she would not have believed it possible. Yet that incredible inching forward, that rubbing of his hard flesh against the secret passage she'd hardly known she possessed, set off the most astonishing reaction within her. She literally flowed with pleasure—oozed with damp desire—so that when he began to withdraw, the pleasure was even more acute than before.

"Better?" he asked in one heated word against her ear.

Wynne nodded her answer. There was no speaking it. She could barely breathe for the astounding sensations rippling up inside her. Almost all the way out he pulled, until she thought he meant to leave her. But he didn't.

With a low groan he thrust back within her, a little quicker this time, causing her to gasp with pleasure.

"Better, sweetheart?"

She nodded again, then raised her hips to take the full length of him. Out he pulled, then in, even faster and more smoothly than before.

How had she feared this? she wondered as blind passion caught her once more in its grip. They fit together like one being. Like two parts requiring only the completion of the other.

She wrapped her legs around his tensed hips, hooking her feet together. With a hoarse groan Cleve began a more urgent rhythm until they were locked in an almost insane cycle of thrust and withdraw. Accept and release.

Again the storm found her, wild and strong, raging inside her, fed by Cleve's maddened thrusting. Then he cried out, and as if in answer the storm broke over her, a hurricane of huge proportion. A tornado, unmindful of the repercussions of its fury, sucking up everything in its path.

In the aftermath, in the wreckage left behind by the storm of their joining, they lay spent and exhausted, like flotsam on the beach. Like forest litter, broken and abandoned.

Cleve lay, damp from his efforts, half sprawled upon her. His face was lost in her hair, his breath hot and hard against her neck. One of her arms curved around his neck and shoulder. Her fingers were buried in his hair. So, too, did one of her legs still circle his hips, while the other lay alongside his, sensitive to the hair-roughened feel of his thigh and knee and calf.

She could have lain that way forever, for she was filled with the most incredible sense of completeness. Contentment overtook her, like a magic she'd never truly understood. Until now.

She felt his sigh, a great groan of repletion, and she smiled to know he felt as she did. With only a slight twist of her head she found his strong, corded neck. She kissed his damp skin, feeling the steady pulse and tasting his salty flesh. She licked, and then bit, filled with a strange, almost giddy desire to evoke a response from him.

And respond he did. She felt an odd flexing within her, once, then again, as his relaxed manhood flickered back to life. He shifted, and her eyes flew open in shock.

"Oh!"

"If you do tease a man," he murmured, tugging at her earlobe in the most erotic fashion, "then you must be prepared to accept the consequences."

Instinctively she arched to meet his growing demand and was rewarded by a sweet, sticky stroke that brought a moan of pleasure to her lips.

"Consequences?" she managed to say with a suggestive smile.

He raised himself upon one elbow and took her face between his hands. But his smile had faded, and Wynne knew at once that he was not teasing any longer. "There are consequences for everything we do, Wynne. This." He slid slowly all the way into her, and then out, making her gasp from the fiery delight. "This has a consequence we both must accept."

But Wynne did not want to hear. She didn't want to speak or see or care about anything but how he made her feel. Most certainly she did not wish to think about the future.

She caught his head in one of her hands, tightening her fingers in his hair and forcing his face down to hers. This time she was the aggressor, forcing her tongue between his lips, stroking boldly, surging fully into his mouth, then drawing his tongue back into her own mouth. She seduced him as he'd done her, until his hips began to move in a like rhythm and they were back to the wild mating of before.

This time it took longer. Though their movements were steadier and the rhythm slower, the results were no less exquisite. The first time had initially been filled with fear. Later wonder. This time, however, seemed more a confirmation. Cleve was more deliberate and possessive as he drove her higher and higher. He was like a man obsessed with bringing her to that peak, that moment of soaring pleasure.

Yet even as she cried out in that absolute ecstasy, a shadow flitted over her soul.

Consequences. The word sounded silently in her head, mirroring their rhythmic thrusts.

Consequences. There would always, always be consequences.

17

The consequences of such indiscreet behavior as she had participated in were vast, though not solely in ways that Wynne would have predicted.

She sat stiffly on her peaceful little mare, gritting her teeth, even though the day's journey was done. She was simply in too much pain to move. It hurt to sit. It would hurt to dismount. It would definitely hurt to walk to a soft spot of grass only to sit once more.

The three boys were already down and running about, scaring up a small hare and flushing a hen harrier from her shelter in the heather. Isolde and Bronwen looked around at their new campsite, then came straight toward Wynne.

"Wynne, Wynne. Can we pick the place to put the tent this time? Can we?"

Wynne forced a pleasant expression to her face, though her bottom ached like the devil. "Why don't you speak to Cleve about it? Or Druce," she added, aware that she should not invest all authority to Cleve. At least not before the children.

"Cleve. Cleve," they chorused as they turned and ran to where he dismounted among his men.

Wynne watched as he squatted before them, nodding and smiling, then giving each of them a fond pat on the head. They scampered off toward where Barris and the now-recovered Henry unloaded the jennets, but her gaze remained on Cleve. He rose to his feet, then with a final stroke and tickle for his destrier, he started toward her.

Wynne couldn't remove her eyes from him, nor had she been able to do so the whole day long, though she'd kept her distance from him. Last night they had slept a short while together, but when the strange, misty glow of the false dawn had showed, Wynne had risen from their tangled bed and fled back to the tent.

Dear God, but she had truly done it this time, she had fretted, lying there amid the sleeping children. If her situation had been unhappy before, it must be tenfold more so after what they'd done.

Yet Wynne had been unable to be completely dismayed. Even now she had only to close her eyes to remember how he'd touched her and how he'd made her feel. Would she honestly wish to undo all that had passed between them this past night? Now, as she perched painfully astride her mare and stared down into his darkening eyes, she knew she would not.

"The riding has been uncomfortable for you," he said as he rested one hand upon her knee.

Wynne tried to shrug, but even that hurt. She grimaced instead. "Just get me down from here."

In a trifling moment he had his hands firmly around her waist, lifted her high, then placed her on her feet before him. When her knees began to buckle, she grabbed desperately at him, but he saved her from falling and pulled her close.

"We should have rested another night at Offa's Dyke. I warned you that you might find the ride, ah . . . difficult."

Wynne met his amused gaze. "You have warned me of many things," she answered crossly. "But I shall make my own decisions. And go my own way."

His amusement faded, for he knew she spoke of more than simply the obvious. Their only conversation earlier that day had been similar, him urging her to rest another day and her responding to his patronizing tone with embarrassment, covered by a curt, dismissive air. Then, as now, she'd said things better left unsaid.

"Go your own way," he repeated her words caustically. "Yes, so you say again and again. But beware, my sweet witch. For all your virginal restraint before last night, such talk as this does reek more of the whore."

"How dare you!" She tried to yank free of him but to no avail. "You pursue me and hound me. And now you dare to chastise me that I acquiesced—"

"I chastise you not that you gave yourself to me," he bit right back at her. "But that you seek so quickly to cast that aside and go your own way, as you say. You act as though what has passed between us was an act of no importance, an urge like hunger. Eat the meal and then promptly forget what you just feasted upon. But our ways are now entwined, Wynne. I told you there were consequences to what we did, and so there are. Do not try to avoid that fact."

Wynne shut her eyes and turned her face away from his angry scrutiny. He spoke a truth she could not dispute— save, perhaps, in their differing expectations of what those consequences would be. He thought they were now somehow bound together. Their lovemaking had initiated some sort of physical permanence in his eyes. But she knew that though the ties that existed between them were powerful, they were emotional, not physical. Oh, yes, she felt that soaring physical longing for him, that aching yearning that swelled from the deepest recesses of her private being to encompass her entire body. But it was her heart that felt it more profoundly than anywhere else. Her heart. Her emotions. That was the connection they would always share. That was the consequence she would have to live with all the days of her life.

"There are consequences," she admitted with a heavy heart. She shifted in his grasp, making certain that her legs would hold her. Then she lifted her face back up to his and met his black look with a determinedly pleasant expression. "I know there are consequences, Cleve. I feel them most uncomfortably even as we speak. But you must allow me my freedoms. I've belonged to no one. Not ever. I've been on my own since I was but a child of twelve. I will not be possessed now. Not even by you."

To her relief he did not prevent her from backing away from him. He merely looked at her as if he would learn every thought in her head, every emotion in her heart if he did but stare long enough.

To be truthful, Wynne was much flattered by his blatant possessiveness. He was a man any woman would want to belong to—*if* a woman wished to belong to a man.

But she did not wish to belong to anyone; nor would any self-respecting Welshwoman. That was for frail and fearful English maidens, not for a strong woman of *Cymru*. And certainly not for the Seeress of Radnor.

" 'Tis not my wish to possess you in that way, Wynne. I do not seek to steal your very self from you. But I would not lose what we have begun." He reached out and let one hand run up her arm, from her wrist up past her elbow to her shoulder. Even through the sleeves of her kirtle and gown she felt the special warmth his touch imparted.

It was the magic, she thought as their eyes held and her skin came afire. The most powerful magic in the world. Why must *he* be the one who stirred it to life within her?

But he was, and if she'd wondered the whole long day why she'd gone to him in such a reckless and forward fashion, she had the answer now. It was magic.

He stepped nearer so that they were but inches apart. She could have sworn that her body felt the imprint of him though they did not touch. But she knew how it would feel. His hard thighs against her legs. His brawny chest against her softer breasts. His rigid manhood . . .

He bent to her as if he might kiss her, and she strained upward in anticipation. But a giggle and a loud "Shhh" brought them swiftly apart.

"I *told* you to be quiet," Bronwen fussed at Madoc.

"*I* didn't do anything!"

Bronwen's scowl faded to a sheepish grin when she looked up at Wynne and Cleve. Her usual shy expression was completely overtaken by a dreamy infatuation, and Wynne feared she knew precisely what the girl imagined.

"What is it you need?" Cleve inquired with an unconcerned grin.

"Oh, well. It's all right," Bronwen demurred. "We don't want to interrupt you."

"Maybe he *wants* to be interrupted," Madoc said in a matter-of-fact tone. "Girls may like to kiss, but I don't think boys do."

" 'Course they do," Bronwen replied. With her fists on her hips and her face patient, she looked the image of a scolding mother. "Well, when they grow to be men, they do. How do you think they get to have children of their own?"

Madoc gave her an equally exasperated look. "It's not from kissing, stupid. Don't you remember what Wynne said? About the English soldiers and our mothers—" He broke off at the memory of that violence and gave Cleve a suddenly suspicious stare. "What are you doing to Wynne?"

"Now, wait a minute, Madoc." Wynne stepped away from Cleve and crouched down before the boy. She took his hands in hers, wondering how she might explain. The last thing she wanted was for her children to think that all men were rapists. "Kissing can be . . . well, very nice," she began. "It's . . . it's the right way for a man and woman to . . . to . . ."

"To show they love each other," Bronwen finished. She shook her head at Madoc. "Boys are *so* stupid."

"We are not!" he shouted back.

"What's the matter?" Rhys called as he ran up to them. As he joined the argument between Bronwen and Madoc, Wynne stood up. She had to be more careful, she told herself. Practically kissing Cleve in broad daylight and in view of everyone, children and men alike. She peered cautiously toward where the men unloaded the horses, then promptly looked down at the toes of her dusty boots. Druce was grinning. So was Barris. Cleve's men looked a little uncertain, but there was still a leering sort of curiosity in their avid gazes.

Oh, but she was an utter fool!

"Kissing can be very nice," Cleve whispered softly in her ear. He slipped an arm around her waist before she could spring back in dismay. "It's the right way for a man and a woman to show—"

"That they love each other?" she snapped, unnerved by how he managed always to strike just the right chord in her, whether with a touch, a look, or just the husky sound of his voice. "Love has nothing to do with it," she vowed as she wrested free of his disturbing nearness.

He studied her. "If you were perhaps more experienced with these matters, I would give your arguments some credence. But we both know you're not."

She was saved from responding to that self-serving statement when Arthur insinuated his slight form between the two of them.

"Are you two going to get married to each other?"

His expression was so solemn and his eyes so intent that Wynne was at a loss as to how she should respond. Of course they were not going to get married. That was preposterous. She glanced at Cleve, hoping to appeal to him for help. But to her surprise he, too, was taken aback by Arthur's innocent question.

At once Wynne's dismay hardened to anger. What an unfeeling, self-centered brute he was! Of course their kiss would not lead to marriage, for his intentions were not that noble. For all his talk of consequences and entwined futures, he had only one plan for her: that of casual mistress. A woman upon her back for him to ease himself upon, much as this Lord Somerville had eased himself upon some poor Welsh maiden, then left her, pregnant and alone, once he was tired of her.

She stiffened in fury, then turned to Arthur. "Kissing does not always imply love. Nor is it a promise of marriage." She swallowed hard, forcing herself to soften the curt edge to her voice. "Sometimes a woman must kiss a few men before she finds just the right one—the one she wishes to marry and raise a family with," she added, shooting Cleve a venomous look.

She took malicious pleasure at the disconcerted expression on his face. When Arthur stared up at him, confusion and disappointment on his young face, Wynne could have sworn Cleve actually squirmed.

"Don't you *want* to marry Wynne?" Arthur asked, hope still wavering in his voice.

Cleve cleared his throat. He focused on Arthur, ignoring Wynne completely. "It's not that simple, lad. Sometimes . . . sometimes . . ." He glanced at Wynne, and their eyes held. "Sometimes a man *also* must kiss a number of maidens before he finds the one he would spend the rest of his days with."

They left it at that, though Arthur was not entirely appeased by their vague words. Cleve went off with two of his men to hunt. Arthur climbed a young oak tree and stared up into the cloudless evening sky. Wynne set the other children to gathering firewood and busied herself with food preparations. But every word Cleve had said repeated itself in her head, like an endless echo that would not fade.

What had he meant? Was she just one among the many women he must have a taste of before he settled upon a wife? Or did he mean that now that he'd tasted several, it was she with whom he would willingly spend the rest of his life?

That did not necessarily imply marriage, of course. He'd not said the word, and she was sure it must be for a reason. He did not wish to marry her, but did he wish to keep her in some other fashion?

Or was she only imagining that because it was at least a more flattering concept than outright rejection?

"*Rhegi*," she swore in frustration. Then she yelped in pain as she sliced into her left index finger with the razor point of her knife.

"Are you hurt?" Druce asked.

She gave him a suspicious look as she sucked at the

wound. "I'll survive," she muttered as she glanced down at the thin line of dark red blood that oozed from the cut.

"You should be more careful with knives." He settled himself amiably onto a grassy spot, leaning on one elbow as he watched her.

Wynne glared at him. "Don't you have something else to do?"

Druce grinned. "Actually I've set aside the next hour or so purely for gloating."

"Gloating?" she asked in initial confusion. Then her lips thinned, for she knew. "Don't waste your time. Or mine."

"Ah, England. Who would think this land could be so fair? Who would expect it to offer such rewards to a group of *Cymry* such as we?"

"England has nothing for us," Wynne snapped. "Nothing whatsoever."

"Not true, Wynne. You know you do but avoid the truth. For one—or two—of our boys, England promises great wealth. For you, well, you have found your one true love."

"I have not!"

"And for me," he continued as if she had not spoken, "for me it offers adventure. Perhaps riches as well. Marriage to a beautiful heiress. Or something," he finished with a carefree shrug.

"This English air does obviously make you daft," she spat.

He studied her with the same nearly black eyes she'd known since they were children together, and without warning Wynne felt a barrier fall. Her quick anger became just as quickly a weary resignation. Druce was one of her oldest and dearest friends, and she desperately needed a friend right now.

He must have seen the change in her expression, for his brows drew together in concern. "Wynne? What is it?"

She gave a huge sigh, stared at him another long second, then turned to squint at the eastern horizon. "I don't know what to do," she admitted in a small voice.

He sat up straighter and peered at her. "About what in particular?"

She shrugged. "About anything. About this Lord Somerville." She paused, then turned her head to meet his encouraging gaze. "About Cleve."

Druce nodded, and a tiny grin lifted one side of his mouth. "I'd say you're doing very well with our Sir Cleve, just by following your basic instincts."

Wynne let out a rude noise and turned away from him. "Men are idiots," she muttered.

"No, just wait a minute, Wynne. Think about it. You've got him completely befuddled. He wants you in the worst way. What more could you want?"

"But I don't *want* him to want me!"

He laughed outright at that. "You do but lie, Wynne ab Gruffydd. To me and to yourself."

They sat in silence a little while. Wynne's full sleeves belled slightly in the freshening evening breeze. The sounds of the camp settling in surrounded them, as did the cry of a lost woodcock and the green rustling of the leaves above them.

She *was* lying to herself, she admitted, rubbing her neck wearily. She did want Cleve to want her, because she wanted him so badly. But that was her body's reaction, and it had nothing to do with common sense or logic.

Druce shifted slightly and cleared his throat. "Last night . . ." he began, but trailed off.

A quick rush of blood suffused Wynne's cheeks with hot color. She licked her lips nervously and chanced a quick glance at him. "What about last night?" she asked in little more than a whisper.

To her partial relief he seemed almost as uncomfortable with the subject as she. "Well, was he . . . you know. Did it . . . Did he—" He took a quick breath. "Did he hurt you?" he finally blurted out.

Wynne focused on the horizon with renewed determination. "No. No, he didn't hurt me. He was . . . he was very gentle."

"Gentle?"

Wynne rounded on him in defensive irritation. "What is it you wish to know, Druce? Would you like a detailed description? Shall I regale you with every . . . every . . ." She trailed off as embarrassment and confusion battled for control. None of this was Druce's fault, she realized. It was pointless to be angry with him.

There was another long pause. Then Druce rose to his feet. "I shall sleep outside your tent for the rest of the journey."

Wynne tilted her head up to meet his determined expression. "That shall solve nothing at all."

But he only grinned, that familiar boyish grin that had charmed almost every maiden he'd ever turned it on. "You are wise in some ways, Wynne. But in the workings of men's minds I've considerably more experience than do you. I shall guard you night and day, from now on."

"But I don't need to be guarded."

Her words, however, fell on deaf ears. Druce ignored all her protests, and indeed, infuriated her with his superior smile. Wynne finally was forced to ignore him in return, pointedly turning her back on him as she sliced turnips, carrots, and garlic with reckless vigor.

A pox on all men, she fumed, dividing one large turnip with a healthy whack. Would that she never had to deal with men ever again, she wished as a trio of carrots succumbed to her blade. Yet as the evening shadows grew, slowly enveloping them in the lavender, then purple of the long summer twilight, her anger could not hold. Was ever there so tangled a web as this one she found herself ensnared in?

Cleve sat on one side of the low campfire, staring at her relentlessly. She sat on the other side, surrounded by children, and with Druce and Barris on either side of her, avoiding Cleve's bold gaze as best she could. But she felt his eyes upon her—while she served the rabbit stew into small tin bowls; while she sat on a rug, eating her meal, though without much appetite; while she shepherded the children to the nearby stream for their evening ablutions.

Druce and Barris, however, kept a constant and prominent position between her and Cleve, and she wasn't certain whether to be relieved or upset. When there were no plausible reasons left for remaining up, she crawled into the tent with the children, only this time she didn't sit in the opening, staring at the Englishmen who still kept company beside the dying fire. She would have had to peer past her two countrymen to see where Cleve sat, and she refused to do that.

She wasn't that desperate for the man. Was she?

Druce wondered the very same thing as he stretched out on a coarse fustian blanket just before Wynne's tent. If the jerkiness of her movements and the stiffness of her bearing were any indication, however, she was well on her way to being completely besotted with the man.

Druce grinned up at the dark velvet of the night sky. Cleve, too, was a study in repressed desire, for his eyes had not once left Wynne the entire evening. Just that one taste of each other they'd had. And look how hungry they were now.

Barris had thought his plot a little mad at first. Keep Wynne and Cleve apart in an effort to drive them together? But Barris had shrugged in good humor and agreed to go along with his older brother's plan.

"Given up on her yourself, then?" Barris had quipped when Wynne had been temporarily out of earshot.

Druce had just laughed. "She's a comely wench, Barris. But she and I are better suited as friends. This Englishman, however, would make her a good husband."

"She hates the English. She's always hated them."

Druce had conceded as much, but he suspected that his primary obstacle would not be Wynne's avowed hatred of the English so much as Cleve's expected reward from this Lord William. Druce had only a few days to raise Cleve's need for Wynne to the breaking point.

If he'd read the tension that had crackled across the campsite tonight correctly, however, that should be more than enough time.

18

They rode into Kirkston Castle just ahead of a fierce summer storm. Clouds, heavy and gray, had welled up from the southwest during the afternoon, threatening the weary band of riders with blustery winds, erratic sheets of lightning, and the ominous rumbling of thunder.

It was a bad omen, Wynne feared as she stared at the stark stone walls that rose so abruptly from a protective circle of black water. She'd heard of moated castles, but never seen one before. The sight only depressed her more. Kirkston Castle seemed an impregnable fortress. A river rushed behind it, and the diverted water of the moat ran around the rest of its perimeter.

Though the bridge extended welcome across the dark waters that surged so restlessly in the storm-driven winds, once that bridge was pulled up, there would be no way to get in or out.

Getting out. That was what concerned her the most.

Rain splattered down in hard, fat drops. The smell of the dust, wet now by the hastening raindrops, rose up to surround her. It was a familiar smell, however, one she knew and reveled in at home, for it presaged the storms of Wales as well.

Perhaps this very storm had shed its tears upon Radnor Manor, she thought wistfully. Perhaps.

Somehow that thought heartened her, and as the horses sensed the end of their journey and picked up their pace, she forced herself to sit more erect and ready herself for what was to come. At least they would have good accommodations and better fare. This Lord William was said to be a wealthy man. His castle certainly looked a prosperous place, for the fields they'd passed had been neat and orderly, and the crops well tended.

She pulled her hood up as the rain began in earnest. She turned to glance at Druce, who'd ridden at her side these past six days, but he was gone. Barris as well had let his laboring mount fall back a small distance.

Even as she looked around, another rider approached her side. To her surprise Cleve fell in beside her, matching his taller destrier to her mare's pace.

"I see your hounds do not guard you so closely as usual," he said, a contemptuous expression on his face.

Wynne lifted her chin and turned to stare somewhere beyond her horse's ears, but she kept her silence. She was torn between admitting that Druce and Barris did this of their own volition and the fear that by placing the blame solely on them she would sound too plaintive and thereby look precisely as she was: a pitiful lovelorn fool. Oh, but there was no justice whatever to be had in this world. Not for women.

"I suppose they feel you are safe once we are under Lord William's roof," he continued in a rough tone. "Well, they are mistaken."

She turned in alarm to stare at him. But was it truly

alarm that caused her heart to quicken so? Was it alarm, or perhaps more accurately anticipation?

He smiled then, a dangerous, wicked smile, and she felt its effect clear to her boot-clad toes. "What do you mean?" she blurted out.

"What do I mean?" He arched one brow in grim humor. But she sensed somehow that his humor was directed more at himself. "I mean that I want you, Wynne ab Gruffydd. One night was not enough for me. Nor for you."

His steed was so near to hers that their knees jostled together. Then he leaned over to take her hand in his, and his voice came low and husky, private words meant only for her. "Evade your guard dogs. Come to me, so we may . . ." He trailed off, fastening his gaze to her mouth when she nervously licked her lower lip. "So we may continue."

Wynne felt as if her heart might burst free of her chest, so mightily did it pound under his potent scrutiny. She swallowed and met his burning gaze with no thought for deception or coyness.

"Come to me tonight," he commanded softly. "Find a way."

"What of . . . what of Edeline?" She whispered the English maiden's name almost fearfully, though she knew she should have been turning him away coldly.

When he frowned and did not answer, however, she tore her gaze from his and stared at the castle they approached. A capricious wind tugged at her hood, forcing it to fall about her shoulders. Though her hair immediately blew in blinding waves around her face, she was glad. It at least blocked the truth of his loyalties from her view. This castle and its lord. This prized English bride of his.

She heard before she saw the armed contingent of

knights that poured through the narrow castle gate. By the time she had her hair twisted in a thick coil and shoved down into her mantle, and her hood back in place, they were surrounded by a jovial crowd of Englishmen.

"What ho? Success, Sir Cleve?"

"It appears five-times success," another voice jested.

"Aye, we met with success," she heard Cleve admit.

"Which little bastard is Lord William's? Or are they all?" one burly fellow asked, leaning to pluck Rhys from where he rode before Derrick.

"Let me go!" Rhys cried as he was held aloft, his arms and legs flailing in quick fear.

"Get your filthy hands off him!" Wynne shouted as all her old hatreds of the English came back in a rush.

At the same time, Madoc screamed, "Leave my brother alone! Let him be, you great oaf!"

Into this sudden pandemonium Cleve forced his destrier, and with an abrupt movement snatched young Rhys from the grinning knight's hands. "You manhandle him who may well hold your fate and that of your family in his hands someday." Cleve glared a warning at the man. "Keep your hands to yourself. That goes for all of you. These children are weary and very likely frightened to be in strange lands."

"And what of the wench?"

Wynne looked up in outrage to see a young, barefaced knight just beyond her mare's head leering at her. Druce angled his horse between her and the knight, and she saw his hand move to his sword.

"Rein in! Both your mounts and your tongues!" Cleve thundered, drawing everyone's attention. "Let us enter and greet Lord William. Your questions will be answered then. Meanwhile you do but confirm the belief of these

Welsh people that all in England are cruel and thoughtless. I had hoped to prove them wrong."

He could never prove her wrong, Wynne fumed as they finally moved forward again. The English knights fell behind the wary party, but as they crossed the heavy plank bridge, she knew that her ordeal had just begun. Like the ominous tolling of a bell, the many hooves of the horses seemed to signal the low, dull warning. These were sad times indeed.

Inside the forecourt a crowd of castlefolk awaited them. Sweet Mother, how vast were the retainers of this Lord William, she realized. His castle was large enough. His fields spread as far as the eye could see. But the numbers of his people!

Cleve led the way through the murmuring throng, toward a raised step before a tall pair of wooden doors. A heavy man stood there. Lord William, she judged, if the quality of his robes was any indication. Four women clustered around him and three men. Of them all, only Lord William smiled. The others eyed the bedraggled party with various degrees of curiosity, doubt, and even suspicion.

And why not? Wynne thought grimly. One of her children could become Lord William's heir, thereby relegating his daughters—and their husbands—to a lesser role in the man's estates. Her gaze narrowed, and she scrutinized the group with a new intensity. How safe would it be for a little child among such a jealous family as they must be? How safe could this Lord William keep her child?

Lord William stepped forward at that moment, and it was then Wynne saw that he walked with a cane. One of his legs had an odd bend at the knee. A broken bone healed badly, she suspected. He was old and in ill health.

How could he safeguard a child if other, younger men should wish the boy dead?

She kicked her mount forward, compelled by her new fear to enlist aid, and it was to Cleve she unthinkingly went. She reached out to grasp his sleeve.

"Cleve! Cleve!" she cried, tugging at him until he turned in her direction. "I'm afraid. For the children."

He frowned. "Don't worry, Wynne. The men's rough curiosity was ill considered, I'll admit. But they meant no real harm."

"No, not them."

But it was too late. They had halted before Lord William, and now that one addressed Cleve after granting her only a cursory glance.

"Welcome, Sir Cleve. Welcome all," he greeted them. "Your messenger announced your arrival. But he did not say that you brought an entire nursery with you." Lord William could not hide his bewilderment.

Cleve grinned at his overlord. "There is much to tell you, milord. But I would rather greet you in private, if that is your wish."

The man nodded, but his brow creased in thought. "I count five children."

Cleve also nodded. He sent Wynne a sidelong glance. "I will explain everything to you."

Lord William let out a noisy breath. "So be it. Anne, Bertilde. See to our guests' rooms. Catherine, Edeline, they will wish some sustenance while Sir Cleve and I speak, but not in the hall. Clear the hall. The meal proper shall wait on us."

The four women jumped to his command. For a moment Wynne forgot her fears as she tried to determine which one might be Edeline. But then she reminded herself sternly that she did not care. Who Cleve was to wed mattered not a whit to her.

"Come with me," Cleve said, taking hold of her horse's bridle.

"I must see to the children first," she replied. "You and your arrogant Lord William will just have to wait."

But he ignored her completely, and that cut her to the quick. "Druce. Barris. You can supervise the children while Wynne and I speak with Lord William." Then he addressed the wide-eyed children. "Arthur, there is nothing to fear here. I want you to be brave and set a good example for the rest. Rhys and Madoc, you were both very brave outside. Can you be just as brave inside?"

The twins shared a look, then slowly their two heads bobbed assent.

"And you girls, Isolde and Bronwen. You shall both be treated as fine ladies at Kirkston. If you wish a bath, or a pastry, you have but to ask. Druce and Barris will be near. And Wynne and I shall return very soon. Will you be all right?"

Not to be outdone by her brothers, Isolde nodded gamely. Bronwen clung to Barris, but she, too, finally murmured her agreement.

Had it not been for her reluctance to upset the shaky calm Cleve had wrought, Wynne would have objected, and loudly, to his presumption. But the children were too round-eyed and their peace of mind too precarious for Wynne to risk unsettling them once more.

She waited, fuming, as he dismounted, then came to help her down. His touch was sure and easy as he lifted her from her mare, and she had to try very hard to ignore the shiver of recognition she felt to have his hands upon her so. But once on her feet, she shook off his grasp and gave voice to her fury.

"Do not think to treat me like a piece of baggage," she muttered in the shelter of the horses.

He gave her a considering look. " 'Tis time to trust me, Wynne. I told you the time would come, and so it has. Leave this to me."

"Leave it to you? Just hand over one of these helpless children to you and this . . . this band of thugs and runagates?"

"Does Lord William look the thug?" he asked in a maddeningly calm voice.

"He is old and infirm now, but seven years ago— What of seven years ago? He was a thug then. And a rapist!"

It was at that inopportune moment that Lord William appeared from around the rump of Wynne's mare. He was stiff with anger, and it was clear he'd heard her last words.

"How unfortunate that she speaks our language so well," he bit out angrily. "You would do well to put a guard on your tongue, wench. Here in England we do not condone such disrespect from our womenfolk."

Wynne rounded on him, her chin outthrust and her fists clenched, fully prepared to let fly with all the furious words that begged to be set free. She meant to flay him with them. But Cleve stood at her side, and he obviously guessed her intentions. Before she could open her mouth he jerked her roughly to his side.

"She is tired, milord—"

"I'm angry, not tired."

"She is distraught over this matter—"

"I am outraged that someone could try to steal—"

"She has raised these five children all alone."

"And not one of them bears a drop of your blood—"

With that last of her interruptions Cleve clamped his hand over her mouth. Though she struggled and clawed, and elbowed him in his ribs as hard as she could, his hand did not give.

"She has been mother to them all these six years past," Cleve spoke as fast as he could. "She cannot yet resign herself to parting with even one of them."

"Then why did you bring her along on this journey? And why bring all the other children?" Lord William snapped. "Achh! I do not wish to stand here and argue like two dogs over a bone. Bring the wench inside." So saying, he turned and limped away.

Wynne's gaze followed him, shooting daggers at his broad back, wishing she could strike him down with only her eyes. She would break his other leg. Or pluck out his heart from his chest, except that he had none.

Her silent invective was cut short, however, by a furious oath from Cleve. He whirled her around and pushed his face almost nose to nose with hers. "Are you a complete fool? Or perhaps merely out of your head!"

"Both, it appears! A fool to think anything good of you. Anything! And out of my head with fury. I should have poisoned the lot of you—"

"Keep silent, woman." He shook her so hard her teeth rattled. "Keep silent and do not speak again until you've thought out your words."

Inexplicably tears started in her eyes. Had she been able, she would have brushed them away. But his hold on her prevented it, so they spilled hot and salty down her cheeks.

"Ah, sweet mother of God," Cleve muttered. For a moment their eyes met and held, and she saw the conflicting emotions he felt. "Wynne, just . . . I don't know. Just try to calm yourself. Speak to Lord William— No, let me do the talking. Just answer any question he directs to you and try to keep your emotions under control."

"Wynne?" Druce and Barris appeared, the children in a cluster behind them. "Shall we stay with you?"

She took a shaky breath and tried to blink back her tears. "No. No, I . . . we . . . we shall speak a little while with this Lord William, and then I'll seek you out." She wiped her face with the backs of her hands when Cleve released her, then she turned to her friends and children with the ghost of a smile on her lips. "I'm all right, and so shall we all be. Go along, now."

Once they had departed, she took several slow, calming breaths. "Are you ready now?" Cleve asked.

She refused either to answer him or to look at him. She was not ready. How could she ever be ready to lose one of her children? But she was as ready as she'd ever be to confront Lord William. Without a word she turned away from Cleve and strode stiffly toward the stone steps and the double wooden doors behind which her worst enemy awaited.

The great hall at Kirkston was easily three times the size of the hall at Radnor Manor. The ceiling soared high enough that a full gallery was fitted at either end. In the middle of one long wall was a huge fireplace, large enough to roast an entire boar, Wynne estimated. Lord William's wealth was evident everywhere she looked. The display of plate upon the surveying board. The huge embroidered tapestry hanging above the wide mantel. Even the generous number of candle branches attested to it. His housekeeping, too, was well managed, if the freshness and abundance of the rushes were any indication.

But the fineness of his abode only caused her to hate him all the more. He already had so much. Must he have one of her children as well?

The lord of the demesne had seated himself on a substantial chair made of English oak and oxhide. Two servants hovered near him, setting pewter mugs and a ewer on the table before him, but at a sharp gesture of his hand they scurried away. Only when the hall was absent of all but the three of them did Lord William speak.

"Which child is mine?" From beneath his thick, beetling brows his eyes jumped from Cleve to Wynne, then back to Cleve. "Which is mine?"

"One of the boys, sire," Cleve replied. "We've narrowed it down to either the twins or the other boy, Arthur. But beyond that . . ." He shrugged. "If you could remember some further detail. Perhaps something of their mother, or the circumstances of—"

"The circumstances of what?" Wynne broke in. "Do Englishmen put to memory each time they brutalize a woman? Rape her? Do they commit the act to memory so they may trot it out to savor again and again—to boast and brag? Your victims' suffering never ceases, yet fat old men like you recount their exploits—"

Cleve's harsh grasp on her arm put an end to her diatribe. But in truth Wynne could hardly go on. Too many awful memories of the past assailed her. Sweet Maradedd had saved her younger sister, but at what a cost to herself.

Keeping a death grip on her upper arm, Cleve addressed Lord William. "Milord, I implore you not to judge her words too harshly. We have traveled long and hard, and she is not pleased to lose a child she has loved so long—"

"So you said before," Lord William barked. He leveled an angry glare upon Wynne. "Who are you, wench? How came you to have possession of a child of mine?"

The very presumptuousness of his words chased Wynne's overpowering sorrow away and replaced it with a burning rage. "They are all the results of English rape upon Welshwomen. *Milord.* Their mothers are gone—all except one who was but a child when she was so viciously raped—"

"You?" he interrupted.

That brought her up short, and she began to shake with impotent fury. "No. Not I. I was saved by my elder sister. She hid me. In my stead she was raped. Over and over. By more men than could ever be counted."

For a long moment her words hung in the air, ugly and cold, like an ominous storm cloud caught within the hall. Hovering. Waiting to destroy them all.

"I did not rape my Angel," Lord Somerville vowed in a voice gone thick with emotion. "No. Not ever."

A bitter smile twisted Wynne's lips. "I wonder if she would say the same."

"Hear the man out," Cleve whispered. His hand slid up and down her arm a fraction, as if he hoped to encourage her.

"She loved me," the old man swore, surprising both Wynne and Cleve with his vehemence. "And I loved her," he added more softly.

For a moment Wynne was hard-pressed to reply, for Lord William's face was contorted in an agony of remembrance. But her brief stab of pity for him was swiftly replaced by the more comfortable emotion of contempt.

"You loved her? You raped her—no, even if your claim not to have raped her is true, you still left her, alone and pregnant, shamed before her people. For seven years you did not care for her. Now you want any child of that union. Any *son*, that is. You will understand, of course, why I scoff to hear that you loved her."

Again Lord William surprised her. She expected anger and outrage at her impudent sarcasm, at her clear disgust. But he only stared at her, a haunted expression on his face.

"Did she . . . did she ever speak of me?"

The heat seemed to dissolve from her anger. Even Wynne could not ignore the abject misery she witnessed in the aging lord opposite her. She started to speak, then hesitated and shook her head in confusion. For an instant she met Cleve's piercing stare, and once again his hand slid along her arm.

Oh, but this was too illogical. Too confusing.

She focused again on Lord William, willing away any softening of her feelings for this man. Toward both of them.

"I did not ever meet any of the children's mothers. Save my own sister, who was mother to Isolde."

He held her eye. "Where are they, then? Why do you have these children?"

Wynne considered her answer. But in truth there would be nothing lost in speaking the truth. She'd done as much to Cleve, and still there was no proof of who fathered any of her children.

"My sister is dead," she began, keeping her explanation brief and her voice cool. It was the only way she could keep the horror of those times at bay. "She was never right after the rape. She flung herself from a cliff once the child was born. Bronwen's mother was but eleven when she was raped. Her parents told her the babe died and they gave the child to me to raise. As for the boys, their mothers are dead." She saw him wince, but pressed on. "Arthur's mother died a few days after giving him birth. The twins' mother died when they were barely walking. Her husband would not raise them once she was gone."

She took a deep breath, relieved as always that her dreadful tale was done. But her gaze never left Lord William. "I raised them all as my own. I am mother to them. They know no other than me."

If she'd thought to shame him, she realized right away that she'd failed. He did not bluster as before. His arrogant and possessive demeanor had been reduced to one more humble and beseeching. But he did not forget his quest.

"Which child—which boy—is my Angel's?"

Once again her anger flared. But before she could respond, Cleve spoke up.

"We cannot be certain, milord. That is why I brought all of them to Kirkston. Perhaps together we can determine the answer to that."

Lord William's gaze remained on Wynne. "And shall you aid us in this task?"

Slowly she shook her head. A lump formed in her throat, and she closed her eyes to avoid the man's beseeching gaze. But that was a mistake, for she was at once overcome by a horrifyingly clear vision of the manor house in Radnor Forest. So vivid was the vision, she could have sworn she was back home. Only there was something wrong.

Wynne jerked her eyes open when she recognized just what it was. There were no children in her vision. No childish voices or giggles. All was quiet and still, just as this hall was. Quiet as death. Empty of life.

Lord William faced her with an almost desperate expression on his coarse, lined face. Cleve waited just at her side, yet she sensed his tension and his anticipation. It emanated from him and seemed to mirror her own confusing emotions. For an aching moment she wondered why he of all men must tap so deeply into her emotions. He tore at that part of her heart that was her very own. And now Lord William tore at the rest of it, that portion that so fiercely loved her children.

Between the two of them they would surely kill her.

Once again she shook her head, steeling herself to speak and behave as if she were not bleeding inside. "I cannot help you."

19

They partook of a sumptuous meal. The five children, Wynne, Druce, Barris, and Cleve all joined Lord William and his daughters and sons-in-law at the high table. But it was not a jovial meal.

Lord William ate silently, staring alternately at Arthur and then at Rhys and Madoc. Cleve sat beside a lovely young maiden, fair-haired and blue-eyed, clearly the youngest daughter, Edeline. The other daughters, most notably Bertilde, were not shy about their dislike of Wynne and her "passel of brats," as one of them had muttered outside of her father's hearing. Their husbands reflected the same resentment on their ruddy English faces.

Perhaps she should solicit *their* aid in returning all her children to Wales, Wynne thought as she pushed a thick piece of venison around her trencher with the point of her knife. Yet that would not help, for even if they could be trusted not to harm her boys—which risk she was not about to take—Lord William and Cleve, not to mention Druce and Barris, would never let this matter die. They were all determined to see Lord William's heir identified and given his rightful place in the man's household.

She sent an aggrieved look toward Druce, then of its own accord her gaze slid to Cleve. Men were truly the most troublesome of God's creatures. Their lands, their castles, their sons. That was all they cared about.

No, she amended as Cleve's gaze collided unexpectedly with her own and her heart began to thud in the most perverse manner. They also cared about women. But only insofar as women provided either pleasure or heirs. She had only to recall Lord William's treatment of the long-dead Angel—or whatever her Welsh name had actually been.

She stood abruptly, breaking the hold of Cleve's dark stare. "Come along, children. 'Tis time we make our ablutions and find our beds."

"But . . . but what of the entertainments?" Lord William sputtered. "I've musicians at the ready. And acrobats."

Wynne stiffened, and her fingertips pressed against the heavy trestle table. "The children are tired and more in need of a good rest than such entertainment. They've had sufficient excitement for one day."

Even as she spoke, Rhys covered a huge yawn with one hand. She sent Lord William a challenging stare. "You will of course concede that I know the limits of these young children's endurance far better than do you."

She saw a glitter of irritation in his eyes, but she did not budge. "Ach, then go ahead," he barked. He waved her away with one sharp gesture, then drank deeply from his goblet. But his eyes followed the progress of the column of children as she herded them down from the raised dais. Had she been stronger and more in control of the circumstances, she would have been most amused by the various emotions that played across the faces of those others remaining at the table. Anger, suspicion, mistrust. Admiration and envy.

She hesitated and peered more intently at the crowded table. Admiration and envy? But it was true. Druce was staring at the young Edeline with the most profound expression of admiration on his face. She'd never seen him so clearly captivated by any woman before. And the maiden in question—Edeline—why, she was gazing at Wynne with an unmistakably wistful look on her innocent face.

Wynne could not make sense of it. Was this the young girl who wished for the deadly nightshade to deepen her eyes? She hardly appeared the coquette.

Edeline lowered her eyes when Wynne looked at her. Then, as if the girl could not prevent it, she peered cautiously over at Druce.

Had the situation been different, Wynne would have laughed. It was that ludicrous. Cleve's affianced was casting longing gazes at the boyishly handsome Druce, while Cleve sent equally potent looks toward Wynne. Lord William gazed with paternal hunger at her sons, while his legitimate family glared at them all.

She shook her head in disgust and pointedly turned her back on the lot of them. Perhaps Lord William should accept Druce as his heir. It would most assuredly please his unwed daughter.

"Do we have to wash?" Isolde asked, sleepily rubbing her eyes with her fist.

Wynne stared down at her exhausted niece and smoothed a wayward lock from her brow. "Just enough to get the road dirt from behind your ears and between your toes, sweetling. Once you're all clean and have fresh gowns on, you'll sleep better than ever."

"Will you sleep with us?" Bronwen asked, an anxious look on her slender face.

"I'll stay with you every single moment," Wynne promised. "We'll all bathe well, eat well, and sleep well while we're at Kirkston," she continued, trying hard to sound encouraging.

"Lord William says we shall ride out with him tomorrow," Rhys began.

"To view his vast estates," Madoc finished.

"And we shall have our own ponies," Arthur added. "I shall have my very own pony. You know, Cleve says I have a horseman's hands."

Wynne only nodded as she directed them toward the kitchen and the shed beside it, which held the bathing caskets. *Bribing them, was he?* And even Arthur was susceptible, thanks to Cleve's earlier encouragements.

Two maids hustled from the kitchen at Wynne's approach. "Ah, milady. You're a'ready here. An' with the little darlin's." The older and stouter of the two beamed. Then she stopped and made an awkward curtsy. "I'm Martha. This here is Dagmar. Milord had us to heat water and prepare the linens. We're to help you with the young'uns."

Though she would have liked to turn away their help, a quick glance at the five exhausted children changed Wynne's mind. She gave the woman a curt nod. "I had laid out their clean gowns in our chamber. If you would fetch them. And my own," she added.

While Dagmar scurried away on that mission, Martha helped Wynne prepare the children for their baths. Like sleepwalkers each of the children reacted when nudged or prodded, raising their arms for their tunics to be removed, sticking out first one foot, then the other for stocking and shoes to be tugged off. Only when the boys were down to just their braies was there any objection raised.

"Go out, now. We can climb into the tub ourselves," Arthur demanded, clutching fast to his rolled linen waistband. When the maids only stared blankly at him, however, he frowned. Then he repeated his words in halting English.

With his skinny legs and skinny chest he looked a meager fellow to be challenging the robust Martha, and a wry smile found its way to Wynne's otherwise glum features. "Yes, Martha," she interjected before Rhys and Madoc could chime in. "They are quite old enough to manage the rest on their own."

The old woman clucked her tongue, but then she gave Wynne a good-natured wink. "I've bathed ever' man of this castle, startin' with milord hisself, and him but a babe in arms. They's all got a time, near about five or six years, when they don't want no help. But then, 'round about the stirring of their manhood, they come back to Martha for their backs to be scrubbed." She cackled with glee. "Guess they want a woman's hand on 'em by then, e'en an old woman's!"

By the time Martha had backed from the room, Wynne's smile had broken free, full and genuine. The girls were laughing, too, and even the boys appeared more relaxed when Wynne pulled the fustian curtain between the two huge caskets of water.

"She's nice," Bronwen murmured as Wynne helped her into the warm and fragrant waters of the women's tub. "She's like Cook, all smiles and happiness."

"I wonder what Cook and Gwynedd and everybody at home are doing right now," Isolde murmured, sinking up to her chin in the swirling bathwater.

Wynne wondered too. "Cook is probably helping

Gwynedd into a nice warm bath, just like this," she answered as a wave of homesickness caught her. In all the days of her journey she'd been too unsettled, too worried and angry and frustrated, to allow herself to miss Radnor Manor. But now as she removed her girdle and untied the side laces of her soiled gown, she was overcome by it.

It was Martha's fault, of course. The old servant had that same warmth and matter-of-fact attitude shared by so many lifelong servants who knew how vital they were to the households they kept. Just like Cook.

She rolled down her stockings, then peeked around the curtain at the boys. Three damp heads rested against the sides of the tall wooden tub. There was no horseplay, no splashing or ducking of heads. They were simply too spent.

"Wake up, sweetlings," she called. "Use the soap and the bathing linens quickly, then we'll see you soon to your beds."

"I'm too tired." Rhys sighed. Then his brother jumped with a splash.

"Who did that? Who pinched me?"

Arthur smiled through heavy-lidded eyes. "I think there's a crab in this tub. 'Tis an old English custom, to put a crab in the bath," he added mischievously.

"You lie," Madoc retorted. "He lies, doesn't he, Rhys?"

Rhys couldn't hold back his mirth. "Here's your crab," and he sent his hand across the water, making pinching motions with his fingers.

"Are there really crabs?" Isolde cried from the other tub.

Wynne shook her head at the boys' antics. She supposed nothing, not even exhaustion and completely foreign environs, could long keep that trio down. She let the curtain fall, then turned to the girls. "They do but tease and play. Come," she added as she removed her own clothes and her amulet. "I promise to pinch back any crab that I find swimming around in our bath."

She let out a groan of satisfaction when she settled herself onto the bench in the tub. The water was warmer and more relaxing than she'd guessed. Mint leaves and rose petals floated on the surface, and the faint scent of them filled her head as was intended, cleansing her mind of troubling thoughts and driving her demons away, at least for a little while.

She let her head sink below the surface, shaking her head and combing her fingers through the tangled length of her hair. "Ah, that feels good." She smiled at Isolde and Bronwen as she reached for the soap. "Shall I wash your hair before I do my own?"

"I can do my hair by myself," Isolde answered.

"Me too," Bronwen echoed.

"Boys, be sure to wash your hair, your ears, and under your necks."

"Under your arms," Bronwen added.

"Between your toes," Isolde grinned.

"You don't have to tell us what to do," Arthur replied from beyond the curtain wall. "We know."

As Wynne lathered her hair, she sniffed at the bar of soap. It was of a very good quality. Hard and even. She wondered if it was made at the castle. She would have to ask Martha, for her own soaps were not nearly so fine-textured. She ducked underwater again, rinsing her hair and rubbing her scalp hard, when a commotion outside brought her sputtering to the surface.

"Which one was it? Which one?" came Lord William's excited voice from the kitchen beyond.

"Wait, milord. 'Tis not seemly—"

But Martha's nervous words were ignored. Lord William burst into the bathing chamber, much to Wynne's complete outrage.

"Begone from here, you . . . you crude Englishman. Can we not at least bathe in peace?"

" 'Tis my castle," Lord William bellowed. " 'Tis my son! Now, which one was it?"

As Wynne sat there, naked in the tub with the two terrified girls trembling in her arms, a veritable crowd of people pressed into the small bath house. The curtain between the tubs was thrown aside, and to her horror both tubs were surrounded by an avid audience.

"Milord, if you please," Martha began, casting an uneasy eye from her master to Wynne and back again.

"Yes, Father," Edeline murmured, clutching at her father's arm. "Can this not wait long enough for them to at least clothe themselves?"

"Show me their feet," Lord William demanded, shaking off Edeline's arm and ignoring her completely. He advanced to the edge of the tub and grabbed Rhys. "Show me your feet!" he insisted.

But Rhys was too afraid to comply. He fought to be free of the man's frantic grasp. Then, when that failed, he bit down on Lord William's hand. Hard.

"By damn! By damn, he bit me!" Lord William shook his hand at the pain and peered at it as if expecting to see blood, or at the very least tooth marks. Then he raised his head and swung it around, eyeing the apalled spectators. "He bit me! God's blood, but he's a true fighter, that one is. Is *he* the one? Is *he* my son?"

"No!" Wynne cried, finally finding her voice amidst these mad proceedings. Had the entire world turned upside down? "They're none of them yours. None of them!" She started to rise, for she needed to save the trio of boys from this ruthless barbarian of a man. But a large hand on her shoulder kept her firmly in her place.

"Milord, this is not the way to handle this matter." Cleve stood steady when Lord William turned an impatient frown upon him. "If everyone will clear the chamber," he continued, "we can see your question promptly answered."

For a moment there was absolute silence, save for the nervous shifting of feet. Then Martha clucked her tongue and began to wave her apron in a shooing fashion. One by one Lord William's daughters, sons-in-law, and curious retainers shuffled away. When only Cleve, Lord William, Druce, and Barris remained, Martha closed the door.

"Now, back with the rest of you. All of you," she insisted, glaring at her master. "I never thought to see the Lady Alvinia's son act in so unseemly a manner. Terrifying women and children at their bath. Were she to see you now, why she would . . ." Martha trailed off once it was clear Lord William was appropriately subdued. She drew the curtain, then rounded on Cleve, who stood beside the tub, his hand warm upon Wynne's bare shoulder. "You too," the old servant ordered, scrutinizing him closely.

Cleve's hand gentled on Wynne's shoulder and slid lightly, rubbing beneath the water's surface, slipping along her flesh. His fingers stroked lightly up the sensitive skin along her neck until he cupped her chin, forcing her to face him.

"Give us a moment, if you please," he said to Martha, though his eyes never strayed from Wynne's.

There was another disapproving cluck from Martha, but she obliged. Though Lord William's muttered demands and the old woman's soothing murmurs came through from beyond the curtain, Wynne's every sense was attuned to Cleve. He was the only one who could help her.

"Don't let him do this, Cleve. I beg you. Please, don't let him take any of my children."

Though her eyes swam with desperate tears, she saw clearly the regret on his face. For a moment she believed he would do it. He would intercede and somehow, in some way, he would make things right again. But then he swallowed and shook his head.

"He wants to know his child, Wynne. To give his heir the full benefit due him. How can that be wrong?"

"No!" Wynne jerked away from him. She wanted to leap from the water, to attack Lord William. To kill him with her bare hands if necessary. But Isolde and Bronwen were weeping in her arms, and if the sounds from the men's bathing area were any indication, the boys were doing the same with Druce and Barris.

"Get out of here," she ordered, glaring at Cleve over the girls' wet heads. At that moment, as he stood there tall and expressionless, his gray tunic wet with water, she truly hated him. He'd brought her to this bleakest moment of her life, him with his easy smile and seductive glances. He'd wooed the children first, then he wooed her. But it had all been in the name of achieving his initial aim.

Their gazes met and held, hers cold as winter, his shuttered, hiding whatever emotions he felt. *If* he indeed felt any at all.

She took a slow, shaky breath. "Make everyone leave. Everyone. I'll dress the children. Then and only then may your English lord enter."

"Trust me, Wynne. 'Tis time to trust me. I can help you in this."

A flicker of emotion showed in his eyes, but Wynne did

not care. Her smile was bitter. "You only wish to help yourself. Just . . . just leave me be."

After a moment he sighed and shrugged. Then he turned on his heel and moved past the curtain. She heard him murmur and Lord William's indignant reply. "I just want to see their toes!" But Cleve's reply was firm, and after a little shuffling the door closed with a thud.

"Arthur? Rhys, Madoc? Are you all right?"

"Can we come in with you?" Arthur's voice came, thin and wavering.

"Of course, love."

Water sloshed, and three sets of feet hit the stone floor. At once the boys barreled past the curtain and clamored into the women's tub, bare bottoms gleaming in the dim light. As she clutched them all to her as best she could, Wynne remembered another time, four years earlier. How overcome with responsibility she'd felt as five toddlers had clung to her for comfort. She'd been so inadequate to the task then, but she felt even more inadequate now. She wanted so much to protect them—from the horror of their terrible conceptions, from the difficulties life would present them. But she couldn't do it. Not anymore. She couldn't even keep them with her any longer.

Her tears mingled with theirs as they huddled in the tub, no longer comforted by the warm water and the pleasant fragrances. This was England, and they were surrounded by enemies.

"Why—" Madoc hiccupped, then began again. "Why does he want to see our toes?"

"Is he going to make fun of them?" Rhys added.

Wynne tried to swallow past the lump in her throat. She was so accustomed to the slight difference in the twins' toes that it hadn't occurred to her that it might be an inherited trait like any other. Oh, why hadn't she foreseen this? "I think that perhaps he has the same sort of toes."

Arthur straightened and pushed his wet hair from his eyes. "You mean Lord William has duck toes?"

"They're not duck toes!" Bronwen cried in sudden defense.

"Hush, my darlings. Hush. Of course they're not really duck toes. But they do have that extra bit of flesh between them, and I suppose, well, that you probably took that trait from one of your parents."

She pressed her lips together, willing her voice to stay steady. "I have my father's blue eyes. Arthur, Isolde, and Bronwen all carry some English traits in the color of their hair or their eyes. But you two, Rhys and Madoc, you are so dark-haired and dark-eyed. You have always appeared Welsh through and through."

"Except for our toes," Rhys said.

"I think so."

They sat in silence a moment. The sobbing had ceased save for an occasional trembling breath, and the hiccups also were easing. Then Bronwen pulled a little away from Wynne.

"Will Rhys and Madoc have to stay here with their . . . well, with their father?"

The words of denial Wynne wished to speak died unsaid. Their father. Could it be true? Could that great blustering oaf actually have fathered her sweet, troublesome twins? Unbidden, his tremulous question about their mother came back to her. He'd wished to know if she'd ever spoken of him. And his face had gone gray to hear she had died. He'd gone so far as to claim that the woman had loved him.

Wynne gazed down at the twins' dark heads. She was far too confused to keep her thoughts in order. If the woman *had* loved him . . . And he seemed in his own crude fashion to have cared for her . . .

She swallowed against her terrible choking fear and tried to pick her words carefully. "Perhaps . . . perhaps they will wish to stay *if* Lord William is their father. But I will not see any of you forced into a life you do not wish," she added vehemently. She forced her tears away. "Come, now. Let us complete our bathing and greet Lord William once more."

"I wish Sir Cleve was my father," Arthur remarked, more to himself than to anyone else.

Wynne helped the boy climb from the tub. "There are many, *many* more worthwhile men in the world," she muttered. "Welshmen."

"Shall you not marry him after all?"

Wynne frowned. "Use that toweling to dry yourself, Arthur. And I never intended to marry him. I told you that. Anyway he is to wed the Lady Edeline."

Arthur sighed, and after a last wistful look he did as he was told.

"Lady Edeline is very beautiful," Isolde said once the boys were out of sight.

"Druce was staring at her all through the meal," Bronwen added.

"Well, she is betrothed to Sir Cleve," Wynne retorted as she rose dripping wet from the tub. "And that is that."

Wynne had convinced herself of that very fact when she bid Lord William, Cleve, and the others to enter the bathing chamber. The children hung behind her, all clean and dried, with damp hair combed back from their wary faces, and fresh gowns and tunics on. But they were all barefoot.

Lord William, too, had shed his shoes, and his toes fairly wiggled with anticipation. But it was the expression on his face that disturbed Wynne the most, for his aging features were suffused with a longing and a hopefulness that made him appear almost young again.

Her gaze shifted of its own accord to Cleve, and she recognized the concern in his eyes. But it was too little, she told herself. And it came far too late.

"Come here," Lord William commanded in a hoarse voice barely more than a whisper. "If you have funny toes —duck toes, my mother used to call them—then show yourself to me."

Wynne's heart pounded so hard, she surely thought it would explode. She could not move. But Arthur did. He nudged his brothers forward. "Go on. Show him. He's your father."

Wynne did not witness the rest. She could not. Rhys and Madoc stepped hesitantly forward, encouraged by Lord William's wondrous smile and Cleve's reassuring presence. They compared toes—old, hairy toes with long, yellowing nails against plump, little toes, rosy from the bath. But all were made the same by the odd flange of flesh that connected the second and third toes together.

With a glad cry Lord William fell to his knees and embraced the startled twins. But Wynne's tears blinded her to their reunion. She clutched her remaining children to her breast, unable to contain her sobs any longer.

"My sons!" Lord William wept with heartfelt emotion. "Oh, Angel, my Angel. At last I have our sons!"

20

Kirkston Castle was not a place arranged for privacy. Although Wynne slipped down the dim stone stairwell, servants and retainers abounded, curled in their rugs and robes, asleep wherever a niche presented itself. In the hall itself Lord William still sat, toasting his great fortune—two sons!—with whoever managed still to match him toast for toast, drink for drink. Even the forecourt was not empty, Wynne found. A merry bonfire flamed high, and the servants who had not yet succumbed to sleep milled around in excitement. The birth of a son was always a joyous occasion in any noble household. With the arrival of *two* sturdy sons, however, Lord William's castlefolk clearly anticipated some display of generosity on his part.

And well he should be generous, Wynne thought, leaden-hearted. Not often was a man blessed with such fine sons as Rhys and Madoc—not that the man deserved them. He'd done no more than spill his seed, and indiscriminately at that.

Yet he claimed her precious boys as his now, and no one was inclined to challenge him save her.

Wynne pulled her hood about her face and wrapped her

mantle tighter around her arms. But the cold that enveloped her, setting her teeth to chattering, came not from without but from within. Her heart—her very soul —was frozen. She could no longer feel anything at all. But it was the only way she could function, at least until she could find some private place to collapse in helpless grief.

As if she hadn't cried enough already, she thought as she peered about through red-rimmed eyes. She'd cried before them all, revealing her complete devastation and upsetting the children. When had she first begun to lose all control over her emotions?

The answer was obvious. When Cleve FitzWarin had made his fateful ride into Radnor Forest. From before she'd even laid eyes on him, he'd begun his insidious attack on her emotions. And now he'd won.

She edged around the bonfire, staying beyond the reach of its flaming light, keeping well to the shadows. Past the kitchen and the bath house she crept, searching—she did not know precisely what she searched for. Around a heavy timbered corner and then along the rough stone outerwall, she let her left hand trail along the cold stones as she moved through the darkness. Once she heard a man's voice somewhere above her. A guard on the ramparts. Was there no place for her to find solace?

Then, in the pitch-darkness of the overcast midnight, her hand met with wood. She stopped and ran inquiring fingers around the weathered surface. It was the postern door—probably leading to the river, if her bearings were correct.

She found the heavy ring and pulled. To her surprise the door opened with very little protest. She peered inside, then driven by her desperation, she stepped within the depths of the thick castle wall. At once she stubbed her toe on a bucket, and when she reached out to prevent herself from falling, her hand knocked down several slender poles. Fishing poles, she realized, once she'd righted herself. This door must indeed lead to the river.

Through a door, twin to the first, she went, and suddenly she stood outside Kirkston's mighty walls, perched on a little stone landing.

It might have only been her imagination, but Wynne doubted it. The air was indeed clearer here, fresher and cooler. She sucked it into her lungs in great drafts, feasting upon the scent of the forests and fields, the river and sky.

The storm had left that washed scent over the earth, and the river plunged and fought the banks on its downward course to the distant sea. Did this river lead to Wales? she wondered, caught in a huge wave of homesickness. Could she simply fling herself into its watery embrace and be delivered into her homeland?

Oh, that would be so easy. But it was only wishful thinking.

Not conscious of her movements, she shed her hood and mantle. Next she removed her shoes and stockings. Then she gingerly stepped down the steep ladder that slanted from the narrow landing to the rocky spit of land that edged the straight castle wall.

Two small boats lay upon the steep incline and rested now upside down. Wynne saw their pale bottoms but dimly in the darkness. However, the rushing water she sensed well enough. Like a living creature it heaved and twisted, glinting back whatever meager light the heavens offered.

How angry that river seemed. How mournful.

She moved forward, feeling her way with her toes until she felt the icy spray. Further she went, hiking her skirts above her knees and reveling in the frigid tug of moving water on her ankles and calves.

The sounds of the river enveloped her, and its winter-cold caress consumed all her attention. Kirkston Castle no longer rose at her back. This was not England at all. She was, for that moment at least, in her beloved forests, standing barefoot in a river she claimed as her own.

Then without warning another presence filled her, and she knew—as she'd known that very first day—that Cleve was there.

She didn't turn. She stayed as she was, wishing she could will him away, wishing she could send him to the most distant edges of the far-flung world. Far beyond the reaches of Christendom itself. Yet in the very same moment she was perversely gratified by his nearness.

"Are you all right?" he asked, his voice a quiet sound against the wild, rushing night.

She shook her head in answer. What use in pretending? So he might ease his conscience?

She sensed when he moved closer. If she reached out behind her, she could have touched him. But she stared straight ahead, peering through the darkness, across the waters to the invisible shore beyond.

"Wynne." His voice came from even nearer than she'd suspected. "I know this day has been . . . well, hard for you."

A bitter smile flitted across her face. "Hard? Perhaps that is the word you would choose. But then, I'm surprised you even admit to that, convinced as you've been all along that this was best for my children." She paused, and swallowed the lump rising in her throat to choke her. "As if *you* could know what was best for them."

"Ah, Wynne. In many ways I do know. I *was* them, remember?"

She whirled to face him at that. "It's not the same!" she cried, almost relieved to confront him at last. "You had your mother. You never lost her. But I . . . I have lost them!"

Though the darkness lay like a chasm between them, she accused him with her eyes and knew he received the message.

Yet he forged on, relentless as ever. "Do you mourn for them or for yourself? And think hard on your answer before you give it. Do you fear they shall suffer their loss less than shall you?"

Wynne drew herself up, but she was unable to completely still the trembling that overtook her, head to toe. She clenched her hands into fists so hard that her nails gouged her palms. "They shall not suffer a roof over their heads. Nor food for their bellies. Fine garments. Fine steeds. Everything that man may purchase they will undoubtedly possess. But what of a parent who loves them—?"

"Even you cannot doubt Lord William's true affection for Rhys and Madoc," Cleve said, interrupting her impassioned words.

"He is a stranger to them. And yes, he is glad to have them. But what of a year from now? Or two? Or five? When they are ill or frightened? Will he give them comfort as a mother would? As I would?" She paused for breath and thrust a wind-whipped lock of hair back from her cheek. "Even you had a mother."

"But they need a father now."

"Not him," she vowed. "Not an Englishman."

In the silence between them the river chortled, cold and mirthlessly onward. She knew her last words had been as much an insult to Cleve as to Lord William, and she would not deny to herself that she'd meant them as such.

She wanted to hurt him. She fairly ached to hurt him as he'd hurt her.

But he seemed even more determined to remain unaffected by her words.

"Perhaps they need both," he offered. His hands spread wide in appeal. "Perhaps it need not be so final an arrangement as you fear. If you would consent to stay . . ."

He let the words trail off, let them be lost to the night elements. Yet that husky suggestion remained with Wynne, echoing in her head, both a promise and a threat resounding in her soul. She took a breath, bolstering her suddenly weakened resolve. But Cleve seemed able to sense her every emotion. He knew where she was the most vulnerable.

"Stay here, Wynne. Stay near to your sons. I can arrange it."

She shook her head, fighting the terrible allure of it. To be near them always. To be near Cleve.

"No, no," she muttered, wishing he did not fill her vision so. She glanced around, almost desperate now. Then, when no solution presented itself, she jerked about to stare once more across the black, swirling river. Her fingers curved desperately around the ancient Radnor amulet, and she took a step deeper into the icy water until it lapped at her knees. If only she could escape. From Kirkston Castle. From Cleve.

But it was not to be. Cleve's hands found her shoulders, and without speaking he guided her back onto the shore. Only when she was seated upon one of the upturned boats did he release her, and then it was to pace restlessly upon the gravel-strewn bank before her.

"The thing is, if you stayed it would solve a multitude of problems."

"Yours? Or mine?" Wynne responded derisively.

"Ours, Wynne. Ours." He crouched on his heels before her and took her cold hands within his own. "Your children are all half English. To raise them on English soil would not be so terrible a thing. And they would be well taken care of. All of you would."

"By you?" Wynne ventured in a voice she meant to be mocking, but which, even to her ears, sounded dismayingly weak.

"By me."

For that moment it all seemed so easy. If she stayed, she would have to give up no one. Not the twins. Not Cleve . . . But just as quickly she realized that she would be giving up a home and a life of her own. She would be giving up herself to this man, and for what?

"And what of me? What would I do with my life here? Have you thought of that? How would I bear it—to live in England? Away from my forest. Away from my Wales."

"I would . . ." He hesitated, and his thumbs rubbed along the sensitive flesh of her inner wrists. "I would do anything—everything—to make you happy here. We would be together, and you would soon come to see that England is not unlike your Wales. Our life here could be good."

If she could simply have closed her eyes and willed his words to be true, Wynne knew she would gladly have done so. If her skills as Seeress were all they'd at times been purported to be, she would have made his pretty vision come to pass. But there was that part of her that was sensible, logical. Practical. What he dared to imagine was an impossible dream.

"Our life," she began. "Our life could never be. There is no future for us together. Or do you forget the Lady Edeline?"

His hands tightened almost imperceptibly about hers. Then he sighed. "No. I do not forget Edeline."

Wynne steeled herself to go on, though a new ache had unaccountably risen in her chest. " 'Twill soon be announced—your wedding. She shall make a lovely bride, if not an altogether willing one."

"What do you mean?"

Envy was what drove her to speak so. Envy and hurt. It was so obvious, so clearly apparent, that Wynne did not even attempt to pretend otherwise. "I mean that she is the one who asked for belladonna—the deadly nightshade. She is the one who casts her pretty darkened eyes in other directions than yours. Even Druce has not escaped her notice."

She smiled grimly in the face of his silence. "Do I take it that you are jealous of her straying attentions?"

"You may take it any way you like," he growled. "My marriage to Edeline is necessary if I am to keep you here. Her dowry lands, joined with the reward Lord William has promised me—"

"I will not hear this!" Wynne jerked to her feet and tried to sidestep Cleve. But he would not release her hands, nor when he stood would he let her pass.

"Wynne, listen to me. If you would just be sensible about this."

"No! No, I will not be sensible. Not if I must demean myself. Lose all my self-respect. I am a woman, Cleve, not a possession. You English are all the same, rapists or no. You think a woman is to be owned, to be used and kept as will satisfy your urgings of the moment. But I am not some simpering—simpleton—Englishwoman. And I will never—" Her voice broke and her words came out on a sob. "No, never," she finished brokenly.

In that moment, an instant of sudden clarity—perhaps

it was one of her visions—Wynne knew what she wanted of Cleve. She would have him for her own husband, to live in her forests and father their own children. She wanted to lie down with him and let him fill her again with his warmth and power and the very beginnings of a new life. He would make such a good father; he was a magnificent lover. He could be a very good husband if he so desired.

On that thought her animosity and need to hurt him fled. If she could, she would have healed them both of their wounds by the very strength of her longing for him.

Oh, Cleve, the cry came silent from her very soul. *Why couldn't things have been different for us?*

As if he heard her cry, he pulled her fully against him. "Say you'll stay," he groaned the words against her mouth. His hands roamed her back as if he marked every rib, every muscle, every curve. He cupped her derriere, proving to her the depths of his own desire with the hard thrust of his hips against her belly. His tongue delved deep, and when he found welcome, he stroked urgently within her lips, slipping in hot, wet forays, deeper and deeper, seeking to know all her secrets.

Wynne accepted his every sensual aggression and wanted still more. Yet even amidst such an agony of longing, she nonetheless knew that there was one secret she must never let him know. Though she succumbed both to the physical and the emotional pleasures of his nearness, she kept that one bit of herself apart. If it were hard now to leave him, how much harder would it be if he knew her secret fantasies of them together? Of him loving her. Marrying her.

But that would never happen, and she well knew it. He could not be a husband to her. And she would not be merely a mistress to him.

She arched against him and tightened her fingers in the warm strands of his hair as he broke their kiss. They both gasped for breath. The very violence of her feelings for him was bewildering, and without thinking she began to kiss his neck and throat.

"By damn, woman," he panted when her teeth nipped the smooth flesh alongside his neck. "Sweet Jesu," he groaned when she moved her lips to the prickly skin beneath his chin. One of his hands moved down from her shoulder to run along her back. Then his other hand found her right breast, and the power of their previous joining came back to her in glorious detail.

Her hands slid down to his hips and urged him forward until their loins pressed close once more. Then in a bold move she had not herself anticipated, Wynne slipped one of her hands between their bellies and let herself touch the hard ridge of his manhood.

"Witch," he muttered in a harsh tone. But to Wynne the word was the sweetest of caresses, a delight to her ears, a balm to her soul. If she did not prompt him to abandon his lifelong goals for her sake, at least she made him forget them when they were together like this.

A streak of lightning split the sky beyond the river, and then another, much closer. The night flashed brilliant with white light, then plunged them into darkness once more. But the blackness was heated and made transparent by the pure awareness between them.

She rubbed her flattened palm against him and heard his groan—felt it—upon her lips. His hands caught her head, tangling in her wind-blown hair and tilting her face up to his. Like a wild man he devoured her, and like a wanton she offered herself for his pleasure—and her own.

"I'll make you stay," he murmured in her ear as he dragged her to the ground with him. He pulled her to lie upon him and bent one knee to press up between her parted legs, forcing her to straddle him. "You'll stay. You'll want to stay."

Wynne kissed him hard—anything to stifle those words that cast such a chill upon their fiery mating. But Cleve would not desist, and his hands cupped her face to halt her frantic kisses.

"Say you'll stay," he demanded. He kissed the curve of her neck and the hollow of her throat. "Say you'll never leave me, Wynne. Say it."

A huge bolt of lightning, accompanied at once by a crack of violent thunder, made them both jump. But though Wynne hoped it would divert him from his painful question, it was not to be.

He rolled them both over, covering her completely with his hard and virile body. Though she recoiled from his words, her body reacted on its own to the exquisite pressure of his arousal against her belly.

"Don't talk anymore," she whispered. "Just kiss me." She circled his neck with her arms and tried to draw his face down to hers, but he resisted. His leg shifted to rub seductively against the juncture of her legs, and she writhed helplessly in reaction.

"Stay with me, my sweet Welsh witch. Say you'll stay, and I promise to make you writhe this way every night. Stay, and I shall shower you endlessly with kisses. With caresses. Like this." He nuzzled the warm place between her breasts. "Like this." He found her taut and protruding nipples through the fabric of of her kirtle and gown and bit on the aroused crests—first one and then the other— until she was panting and twisting in mindless desire.

"I'll keep you sated with my loving so that you'll forget anyplace except where we are together."

He'd done that already, she knew in some vague part of

her mind. She was never conscious of where she was nor of what was right or wrong when he loved her this way. But to lose oneself so . . . It was too dangerous. Too frightening.

She looked up at him, and when their eyes met, they held in a long, telling connection. As if it literally fled her body, Wynne felt her resolve weaken, and that nagging voice of caution in her head was silenced at last. "Oh, Cleve," she whispered as tears formed in her wide eyes. "I . . . I . . ."

An ear-splitting crash drowned out the last of her words. Lightning struck a tree directly across the river from them, and with a bright flash and a shower of sparks, it toppled into the raging river. So near had it come that the hair stood out on Wynne's arms and the overcharged air seethed with restless energy.

Cleve had jerked in startled response and had thrown himself flat over her, protecting her head in the crook of his neck. Now, as they both looked up, an icy sheet of rain abruptly pelted them, pushed forward on an angry wind.

They'd been warned by the advancing lightning and distant thunder. They'd been given fair notice by the surging river riled by the storm brewing in the hills above them. But it had taken the mighty fist of God, she was later to think, throwing bolts of lightning upon her and dousing her with rain, to finally drive sense into her head and to save her from her own weak desires. She had been ready to consent to stay with him, to agree to become his mistress, the woman he turned to *after* doing his duty to his wife.

As Wynne sprinted across the mud-slick courtyard, fleeing Cleve while he wrestled with the two postern doors, she searched for some comfort at her unlikely salvation. For saved she had indeed been. Saved from a life of illicit pleasures and bastard babies. Saved from years spent longing for what could never be. He did not mean her to marry him; he'd never once spoken the words. But instead of comfort, she felt only an awful emptiness.

She stumbled over one groggy servant in her pell-mell flight through the great hall, then nearly stepped on another curled upon the bottom tread of the stairs. But she fled onward, unmindful of the wet trail she shed. She only knew that she must find her children and hold on to them. They were her life, not Cleve. And Wales was her home, not England.

In the darkened chamber she stripped herself of her wet garments and donned a dry kirtle. Then she bound her wildly tangled hair in a strip of old linen and, trembling all the while, found Rhys and Madoc. They grumbled when she slid them apart. One of them flailed out, and she made out the words "a horse. No, two." But once she lay between them, they both settled down.

They were warm, and she was safe. That thought circled around and around in her head as she tried to calm her rapid breath and still her galloping heart. They were warm, and she was safe.

But such a cowardly thought made her ashamed of herself. Their safety was more important than her own. She must bury her fears—and most of all her inappropriate desires—and tend sensibly to her sons' futures.

She slid an arm about each of them, pulling them close until she smelled little boy mingled with rose water. How dear they were to her. Only yesterday they'd been a pair of squirming babes in her arms, and already they were tall, hale lads, eager to master every new skill or challenge they met. Soon they would be strapping youths and then men.

Was she wise to oppose Lord William's claim on them

—and perhaps lose them the vast inheritance the man would bestow upon them?

She stared up at the dark-beamed ceiling and reluctantly let herself imagine her worst fear brought to life: If they stayed and she left . . .

The minutes passed. Outside, the storm howled against the sturdy stone tower. But inside her heart she faced a storm infinitely worse.

Finally the tears ceased. Finally she accepted what the fates so unfairly decreed. But she would drive a hard bargain with that man—their father—she vowed. He would concede much if he would keep her boys with him. They would have every advantage—books, tutors, not just horses and weapons.

And one thing more, she decided as Cleve's image intruded once again, despite her best effort to keep it at bay. Since they would already be possessed of castles and demesnes, Lord William must vow to give them complete freedom to marry as they pleased. To marry for love alone, not for money or lands or political expedience.

She took a trembling breath and willed away the emotions that threatened to swamp her again. Rhys and Madoc would never find themselves torn between two women, wanting the one for her fortune and the other for herself. Whosoever they eventually wed, at least Wynne would know it was for love and happiness.

For she knew that they, like Cleve—like most men, she feared—could easily choose a wife for practicality and a mistress for love.

Lord pity the women—both wives and lovers—hurt by such cruelty.

But not her. Not any longer. Her heart was closed to Cleve now, and it always would be. And even if she should ache for him inside, she would never reveal it. No, not ever.

21

"We need to talk." Wynne spoke the words to Lord William in her haughtiest tones. The early-morning sun streaked through the narrow windows to illuminate a hall still redolent of the previous night's celebrations, and the one who had celebrated the most vigorously was plainly the lord himself. He sat in his huge chair, his robes in disarray and his hair standing in erratic gray spikes about his haggard face. Yet despite what must have been an aching head and a foul-tasting tongue, he managed nevertheless to appear very well contented.

"So we do. So we do." He waved her to a chair at his left hand, then gazed about through bloodshot eyes. "Where is my ale? And bread? I'll have cheese as well!" he bellowed to the few servants who stirred at such an early hour. Then he grasped his head between his hands and groaned. "You select a troublesome time to speak with me, mistress witch."

Before she could react to that impertinent term, he grimaced. "Pardon, mistress. Pardon. I did but repeat in an unguarded moment something I had last night overheard."

"From Sir Cleve, I'll warrant."

Lord William shrugged under her irritated scrutiny. "Do not fault him for having found my two sons for me. If it had not been him, it would have been another." His expression grew more watchful. "For I *would* have found them, no matter what."

Wynne lowered herself into the hide-covered seat. "Perhaps. Your determination is obvious," she added, resolving not to antagonize him simply for the sake of vengeance for her own loss. She had a more important purpose this morning.

A ewer of ale was placed between them along with two cups and a tray of bread, cheese, raisins, and almonds. Lord William took a long pull of his drink, exhaled a huge sigh, and wiped his mouth with the back of one heavily embroidered cuff. Only then did he appear ready to hear her speak. Her first words, however, would be the most difficult, and she cleared her throat nervously.

"It appears that Rhys and Madoc may well be your— the result of—" She broke off.

Lord William's brow lowered. "They were not conceived in rape." His eyes bored into hers, unflinching in their intensity. "My Angel was . . . she was everything to me."

"Then why didn't you marry her?"

He straightened, and she saw the pain in his face. "I already had a wife. But I asked Angel to come with me. I knew she bore my child—my children. Only she would not come to England."

How alike men were, Wynne thought as she fought back her own stab of pain. They considered the role of mistress to them almost an honor. She shook her head.

Lord William must have taken her motion for commiseration, for he continued. "I would have been so good to her. Only . . . only she would not raise her children as English bastards." His lips thinned as he said the words, and he passed his hand over his face as if he might scrub away the oppressive memories. "At any rate I left her with all the coin I had. I knew she meant to wed with a man she'd known before—if he returned from the wars—and it enraged me. Still, I would rather her happily wed to another than dead."

Wynne could not help responding to the plaintive note of loss in his aged voice. Though she would like to have seen him suffer, she found herself reassuring him.

"She was happy while wed. And her husband loved her. It was just that after she died trying to birth his own son, well, the distraught fellow could not bear to raise someone else's. Or so I was told by the two women who brought the twins to Radnor Manor."

Lord William nodded, and for a moment they were quiet together. A cock crowed somewhere without the castle, and one of the servants poked in the massive hearth, searching for embers to rekindle the flame. Then Lord William pushed his cup away from him.

"Did my sons sleep well?"

"Yes. All the children did. They sleep yet, for they were sorely tired by their journey."

"Today we shall celebrate the whole day long."

Wynne raised one brow knowingly. "Are you certain you are quite up to it?"

The softness fled his face, and before her very eyes he became the stern lord of Kirkston. "Do not dare to doubt it. There is not the man in my vast holdings to best me at anything I choose to do." At her disbelieving look he relented, but only slightly. "Riding is hard for me since I broke my leg. But nothing else," he insisted.

Wynne shrugged. "The day will come when Rhys and Madoc shall take pride in besting you at everything."

He grinned at that. "Aye, so they will. And I will take pleasure in ceding to them. Though I will not make it easy for them."

"I would have an agreement between us." Wynne changed the subject without warning. He eyed her suspiciously, but she continued on unperturbed. "I have cared for these boys up to now. I know them best, and I know what is best for them."

"If you wish to remain here to be with them, I will not oppose it."

Wynne frowned. "I am *Cymry*. My home is not here."

"But Cleve said—"

"Your Sir Cleve is a fool," she snapped.

He leaned back at that, saying nothing. However, Wynne did not appreciate the gleam that lit his eyes, as if Cleve had been telling him things about her that were better left unsaid. She continued, struggling to regain her composure. "The thing is, if you would keep the twins, then I would have certain concessions from you."

He eyed her noncommittally, "I have no need to make any concessions to you. However, I'm feeling generous today." He paused. "Name your price."

Once again her anger flared. "God save me from fools! I do not wish your *coin* nor whatever other riches you may boast of. I speak of my children's happiness, now and long into the future. You may not throw coins of appeasement at *me* and expect to have bought a clear conscience."

Lord William's face mottled in shame, and she knew he realized she spoke as much of the boys' mother, Angel, as she did of herself.

"What do you want, then?" he bit out the words, glowering at her all the while.

"They shall have tutors."

He waved his cup about. "Of course they shall have tutors. I am a great lord, and they are my sons."

"Tutors for Latin. For reading and religion. Music," she continued, unaffected by his bluster. When his brows lowered as if to take exception, she only smiled. "I am reassured that you shall make of them fine horsemen. No doubt they will meet your rigorous standards for jousting, swordplay, and skill with every other weapon yet devised by men. The management of your people and lands, and even the dispensing of justice, you will impart with a thoroughness I hope never to find fault with. But I, who have made of them the honest and inquisitive, wonderful boys that they are, I demand that they be tutored as I would have seen them done, in matters that shall make of them truly fine men."

He sat in silence when she finished her speech. Only the thoughtful drumming of his fingers on the sticky trestle table gave evidence that he considered her demands at all. Finally he gave a nod. She thought he may have smiled ever so slightly.

"As you wish, Wynne ab Gruffydd. The boys are brave and loyal. You've given them as good a beginning as any children could have. I'll see that they're tutored by the most learned monk I can find."

"There is one more thing," Wynne said, fearing to become too confident by her initial victory. Hiring a tutor was a small enough concession for so wealthy a man as Lord William. But denying him control of his sons' futures—for that was how he would see it—that was another matter altogether.

"Well? Out with it, woman. I would seek my bed awhile before the festivities begin in earnest."

"You must promise me—no, you must vow to your sons

and God—that when the time comes, they will be free to select a bride of their own choice."

She held her breath, awaiting his angry retort. When it did not come, however, she thought he'd not heard her aright. "That means you may not betroth them for reasons of money or lands—"

"Nor for political purposes," Lord William added, nodding. "I agree to your terms."

Wynne stared at him, thunderstruck by his easy acceptance. Then suspicion set in. "Do not think to appease me, Lord William. I will demand the right to visit them—and have them visit me. I will know if you break your word."

"A Somerville never breaks his word!"

His vociferous outburst caused heads to turn throughout the hall. Those who had slept now sat up. Those who'd busied themselves clearing away the previous night's debris worked all the faster. But Wynne was not frightened by Lord William's angry display. She was too surprised to be frightened. He meant to honor her request —her demand. He meant to allow her boys—his sons—the freedom to choose their own wives where their hearts lay. She didn't even try to disguise her delight.

"You will never be sorry that you have decided so," she replied, her face lit both with gratitude and with happiness. "They are good boys, and when they wed, they shall surely choose good wives."

Lord William's fierce expression eased under her sunny smile, and he reached for the ewer and filled his cup. He drank the entire portion, placed the cup carefully back on the table, then gave her a direct look.

"I wed once for money and lands. For opportunity. It gained me all I wanted—even more. But Angel . . ." He paused and cleared his throat. "Angel gave me love. It was worth all the rest."

He pushed away from the table and stood up abruptly. At once a servant appeared holding Lord William's cane out to him. Wynne watched in amazement as the man limped away. The most perplexing emotions circled in her head, too convoluted to be made much sense of. That he'd loved his Welsh mistress was undeniable. That he would love her sons—their sons—was becoming more and more clear. Rhys and Madoc would have the best of everything. They would grow into men who could read as well as fight. Who would employ scribes for convenience, not for necessity. And who, most especially, would be at liberty to love freely.

Quick tears stung her eyes, and she dashed them away before anyone could see. Aunt Gwynedd had been right. Rhys and Madoc were well served by knowing their father. Druce had believed it, as had Cleve.

Her soft sentiments hardened, however, when she thought of Cleve. Lord William might have come around to believing in the value of a marriage based on mutual love, but Cleve FitzWarin would never do so. She'd been a fool ever to hope for such a thing, and as a result she'd almost made a dreadful mistake last night. If the storm had not prevented it, she would have promised him all he wanted. She would have become that lesser person, that shadow lurking beneath his wife.

Even as she thought of Cleve's future wife, the very girl moved across her line of vision. Wynne stiffened, as did Edeline also, when she spied her. The two stared warily at one another. Then Edeline drew herself up and turned purposefully toward Wynne. She stopped on the opposite side of the table.

"Mistress Wynne," she began cautiously. "I hope you

will not take my father's temper amiss. One of the maids told me he shouted at you."

Wynne smiled back at the girl. Although they were nearly the same age, she felt infinitely older and wiser. The girl's very innocence made it impossible for Wynne to hold Edeline accountable for Cleve's single-minded pursuit of her fortune.

"Your father and I understand one another. There is no need for you to apologize for him."

Edeline chewed her lower lip, staring all the while at Wynne. For a moment Wynne wished she'd spent more time on her appearance before rushing to confront Lord William. Her hair was braided in one long plait hanging over her shoulder and tied with only a plain bit of cord. Her face was scrubbed clean but not whitened with rice flour as was Edeline's. Her gown was simple, unlike the other girl's fine raiments, and Wynne wore no jewels save the ancestral amulet that always hung around her neck. Still, she was not competing with Edeline for anyone's attentions, so what did it matter?

"Could we walk apace?" the girl hesitantly inquired.

"Why certainly. Yes." Wynne rose. "Is there something in particular that you wish to discuss?" she asked, fearing suddenly that the girl wished to speak of her betrothed, Sir Cleve FitzWarin. Wynne knew, despite her resolve, that she was not strong enough to do that. Not with Edeline.

To her surprise a warm flush pinkened Edeline's fair features. "Not here," she pleaded. "Let me show you the gardens. We'll be able to speak more freely there."

It was hard to say who more dreaded the coming discourse. Despite her own wounds Wynne was not blind to Edeline's discomfort, and that helped her to bury her own feelings. As they crossed the yard, she saw Druce perched upon an upturned bucket beside the stable door. He hailed them, and she paused to await him. When she glanced at Edeline, however, she saw the girl's face go scarlet. Edeline's eyes were huge and glued to the young Welshman's approach.

That furious blush explained everything to Wynne. There was no need for Edeline to use drops of nightshade in her eyes when Druce was about. And judging from Druce's avid gaze, he saw nothing but the slender English maiden.

Would that Lord William would be so generous to his daughter as he was being to his new sons, Wynne mused. If Edeline could choose, it was clear where her heart's selection lay. But there was Cleve to consider in this messy triangle. Even if Lord William were inclined to extend such generosity to his youngest daughter, he would not break his word to the man who'd brought him his sons. He would never deprive Cleve of his justly deserved reward, and Cleve would never give up his prize.

"Greetings on the new day," Druce said. He whipped his cap from his head and made a hasty bow. Wynne couldn't prevent the shadow of a smile from curving her lips. Where was the masterful young man, so confident of his skills with the village maidens, the fellow who twisted their hearts about his smallest finger? The Druce who stood before her now, giving her a sheepish grin before he fixed his gaze on the trembling Edeline, was another lad entirely. Had the focus of Druce's ardent pursuit not already been taken by another—and far beyond the reach of a poor Welshman anyway—Wynne would have been completely happy for him. As it was, however, she could only feel a sad heaviness for this misaligned pair. Druce and Edeline. She shook her head slightly as she glanced from one to the other. Their fledgling romance was doomed; that she knew. But she was just heartsore enough herself to wish it could succeed. Someone ought to find happiness with the one they loved. Lord William had not done so, and she clearly would not either.

Not that she loved Cleve. It was mainly a physical attraction. Nevertheless they could not be together—nor could Druce and Edeline. But Rhys and Madoc would, as would all her other children. They would all marry for love and no other reason.

"Might I walk with you?" Druce was asking when Wynne finally focused back on the conversation. Though he directed his question at Edeline, Wynne answered him.

"Edeline and I have a matter to discuss. 'Tis private," she added. Though she knew her obvious dismissal of him crushed his hopes, it was for the best, she decided when he sent Edeline a last, lingering smile. It was foolish for him to hope beyond his means.

"Oh, but that was too cruel!" Edeline rebuked her once Druce was out of hearing range. "You're every bit as hardhearted as my father!"

The girl whirled to stalk away, but Wynne, despite her initial shock at such an outburst from the previously meek girl, stopped her with a hand on her arm. Wynne was inexplicably heartened by the spark of anger and defiance she saw on the girl's face.

"Perhaps it was cruel. But not as cruel as to delude him into thinking he might have what we both know shall ever be beyond his grasp. 'Tis you who are cruel to encourage him in such a manner."

Under Wynne's severe gaze Edeline's temper dissolved, and quick tears flooded her eyes. "Oh, 'tis not fair. Not fair at all."

Once more Wynne felt infinitely older than the sheltered maiden before her. She sighed then and relented.

"Come along. Let us adjourn to your garden and have that talk."

" 'Tis useless. You have already made that clear."

"Dry your eyes and display some backbone," Wynne snapped in irritation. How had she become cast in the role of confidante to the very girl who laid claim to Cleve? Edeline was right. It was not fair. No, not at all.

Once they were seated on a plain wooden bench, worn by years of exposure and devoid of either back or arms, but sheltered and secluded against the rear of the armorer's shed, Wynne faced the sullen Edeline.

"Will you speak as you had planned, or shall I be forced to guess what it is that troubles you?"

Edeline raised her chin and stared resentfully at Wynne. "I think you would keep them both for yourself. Cleve and Druce. 'Tis not fair."

"I? Oh, but you are most truly a youngest daughter. Spoiled and willful, thinking only of yourself." She glared at Edeline's pale face. "I have neither of them—as you so badly state it. Nor do I want either of them. Druce is my friend—the nearest I have to a brother. But no more than that. And as for your Sir Cleve—well, he is plainly yours, not mine."

Edeline swallowed, and averted her eyes. When she looked up, her gaze was less accusing, but still miserable. "Sir Cleve's eyes follow you everywhere. I have seen it and I know what it means. He wants you, not me."

"Do you want him?" Wynne countered, for she was unwilling to address Edeline's statement directly.

Edeline fiddled with the embroidered length of her girdle and restlessly braided the loose tassel at its end. "I am promised to marry him."

"But do you wish it?" Wynne prompted, driven by a perverse need to know.

Edeline slowly shook her head. When her eyes met Wynne's, they were devoid of all hope. "I dreaded it before, because I knew he valued my dower lands more than he valued me. Though I have known all my life that such is to be expected in any marriage, still I did pray that it might not be my lot. And now that I have met Druce . . . I think I should rather die than be given to any man but Druce."

Despite the girl's dramatics, Wynne could not help but be moved by her sincerity. "You've known him but one day, and not spoken with him at all. Oh—" she broke off when Edeline's fresh blush proved her assumption wrong. "You have spoken. Well, even so, 'tis still awfully soon to tell."

"How long after you met Cleve did you know that he was the one for you?"

Wynne shrugged. Not long at all, she feared. Then she jerked her head up and met Edeline's watchful expression. "He—that is . . . I know no such thing. He is not for me."

Edeline did not look convinced. "We are both in the same fix, you and I. It does not help your cause to be less than honest about it."

Wynne stiffened. "If you wish to pursue Druce, so be it. But do not think to involve me in your schemes. I have no designs on the man to whom your father has betrothed you, nor on Druce either. If you would gain your heart's desire, I suggest you confer with your father. Now, if you will forgive my rudeness, I have my children to see to."

Wynne's heart hammered an unsteady rhythm as she fled her interview with Edeline. Pity the man who married that schemer, she fumed, dabbling in matters not of her own business. What right had the girl to question her about either Druce or Cleve?

Yet Wynne knew that her anger at Edeline was misplaced. The girl was guilty only of speaking a truth that Wynne did not wish to hear, and of longing for a future that Wynne feared to hope for. Even if the girl managed to maneuver her father into accepting Druce's suit—which was impossible given Cleve's standing with Lord William—what good would that do for Wynne? Cleve wished to wed a well-landed Englishwoman. A noblewoman. Would he ever turn to Wynne? And even if he did, it would only be as a second choice. Wynne knew she could never resign herself to that.

As she hurried past the stables, she spied Druce loitering beneath one of the lean-tos. As soon as she passed, he was on his way in the direction whence she'd just come. Well, then, let the new lovers have their brief moments of heaven in each other's presence, she decided. Too soon would they face that bleak hell of separation.

With that dreary thought uppermost in her mind she entered her chamber to be greeted by a most unhappy crowd of children.

" 'Tis *our* castle, and we—"

"—wish to have the biggest bed," Rhys finished Madoc's demand. He and his brother stood upon the one high bed in the room, daring by their belligerent stances any of the others to advance nearer. Arthur was busy tracing the pattern of seams in the stones that formed the outer walls of the room. How to build the castle itself seemed a far more immediate problem to him than how to claim the softest bed from his brothers. Isolde, however, was in a high temper.

"Just because your father is rich doesn't mean you can order us about. Nor does it mean this bed is yours." She glared at the smug pair. "Just you wait. When I get home to Radnor Manor, I'm going to tear your old pallet bed to shreds and then . . . and then I'll throw it in the pigsty!"

"Oh, Isolde," cried Bronwen in true distress. "You can't do that."

"Actually it makes very good sense," Arthur interjected, though he stared now at the rough beams that supported the floor above them. "Rhys and Madoc won't be sleeping there anymore."

His words, so straightforward and logical, silenced them all. Even Wynne was taken aback at the thought of their empty beds in the sleeping loft above the hall at Radnor. When Bronwen spied Wynne, she dashed to her and grabbed her skirts. "Do they have to stay here? Can't they come home with us and sleep in their old beds?" She sent a fierce look about the spacious chamber. "I *hate* this old castle. It's . . . it's too big. And too ugly. I hope it all falls down."

"It's very well constructed," Arthur remarked. "I don't think anything could make it fall down."

"Oh, do be quiet, Arthur," Isolde snapped, tossing her sleep-tangled hair. "You always get everything confused."

"It won't ever fall down," Madoc vowed. He jumped up and down on the bed as if that somehow verified his statement, but a quick frown from Wynne stilled him.

"Down, you two. And before you think to order others about, I think we should have a long talk with Lord William—with your father," she amended. "If my discussion with him this morning was any indication, you shall both be kept far too busy to find time for giving orders to anyone else."

When they appeared adequately subdued, she relented and gave them all a smile. "Come, now. Let's prepare for the day. Lord William promises a celebration. I think, too, that perhaps he might like a little time alone with his new sons."

When they finally descended to the hall to break their fast, a vast assortment of eyes followed them. The servants clucked and whispered over the identical twins, newly found and known now to be heirs to the master's vast fortune. The outraged expressions of the displaced sons-in-law and their equally dispossessed wives had mellowed over the course of the night, Wynne noted with some relief, replaced, it appeared, by a mingling of irritation and resignation.

Conversation was low during the brief meal, just a murmur of voices rising and falling. When Lord William came down the stairs, however, leaning on his cane yet nonetheless projecting an aura of good spirits and hearty vigor, all discourse died away. Here were father and sons united at last, and in the sight of all.

Though Bronwen and Isolde shrank from the sight of the man they perceived as taking their brothers from them, Rhys and Madoc stared at him in frank curiosity. The night's rest had clearly restored their natural ebullience. Lord William stared at them just as boldly, but his widespread smile softened his otherwise intimidating figure. His faded blue eyes were lit with new color, and his step seemed light despite his ample girth and lame leg.

"Well, lads, and how would you celebrate this first day in your new home?" Lord William began, enunciating slowly so that his sons might more easily understand his words, so foreign to them. "The kitchens shall prepare whate'er you like best. The minstrels and jongleurs shall entertain as you demand. Would you ride? Or play games?"

Wynne saw the look that passed between Rhys and Madoc, and despite the well of sadness in her heart she could not keep from smiling. The pair understood, all right. Lord William was in for a rough ride with these two. By the time he finished indulging them, as he so obviously intended to do, they would be well in command of their father and every other adult who thought to control their mischievous natures. God pity their poor tutors.

"Could we see jousting—"

"—and hawking?"

"Have you hounds for hunting?"

"May we have hounds of our very own—"

"—and our own horses as well?"

Lord William's gaze leaped from one dark-haired son to the next, and slowly his grin began to fade. "How shall I ever tell you apart?"

"I'm Rhys—"

"—and I'm Madoc," the pair responded after only the briefest pause. Still, it was enough hesitation to alert Wynne. She rose from her chair to approach the two. But as she reached their side, so did Cleve, and she stumbled to a halt. His eyes swept over her, at once devouring and accusing, setting her heart racing in an uneven rhythm. Oh, why couldn't she put him out of her head and out of her heart?

His cool gaze left hers, and with each of his hands he tilted the twins' faces up to him. "This is Rhys," he said to Lord William, indicating quite the opposite of what the boys had stated. "If you will notice, milord, he has a scar on his left eyebrow. Here. 'Tis tiny, but telling."

Lord William's own brow lowered in annoyance with his sons, but when the dark-eyed pair turned their sheepish gazes upon him, that emotion fled. "Clever boys, my sons. Brave, loyal, and quick-witted." He began to laugh and fondly rumpled the boys' hair. "Jousting, you say. And hawks and hounds. All right, then. So be it. Harold.

Thomas. Reginald," he called his sons-in-law. "See to it. Arrange for the joust and any other sporting events. Anne, Bertilde, Catherine. See that a day of feasting is arranged for one and all. We shall have a fair in the low meadow beside the river."

"Shall Edeline have no chores?" Bertilde complained, tugging upon her father's sleeve. But he waved her away.

"Edeline is to be officially betrothed this day. She and Sir Cleve will be feted before one and all." He spread his arms wide, causing the disgruntled Bertilde to catch his cane before it fell. "Ah, but life is good to me," Lord William expounded as his eyes swept the crowd in the hall. "God is good to me, and I would have one and all share in my blessedly good fortune."

But for Cleve's disturbing presence beside her, Wynne might actually have shared in that sentiment. After all, she had negotiated as good an arrangement for her sons as any a mother could have wished, short of seeing to their everyday lives herself. And even she must now admit that Lord William's parentage offered the pair myriad benefits, far beyond her ability to provide.

However, Cleve *did* stand beside her, and it was his betrothal that Lord William boasted of almost as happily as he did the presence of his sons. Under the circumstances Wynne was hard-pressed to maintain even the semblance of a civil expression on her face. Her gaze avoided Cleve entirely. But seeking Edeline's grave features was nearly as awful. Edeline stared wide-eyed at Cleve, then her gaze slid to another, and when Wynne followed the direction, she found the equally stricken Druce.

Life was good to Lord William, she acknowledged as she watched him lead his young sons off for a leisurely tour of the castle and grounds—belatedly gesturing for

Arthur to come along as well. Life was good for Lord William, but for others in the hall it was wretchedly unfair.

Edeline disappeared, white-faced, up the stairs to her own chamber. Druce kicked over a chair, then stalked off in frustration. Cleve turned to confront Wynne, but she had anticipated that and was too quick for him. She herded the two girls toward Barris, not heeding by word or posture Cleve's call. Though Barris gave her a searching look and she knew Arthur yet sent a plaintive look back at Cleve, she ignored them all.

"The day is bright," she stated firmly. "Let us walk about and see what herbs may spring from this English soil."

And perhaps she would come upon some magical herb, one that would leap into her hands, proclaiming itself as a true love potion, one that could compel another's will to one's own and truly command another's love and eternal devotion.

Yes, and perhaps the sun and moon would collide this day in the heavens. The one was as far-fetched as the other.

22

Across the narrow drawbridge and a little north of the castle, past where the river water was diverted to form the moat, the meadow gave way to a damp woodland. It was here that Wynne steered her young charges. The castle bustled with too much activity; the overflow spilled out into the meadow, and from their place near the riverbank they could still hear the shouts and laughter of the workers.

The castle folk were in a high good humor, preparing for the unexpected day of recreation. A line of men swung scythes in remarkable harmony, creating, step by step, a wide cleared area suitable for any sort of play that Lord William desired—or, more accurately, that Rhys and Madoc desired. A constant stream of carts made its way out of the castle, bearing tents for shade, planks for tables, great barrels of both ale and red wine, and every manner of food the kitchens could produce on such short notice.

Even Wynne couldn't restrain the tiniest spark of excitement, which drew her eyes back again and again to the meadow. She'd never attended a fair of this sort. She'd been to several town fairs—three in all. She'd gone twice as a girl with her parents and sister, but only once in recent years. She'd not had the time to make the three-day round trip to Brecon. And the meager market day at Radnor hardly counted. But this . . . this was something. A fair not part of a market but meant only for celebration. If only it were to celebrate something she was truly happy about.

"Oh, look. There is parsley fern here too. Just like at home," Isolde called.

"And dragonflies too. All colors and—oh, just see how big that one is. All green and red!" Bronwen cried, clapping her hands gleefully.

"There's a prince heron," Barris whispered, pointing out the stately water feeder as it stood, still as stone, wary about these noisy visitors.

Wynne stood knee-deep in some spiky grass of a variety unknown to her. But the trees that soared high around her were the same familiar oaks of her home, and the low, pointy-leaf plants that circled their dark-gray trunks were common wild strawberry. This long distance had they come, into another land with a different language and altogether different ways from their own, yet the forest and all its creatures were not so foreign as she would have thought. Even the flock of raucous birds that rose in a cloud at their approach were the dark-winged ravens of her own woods.

"I see a buzzard nest." She signaled to the girls. "There, above the second branching of that tree. Just to the right. The right." She tapped Bronwen's right shoulder.

"Oh, yes," Bronwen breathed, once she'd turned her head in the correct direction. " 'Tis so large. Are there any nestlings within?"

"No, not at this time of year," another voice answered.

To everyone's surprise Edeline materialized from beyond a thicket of holly. "That particular nest has been in use at least seven seasons. The young birds flew off a fortnight since, perhaps two."

Bronwen was the first to reply. "Do you like birds? Arthur likes birds as well. He wants to fly just as they do." The child crouched in the undergrowth, her fair hair brushing the tips of the tall grass. As she looked up at Edeline, Wynne was struck by how very English Bronwen appeared, very near to Edeline in her coloring and fragile build.

Edeline smiled at the little girl. "Flying. Now, wouldn't that be something fine. Perhaps if he learns how to do it, he will teach the rest of us as well." Then her gaze shifted to Wynne, and her easy manner drained away. "May I confer with you?"

"I cannot help you," Wynne replied. "I told you that before. Speak to your father."

"I will. I will. But I need something, and, well, you are a Seeress, or so I am told."

"Oh, by everything that is holy!" Wynne muttered in exasperation. She eyed Edeline uncharitably. "Here, give me your hand. I shall foretell your future." When the girl dutifully stuck out first one palm and then, nervously, the other as well, Wynne snorted in disgust. "I need not see your pale, uncallused palms to foretell what lies in your future. You shall marry an arrogant, though handsome knight and have three or four children. Perhaps five or six. And you shall never want for anything."

"Save for happiness!" Edeline cried, clasping her hands into a knot. "I shall want for happiness, as shall you."

"Aye, Wynne, she makes a very good point," Barris put in. "You and she—and Druce—mope about till I feel as if a heavy cloud hovers above us all. For the love of God, help the girl. Druce is your friend, is he not? Will you ignore his misery as well?"

In frustration Wynne thrust one hand through her thick hair. "And just what is it you expect me to do? I have influence with neither Lord William nor Sir Cleve, and those two are quite firmly set upon their chosen course."

"But Cleve loves *you*," Edeline cried. "I'm certain of it."

Wynne started to respond, but abruptly closed her mouth. How was she to reply to such an outrageous remark, especially when she wished so to believe it was true?

"He does love you," Bronwen echoed in her solemn baby's voice. "I know he does."

"I can make a love potion for you," Isolde added with an earnest bob of her head. "Probably it would work better if I made it instead of you making it for your own self."

Wynne pursed her lips in rueful consideration. "Yes, my little darling, it probably would. But for now why don't you two go on with Barris while Edeline and I finish our discussion."

By the time the two children reluctantly headed off with the grinning Barris, another figure came cantering across the meadow. When Druce spied the two women, he urged his steed straight toward them, and before the animal could properly come to a halt, he threw himself down from the saddle.

"Edeline—" he began in a tortured tone. Then he turned to Wynne. "Wynne, you must help us!"

With a cry of pure frustration Wynne threw her hands up in the air. "And what is it *I* am supposed to do? Why do you turn to *me* when 'tis clear—and has been for a fortnight—that *I* am the least able of us all to achieve my own aims! I did not wish to come to England, but here I am. I did not wish to lose a son—or two—to Lord William, but so has become my fate. Why do you now think that *I* can be of any help to you in your doomed romance?"

" 'Tis not doomed!" Druce countered, his face gone dark and shadowed. He pulled Edeline to his side with a desperate movement, yet within the roughness of his embrace there was the unmistakable touch of tenderness. He stared down at the English girl and she up at him with such a look of radiant happiness and yet abject misery that Wynne averted her eyes. She could hardly bear it. But even casting her anger and frustration—and envy—aside, what could she actually do to help the two of them?

As their avid gazes clung, Wynne cleared her throat. "Have either of you considered going together to speak to Lord William?"

Druce shook his head. "Cleve is the one we must convince first. If he agrees, it will be easier to convince Lord William."

"It will never be easy to convince Lord William," Wynne countered. She kicked at a nodding seed head of cat's-play. "Do you truly think he will accept a poor Welshman as his son-in-law when any number of noblemen court his pleasure and would love nothing better than to be related to such a wealthy and powerful lord? Even Cleve had to earn the right to her hand by first finding Rhys and Madoc."

Druce's expression turned stubborn. "Leave that part to me, Wynne. All I'm asking is that you remove Cleve as an obstacle on our path to happiness."

"And just how am I to do that?"

"You did it once," he replied with a knowing look.

Wynne's eyes widened in dismay at his bold words, and her face burned a painful shade of scarlet. How could he say such an awful thing to her? Did he mean for her to offer herself to Cleve like some . . . like some . . . Her breath caught in her chest. To offer herself in the same wanton fashion as she'd done that first time?

Wynne bit down on her lower lip and blinked hard, fighting back the sudden rush of emotions that threatened to overwhelm her. "It will not work," she muttered hoarsely. She returned her reluctant gaze to the pair of them. Edeline did not appear scandalized by Druce's revelation—perhaps she'd not understood. But the girl's next words dispelled that hope.

"I do not feel about Sir Cleve in the same way that . . . that you do." Edeline's eyes turned up to Druce, and it was her turn to blush. "But Druce, well, he . . ."

Her words trailed off, but Wynne understood. She feared she understood better, even, than did Edeline herself. When the heart pulled you and the loins contributed their own perverse longings also, well, there was little hope of opposing those two mighty foes. Logic failed in the face of their superior strength.

She swallowed, then cleared her throat. "I will attempt to reason with Sir Cleve. And that is all," she added with a scowl. "Though why the pair of you could not do so I cannot fathom."

"You will have more sway with him," Druce replied.

Wynne shook her head. "You delude yourself, Druce. And you as well, Edeline. He wants one thing only. Land and power. Power and land."

"That's two things," Edeline put in.

" 'Tis one and the same," Wynne snapped. "Oh, just leave me. Leave me and let me think." She spun about and marched to the riverbank and stood there, arms crossed and back stiff.

"All right, then. We're going, Wynne. But remember, you agreed. Today would be a good day," Druce added.

She sent him an icy glare. "If it is a miracle you wish, best you take yourself to the chapel to pray."

"But if Father makes the announcement today, it will make things even more impossible," Edeline cried.

"Oh, bother with the two of you," Wynne swore. "Stay in your chamber, then. Claim illness. Whatever. Your father will be less likely to announce his glad tidings if the bride is not present. And as for the groom . . ." Her voice trailed off as a truly vindictive thought took hold. A bitter smile curved her lips ever so faintly. "If the bridegroom is too much in his cups to be present, well then . . ." She shrugged and gave Druce a meaningful look.

"What do you mean—oh." Druce straightened as understanding dawned. "You would drug him?"

"Oh, no. Not *I*," Wynne demurred. "*You* shall do the deed this time." Then she turned away from them once more. "Now, leave me."

"Druce, what does she plot?" Wynne heard Edeline ask as the lovesick pair started back toward the castle.

"You need not know, my sweet. But she will handle it. We may trust Wynne."

A sharp pain pulsed behind Wynne's eyes as she stood alone on the steep bank of the river once they were gone. They could trust her. Indeed! She could not trust herself when it came to Cleve FitzWarin, yet they fully expected her to solve their problems with the man. Oh, how foolish were young lovers. And she had been the biggest fool of all.

All she was doing was buying a little time for the moonstruck couple. They would gain a day or two together, but in the end . . . In the end Cleve would marry Edeline. It was his fondest desire, and no amount of reasoning or pleading or even seduction on Wynne's part would alter that fact.

She could only hope that Edeline's brief romance with Druce was not too deeply rooted. As for Druce, he had been with any number of women. Surely he could recover from this broken romance without too much pain. After all, she planned to recover from hers. What other choices did the two of them have?

At high noon the bells of Kirkston's Chapel to Saint Peter began rousingly to ring, summoning castle folk and village folk alike to the hastily assembled fair grounds. Wynne saw Cleve once from afar, but she slipped off in another direction immediately. Her sole purpose for attending the festivities was to give Druce the small packet of herbs that he was to dissolve in Cleve's wine. Barris had promised to shepherd the children with Druce's aid once that one's task was complete. Edeline already lay abed in a closed room with a damp cloth on her brow.

Wynne had heard Lord William's frustrated oath on hearing the girl was indisposed, but she had wisely kept her distance. How would he take to his future son-in-law's inability to maintain his wits today? He would no doubt be furious with Cleve, but Wynne reassured herself that the man's anger would swiftly pass. After all, he had his two young sons to occupy his thoughts.

Despite the general disorganization of the hastily planned recreations, a gay atmosphere prevailed. Competitions were begun. Races. Wrestling. Even eating contests and drinking as well. The best of Lord William's archers competed for a gold coin, and it was amid their numbers that Wynne finally located Druce. He and Barris had their heads together, and all five children clustered about them.

"You can do it, Druce. You can beat that—"

"—old gray-beard Englishman."

"His gray beard will not hurt his aim," Arthur remarked to Rhys and Madoc. "And we are all at least part English."

"Not Druce and Barris," Isolde threw in. "They're all Welsh."

"So is Wynne."

"So I am," Wynne agreed with Bronwen and drew the little girl fondly to her side. "Rhys and Madoc, I think you should cease considering this a competition between the English and the Welsh. 'Tis but a contest between very good archers."

Druce grinned up at her and plucked a resounding twang from the taut line of his longbow. "Aye, we are all but archers. But 'tis well known that the best archers are *Cymry*, and today I shall prove it to one and all."

"Especially to Lord William?" Wynne asked with one raised brow.

Druce's grin faded somewhat, but his cocky expression only displayed more determination. "Right you are, wise Seeress of Radnor. Tell me, can you foretell the outcome of this day's work?"

Wynne met his dark gaze. That he would win the archery competition was more than a little likely. But whether he would win the prize he most desired—that was a future she could only guess at, and at this moment her guess was no.

"Here," she said, not answering his question. "Take this packet of herbs and use them in your quest."

"Will they make his aim truer?" Barris asked, wide-eyed.

Wynne glanced at him, surprised that Druce had not taken his brother into his confidence. At that precise moment Cleve joined their circle, drawing Wynne's thoughts away from Barris. So the beast approached the bait. Even should he take it, however, would it truly do any good? Again, she feared the answer was no.

"Wynne's concoction made my aim truer during our hunt at Offa's Dyke," Cleve said, watching her with his unsettling gaze. "Perhaps I should warn Lord William's champion of the unfair advantage you have given Druce."

Wynne thrust her chin forward, for she would not reveal even one of her softer emotions to him. But her fingers tightened together with the effort. "If Druce's competitors are desirous of my skills, they have but to request my aid."

He kept his eyes locked with hers. "If I were a competing archer, I would most assuredly seek out those extraordinary skills of yours."

On the surface his words were courteous and correct. But Wynne knew he implied something far more intimate than the mere administering of some herbal remedy. Judging from Druce's shrewd look, he, too, knew. Relief flooded her when Arthur stepped forward, commanding Cleve's attention.

" 'Tis good you will not test your aim against Druce," The child stated in all seriousness. "He is the finest archer in all of Radnor Forest."

"No one can best him," Madoc boasted.

"No one," Rhys echoed.

Druce stared boldly at Cleve. Wynne recognized the battle that raged within her childhood friend's chest—the normal male need to best even his closest friend at sport was aggravated by his real need to best this particular man in the struggle for one special woman's hand. To make matters worse, however, Druce had to conceal the true nature of his competition with Cleve, at least for a while longer.

Since Druce had taken possession of the herbs destined for Cleve's wine cup, Wynne thought it best to lighten the conversation. "I for one shall toast Druce's success when he wins Lord William's coin. Will you do the same?" She posed the question to Cleve.

He grinned at Druce, then turned the force of his smile on Wynne, causing her to swallow hard. "May the best man win," he replied.

Seeing his chance, Druce put a hand on Arthur's shoulder. "Go refill our cups, Arthur. Here." He signaled Rhys and Madoc to help. "If you would be knights someday, first you must learn to serve. Am I not right, Sir Cleve?"

"Most assuredly. Here's my cup."

Barris and Druce added their cups, and the three boys scurried off at once. When Cleve's eyes returned most disconcertingly to her, however, Wynne shifted uneasily. "I think I shall take the girls to examine the weaver's new loom. 'Tis a most cunning assemblage and produces a very fine cloth."

"But, Wynne," Isolde protested. "I want to see Druce win—"

"And so you shall," Wynne promised. "But until the competition begins, he does not need to be distracted by our presence."

" 'Tis no distraction," Druce countered, sending Wynne a meaningful look.

"Oh, but I'm sure it must be," she insisted, a grim smile pasted firmly on her face. "Come along, girls, I promise we shall not miss seeing Druce compete."

All three men's eyes followed Wynne's departure. Barris was the first to speak, prefacing his words with an excessively heavy sigh. "She does not notice me. No matter what I do, she sees me only as a boy. I'm but a year younger than she."

Druce took up the ploy at once. "I have given up on her myself. Perhaps you will have better luck, though. And don't forget, we have that lengthy journey back to Radnor. Who knows what may happen? And she shall need comforting, after all."

"I thought you would leap to fill that void," Barris continued. He glanced at Cleve's darkening face. "What say you, Cleve? You seemed well enough taken with her on the journey here. Should I vie against my brother for the fair Wynne's attentions? Or shall she rebuff me as well?"

"I would hardly say she rebuffed me," Druce stated. When the three boys ran up, red wine sloshing from the pewter mugs, he took two of the mugs. "Where's a rag to wipe these? And another thing, Barris, she did not precisely rebuff Cleve either."

"What do you mean?" Cleve challenged to Druce's turned back. "Do you imply some impropriety?"

Druce looked over his shoulder at Cleve, an innocent expression firmly in place. "No, no. You mistake my meaning. Here." He turned and handed Cleve a cup. "Take your wine. What I meant was that you knew your betrothed awaited you in England. Your flirtation with Wynne was mild, not of a nature even to require a rebuff. Was it?" he added, watching Cleve over the rim of his own upturned mug.

Cleve's hesitation, followed by his full quaffing of the contents of the cup, described to Druce better than words the struggles that tore at the man.

"Our Wynne has not yet found the man whom she will gift with her love—as well as with all her other lovely charms." he added with a grin. "Who knows, Barris.

Maybe it shall be you. By the by, Cleve, how do you find
the sweet maid to whom you shall be wed?"

"She is . . ." Cleve shrugged, clearly distracted by either guilt or worry. Or both, Druce hoped, warming to
this task of goading Edeline's betrothed. Though he liked
Cleve very well, when it came to Edeline—and Wynne as
well—they stood on opposing sides of a drawn line.

"She is what?" Barris prodded.

Cleve frowned. "She is fair and well-mannered. But she
is . . . she is very young."

"Most men find that commendable," Druce pressed on.
"She may bear you many sons."

" 'Tis not precisely her age," Cleve replied. "Wynne is
nearly as young. 'Tis more, I don't know, something in
her bearing." He sat down, rather abruptly, on a three-
legged stool. "Arthur, lad. Will you fetch me another cup
of wine?"

By the time Arthur returned, it was clear to Druce that
Wynne's herbs were taking effect. He gave Barris a quelling stare when that one began to look concerned. This
was Druce's chance to question Cleve, and he did not
mean to lose the opportunity.

"Wynne is an unusual woman," Druce prompted.

"Oh, aye," Barris added. "The lads at home do trail
after her as if she were some sweet dessert that they fain
would take a taste of."

"Who?" Cleve demanded. "Say their names and I'll
teach them to keep their distance from her."

Druce grinned at the slurred sound of Cleve's words.
"You won't be there to prevent it," he reminded the befuddled man. "You will be well married to Edeline, remember? While Wynne is returning to Wales."

"I will not let her leave me," Cleve stood up, then
would have toppled over had Barris not propped him up.

"Are you going to keep Wynne here?" Arthur asked, an uncertain expression on his young face.

Cleve stared down at the boy, and Druce held his breath. He hadn't meant to alarm the children by his questioning of Cleve. But Cleve seemed to retain some remnants of his wits, for he focused on Arthur and gave him a reassuring smile.

"I wish all of you could stay, my lad. You and Wynne and all the children. Even Druce and—" His legs went out on him, and Barris laughed out loud.

"Soused! He's soused. Who would have thought him unable to hold his drink?" He lowered Cleve's limp form to the ground and leaned him against a cart wheel. "Now what shall we do with him?"

"It was not just wine he drank," Druce whispered to Barris. "But do not speak of it. Just help me move him to some quiet place."

As the three boys watched round-eyed, Druce and the curious Barris lifted Cleve between them and, with one of his arms draped around each of their shoulders, walked him—dragged him was a more accurate description—to a shaded spot beneath an ancient oak. There they laid him to sleep off the ill effects of Wynne's concoction.

As Druce returned to the archery field, he was buoyed up by an enormous sense of optimism. The betrothal would not be announced, not when both parties were equally indisposed. He would prove his merit before Lord William's eyes. Then tomorrow Wynne would work things out with Cleve.

That was the only sticking point in his plan. Wynne must work things out with Cleve.

23

Truly Druce did expect miracles from her, Wynne fumed as she crossed the yard, making her way through the deep twilight to the lean-to barracks against the castle's outer wall. First she dosed Cleve FitzWarin with enough of her sleeping potion to topple a destrier. Now she was to ease his pounding head and roiling stomach with an altogether different tonic. Not that she wasn't up to the task. That was no real feat. Rather she was frustrated by the futility of it all. Plus, she dreaded being alone with Cleve. Somehow he always managed to turn such circumstances to his advantage.

But not tonight, she vowed as she slowed near the barracks' entrance. She would perform her task and leave. Besides, what did Druce think, that Cleve would renounce his well-dowered bride in favor of a Welsh maiden blessed with neither title nor riches? She shook her head in disgust. Truly Druce was too besotted with love to be in the least logical about the situation.

Still, she could not begrudge Druce his desperate need to try something—anything—to achieve his heart's aim. After all, Edeline returned his love. If Cleve only returned *her* love, Wynne, too, would struggle against all obstacles in order to win him. But what Cleve felt for her was not love, it was lust. And for her that simply was not enough.

A heavy weight settled in her chest as she approached the barracks where the unmarried knights and foot soldiers lodged. Dark shapes spread about in random fashion attested to the potency of Lord William's free-flowing ales and wines this day. Men slept where they'd fallen, crumpled into heaps or stretched out in vociferous slumber. The discordant harmony of their snoring was almost funny. Almost.

Wynne halted before the doorway, surveying the slumped and snoring form of a man half in and half out of the building. How was she to find Cleve among all this excess of drunken male forms?

"He is here," a young voice called, answering Wynne's wordless query.

"Arthur? What in heaven's name—"

"Here, Wynne. I found him."

Wynne stepped over the oblivious drunk in the door, and once her eyes had adjusted to the dark interior, she spied Arthur. "You should not be here," she whispered as she hurried toward him and the hulking shadow she assumed was Cleve.

"His head is hurting real bad," Arthur replied, unmindful of her scolding words, and his worried tone touched Wynne's heart. Arthur suffered for his idol now. Later it would only be worse.

"I shall mend his aching head," Wynne said, giving Arthur a reassuring hug. She started to urge him away from this place, but then thought better of it. With Arthur there, Cleve would scarcely try anything untoward. Not that he was likely to, given the aftereffects he was now suffering. Still, there was no sense taking any chances.

"Here, my sweet lad, hold my purse for me," she instructed the child. Then she turned her attentions toward Cleve. "Are you able to stomach a remedy?"

He looked up slowly from his place on a sturdy bench, his head hanging low between his hands. Had ever a man appeared so wretched? She had to physically restrain herself from reaching out to stroke his face.

"You had a hand in this," he stated in a low, thick voice.

Wynne heard Arthur's quick gasp of comprehension and immediately regretted allowing him to linger here. What would he think of her now? This was the third time she'd turned her special knowledge against the boy's idol.

" 'Twas for Edeline that I did it," she retorted defensively. "The girl would delay the betrothal announcement."

Although Arthur's stiff posture eased at that, Cleve's did not. " 'Twas a useless gesture," he grunted. Then his eyes narrowed, and he watched her closely. "Did you truly do it for her? Or was it for yourself?"

Wynne knew the honest answer to that question, but not for the world would she reveal as much to him. Her love for him would forever remain her secret.

"Why must you marry Edeline?" Arthur piped up. "I think you should marry—"

But Wynne interrupted the child before he could put into words her own thought. "I would have a favor of you, Cleve. A promise," she said.

"You poison me, then request a favor?" he asked sarcastically, glaring at her through bleary eyes.

"Not for me," she retorted tensely. She swallowed hard and willed herself to remain calm. "For Rhys and Madoc. Will you keep a watch over them? Safeguard them? I know now that Lord William loves them well. But his family . . . well, they will surely resent them, and I . . . I . . ." she trailed off.

"No harm shall come to them, Wynne." He pushed himself upright and faced her in the shadowy barracks. "I promise you that. But if you would only reconsider—"

"Here." Wynne thrust a small vial at Cleve, interrupting him before he could repeat his impossible offer for her to stay. She could not bear to hear it, nor did she want to put any ideas in Arthur's head. "Drink this. Half now and the remainder in an hour or so. 'Twill ease your symptoms enough that you can rest." Then, before he could respond, she grabbed Arthur's hand and hurried the two of them away.

Arthur sat on the high bed he shared with Rhys and Madoc in the chamber Lord William had granted his new sons. Rhys and Madoc yet tussled and rolled about, mimicking the wrestlers they'd watched during the afternoon.

"I win!" Rhys crowed from his position atop Madoc.

With a grunt Madoc pushed his brother off him. "You cheated. And anyway I can best you at the targets." He pulled back an imaginary bow string and let fly with an invisible arrow. "I'm Druce and I'm the best of all the archers!"

Arthur watched as Rhys fell down, clutching his stomach in an appropriate display of agony. "You know, it's too bad Druce can't stay here and teach you how to use the longbow."

The twins both looked over at him. "Perhaps our father will let him stay," Madoc answered.

"Yes, he's the best archer of them all. He really showed them. He could be the *captain* of the archers."

Arthur nodded. "That would be a very good idea. Only I don't know if he'll stay."

"Yes, he would," Rhys stated. "If we all begged him to, he would."

Arthur gave them a considering look. "I think Druce likes Lady Edeline."

"The one Cleve is to wed?"

Arthur nodded gravely. "I don't think Druce will stay unless *he* can marry Edeline."

The twins stared at him. "Why?" Madoc asked.

Arthur exhaled in exasperation. "Because Druce and Lady Edeline love each other, just like Cleve and Wynne do. Only your father has promised Lady Edeline to Cleve, so . . . so everything is all mixed up and nobody is happy."

Rhys and Madoc shared a look. "So if Lord William changes his mind and Edeline could marry Druce—"

"—then Druce could stay here. With us."

"But what about Cleve?" Madoc asked.

"He could marry Wynne and come back to Radnor Forest with us," Arthur said with a hopeful smile.

"I thought he wanted to marry the Lady Edeline."

"Well, he sort of does. But he loves Wynne best. And she loves him," Arthur replied. "Besides, you already have a father. It's only fair that I have one too. And I want Cleve for my father."

The twins glanced again at each other, then shrugged in unison. "All right, then. What do you want us to do?"

The day dawned as gray and dismal as Wynne's mood. Over the entire castle a subdued mood prevailed. Too many aching heads and unsteady stomachs made for a small group at the morning meal. Only the children and a few of the older servants seemed unaffected by the previous day's excesses.

Wynne was as perversely affected as anyone, though

not due to any overindulgence in either food or drink. Through the long hours of the night she'd examined her predicament and had come to the unhappy conclusion that it was time for her to return home. It was painfully clear to her that Rhys and Madoc would not long suffer in her absence. Together they would take very good advantage of all Lord William's parentage could offer. But she and Arthur, the two girls and Barris, and even Druce had been in England long enough. She intended to plan their departure this very day.

To her dismay, however, before she could search out Lord William's manservant to request an audience with him, Cleve FitzWarin blocked her path.

"A word with you, Wynne. If you please," he added with exaggerated courtesy.

Wynne stared up into his face, noting the lines of weariness around his mouth and eyes. He, too, had passed a long and restless night, it seemed. But at least his color was good. She forced herself nevertheless not to care whether he was well or ill. Mimicking his polite tone, she replied, "I'd rather not speak with you, if you please."

"Why?" He shifted to block her again when she would have sidestepped him. "Why avoid me now? First you seek to poison me, then you heal me. One day you seek me out, the next you avoid me at all costs. Christ, Wynne, you do drive a man to madness!"

Wynne stared up at him, first in dismay, then in frustration. "I am not the perverse one here. You are. And I am hardly the one who has sought *you* out. I've but tried to protect myself and my family from your unwanted attention. And furthermore, if I wished truly to poison you, you would not look nearly so hearty this morning!"

He gave her a long, assessing look, as if he did measure the depths of her emotion and gauge his own response accordingly. Then he sighed and raked his fingers through his uncombed hair.

"Come ride with me. We can talk."

Wynne shook her head. "No. I've other plans, and besides, we've nothing to discuss."

"Don't turn coward on me, Wynne. You've been a most worthy opponent up to now. You know we've much yet to discuss between us. Why do you fear it so?"

She could hardly give him an honest answer to that question, so Wynne wisely kept her silence. But she feared his dark, intense stare stole the answer from her heart, for she could not tear her gaze from his. Once more she was overcome by that creeping magic of his, that numbing yet exhilarating sense of connection he managed so easily to forge between them. The time had come to part from him, yet she could not bring herself to say good-bye.

"Come ride with me," he repeated as he reached for a flyaway tendril of her waist-length hair. He tugged on it playfully, but his eyes were earnest. "Come ride with me, Wynne. I've something to show you that you will want to see."

Wynne shook her head again, but more weakly. A self-conscious blush colored her cheeks as her vivid imagination pictured precisely what he meant to show her.

Why must he of all men affect her so? Why couldn't some straightforward Welsh fellow do to her heart's pace what this difficult, devious Englishman did? A practical woman such as she should be drawn to an uncomplicated man with honorable intentions. Yet here she stood, succumbing once more to his potent gaze and magical touch. He wanted but one thing of her, and fool that she was, she wanted to give it to him.

"You've nothing at all that I want to see," she lied as best she could. But he only smiled.

"I fear you do misread my words," he replied. "I wish only to show you a quiet glade near here. It is very like your own glade at Radnor, damp and overgrown with a wealth of plants. Come ride with me there, Wynne. 'Tis not too far. Come ride out to that glade with me."

She wanted to say no, to insist that other tasks awaited her. She had no time to ride about the countryside and no wish to be with him, under the circumstances. But she was suddenly assailed by the terrible knowledge that this would be her last time with him. She would leave tomorrow, never to see him again. That realization was so unbearable that her words of denial died unsaid.

She reached for her amulet, unaware that she did so, then stared up at him through eyes misted with emotion. "Why are you doing this to me? Why?"

"Because I must," he muttered in a voice gone low and husky. He released the lock of hair he'd wound around his finger and let his knuckle slide ever so lightly along her cheek. "Ride with me, Wynne."

She did not fight him when he steered her toward the stables. His hand held her arm in a manner no one would have considered less than absolutely proper. Only she and he sensed the tension that crackled so intensely from that slight contact.

This ride would be their good-bye, Wynne told herself as she let him guide her. She stood silently as he called for two horses, then watched as he assisted the stable boy with their harnessing. In some private glade, away from prying eyes, they would take their leave of one another. He no doubt thought to convince her to stay, but she knew that was impossible. She would take him to her one last time—take him to her heart and to her body. But it would be in farewell.

And perhaps . . . perhaps she might get a child of him, the thought came unbidden to her.

She gasped, and clasped one suddenly shaking hand to her stomach at the very idea. He looked up at her then, not smiling at all, yet nonetheless conveying a wealth of emotion to her, and she knew without a doubt that it was meant to be thus. She could not have him, at least not on terms acceptable to her. But she could have a child of him.

There was a bittersweet satisfaction in that. Her terrible sorrow, her impending sense of loss, were not assuaged, yet there was a certain solace in knowing she could at least keep that portion of him for herself. And know it she did, in the same inexplicable way she'd first known of his presence in her forest.

He was the one love of her heart, and their child would be her sole comfort when Cleve was gone from her life.

More than one set of eyes watched the two of them depart on horseback from the castle.

"You see," Arthur said to the other children who crowded silently at the deep window of the twins' chamber. "I told you they should get married."

"You see," Druce said to Edeline from where they lurked behind the kitchen. "I told you Wynne would not let us down."

Only Lord William frowned blearily from where he stood just within the propped-open door to the great hall. Yet even he understood that a man had certain needs. Better that the fellow ease himself on a pretty wench like the Welsh girl than to soil his bride before the wedding ceremony took place. Edeline was his last daughter, his sweet and amenable favorite, who resembled her fragile mother more with every passing day. Better for her virile bridegroom to dull the edge of his lust on another woman. And after all, like her mother, what Edeline did not know would not ever hurt her.

He only hoped Cleve did not get a bastard on the Welsh girl. Best that a man's sons sprang from his wife's belly and no other. He better than anyone knew the truth of that.

24

The glade was cool and damp, shaded by a circling ring of towering beeches and softened by a floor of creeping fern and carpet moss. A sparkling pool lay at its heart, and even Wynne could not deny the beauty of the place. A young doe raised her wet muzzle at their entrance, then with a dismissive shake of her tail, bounded away. A flock of crows raised raucous welcome, but they quickly tired of that. By the time Cleve dismounted, only the buzzing of several industrious bees and the croak of a hidden toad broke the ethereal quiet.

Wynne remained on the gentle palfrey Cleve had selected for her. During the hour-long ride their conversation had been stilted. He'd pointed out landmarks of interest—the distant spire of Saint Mary the Virgin in Derrymoor; the ruined castle at Balingford, one of the many adulterines of King Stephen's time; the ancient road that led north to Manchester, Lancaster, and the wild country of the Scots far beyond. But Wynne's replies had been little more than nods and shrugs. What cared she for England's vast resources? She wanted only one thing of this land now, and that was a child sired by a certain English knight.

Though she knew her rudeness was foolish under the circumstances, Wynne was nevertheless unable to control it. She'd contracted a dreadful case of nerves, and now as she watched him approach her mount, her heart pounded so violent a rhythm, she was certain he must hear it.

" 'Tis . . . 'tis indeed a lovely spot," she stammered as he drew to a halt beside her.

"Aye, but there is even more I would have you see." He rested one hand on her left knee while he studied her face with sudden uncertainty. But Wynne barely recognized that unexpected emotion in him, for she was too overcome by her fiery reaction to his touch. Anticipation was surely a more potent aphrodisiac than ever the most powerful herb, she dimly realized. If he only knew how sensitized she was to his touch, how eager she was for his caress.

When he reached his other hand to her, she leaned into his grasp. In an instant he had her down from the saddle, standing before him in the soft, springy earth. For a lingering moment they stared at each other, not speaking words yet conveying nevertheless a world of emotion. Wynne stepped nearer, expecting his hands to slide from her waist to around her back, expecting him to lower his face to meet her upturned lips.

But Cleve instead tightened his hands on her waist and held her awkwardly at arm's length.

"I . . . I have something for you. There." Nervous again, he gestured with his head.

Wynne swallowed her disappointment, then followed the direction of his gaze. At first she did not see the cottage, so hidden was it beyond a pair of apple trees. In addition its stone walls blended into its setting, for it was grown up with vines and mosses, and sheltered beneath a widespread oak growing at its near corner.

It was clearly abandoned, for no kitchen garden bloomed, nor did the chimney reveal even a trace of smoke. As he urged her toward it, she saw that the thatch was old and the wooden door long removed. But it was a sturdy place and large enough for two rooms, not simply one. Had he prepared a pallet for them here?

They paused at the entryway, and peering in, Wynne saw that the place had recently been swept clean. A pile of leaves and dust and animal leavings mounded just beside the stone stoop, and a broom rested yet against the doorframe.

" 'Tis humble, I know," Cleve began. "But it is large and well built. I'll have the roof repaired, as well as whatever else is required." He captured both her hands in his, then backed into the cottage, pulling her along with him. "There's water nearby, the woodlands you love. And I would not be far away. Plus, you would be near to the twins."

Wynne halted in the middle of the fair-sized main room. She'd expected him to try one last time to tempt her to stay. But she'd anticipated a well-planned seduction, a sweet, physical enticement, meant to soften all her objections. On the ride over she had steeled herself to enjoy the seduction, yet not succumb to anything more than that.

This, however . . . this was far worse than what she'd prepared herself for. It seemed he'd come to know her so well, for this lovely glade was one she could almost picture herself in. The children would adore it, and she could clearly imagine herself, standing on this very front stoop, watching as Cleve rode up. Waiting for his return to her arms.

Yet how often would that be? she wondered as reality returned with unpleasant force. Where would he and his wife reside, and how frequently could he spare time for his . . . his mistress?

She took a shaky breath and swallowed the lump that had formed so quickly in her throat. To hide the sudden mist in her eyes, she made a slow circuit of the room. Strong walls, broad hearth. Even the floors were good, flat boards laid over a stone base.

But no matter how fine the accommodations, they were missing one essential. This house would always lack a husband. Cleve did not offer her love and marriage. He offered her lust and a well-constructed cottage. Though he thought it enough—and a part of her was willing to accept it as enough also—she knew it was not. She already had a cottage—a manor house in fact. And as for lust, she feared that was a far too common emotion. Love was far the rarer, and it was love she must have.

With a determined lift of her chin she turned to face the man who meant to break her heart. " 'Tis a lovely place, and with some work it shall make a handsome home."

He stared at her through the dim and dusty atmosphere. "Does this mean you'll stay? Is that what you're saying, Wynne?"

She forced a smile to her face and fought the burning tears away. He looked so dear at that moment. So tall and virile, with the light of eagerness burning in his devouring gaze. At least he wanted her, she told herself. At least she had that to remember and cling to.

Without answering his question she crossed the room to him. Her hands cupped his face to bring his lips near to her own, and at the first touch of them his arms circled her in a breathtaking hug. Like an explosion they came together, every repressed emotion swelling to bursting, every starving sense filled to saturation in one violent melding.

"Jesu, woman. I will never have my fill of you," he whispered against the seeking heat of her mouth. Then his lips pressed down on hers as his tongue surged deep into her mouth. Neither of them held back as their tongues thrust and parried, slid and danced together. His boldness was driven as much by triumph as by desire, she suspected, while hers was formed of love and impending loss. But he did not need to know that, and anyway that did not lessen the overwhelming physical pleasure of it.

His hands slid along her back: one up to become lost in her hair as he held her steady for his sweet, invasive kiss; the other down to cup her derriere and press her urgently to his loins.

I love you, her heart spoke directly to his as she clutched him closer. *I love you*. But they were words she could never speak out loud.

Yet for one fanciful moment she thought he might actually have heard, unspoken though the message was. He pulled breathlessly away, just an inch or two, and searched her eyes as if surprised or confused.

"Wynne," he began hesitantly, although his eyes burned into hers with fierce emotion.

But Wynne knew the time had long passed for talking. The courses of their lives had been set long ago. They were born of the wrong lands and in the wrong time, and events of the past weeks only served to seal their separate fates further. Overcome by sorrow for what could never be, Wynne reached up on tiptoes to kiss him again. She slid her tongue out to trace the seam of his lips, to silence his words. Then she closed her eyes and willed him to do the same. This time was for remembrance, for imprinting every detail of him into her mind so that, awake or asleep, she would ever be able to summon the memory. The day might come when he would forget, but she never would.

As he met her questing kiss and his body pressed demandingly against hers, she knew also that this time would be for love. At least for her. He might never recognize it as such—in truth she didn't want him to. But she knew.

With a groan against her mouth Cleve lifted her so that her feet no longer touched the floor. She reveled in the violent emotions that erupted between them. No magic had ever been stronger than this. No spell she had ever cast had matched the power of this moment. He'd charmed her from the beginning, from his first step onto her lands.

The tiniest gasp caught in her throat. He walked them back into the second room of the cottage, deepening the kiss with every step, devouring her with lips and hands and the very force of his will. But it was not entirely for passion that she gasped in startled realization.

Her lands. Her Radnor Forest. Come to her through the women of her family. Just as the line of seeresses carried that spark of dark knowledge, so did it also convey rights to the vast lands of wild Radnor Forest, from one generation to the next. The far-flung hills and valleys nurtured all within its bounds. But the people of those lands turned to Radnor Manor for guidance, just as Lord William's people turned to him.

In her own way—in the unique way of the Welsh—she was as much an heiress as Edeline.

Cleve halted at a raised bed furnished with a simple mattress and clean linens. He put her on her feet, but his arms did not entirely release her.

"Many nights we shall share in this very room," he

whispered hoarsely. His fingers loosened her coif so that the last of her hair was freed to spill down into his hands. "Sweet witch, you long ago caught me within your magic web, but I vow to weave as potent a spell around you."

Wynne stood still beneath the heady caress of such sweet words. But even as they warmed her battered heart and she held to the comfort of them, she nonetheless could not shake the troublesome thoughts that assailed her. If he knew what lands might be gained through a marriage to her, would he veer from the course he had so long been set upon? If she told him, would that change everything?

One of his hands worked to release the tie at the neck of her bliaut, while the other pulled her face up for another kiss. Like one starved he devoured her mouth, and like a living sacrifice Wynne offered herself body and soul for the taking. The bliaut slipped off one shoulder, then the next. As it slithered down her body, he worked the fastenings of her kirtle. Wynne shifted and twisted as necessary to aid him, yet their lips still clung and their tongues still danced in an ancient rhythm.

For this man she would offer herself like a maiden of old. She would fling herself upon the fire for him, or cast herself upon the blade. But could she use the lands of her mother's family to lure him forever to her side?

She gasped when he palmed her loosened kirtle down her shoulder and arm and let it slide over her bared breast. As if she were two separate parts of the same person, she arched instinctively under his possessive caress. Her body desired him—so fiercely, she truly thought she might go up in flames from the burning need in her. Her heart, too, desired him. But there was that part of her that could not bribe him to take what she so desperately wished to give. Her love was something apart but no less real than her physical need for him. Only if he wanted her love—for love's sake only—could he take it. Not for desire. Nor for lands either.

A piercing pain, as real as a dagger through her heart, brought a cry to her lips, and unbidden tears rose in her eyes.

He paused again. Did he sense her every emotion? she wondered disjointedly. But Wynne refused to let the moment last. She slid one hand down to his girdle and the other lower, tentatively rubbing along the hard bulge that strained his braies.

At once he surged against her hand, and a groan broke free of their joined lips. "Sweet Jesu, Wynne. Don't do that."

With an effort he pulled away from her. They stood one long seething moment, she bared to his eyes as the kirtle was freed to slip down past her hips and settle upon the floor, and he gasping for breath and fumbling with shaking hands to release his own clothes. The tunic he flung aside. The chainse he whipped recklessly over his head. Then, clad only in boots and braies, he reached for her once more.

"You are magic, woman," he murmured as his hands lightly traced parallel paths down her shoulders and arms to her hips. He splayed his fingers wide, letting his thumbs press the soft flesh of her belly while his fingers curved around to the upper swells of her derriere. All the while his eyes swept over her, seeming to possess her lips and breasts and more with their burning touch.

"You are magic," he repeated. "Dark and blistering, drugging me. You make me want—" He broke off, and she saw him swallow and shake his head. His eyes bored into hers.

"Do you know the things I want to do to you?" he

asked in a tortured voice. "Can you sense what I would have of you? There are things between a man and a woman, things never spoken of in the women's quarters."

His hands moved down so that his fingers delved beneath her buttocks into the warm place between her legs. A low moan—her own?—broke the stillness, and her eyes fell closed. She wanted to know everything that might be between a man and a woman, so long as he was that man and she that woman.

"I want to worship your body, Wynne. To touch and kiss and know you in every way. Sweet and loving, hard and demanding. Do you understand? I want to bend you to my touch and know that whatever I demand of you, you will comply."

A violent quiver shook her, but it only served to further incite him. He fell to his knees and pulled her against him. One of his fingers slipped farther, up inside her, and she thrust instinctively against him, almost collapsing from the heat that pulsed through her. Her hands clutched his sweaty shoulders, and when he nuzzled her amulet aside to get to her breasts, her fingers dug deep into his skin.

"Say you'll submit to me, Wynne. There will be no secrets between us, not of the body nor of the mind. Offer yourself to me completely, and I promise I shall do as much for you."

His finger began a rhythmic stroking deep within her velvet folds, while his other hand found her right breast. One aching nipple he teased with his tongue, while the other he rolled between his thumb and forefinger, until she was writhing in a blind agony of desire.

"Say you will be mine, sweet witch. Say it," he persisted between hot, sucking caresses.

Wynne ground her belly against his heated body. She would give him everything, if only he were ready to accept it. "What shall I have of you?" she whispered against the dark silk of his head. She raked her hands through his hair, then knotted her fingers within it and with a rough tug forced him to look up at her. "What shall I ever have of you?" she cried in desperation.

"Everything," he swore, meeting her stark blue gaze with fiery intensity. "Even in mastering you I seem ever to be but your slave. You have only to demand it of me—" He broke off with a muffled oath. Without warning he stood up, lifting her high in his arms as he pressed his cheek against her breasts.

"I have no right to you save what you grant me." He laid her down upon the bed, then braced himself over her and stared down into her huge eyes. "Grant me those rights—every right. To your body." He stroked one finger down her throat, between her breasts and then brushed his knuckles lower to the top of the curls that marked her most secret place. "To your mind." The same hand moved to caress her hair back from her face, and he lowered himself to kiss her brow. "To your heart," he finished in a hoarse whisper. He pressed a chaste kiss to the upper slope of her left breast, then slowly lowered himself to lie over her—heart to heart, she thought as love welled painfully in her chest. How she ached to vow her love then and there, to tell him of the lands he might claim through a marriage to her. Their children might not be born to English titles, but they would be heirs to a history fully as noble and proud. A Welsh history.

But then what, she wondered as misery overset her foolish imaginings. Though he lay upon her in perfect intimacy now, his cheek pressed near to hers, she knew her happiness could not be gained thus. He must choose her for herself as she'd chosen him. Not for family, nor title, nor lands. Only for love.

He lifted his head, and she opened her eyes to meet his gaze. "What shall you grant me, Wynne? Tell me."

She swallowed as she searched his agate-brown eyes. "Whatever you would have of me, my lo—my lord. And more," she added, conscious of how near she'd come to saying what she could not reveal.

"And I'll grant you as much," he swore before he lowered his face to hers. "More," he finished as their lips met in fiery collision. His mouth slanted across hers with startling vehemence, forcing her lips apart and taking absolute possession of her. Like some warring angel he laid claim to all her senses, robbing her of every thought, every memory, save of him.

Wynne responded to his urgency with a demand equal to his own. She welcomed every thrust of his tongue, every stroke of his hand. She arched in reckless need beneath his rock-hard body and fumbled desperately at the waist of his braies. He raised his hips slightly so that she might find the tie, then helped her drag the cloth down his hips.

How he shrugged out of them she did not know. She was too aware of the demanding length of his fully aroused maleness to note the details of anything else. He was there, poised above her, ready to possess her, and she was ready. This time was for love, she thought as emotions clogged her throat. This time was for love.

Then he pulled one of her knees up and, like one truly maddened with desire, he thrust possessively into the damp, receptive core of her. Wynne groaned with the fierce pleasure of it—the joy of being joined to him this way.

"Sweet Jesu," he muttered. "Are you angel or demon to so possess my soul?"

Again her joy surged even higher and more intense, for

it seemed that she did possess him as fully as he possessed her. That must be the source of perfect happiness, of perfect love, she thought. To possess and be possessed equally. To give and receive as much from another.

Then he moved his hips, starting that achingly perfect rhythm, and she thought no more. All was centered in the place of their joining. He sunk deep within her, then withdrew. He thrust again and slowly pulled out. Like a perfect promise and the threat of leaving, he tortured her needy body. He might give, but he could also take away. She might have all, but she could lose everything. In and out he drove, and with every exquisite stroke and every excruciating withdrawal he pushed her beyond the limits of her control.

Her legs wound about him, locking around his body so that he might never leave her. Her arms, too, held tight, clasping him as if in a mortal confrontation. And on and on he thrust, until they were both sinking into the plain mattress, oblivious to all but the dark, spiraling magic they'd created.

Then the magic burst through, higher and farther than even magic was meant to go, and Wynne cried out in a mindless frenzy. "I love you," she sobbed as his mouth ground against hers. His tongue surged into her mouth, mirroring the rhythm of below, and she felt as if she were truly bursting from the very intensity of it. Her entire body reverberated with a nearly painful power. On and on it went, like a tidal wave that crashed endlessly upon her, beating her senseless with its exhilarating strength.

Then he groaned against her mouth and moved even harder and faster than before. "Wynne, Wynne!" he cried her name over and over as he spilled his precious seed within her.

She squeezed her eyes closed, suppressing tears of joy

and wonder as she held him urgently to her. He thrust again, but slower now. Then once more. In a rush the tide receded, leaving them gasping and exhausted, yet replete in a way that was beyond explanation.

Without thinking she kept her long legs wrapped about his hips, holding him within her. She did not wonder about the results of this fiery union of theirs. In her heart she already knew. This perfection could only breed perfection. She would have her child of Cleve. Though she would gladly have him as well, she would take whatever she could with her when she left.

He raised his head and sought her mouth for a warm and weary kiss. "I meant to please you first, before I took my own selfish pleasure, but—"

Wynne kissed him back, slipping her tongue within his lips to silence him. Only when she felt him flicker to life deep within her did she breathlessly break the kiss.

"Yes, I well note your selfishness." She smiled up into his dark eyes. "I am so undone by your selfishness that I shall demand that you pay better attention to me next time."

"Next time?" He moved within her, slowly at first, then a little faster until she gasped with reviving pleasure. "You mean this time," he said with a grin of his own. "Only I shall control myself a little better."

" 'Control,' " Wynne murmured the word drowsily as she concentrated on the exquisite feelings building within her. "That seems the wrong word for what we practice here."

"Do you think so? Well, we shall soon see." He pulled out of her, but silenced her groan of dismay with a finger to her lips. "There are pleasures—extreme pleasures—to be had from the exercise of just a little control. Shall I demonstrate?"

Without waiting for an answer from her, he reached over the side of the bed to find his leather belt. Then he looped it somewhere above her, around a supporting board of the bed. "Hold the ends," he instructed her, tightening her fingers around the two ends of the belt. "Hold on and do not for any reason let go."

Wynne stared warily up at him as he knelt over her, but he only raised a warning brow. "Don't let go, Wynne. You may cry out, try to twist away, or anything else. But don't let go." Then he grasped her hips and slid her toward the foot of the bed so that her arms stretched straight above her head.

At once she understood. She was at his mercy. He knelt at the foot of the bed, proud and virile, his arousal standing before him, both threatening and promising. And she lay pale and vulnerable to him, her breasts thrust high, her nipples erect with desire. How very like a pagan sacrifice she must appear, waiting to be devoured by her wonderful, omnipotent God.

And she was willing. Oh, but she was too, too willing.

"Talk to me, Wynne. Tell me what you want."

"Everything," she admitted. She swallowed as he smiled, and her hands tightened around the leather straps.

"Everything?" His eyes roamed her body, and something leaped in her belly. This time she could only nod her answer, her throat was too constricted with desire.

"Then it shall be as you ask, sweet witch. I shall do everything to you until you scream and pant and faint from the pure pleasure of it."

Wynne closed her eyes when his hands stretched her legs apart, but Cleve kept his eyes open. He was too racked with longing for the woman before him to relinquish even one moment staring at her sweet and delectable body. But it was more than the body he desired. Edeline was as lovely. Other women he'd known had been as beautiful. But Wynne . . .

He ran his hands lightly up each of her legs, stroking his thumbs along the soft inside curves of her calves, then up her knees and thighs until she quivered helplessly beneath him. She was his now, his to possess in every way possible. His to enjoy. His to bring infinite pleasure to.

His to love.

And love her he did, he realized, letting his fingers pause in their torturous exploration. She'd spoken words of love to him, but though he'd not said as much to her, he knew now that his feelings were true. So why did he feel so unsure of her—of what she might do and whether she would long stay with him? She loved him. That should mean she would stay.

He slid his fingers higher, parting the raven-dark curls that protected her sweetest spot. She was so wet and pink, ready for him, demanding his attention, he thought as he slid his body down between her widespread legs.

"You're a feast for the senses, my delicious witch." He dipped his head for a taste, then delved deeper when she gasped and arched in response. "God, but you taste sweet," he murmured as he rubbed the little nub that he knew would bring her even greater pleasure.

"Cleve . . . oh, you must . . . must stop. No."

One of her hands caught in his hair, and he raised his head from its lovely task. "Hold on to the belt, Wynne. Hold on," he ordered.

"Why?" she moaned. "Oh, just come into me."

Cleve fought the desire to do that very thing. He was so hard it hurt. Only by once again plumbing the heated depths of her would he find the relief he sought. But he would give her more first.

"There are pleasures of all sorts, my bewitching girl.

Some of possession; some of being possessed. You shall know them all—"

He broke off when one of her feet slid up the back of his thigh to rub his buttocks. "Damn," he swore. Then he pressed a hungry kiss to the soft flesh of her belly. She would have him exploding with desire if he couldn't get himself under control.

His lips slid down to her secret place once more, aided this time by his hand. He slipped one finger up into her, eliciting another gasp as she twisted in tortured pleasure. His tongue worked swiftly, stroking and rubbing until she was mindless with excitement, while his finger sought her magic place. She was so moist . . . so ready.

Then she arched against him with a convulsive cry, and he felt her explosion against his lips. She quivered in helpless spasms, squeezing around his finger as she peaked over and over again.

His woman, he thought as he pressed the side of his face to her concave belly. His woman now.

When she was still he lifted his head, then slowly slid himself up the damp and slippery length of her. "There is so much to be had between us," he whispered, between kisses along her cheek and temple. Beneath him she felt so warm and alive, though she was well and truly spent and drained. Still, he knew there was more to come.

"Let go of the belt." He stroked his hands up her arms, then twined his fingers in her slackened ones. Her palms fit so easily within his, he marveled. Her body fit so well with his, so perfectly. Then her hands tightened around his, and her eyes opened to meet his gaze.

"Control is a truly wondrous thing," she admitted in a throaty whisper. "Shall I . . . shall I try as much on you?"

He smiled indulgently, but to his surprise she brought

his hands to the leather belt. "Hold on. Tight," she ordered. Then she pushed against his chest until he rolled over. In a moment she lay over him, and he became her captive.

"You are my sacrificial virgin," she stated. "Well, perhaps not a virgin." She grinned and forced herself upright, straddling his lean hips. "Now, we shall see just how good *your* control is." So saying, she began to explore his chest with feather-light touches.

Though he willingly submitted to her gentle explorations, Cleve found himself squirming beneath the heady caresses. When had his ribs become so sensitive a place? How could the hard muscles of his waist leap to fire merely at the rake of her nails?

Then she scooted down to straddle his thighs, revealing the growing length of his manhood. He watched with bated breath as she stared at it, and if anything, he became even more rigid under her perusal. Then she innocently licked her bottom lip, and he groaned out loud.

Wynne smiled at that. "So, you can be teased and tortured as easily as I." She watched his face as her hands slid over his belly to the springing mass of dark hair at his groin. When she grasped him in her warm hand, however, Cleve's eyes clenched shut.

"Damn you, Wynne. Do not prolong this—"

"Why? Can't you bear it?" She slid her hand, slowly, deliberately, up the demanding length of him, paying curious attention to the ridged end. "The skin is amazingly soft and silky here," she murmured.

Cleve had such a tense grip on the belt that he feared he would never be able to release it. he had ceased breathing even. Only when she leaned low to kiss and then taste him did a rush of air burst from his lungs.

"Don't, Wynne. There's no time left—" He broke off with an oath and in an instant released the belt ends, grabbed her hips, and pulled her up to straddle his groin.

"What of your control?" she laughed as she braced her hands upon his shoulders and her hair spilled forward around them both.

"Control bedamned," he answered. Then he raised her hips above his erect manhood and with one movement joined them again.

Wynne gasped, and he groaned. But she understood her role, and in a moment they were moving in exquisite tandem.

The tangled richness of her hair caressed his shoulders and arms, curtaining them in a silken cocoon. Likewise did she sheath him in silken wonder, and as her rhythm quickened, he found her breasts.

She cried out, words meaning nothing yet conveying clearly the desire she felt. First one firm breast did he fondle, caressing its warm weight, sucking its jutting peak. Then the other he found, until her rocking movements grew frantic. His hands gripped her hips, urging her faster and faster, until she cried out in agonizing completion.

It was perfect. She was perfect, he thought amidst the mindless joy of it all. Then his fingers tightened, and he drove the final few thrusts into her, giving her the last of everything he possessed.

When she collapsed upon him, he held her close, so close, he feared to crush her. But she accepted it, and he breathed in the sweet aroma of clean hair, sweaty skin, and deep, lusty sex. If he could but preserve this moment, keep this feeling, then all would be right with his world. If he could but keep her forever . . . Perhaps a child of their own . . .

He smoothed a damp tendril of midnight-dark hair back from her temple. "I love you, Wynne," he whispered, knowing he could never feel this way about anyone but her. Then they slept.

25

"What if there is a child?"

Wynne faced Cleve in the castle yard, her chin raised and her resolve firm. But inside, her heart shredded into a thousand bleeding pieces. "I am well able to ensure there will be no child," she answered in a carefully controlled tone. That was not precisely a lie, she consoled herself as she stared up into his furious face. She was well able to ensure it. She simply had no intentions of doing so.

"Dammit, no!" He grabbed her by both shoulders and lowered his face to the level of hers. "You don't have to do that. Don't you see? If you stay, I'll take care of everything."

"You're the one who doesn't see." She jerked out of his grasp, then faced him, fighting down that part of herself that needed so badly to stay with him. "You're the one who doesn't see," she repeated quietly. "I don't need to be taken care of. I've taken care of myself since I was a girl. I've taken care of five babies. Five children." She shook her head. "I told you I was returning to my home. You cannot make me stay."

But you could come with me. Her silent plea begged to be

spoken aloud, but she would not let it. It was clear what his choice was. As a wife Edeline brought her lands and a title, all those things a bastard-born child such as he had been could only dream of. But his dream was about to become reality now, and Wynne was a fool to hope he'd ever abandon it for her.

She took a deep breath, holding but tenuously to her shaky resolve. "I have already taken my leave of Lord William. If . . . if you would just say farewell to the children. To Arthur," she added, unable now to disguise the pain in her voice.

He stared at her disbelievingly. Then his eyes grew cold as ice, and his jaw tightened. He turned his head to stare somewhere beyond her. "I suppose yesterday was your leave-taking of me?"

Wynne couldn't answer, but he obviously took her silence to be an admission.

"Christ!" he exploded. "You could have had the decency to let me in on your little secret. Instead you led me on—" He broke off, then locked his piercing gaze with her miserable one. "Did my avowal of love come too late?"

Wynne sucked in her breath as the pain in her chest increased tenfold. She'd tried so hard to put those words of his out of her mind, and yet she'd clung to them ever since, wondering if they'd been said at all. Perhaps she'd only imagined them, so desperate had she been to hear such vows from him. Or perhaps, as was more likely, he'd been so consumed with their passion that they'd just slipped out, truthful at the time, but not meant to apply beyond the ecstasy of the moment.

Still, she'd clung to that "I love you," hoping against hope. Not wanting to know the terrible truth and most certainly not wishing to discuss it with him. But here he was, in the watery morning light, dredging it up to be examined.

She swallowed, then cleared her throat. "That has nothing to do with anything. Rhys and Madoc are settled. I am reasonably content that their life here will be . . . good. It will be good for them. And Lord William has agreed to be most generous in allowing visits."

"I do love you, Wynne. Don't leave me."

The simplicity of his words and the stark intensity in his eyes cut through all the logical babble she had surrounded herself with. Like a knife they were, a razor-edged dagger, slicing into her heart and striking a mortal blow.

Unable to bear the pain, unable to respond at all, Wynne flinched as if from a physical blow, then turned and forced herself to walk away. One foot, then the other. *Don't look back. Don't look forward. Just keep moving until you can't go any farther.* All the way to Wales and her familiar woodlands. To the Giant's Trail and Crow's Moor. But she knew in her heart that was not far enough to break the pull he had on her heart. Not nearly so.

Arthur stood against the supporting column of the stable shed. He'd long ago lost interest in his brother's mock battle and had watched Wynne's conversation with Cleve instead. It hadn't lasted long. Nor had it ended well, if Cleve's furious expression and her stiff posture as she left were any indication. Though Arthur was too far away to have heard what was said, he feared he knew. They were still going to leave today. And Cleve was going to marry the Lady Edeline.

"Damn," he swore.

Isolde looked up at his unusual vehemence. She and Bronwen were playing with a pair of half-grown kittens from the stable, but at his frown she abandoned that sport.

She followed his gaze to the retreating Wynne, and her face clouded as well.

"They're not going to get married, are they?"

Arthur rounded on her, his fists knotted. "They are too!"

Had it been either of the twins who'd shouted so belligerently at her, she would have shouted back even louder. But this was gentle Arthur, and she knew he was just upset.

"We can't make them get married," she said patiently.

"Only they can do that," Bronwen added.

"Grown-ups are stupid!" he shouted back.

Even Rhys and Madoc drew up at Arthur's uncharacteristic behavior. "What's the matter—"

"—with you?"

"Oh, shut up!" Arthur yelled. "Just everybody leave me alone."

"Don't you tell me to shut up." Rhys stuck out his chin challengingly.

"Me neither." Madoc advanced on the smaller Arthur. "I'll knock your block off if you say that again."

Isolde threw her hands up in the air. "Boys must be the stupidest things in the whole wide world! Fighting doesn't do any good." She planted her fists on her hips and glared at the twins. "Don't you even care why Arthur's so sad?"

"I'm not sad!" Arthur yelled. "I'm . . . I'm mad."

"You are not," Isolde answered with equal vigor. "You're sad because Cleve's gonna marry Lady Edeline instead of Wynne. Why don't you just admit it?"

There was a brief silence. Then Arthur slumped back against the column and slowly slid down to a sitting position on the straw-littered ground. "They should get married to each other," he muttered, all the anger gone from his voice. "They should."

As one, the other four children gathered around him, dropping to their knees or sitting cross-legged. "Why doesn't he just marry her, then? I don't understand," Bronwen whispered.

Madoc scratched his head. "It all has to do with castles and land, I think."

Arthur nodded disconsolately. "Wynne explained it last night."

"She did?" Rhys asked.

Arthur sighed. "Not about her and Cleve exactly. But it's the same thing as what she said about you and Madoc."

"*I'm* not gettin' married," Madoc interjected.

"You'll change your mind when you grow up," Bronwen stated confidently.

"No, I won't."

"Oh, just be quiet," Isolde scolded. She took Arthur's hand. "What did Wynne say?"

He stared at the ground. "She said Lord William had promised her that Rhys and Madoc would never have to marry anybody they didn't want to marry." He looked over at his brothers. "Remember? She said you could marry just 'cause you loved somebody. Your father can't make you get married to some girl just to get her castle or something."

"So?" Rhys said. "Wynne doesn't have a castle or anything, and—"

"—neither does Cleve."

Arthur sent the other two boys a quelling stare. "That's the problem, don't you see? Cleve wants a castle, and Lady Edeline has one. Plus, your father wants to give Cleve a reward for finding you two."

They were quiet again until Bronwen spoke. "I don't think Lady Edeline *wants* to marry Cleve. She likes Druce best. I saw her crying on his shoulder in the garden just a little while ago."

"Lord William is wrong to make her marry Cleve. It's all his fault," Isolde said.

"But he's lord here," Madoc defended his new father. "He gets to make all the rules."

"Well, that's a stupid rule. And anyway why can't he make a different rule? He could make Cleve marry Wynne and Lady Edeline marry Druce."

"But he doesn't want to change the rules," Arthur explained.

"I bet he'd do it if Madoc and Rhys asked him to."

Everyone turned to look at Bronwen.

"Well, I mean, he gives them everything they want."

Rhys shrugged. "We could ask him, I guess."

"I bet Lord William wishes he had married your mother," Bronwen added with a wise nod.

Silence descended once more as they each thought of the unknown women who'd given them life. Then Rhys spoke. "He asked me if I remembered her."

"Me too," Madoc quietly added. "I don't, though. But I wish I did."

"He said she was the most beautiful woman he'd ever seen. Beautiful on the inside and on the outside."

"I wonder who my mother was," Bronwen murmured, a sad note in her voice.

"Wynne is our mother," Arthur stated. Though the other children had grown quiet with their own somber thoughts, he had brightened considerably. "She's a good mother, and Cleve would be a good father to us." He fixed his hazel-green stare on Madoc and Rhys. "Just because we might have to leave today to go home doesn't mean we have to give up. You two will still be here."

Suddenly he laughed and clapped his hands. "I know! Rhys and Madoc can be the spies."

"What do you mean?" Madoc asked.

"Like a war or something?"

"Sort of," Arthur replied. "But you know, war is not just the fighting and stuff. It's strategy too. That's what Cleve said. He said strategy was very important. And he told me I was very good at understanding strategy."

They left when the sun was at its zenith. Though Lord William had encouraged her to delay till morn, Wynne would not hear of it. Barris's logical arguments fell on deaf ears with her as well. As for Druce, he was so angry, she feared he might not even accompany them back to Wales.

But Wynne could not deal with their troubled reactions. Her own emotions were in too much turmoil for her to think beyond one minute to the next. Gather her belongings. Have the cook pack sufficient supplies. Don't forget the tent.

Her head ached and her stomach clenched in nauseated waves, yet she forced herself to hurry, and to hurry everyone else as well. Finally there was nothing left but to don her traveling mantle and to say her good-byes.

She found the five children in the garden gathered around Lord William. When six sets of eyes turned on her, she felt a renewed spasm of pain. She'd dwelt so much on her own sorrow—she was losing both the man she loved and two of her beloved children this day. But the children were parting from one another as well. Bronwen's face already showed a pink nose and puffy eyes from crying. Like Isolde, she sat on Lord William's knee, while the boys sat at his feet.

Wynne fought down a lump in her throat, promising to

have a good cry sometime later when no one would be around to hear. Only just let it not be now.

"I . . . I would speak with the children a moment," she said in a strained voice.

Lord William stared at her from beneath his lowering gray brows, as if he saw her now for the very first time. He patted the girls, and after they slid from his lap he stood up and shook out his richly embroidered tunic. Then he cleared his throat. "If I did not adequately say so before, well, let me say now that you are to be commended. These children—all of them—are fine and strong. And intelligent also. You have been a good mother to them, and I thank you for it. From the bottom of my heart I thank you."

His fervent words so took her by surprise that Wynne was forced to brush an escaping tear from her cheek.

"I will keep my vow," he added. "About the twins' education and about their marriage prospects. They've just been reminding me that they are to wed by their own choice—for love, as Rhys says. I promise you that I shall not forget. And you, of course, shall be well informed of every aspect of their lives."

He smiled, then shifted awkwardly on his bad leg. Arthur was quick to hand him his cane, and Lord William tousled the boy's head fondly. "You are, every one of you, always welcome at Kirkston Castle or any other of my houses and demesnes. Should you ever need help, I hope you will count me as your ally. Your friend."

Wynne watched through misty eyes as he moved ponderously away. She was doing the right thing to leave Rhys and Madoc with their father. She knew that now. So why did it hurt so terribly?

She fell to her knees with arms outstretched, and at once five small bodies hurtled into her embrace.

"Why can't you stay?" Rhys cried, all bravado gone in the face of their impending separation.

"Don't go, Wynne. Don't," Madoc sobbed against her neck.

Rhys and Madoc so seldom wept, Wynne thought as misery washed over her. They never wept, nor did she used to either. But as she clung to them, she cried, weeping as if her heart had broken, never to be mended again. She held to them and they held to her, a small, fragile family formed against all odds, then broken apart when it had seemed they'd already gotten past the worst life could throw at them.

But nothing was as bad as this. Nothing.

"Now, boys. Listen to me, sweetlings," she managed to say in a choked voice. "We part today, I know. But not forever. For we shall visit. You to Radnor Manor, and we . . ." She paused, fearful to promise to return to this place. What if Cleve should be here too?

"You will come back to visit us—"

"—won't you, Wynne?" the two boys pleaded.

She nodded. "Yes. Yes, of course I will. I love you both too much not to visit you. Now." She took a shaky breath and forced a smile. "Let's dry our faces, shall we? Here, use the lining of my mantle."

Once they were all dried and standing upright again, Wynne looked over her little brood. Such a varied lot: fair and dark; delicate and brawny. "We must leave you now. But in our hearts we'll still be together. We're still a family and . . . and I love you so much."

She pulled Rhys and Madoc into a smothering embrace. "I love you so much," she whispered against their dark curls, breathing in the familiar scent of them, sweet and sweaty. Earthy. It would be so long before she could again do this. "Never forget how much I love you."

It was a solemn group that made its way from the garden to the castle yard. The horses stood ready. Lord William's men who were to accompany them relaxed as they waited, saying their casual farewells to family and friends. Though Barris stood among them, Wynne saw at once that Druce was not there. Nor was Edeline.

But Cleve was.

When Arthur saw Cleve, he broke into a run. Though Wynne would rather have looked anywhere but at their emotional farewell, her eyes would not be forced away. As if they anticipated the long days of their impending fast, her eyes feasted upon Cleve, seeing all the good things—his strength, his vitality. His gentleness. *He would make a wonderful father*, the unbidden thought came once more. A wonderful father and a good husband—that is, if he did not take a mistress, as he'd meant to take her.

That thought sobered her, and she was able at last to tear her eyes away. Though she heard him take his leave of the girls, and Barris as well, she concentrated on her placid mare, settling herself comfortably upon it. Then Barris put the children into the wagon Lord William had provided for their journey, and they were ready to go.

Still the call to depart did not come, and Wynne knew with a sinking certainty why. Cleve crossed the yard, before Lord William and his various daughters and sons-in-law and everyone else, and halted beside her left knee.

"Safe journey, Wynne."

She didn't want to meet his gaze, though courtesy demanded it. Still, it was not courtesy that turned her eyes toward him. It was her insatiable need to look into his eyes one last time. Despite all that lay between them—his need for lands and a title; her need to have him want only her, for herself and nothing else—at that moment she could not see him as anything but the man she loved.

She opened her mouth to speak, then consciously had to force the words to come. *"Ffarwel,"* she whispered as her eyes drank in this last sight of him. "I . . . I wish you well, Cleve FitzWarin. You and . . . and Edeline."

Then she jerked her horse about and, because tears blinded her, trusted the animal to find its way through the crowded courtyard. She heard the wagon start forward, and the restless shuffling of the other eager animals. But they were simply background sounds. In her ears she heard only Cleve's low and rumbling voice. He'd said once that he loved her. But today he'd just said good-bye.

26

Rhys and Madoc stood in the narrow stairhall, pressed against the rough stone wall with stick-swords clutched in their fists. "It's that door," Rhys pointed at a solid, closed portal.

"What if it isn't?" Madoc asked. "What if she's not there?"

"Then we'll keep on lookin' till we find her. We're spies, remember? We have a war to win."

"A war to win," Madoc repeated, his face brightening. "All right, then. Let's go."

They crept toward the door then, and when it seemed safe—no one was about at all this hot afternoon—they pressed their ears to the cracks around the door.

"I don't hear anything."

"Maybe she's asleep."

As one they pushed the door, then jumped when the old hinges creaked in protest.

"Go away," the muffled words came, thick and petulant. "Go away, I said!"

The boys stared at each other, gathering courage. Then

they pushed the door fully open and ventured into Lady Edeline's chamber.

Because the room faced the courtyard instead of an outer castle wall, the window slits were wider and the chamber was well lit, though no candles burned within. It was simply furnished save for the fine bed that dominated the low-ceilinged space. The bed was huge with four massive posts and generous drapings of forest-green bed linens. All in all, just the thing to capture two small boys' imaginations. That bed could easily become a mighty fortress or a storm-tossed ship. Or it could be a hidden mountain hideaway.

The twins advanced forward as one, diverted from their task by the vast possibilities of this high, enclosed bed. But when Lady Edeline sat up abruptly, they stumbled to a halt. Their fortress was already occupied. What were they to do now?

"I said go away," Edeline demanded, glaring at them. But when she spied only two small boys staring up at her with twin faces reflecting both guilt and determination, she let out a frustrated sigh and slapped at the deep, down-filled mattress. She'd expected her father, but these two were almost worse. "What do you want?" she asked, flopping down on her back to stare up at the knot of gathered fabric above her head.

She heard them shuffle forward but did not bother to look over at them. One of them cleared his throat. "We . . . uh . . . we think you should marry Druce, not Cleve."

With a jerk Edeline sat up. "What? No—" she cut off the other one when he would have repeated his brother's words. "I heard what you said. But . . . but why do you think that?"

The two glanced at each other, then both turned their

almost-black eyes upon her. "Can we get up on your bed?"

"It's much nicer than ours."

"Yes of course. Get up right here. Now"—she faced them on her knees—"why do you want me to marry Druce?"

"Because you love him."

"And Druce loves you." One of them jabbed his stick at a thick fold of drapery. "Wynne said *we* only have to marry who we want—"

"—only we don't want to marry anybody," the other one added. Then he tackled his brother, and they began to roll around, balling themselves up in her rumpled bedcovers amidst much giggling and shouts of glee.

"Wait. Just wait a minute," she protested, catching them in her arms. She forced them to face her. "You may play in my bed all afternoon if you like. Only first explain something to me. Did Druce tell you to talk to me? Or . . . or Wynne?"

"Arthur did," they chorused. "He said you love Druce, not Cleve, and Wynne loves Cleve. So you should marry Druce."

"Arthur? You mean the other lad?"

"Arthur is very smart," one of the boys replied sagely, while the other nodded agreement.

"That may very well be true, but Father will never agree to let me marry Druce. Nor will Sir Cleve step aside," Edeline added morosely.

"Arthur says we have to change their minds," the one with the scar on his brow said.

Edeline pursed her lips. "Which one are you?"

"I'm Rhys—"

"—and I'm Madoc."

"And just how does Arthur expect us to change my father's—*our* father's mind?"

"Well, he says we can talk him into anything—"

"—'cause he's so glad to find us—"

"—and because Isolde said he really loved our mother—"

"—a lot."

Edeline sat back on her heels. "He was married to *my* mother. He should never have—" She broke off in mid-sentence and for a moment only stared at the pair before her. Though she resented them on many levels, she could not deny that they were a rather appealing pair, with their dark, curling hair and sparkling eyes. She'd not been able to understand her father's obsessive need to find them. But now, facing them, her resentment began to fade. Maybe it was true. Maybe her father *had* loved their mother. She was certain he'd never truly loved hers.

"How does Isolde know he loved your mother?"

"Because she's got the vision—"

"—just like Wynne."

Edeline let that sink in as she mulled things over, until the boys began to get restless once more. "Rhys. Madoc. Just wait a moment. Tell me, does Cleve love Wynne?"

"Bronwen says he does," Madoc answered. He leaped up and whirled about, then collapsed on top of his brother.

Druce had said the same, she thought as the energetic pair began to wrestle in earnest. If that was true, perhaps Arthur was right. Maybe if she played on her father's sentiments . . .

That would still leave Cleve, of course. But if he was offered some other reward, one that might not include a wife but was nevertheless generous . . . And of course if she acted the shrew toward him. If he was to find her the most unappealing of wives . . .

Cleve pushed Ceta as hard and fast as the gallant steed could go. Wynne had headed west, so he rode east. The more miles between them, the better, he thought bitterly. The farther she was from him, the less he would feel this cruel tearing of his heart. It was as if he were being ripped into shreds, as if a part of him were drawn, despite his will, to the misty hills of Wales, and especially the dark, mysterious forest at Radnor.

But that was an absurd thought. Wales held nothing for him. He would be just another poor, landless knight there. Hadn't he struggled the past fifteen years to do better than that?

He rode until he was exhausted and Ceta could go no farther. Behind them the sun had dipped beneath the topmost branches of the forest, and long fingers of shadows crept forward, covering everything with impending darkness.

He dismounted, then leaned his head against Ceta's heaving flank. "Sorry, old fellow. Sorry," Cleve muttered, cursing his recklessness for pushing a valuable animal so hard. He forced himself upright and began to walk the weary animal, following the narrow road blindly, just walking ever eastward until a light in the distance caught his eyes. Only then did Cleve look around, gaining his bearings. He was near to Purvis, he realized. There was a stream ahead where he and Ceta could refresh themselves, and he could seek shelter at Purvis Castle. After all, once he wed the Lady Edeline, Purvis would become their home. Lord William's retainers there might as well meet their new master now, and he could ascertain how well they maintained the place in between visits from their liege lord.

With that task in mind, he increased their pace, and after a short interlude at the trickling beck, they approached Edeline's dower castle.

Though night had well and truly enveloped the land, a brilliant quarter moon lit the fields before the castle. Cleve paused on the road, examining the small stone keep set high upon an open mound. A stout stone wall would be needed, he decided, perhaps built upon the existing ring mound, if that proved sufficient space for the other buildings he envisioned. A granary. A stone kitchen—not the wooden lean-to that abutted the keep's farthermost side. Stables. A chapel.

He urged Ceta forward, then just as quickly reined in. Inexplicably he couldn't bear the thought of sleeping at Purvis. Not tonight.

But that was idiotic, a rational voice countered, urging him toward the keep. If he did not sleep at Purvis, then where? The open fields or forest? On the hard ground with neither food nor drink to fill his belly?

Yet still Cleve could not do it. Ceta danced in a tight circle, sensing an end to the hard day's ride and a generous portion of feed, but Cleve kept him in rein. He did not want to sleep at Purvis. It was the last place in the world where he could find comfort this night.

With a vicious oath at his own perversity he drew the protesting destrier about. What a maudlin fool he'd become. And all on account of one impossible woman. He would just have to find himself a mossy place to lie down, cover himself with his mantle, and his rumbling belly be damned.

Once he headed west, however, his destination became

suddenly clear to him. He would find the cottage, the commodious abode he'd offered to Wynne.

This time it was the rational portion of his mind that rebelled. To enter that cozy place—to lie where he and Wynne had lain together—now *that* was truly madness.

Yet once fixed on his destination, Cleve knew he could not turn back. Wynne was gone from him forever, but her memory still burned inside his heart. He knew somehow that it always would. How much worse could it be to revel in those memories just this one last time?

Lord William remained in his chair once the last of the day's business was complete. King Solomon had never done so well, Lord William thought as he rubbed his belly. He'd successfully negotiated an agreement between the two freehold tanners in his largest village, Chipping Way. He'd resolved a dispute about water rights, sentenced a pair of thieves to the stocks, and granted three men the right to marry.

When his belly rumbled hungrily, he rubbed the considerable expanse once more. But even as he wondered how long it would be before the evening meal would be served, another part of his mind lingered on the subject of marriages—more specifically on Edeline's impending marriage to Sir Cleve.

What the devil was wrong with the girl? he wondered, not for the first time that day. She was pale as a wraith, hiding in her chamber the livelong day. And when she did come out, a skittish hart could not have been more wary, fearful of hunters at every turn. It was becoming more and more clear, however, that the only hunter Edeline feared was her bridegroom, Sir Cleve.

But why? The man was young and handsome. He had all his teeth, for pity's sake, and all his hair. He even had a courtly manner—save with that Welshwoman. With her he was curt and demanding. Surly, even. And therein, Lord William feared, lay the problem.

"John," he bellowed. "Refill my cup. And bring me a joint of meat from the kitchen." While he waited for the refreshment that would tide him over until the evening meal, Lord William drummed his fingers thoughtfully on the grainy tabletop.

Cleve had disappeared yesterday, shortly after the Welshwoman had left with her three children. Edeline had taken to her bed shortly thereafter. Cleve had ridden off to the east. That had been verified by the midday watch. He'd ridden east while Wynne ab Gruffydd had headed west toward Radnor and Wales. Clearly he did not pursue her.

Yet that meant nothing. Hadn't he himself once abandoned a woman he loved, angry when she would not leave her home and come to England with him? Lord William's brow furrowed as he recalled that long-ago day, still so fresh in his memory. Could Cleve and this Welsh girl be as cursed as he and Angel were? Could they love and yet be unable to overcome their differences?

John filled Lord William's goblet, then left the ewer close at hand. A serving wench placed a trencher before him bearing a fleshy joint of mutton, yet Lord William's appetite had suddenly waned. He should not give a thought to the youthful yearnings of two people not under his care. Yet he did owe each of them a debt. The one had raised his sons into strong, sturdy lads, and the other had found them for him.

But there was Edeline to consider. Her first bridegroom had succumbed to a fever. Cleve would make a good husband to her and a strong addition to the Somerville family. Though the girl was anxious about her impending marriage to him, perhaps in time they would come to love one another.

He was sunk in thought, playing idly with his goblet, when Rhys and Madoc burst into the hall. At once Lord William brightened. With them at least he had no doubts. They were his sons, borne by his beloved Angel, whom he never should have left behind. But at least he had them now, and as so often occurred when they were with him, he had the sure sense that Angel observed him from her heavenly abode. And that she approved.

"Father, Father!" the irrepressible pair chorused as they charged across the slate-floored hall.

"What say you, lads?" Then he grimaced as he spied their begrimed condition. From head to toe they were both filthy, as if they'd rolled about in a muddy hole. And they stank. He wrinkled his nose at their rank odor.

"By damn, have you two taken up residence in the pigsty? What have you been about?"

"One of the cats has kittens. But they won't come to us—"

"We chased them into the barn—"

"—and past the pigs."

They both stared up at him. "Can we each have a kitten of our own?"

Lord William began to laugh, his earlier mood completely forgotten in the joy of being a part of his sons' lives. "If you bathe now—*if*, when you answer the dinner bell, you are clean and neat and do not stink—then yes, you may each claim a kitten all your own."

As if they sensed his generous mood, the boys shared a look. "Can we each have—"

"—a puppy too?"

Lord William's laughter boomed across the hall, causing several of his retainers to startle. But when they spied the identical boys, the servants only smiled and returned to their tasks. Life was always better when the lord was happy.

"Aye, you may each have a pup. Anything at all, my lads. Anything at all."

"Anything at all?" Madoc asked. Once again the boys' gazes met.

Rhys piped up. "May Edeline have anything she wants as well?"

Lord William's brow raised. "Edeline? Why, Edeline already has everything she wishes. And more." But even as he said it, he knew that, in one area at least, that was not true. But surely these two children did not mean that.

"I think she *would* like something else," Rhys said, his face gone grave.

Lord William pursed his lips and stared at his sons. "Do you, now? And shall I be forced to guess, or shall you tell me?"

"She wants to marry Druce—"

"—not Cleve," the pair answered without a moment's hesitation.

Lord William's brow furrowed. "Druce? You mean the Welsh archer?"

Before either of the twins could respond, a commotion at the entrance of the hall drew all their attention. Even the lad raking the ashes from the hearth looked up when Cleve strode in, for it was clear by his tense posture and purposeful stride that some weighty matter drove him.

So he'd come at last. Though Lord William was put out at so obviously being the last to know what was going on around him, he nonetheless was hard put to suppress a satisfied smile. He bent down to his boys and gave them each a fond pat. "Go on and do your bathing quickly. If you're not completely clean by dinner, however, our agreement is off."

"But Father—"

"We'll speak of Druce and Edeline later," he interrupted them. He fixed them with a stern look. "If you want those kittens, you'd best hurry."

Desire for the kittens warred with their need to fully impart the message they'd clearly been prompted to deliver. By whom? Lord William wondered for a moment. But it didn't really matter. He grinned as they scampered off, shouting a bright hello to Cleve as they ran by him.

Cleve's nose curled up as their awful stench assailed him, and that served to increase Lord William's good humor even more. He leaned back in his sturdy chair and stretched his lame leg. Ah, but his life was good.

"Well, Sir Cleve. We missed you last night and again today. Is anything amiss?"

Cleve leaned across the table toward the other man, bracing himself on his knuckles. "Yes, milord," he answered tautly. "Something is definitely amiss."

That was the right answer, Lord William thought as Cleve began to talk. That was definitely the right answer.

27

Isolde looked up from the intricate pattern she traced in the dust with a willow wand. She sniffed, then peered around her as if someone did play a trick on her. "Arthur? Are you teasing me?" she called, but there was no answer. Arthur lingered still in the meadow, she realized when she squinted into the late-afternoon sunshine. He lay on his thinking rock, staring up at a solitary red kite wheeling and circling on high.

Bronwen helped Gwynedd with her spinning; Isolde could hear the quiet murmur of their voices inside the manor. As for Wynne, she had not been in the mood for teasing since they'd left England.

When the odd tingle came again, Isolde straightened up and peered suspiciously around her. Somebody *was* trying to play a trick on her, and she didn't like it. The back of her neck tickled, and now so did the pit of her stomach.

Someone was coming. The thought popped into her head from nowhere. Someone was coming; she'd better tell Wynne.

But Wynne already knew. When Isolde dashed breathlessly toward the damp glade that her aunt retreated to so often, she found Wynne standing very still. Very alert.

"Someone . . . someone's coming," the child panted.

Wynne looked over at the child, and her brows lifted in surprise. "You saw them? Or you just knew?"

Isolde drew back at that. "I . . . I just knew." Her small face broke into a wondering smile. "I just knew!"

Wynne smoothed the child's dark hair back from her cheek fondly, then pulled her close for a tight hug. She seemed ever to be clutching her three remaining children to her these days. Touching them. Kissing them. They'd always been precious to her, but now . . . now that she lived in the shadow of loss, she valued them all the more.

"So you shall follow in your mother's path," Wynne murmured. "I am so glad. Shall we go tell Aunt Gwynedd?"

Isolde nodded. Hand in hand they started off, but then Isolde paused. "What about whoever it is that's coming?"

Wynne tried to swallow the butterflies that rose in her stomach, but without much success. "He will get here soon enough. We'll deal with him then."

"Do you know who it is?"

Wynne knew. She'd known it with a certainty that had at first taken her breath away. Like a fist to her stomach it had caught her unaware. But she was recovering from the initial shock now, and she refused to speculate or wonder why he'd come.

"We shall know who it is soon enough," she replied, deliberately evading Isolde's question. "We'd better hurry. Why don't you go and collect Arthur?" *While I try to confront Cleve FitzWarin before he reaches the manor*, she decided in that moment.

Wynne watched as Isolde dashed off ahead of her, the skirts of her kirtle and tunic flaring about her plump little legs. The children would be so happy to see Cleve. Especially Arthur. But what of when he left? They'd hardly had time to heal from the loss of Rhys and Madoc. Did Cleve now mean to start things with her all over again?

Between the anxious pounding of her heart and the furious knot in her stomach, Wynne was in fine fettle when she reached the Ancient Road. He was coming this way. She could tell. But he would not get past her. Not this time. He could just take himself and his band of ruffians back to England.

But when Cleve finally appeared around a bend in the narrow track, he was alone. No one rode with him, save three sumpter animals packed high with goods, an additional destrier, and a delicate mare, which followed on lead reins.

She stepped from the deep shade of a heavily branched oak, to stand alone in the middle of the worn trail. Though she'd been so certain of her ability to send him away, the sight of him shook her confidence sorely. Added to that, his peculiar traveling circumstances left her confused. Why did he travel alone?

When he spied her, he neither slowed his pace nor increased it. He just bore down on her steadily until he halted his destrier but an arm's span from her.

"Wynne." He said only her name, no words of greeting or explanation. Yet she knew he was glad to see her. His eyes told her that, for they drank in her form as if he could quench his thirst only in that fashion. She also devoured the sight of him, hungry as she'd never suspected for just a glimpse of his perfect masculine beauty. What was it about him that touched her heart so completely? Her eyes moved over him, noting every detail: his dusty clothes; his damp hair; the weary lines in his face. How she wished to smooth those lines away with her fingers and her lips.

In self-defense she closed her eyes, shutting out the sight of him in the vain hope that it might help. When it didn't, she focused instead on the animals he led, watching as they lowered their heads and nosed around alongside the road for something to eat.

The silence seemed endless. To still her distraught nerves, she cleared her throat. "Are you traveling a distance?" she asked, then winced inwardly to initiate such noncommittal conversation. Where had her anger fled? Where was her backbone?

"No." His saddle creaked as he dismounted, and Wynne's gaze flew back to his face at once.

"Stay on your horse," she warned as panic rose suddenly in her chest. "Just turn yourself right around and go back to England. You have no reason to be in Wales, least of all in *my* forests."

He released the destrier's reins and took a step nearer to her. "I have a very good reason for being here," he replied in a low and hesitant voice.

Wynne pressed her lips together and shook her head. He had a very good reason, and yet he was hesitant? That made no sense whatsoever. Then her heart stopped. "Is it the twins? Are they—"

"They're fine. They're fine, Wynne. I promise you."

In those brief seconds when she was so vulnerable, he moved up to her, and now he reached forward to grasp her upper arms. But when he would have pulled her to him, Wynne jerked away. His touch was too strong. Like magic it invaded all her senses, weakening her every time. She backed away from him, afraid of what she might do if his touch lingered too long upon her.

"Go away, Cleve FitzWarin. Go away from here, and

never may your shadow fall across mine again. Go back to England and—"

"Cleve!"

Wynne whirled about at Arthur's glad cry.

"Cleve! You came!" the boy cried as he began to run down the narrow road toward them, his feet churning furiously and his arms pumping. His face was alight with joy, but the very sight of it caused Wynne's heart to plummet anew.

She faced Cleve again, anguish painting her features. "Why are you here? Haven't you done enough damage to me and my family! What more do you want of us?"

He did not answer, and in truth she had not expected him to. By then Arthur had reached them and flung himself into Cleve's arms.

"Why, hello, lad. Hello, Isolde and Bronwen," he added when those two ran up as well.

"I knew you would come. I knew it!" Arthur boasted from his lofty position in Cleve's arms.

"I knew it before you!" Isolde countered. She leaned against Cleve as he put his arm around her. "I knew. I felt it before you even got here."

Wynne observed the scene before her with a sinking heart. The children loved him. She loved him too. Was she doing them all a disservice by refusing Cleve's offer, even if it kept them second in his life? Perhaps even second place was better than no place at all.

A small hand insinuated itself into hers, and she looked down into Bronwen's quiet, smiling face. "I knew he would come too." She beamed. "I knew it."

In a state of complete bewilderment Wynne allowed herself to be pulled along as the children tugged Cleve toward the manor. With a grin Cleve tossed Arthur astride the patient destrier. Isolde, too, he lifted, as she shrieked with delight, and deposited her behind the ecstatic Arthur.

"I have a horseman's hands," Arthur boasted as he wove the leather reins between his little fingers.

"That you do, my boy. Now, show Ceta who's in charge." Cleve turned to reach for Bronwen, but when she drew back from riding the towering steed, he smiled. "You shall ride upon my shoulders then. Would you prefer that?"

Bronwen shook her head. "Let's just walk, all right?" Then she took his hand in her free one so that she held on to both adults. A happy sigh escaped her lips, and her shy smile flitted from Cleve to Wynne and back again. "Let's just walk, all three of us."

What was she to do? Wynne wondered miserably as the little party started up the road. Once more she questioned her motives in refusing Cleve's offer to make her a part of his life. Was pride more important than the happiness she saw in her children's eyes? Would she truly be happier here than she would be in England sharing at least a portion of her time with him?

She knew the answer, and that knowledge both thrilled and terrified her. But there was more to consider than merely herself and her family. What of Gwynedd? What of Wynne's position as Seeress—and Isolde's newly unfolding talents as well? Was she to abandon it all for this man?

The children's chatter rose around her. Cleve's words of caution to the two adventurous riders registered in her ears, only adding to her confusion. He would be such a good father to them. But how could she leave here?

And then, she was not really certain he'd come here to ask her to return to England at all.

That thought brought her up short. She couldn't keep

from casting a sidelong glance at him, wondering what in fact, had prompted his journey here. He was smiling down at Bronwen, and Wynne's eyes traced his profile with loving attention to detail. The straight, proud nose; the lean cheeks and strong jaw. The curve of his lips. Then he turned slightly and met her gaze full on.

Wynne looked away at once, but not quickly enough to miss the searching, possessive light in his eyes. Her heart pounded, a pattern caused as much by fear as by anticipation, for with that solitary look at least one of her questions was answered: he'd come for her. There was no doubt of that. But would she go?

Gwynedd stood on the stone stoop before the manor's front door. "So you have come," she said, her sightless eyes following Cleve's approach.

"I have come," Cleve answered. He took Gwynedd's outstretched hand in his. "Will you grant a weary traveler your hospitality?"

Gwynedd chuckled. "As long as you are in need of it, my son."

At once the entire yard came alive with activity. Cleve lifted Arthur and Isolde down from the destrier. Cook and the other servants spilled out of the kitchens, and like ants upon a bit of sweet pastry they swarmed about his packhorses, unloading his considerable belongings and ferrying them into the manor. Even the children helped until all of his goods were stored. But amidst it all Wynne remained a bystander, observing but not participating. Wondering, but afraid to ask.

"Children, children." Gwynedd clapped her hands, and the three slowed their excited chattering for a moment. "I need three sets of strong hands to assist me with putting away my spinning. Come along. You shall have ample time to spend with Cleve later."

"Oh, do we have to?" Isolde complained.

"I wanted to help feed Ceta," Arthur protested.

But Bronwen cut them off. "You heard Aunt Gwynedd," she said. "She needs our help. Besides, *Wynne* can help Sir Cleve feed his horses."

Arthur and Isolde shared a look of such sudden and complete understanding that Wynne was reminded of Rhys and Madoc. Then the two started nodding and backing away.

"You're right, Bronwen."

"Come on, let's go help Aunt Gwynedd."

They were so obviously anxious to leave her alone with Cleve that Wynne could have laughed. But instead she only swallowed the uncomfortable lump that had lodged in her throat. How could a person both long for and dread the same moment with such equal intensity? She wrapped her arms around herself, waiting for everyone to leave. Waiting for Cleve to speak. Waiting to see what she would do.

He stood waiting, too, and once more Wynne was conscious of his hesitant manner. It seemed so out of place, especially considering how far he'd come to speak to her. She supposed he worried that she would again turn him down, and once more she had the ridiculous urge to laugh. He feared she'd turn him down. She feared she would accept.

"Will you help me with the horses?"

Slowly she nodded. She took the lead reins for the three jennets that he handed her, but she was careful to avoid touching his fingers. His touch had proven time and time again to be too compelling for her. Too beguiling.

They led all six animals across the yard to the fenced area beside the stable. Only when the horses were set free in the yard and the gate closed and latched did he turn directly to face her.

"I . . . I came to see you, Wynne, because . . ." He paused and wet his lips nervously. Then he grimaced at his stumbling beginning. "My God, woman, but you do unman me."

She met his eyes, gone dark now with emotion. She unmanned him? Oh, but there was no logic in the world at all when it came to their dealings together.

"I have left England, Wynne. I've come to Wales to stay. If you will have me."

At such a startling revelation Wynne's mouth fell open in surprise. For a moment her mind refused to function, and she even doubted her ears. But Cleve continued, though he kept his distance from her.

"Lord William has released me from my betrothal to the Lady Edeline. Not that she minded much," he added with a wry expression on his face. "I've messages for Druce from both her and her father—"

"You are not wed to her?" Wynne blurted out, focusing on that single fact above all others.

"No. And I never will be wed to her, Wynne." He started forward, but then stopped as if he fought a terrible battle of restraint with himself. "There is only one woman I wish to wed. There is only one woman I want as mother to my children."

Like a tide, emotions rose up inside her, filling her with an unearthly joy, bringing tears to her eyes and the most unspeakable happiness to her heart. "Me?" she asked in a voice gone low and shaky.

He nodded his head while his eyes devoured her with the force of their possessiveness. "If you will have a poor Englishman who brings you only a few horses, a few coins, and a heart that truly loves you."

In an instant she was in his arms, crying, laughing, holding him as if she would never let him go. Knowing now that she would never have to. Tears streamed down her cheeks, but complete love filled her heart.

"Will you marry me, *cariad*?" he murmured urgently against her lips. They kissed deeply, all their pent-up emotions free at last. "Will you marry me? Say the words, my love. I need to hear them."

"I will marry you, Cleve FitzWarin. I will marry you and be your wife forever. Forever. I love you so." This last she said staring deeply into his eyes, eyes that radiated so much love that her heart fairly ached with fullness. He lowered his head to kiss her again, and this time she held back nothing. All her love she placed into his keeping, knowing now that there could never have been any other ending for the two of them. Their love had been ordained by a force mightier than they.

Dimly the sound of clapping and the excited shouts of children came to her. With a laugh she pulled back from Cleve just enough to turn her head to see her three little imps. They hung out of a window on the second floor of the manor, and she realized they'd witnessed the entire scene.

"You do know that you're getting a considerable family when we wed."

Cleve glanced at the three grinning faces in the window. "I wouldn't have it any other way. In fact," he added thoughtfully, "I've sometimes wondered if the five of them didn't somehow have a hand in things." Then he looked back at her. "Actually I considered asking you to marry me while they were present. I knew they would approve."

"So why didn't you do it before they left with Gwynedd?"

Cleve's hands slid slowly up and down her arms. His eyes were dark with emotion, yet still they radiated the most incredibly heartening warmth. When he spoke, his voice was serious.

"I wasn't as sure about you. But if you *did* accept me, well, I wanted it to be because you wanted to for yourself. Because *you* wanted to be my wife, not because others wanted you to. I wanted to know that you accepted my suit for love's sake alone."

Once more tears misted her eyes. "I love you for . . . for many reasons, Cleve. And one of them is that you will be a good father to my children—and to the ones we shall have together." She smiled up at him, full to bursting with the love she felt for him. "But were I all alone in the world, or mother to a hundred children, I would want only you for my husband."

He pulled her close, and she came willingly, pressing her face to his chest, closing her eyes and simply absorbing his nearness, his warmth, his special scent of dust and horse and sweat, the wonderfully steady pounding of his heart.

"How soon can we arrange the ceremony?" he murmured against her hair. "For I am more than eager to consummate our vows." For emphasis he moved slightly, letting her feel the evidence of that eagerness. "You haven't an overlord, have you? Someone whose permission I must gain?" He tilted her face up to him, and she saw his frown. "There won't be a problem with me being English, will there?"

Wynne smiled up into his dear, handsome face and traced the perimeter of his lower lip with one finger. "We may wed as soon as a priest can be found, for I have no overlord to ask. The forest is mine, passed through the Radnor women and subject to no one but us."

At first his face reflected only relief. Then, as the full meaning of her words struck home, his expression changed to one of stunned amazement, and she laughed out loud, a joyous, happy sound that bubbled up from the depths of her being. "Marry me, Sir Cleve FitzWarin, and you will be known as Lord Cleve." She kissed him firmly on the lips. "My dear Lord Radnor."

When she would have deepened the kiss, however, Cleve held her a little away. "Why didn't you tell me that long ago? Why didn't you tell me that day in the cottage? Had I known that you brought lands with you these past torturous weeks—"

He broke off under her steady gaze, and for a long moment their eyes met and held. Then he sighed and lowered his head to lean his forehead against hers, and she knew that he finally understood.

"You wanted me to come to you for love's sake only," he answered his own question, his voice low and filled with emotion. "And I do, Wynne. I want you for love and love alone."

Wynne nodded as tears filled her eyes. "And I want you for love's sake only."

EPILOGUE

The rising sun glinted through the mist and struck golden against the distant peaks of Black Mountain. Wynne stretched and yawned, then leaned her elbows on the wooden windowsill, propped her chin on one hand, and gave a great, contented sigh. She smiled when a warm hand slid beneath her heavy sleep-tangled hair to rest familiarly at the nape of her neck.

"They'll be here soon," Cleve murmured as he planted a kiss near her ear.

"I feel their nearness," she revealed, glorying in the way he sensed her moods so well. "Rhys and Madoc—and Lord William, and Edeline and Druce—will arrive today. Perhaps this very morning." She leaned back into his broad chest, and he wrapped his arms about her waist.

For a long, peaceful while the two of them merely gazed out onto the manor grounds, watching as the sun pushed back the night's shadows. Cook bustled across the yard, trailed by two hopeful chickens. Bronwen's pup, grown into an ungainly but cheerful mongrel, ambled up, still sleepy and unable to give more than halfhearted pursuit to the irate fowl. Morning was well upon them,

Wynne decided. And it would no doubt prove to be the most wonderful of days.

A soft cooing came from beyond them, and she sighed happily. "Your daughter does beckon you," she murmured, turning in Cleve's embrace.

He squeezed her and planted a warm kiss on her mouth. Then a loud, demanding cry made him laugh. "And your rowdy son does command your presence."

Arm in arm, Wynne and Cleve strolled to the twin cradles that held their two babes. "Good morning, Maradedd. Good morning, Hewe."

At the sound of their mother's voice the twin babies began to cry in earnest. Cleve's face creased with worry.

"They seem to cry, to grow hungry, and even to wet themselves at the very same time. How can you keep up with them?"

"You forget, I've had several years' practice with Rhys and Madoc." Wynne lifted Hewe up and handed him to his father. "Entertain him while I tend to Mara."

With a grin Cleve lifted the wide-eyed Hewe high over his head. "Hello there, lad. What say you? Shall you meet your brothers today? Oh, but they shall love teaching you all their tricks."

Hewe squirmed in infant delight and let out a happy gurgle. Mara laughed as well, and Wynne smiled down at her daughter's cherubic face. "Yes, the two hooligans shall try their best to drag you into all sorts of adventures," she crooned to the now-happy baby. "And you unfortunately shall eagerly trail after them, won't you?" she added, tickling Mara beneath her double chin.

She changed Mara's wet wrappings, then picked up the burbling baby and handed her to Cleve. For a moment she simply stood there, smiling at her tall and handsome husband, whose arms were now each filled with a plump, contented baby.

"You know, I don't think I've ever loved you more than at this very moment," she confessed in a voice that had become thick with sudden emotion.

Cleve's gaze met hers in perfect understanding, love shining in his eyes and the most beatific smile upon his lips. "And you . . . you are more bewitching, more . . ." He shook his head, unable to put to words the emotions he felt. But Wynne knew. She stepped up to him, wrapping her arms about him so that their two wide-eyed babies lay between them and their brows rested against each other's.

"I love you, Wynne," he murmured. "More than life itself."

Wynne lifted her face to kiss him, sweetly and tenderly, all her love imparted in the chaste touching of their lips. But the thoughts that leaped into her mind were not in the least chaste.

"I have an idea," she said, a mischievous gleam in her eye. "After the christening—after the feasting and the games, when everyone is tired and the children are quiet —do you think the godparents would tend the babies? Just for an hour or two?"

Cleve gave her a speculative look. "Aric and Rosalynde probably break their fast in the hall even as we speak. I'm certain they can be talked into an hour or two without any trouble. But tell me, what do you have in mind?"

Though his grin revealed he knew precisely what she had in mind, Wynne decided that a little anticipation would not hurt. "Well, there is this place not far from here. 'Tis deep, dark, and very secluded. A place where two lovers might find complete pleasure in each other's company."

"And play all sorts of devilish games together?" His brows arched suggestively.

"The Devil's Cleft is just the place for a devil such as you," Wynne laughed.

"So long as we stay clear of the parsley fern."

Again Wynne laughed, and this time Cleve joined in as well. Was it truly only a year ago that she'd fought him as her worst enemy, the man who meant to destroy her family and ruin her life? But their battles had only brought them closer together, and now . . . now her life was wonderful beyond all expectations, filled with more family, more friends, and more love than she could ever have known possible.

"No parsley fern," Cleve murmured as they moved together toward the door. "But if you have some other, more *appropriate* potions, my sweet Welsh witch . . ."

Wynne gave him her mysterious smile. "As a matter of fact there is this lovely plant I've discovered. 'Tis called the passion plant. Shall I gather some of its leaves?"

He grinned. "If you like. But I suspect I shall not need it. No, not at all," he added with a long, deliberate perusal of her.

Wynne's senses all leaped under his bold scrutiny, and her heart soared to new heights of love for her lusty English husband. No, they needed no such potions or aids, for their love burned hot all on its own.

And she knew that, like the most potent of magics, it would dwell in their hearts forever.

Be sure to watch for Rexanne Becnel's
next wonderful historical romance,
When Lightning Strikes,
coming next March. We hope you enjoy
the following excerpt from
When Lightning Strikes.

Nebraska Territory, 1855

Abigail Bliss walked alone, struggling through mud that was ankle deep. It sucked at her boots and clung to the hem of her skirt, but today she hardly noticed. Her legs moved mechanically. Left, right; one after the other; propelling her forward at a steady pace. The other women from the wagon company made their way over to her, offering condolences on the loss of her father. But death was a constant companion on the trail, and life must go on. Eventually they all drifted back to their own wagons and their own responsibilities, leaving Abby to walk beside her oxen, alone with her frozen thoughts.

Dexter was ministering to a man who'd broken his hip. The man's family was staying behind today. It was just too painful for the man to be bumped around in the wagon, and besides, he was not expected to live long. By tomorrow Dexter would be saying a service over a fifth grave, she feared. But despite her sorrow for the injured man and his family, Abby was relieved not to suffer Dexter Harrison's constant presence this day. She simply did not think she could bear his hovering one more minute. As for Tanner McKnight—she didn't know what to think.

She hadn't seen Tanner since he'd confronted her this morning with his shattering story about her mother's father—a grandfather she'd never known she had, but who Tanner said had been searching for her. It was too far-fetched to be true, and yet it fit in with her father's strange behavior of recent months. Tanner said he'd been hired to find her and bring her back to Chicago. She realized now why he'd paid so much attention to her—not because he was drawn to her, but to find out if she was the right girl. For the reward money. No doubt he'd thought it would be easy to sway some spinster schoolteacher and convince her to return with him to Chicago.

But she meant to do as her father had requested before he died. She would marry Reverend Dexter Harrison and continue on to Oregon. Tanner would have no choice but to give up and go away.

So why did the thought of him leaving raise such an aching weariness in her chest?

She should be grateful to have finally recognized his true nature. He was a duplicitous rogue. A liar.

An opportunist. So why couldn't she chase him out of her every waking thought?

Trying to do just that, she determinedly turned her mind toward her father and his painful, tortured death. He was at peace now. She had to cling to that one truth or else fall apart from sheer loneliness. Her father and mother were both in heaven now, and they were praying for her. She must not disappoint them.

But what, she wondered, would her mother think of this? What would she think of her own father—Abby's grandfather—and this determined pursuit of his?

"Miss Abigail!" A childish call steered Abby's thoughts away from that troubling subject.

"Why, Carl. I haven't seen you in a couple of days. How have you been?" She affectionately stroked the wet felt of the hat he wore. "How's your sister?"

"Estelle's sick." He sighed. "Mama said for me to leave her alone."

"Sick?" Abby sucked in a sharp worried breath. "Sick how?"

He made a face. "Throwin' up and stuff. You know."

"Does she have a fever?" Abby asked, struggling to keep her fear for his sister from showing in her voice.

"Nope." He hopped and landed with both feet in a shallow puddle, then laughed at the spray he'd caused. "Mama made us pray a long time last night *and* again this morning that Estelle wouldn't catch a fever."

Abby sent up a quick fervent prayer of her own. Thank God. At least it wasn't cholera.

"Can you tell me another story about those two mice?"

Abby smiled down at the gap-toothed little boy. With God's help he and his sister would make it to Oregon and grow to raise children of their own someday. She caught his hand and gave him a fond smile. "You know, I was just wondering how Tillie and Snitch manage on wet muddy days like today. What do you think?"

He grinned. "I bet Snitch catches on to an oxtail and rides there."

"And what about Tillie?"

"Hmmm." His face screwed up as he thought. "Does she ride in the wagon?"

"Under the wagon. On one of those braces between the wheels. See?" She pointed to her wagon, and Carl peered under it.

"That's a pretty good place to ride," he conceded. "But it's kinda boring. Not like being on an oxtail."

"You think so? Well," Abby mused, letting her mind spin with fanciful possibilities, "did I ever tell you about the time Tillie and Snitch got caught in a raging flood?"

"A flood?" His eyes grew round. Then his face

split in a wide grin. "I know. I know. I bet Snitch saves Tillie from drowning."

"Actually, it happened just the other way around. . . ."

By the time Captain Peters called for the noonday break, Abby was feeling calmer. Carl and his never-ending demands for more stories had forced her to put aside her own miseries for a while, and she'd spun all sorts of wild and dangerous tales of mouse escapades.

Now, determined not to slide back into depressing thoughts just because the child had left to get his midday meal, Abby busied herself with tending the oxen, mending a small tear in the canvas wagon tent, and checking the wheels for any sign of wear. At least with the wet weather there was no chance for the wooden wheels to dry and shrink and fall out of their steel rims, as they'd been warned could happen.

She ate a cold leftover potato with just a sprinkle of salt while she waited for the call to proceed. But it started to rain again, harder than ever, and soon the call to circle up came echoing down the line.

"Jerusalem," she swore. Walking was boring. But sitting was even more so. Still, she heeded the call, and when her turn came she aligned her wagon with the rest.

By then the rain was a blinding torrent. Was anyplace in the world dry today? she wondered as she retreated into the damp recesses of the wagon. After donning her oilcloth rain slicker, she freed the oxen from their tracings. Victor Lewis rode up, though he was so covered against the rain that she could hardly identify him.

"I'll herd them to their grazing," he shouted over the steady roar of the storm. "You go keep Sarah company."

Abby nodded her acceptance of his suggestion. She didn't want to be alone with her sad thoughts today. Young Carl's company had been a blessing. She knew now that she could not spend the rest of the day in her wagon, surrounded by so many reminders of her father and a life that was no more. And maybe Sarah's cheerful company and her unremitting joy in her marriage would help prepare Abby for her own forthcoming wedding to Dexter.

She rummaged in the wagon for her needle and thread and a faded cotton blouse she'd torn beneath the arm. She would work on her mending while she and Sarah talked.

The wagon swayed and creaked as the angry wind tore at the canvas top, and bursts of rain gusted in past the flapping curtain behind the driver's box. Abby was leaning over a heavy trunk, struggling to retie one of the curtain's string fasteners, when a mighty blast of wind blew in from behind her. When she turned to attend to that problem, however, she let out a small startled cry. It was not a loose flapping curtain that had allowed the storm in, but Tanner McKnight's unexpected entrance.

For a long silent moment she stared at him, wishing he had not come here, yet absurdly pleased that he had. Beneath the dripping brim of his hat the ends of his hair were wet. His slicker shed rivulets of water onto the floor as well. He looked wild and dangerous, and she could not tear her eyes away.

She rubbed her shaking hands up and down the folds of her slicker before she found her voice. "You shouldn't be here."

He took his hat off and speared his fingers through his dark hair. "You shouldn't either." His midnight blue eyes ran over her, and though she was completely covered by the shapeless slicker, the weight of his scrutiny lifted goose bumps all over her body. How would it be if he'd actually touched her?

"You shouldn't be here either," he repeated. "Let me take you back to Chicago, where you belong now."

Abby stiffened. Of course. He'd come because he had his job to do. His reward to earn. Knowing she was absurd to feel so disappointed, she half turned from him, finished gathering her sewing materials, and stuffed them in the pocket of her apron.

"I don't belong in Chicago," she countered. "Besides, what you are proposing is quite impossible," she added, striving to sound casual and off-hand. "Dexter plans to build a church in Oregon, and I plan to be at his side." *And perhaps one day I will learn to crave his touch as I so foolishly crave yours.*

"You don't really want to do that, Abby."

She looked sharply at him. "You don't know anything about what I want. You don't know anything about me!"

Her stinging accusation hung in the air between them. A raindrop fell through the canvas to plop on the bed, then another. Abby automatically moved a pot to catch them, and in the close quarters the metallic sound of the drops seemed to tick away the seconds. The minutes.

"I know you're far too passionate for the likes of Dexter Harrison."

Abby swallowed hard. When he spoke to her of passion in such low, moving tones, he seemed to strike some chord in her that left all her nerves thrumming. "Dexter . . . Dexter and I, we shall get on very well."

He smiled at that, a taut smile that seemed at once both sympathetic and somehow pained. "You would make the best of it, I'm certain of that. But I hardly think a preacher would let his wife publish stories about a pair of little mice and all their adventures." He paused, watching her. Letting his words sink in. If they didn't echo so closely Abby's own fears, she would have been better able to ignore them.

"Don't you pretend to care a bit about me or my stories. All you want is the money this man—"

"Your grandfather," he interrupted.

She glared at him. "The money this man has promised to pay you."

One side of his mouth curved down ever so slightly. "I do care about what happens to you, Abby."

Why did he have to say that? He didn't mean the words the way she wanted him to mean them, yet her foolish heart insisted on beating faster till she thought she could not breathe.

"Just leave me alone, Tanner McKnight. Go back to your employer and tell him . . . tell him that my mother and father loved each other very much. For whatever reason he objected to my father as a son-in-law, my father made my mother happy. Now they're at peace together—" She broke off and fought down the hard rush of emotion that rose to choke her. "They are at peace together despite his interference. I don't intend to let him interfere in my life any more than they did."

He nodded once, as if he understood and maybe even agreed. But then he said, "Do you love Harrison?"

Abby didn't answer.

He didn't give her time to, she tried to rationalize a few minutes later as she picked her way across the mud slick that was their campsite, heading toward the Lewis wagon. He'd turned around and left before she had time to say that her father hadn't loved her mother right away either. He'd come to love her just as she would come to love Dexter.

Only she feared that in her case it would never happen. She'd already lost her heart to an undeserving rogue who didn't value it in the least.

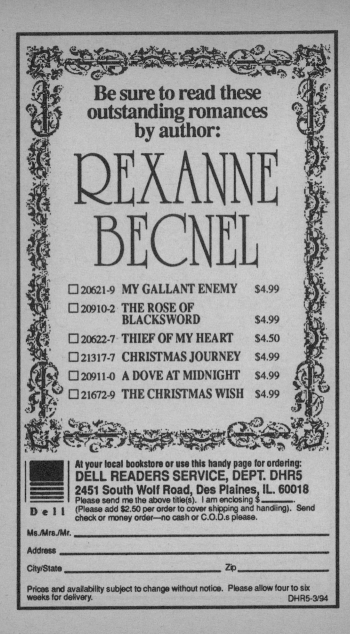